New York Times bestselling author Elizabeth Chadwick has written over twenty historical novels sold in eighteen languages worldwide. Her first novel, *The Wild Hunt*, won a Betty Trask Award, and *The Scarlet Lion* was nominated by Richard Lee, founder of the Historical Novel Society, as one of the top ten historical novels of the last decade. Elizabeth's nineteenth novel, *To Defy a King*, won the RNA Historical Novel prize in 2011.

Also by Elizabeth Chadwick

THE WILD HUNT
THE RUNNING VIXEN
THE LEOPARD UNLEASHED
DAUGHTERS OF THE GRAIL
SHIELDS OF PRIDE
FIRST KNIGHT
THE CONQUEST
THE CHAMPION
THE LOVE KNOT
THE MARSH KING'S DAUGHTER
LORDS OF THE WHITE CASTLE
THE WINTER MANTLE
SHADOWS AND STRONGHOLDS
A PLACE BEYOND COURAGE
THE GREATEST KNIGHT
THE SCARLET LION
THE TIME OF SINGING
TO DEFY A KING
LADY OF THE ENGLISH
THE SUMMER QUEEN
THE WINTER CROWN
THE AUTUMN THRONE
TEMPLAR SILKS

The Falcons of Montabard

Elizabeth Chadwick

sphere

SPHERE

First published in Great Britain in 2003 by Little, Brown
Paperback edition published in 2004 by Time Warner Paperbacks
This reissue published in 2018

1 3 5 7 9 10 8 6 4 2

A CIP catalogue record for this book is available from the British Library.

ISBN 978-0-7515-7566-8

Typeset in Horley Old Style by Palimpsest Book Production Limited,
Falkirk, Stirlingshire
Printed and bound in Great Britain by Clays Ltd, Elcograf S.p.A.

Papers used by Sphere are from well-managed forests
and other responsible sources.

FSC www.fsc.org
MIX
Paper from responsible sources
FSC® C104740

Sphere
An imprint of
Little, Brown Book Group
Carmelite House
50 Victoria Embankment
London
EC4Y 0DZ

An Hachette UK Company
www.hachette.co.uk

www.littlebrown.co.uk

Foreword

The first edition of *The Falcons of Montabard* was nominated for several awards in the UK and the USA, and was one I enjoyed writing tremendously. Indeed, I have loved revisiting it and giving it a swift polish and brush-up. Although nothing major has changed.

My thanks for allowing me the delight of a revisit go to my perceptive editor Maddie West at Sphere, and the rest of team Sphere at Carmelite House for their dedication and enthusiasm.

While plans and preparations for the reissue of *Falcons* were ongoing, my agent Carole Blake very suddenly passed away. Carole was the first publishing professional to read the novel, and there to cheer me on at the RNA Awards for which it was shortlisted. She was with me every step of the way, and I embrace the tremendous debt that I owe to her for every one of my novels.

I now have Carole's dear colleague Isobel Dixon as my agent and I want to acknowledge her contribution as another truly remarkable and insightful person and to say how fortunate I am to have her, and the support of the brilliant team at the Blake Friedmann Agency – may it long continue.

Chapter 1

Port of Barfleur, 25 November, 1120

Sabin FitzSimon stood on the wharfside in the gathering dusk and watched King Henry's ship, the *Mora*, put to sea. A chill wind chamfered the iron-coloured waves with silver as the galley diminished to a dark beetle shape toiling through the troughs. The fading plash of her oars carried back to shore and Sabin smiled to hear the sound because it heralded the success of his scheming. With the King's departure for England, his way was clear.

The young woman at his side moved closer until her hip grazed his. Her hood was drawn up against the cold, and strands of auburn hair had escaped her veil to whip in the stiff salt breeze. Lora was still fresh, still had that glimmer of innocence that was so fleeting in the court whores, and he should know. At two and twenty, Sabin FitzSimon had had them all. It was said at court that Sabin kept a notched tally stick of his seductions, but it wasn't true. He had no particular interest in remembering those who had gone before. His pleasure was in the pursuit, and there was a keener edge to this particular chase, for Lora was a favourite bedmate of King Henry's and Sabin was trespassing on royal territory.

Shouldering a wine cask, a porter emerged from one of the

dockside taverns and strode towards a moored galley. In the deepening twilight, the vessel gleamed like a swan, her prow a proud, graceful curve. Boldly coloured round shields lined the wash strake, increasing her freeboard and protecting her passengers from flying spray. Silk banners streamed at her mast, their colours intense in the last of the light. She was the *White Ship*, the *Blanche Nef*, pride of King Henry's fleet and a fitting transport for his heir William the Atheling and the lively younger element of the court who were still roistering on shore.

'Shall we go within?' Sabin indicated the hostel from which the porter had emerged. 'We could have a room to ourselves while we wait to embark.' His voice was devoid of suggestion but his gaze was eloquent.

She slanted him a look. In the gloaming, her eyes were dark but he knew that in daylight they were the blue-green of a sunlit sea. 'That would be welcome.' The formal words belied the mischief and frank lust dancing in her expression. If Lora's list of conquests was not as long as Sabin's, it was because she had more recently come to the battlefield. It was of her own will that she chose to end the hunt. Had she wanted, she could have sailed on King Henry's ship, instead of remaining to dally with the revellers . . . with one reveller in particular.

He turned her on his arm to face the torchlight spilling from the drinking house. Tipsy laughter and overloud conversation beckoned the couple as they picked their way across the straw-littered mire of the street. So too did the stares of three well-armed soldiers who had also not sailed with the King.

Sabin swept a giggling Lora into his arms, carried her over the threshold and deposited her on a trestle bench. 'A flagon of your best wine if you have any left,' he commanded the tavern-keeper. 'And food to soak it up.'

'There's just one keg, sir.' The landlord wiped his hands on the cloth at his belt. 'But it's supposed to go to Prince William's ship with the rest.'

Sabin fished in his pouch and withdrew a handful of silver – winnings from an earlier game of dice. 'It isn't now,' he said with a wolfish grin. 'A flagon for me and the lady, and share the rest around.' He cast his gaze into the murky corners of the hostel and snorted with contempt to see a youth slumped over a trestle, one hand curled slackly around a cup. Sabin strode over to the table and, lifting the mop of fair-gold hair, looked into the slack, pickled features of his youngest half-brother. 'Simon?'

The youth blinked owlishly. 'Is it time to go?' He belched a miasma of sour wine fumes into Sabin's face.

'No. I was just making sure that you were still alive.' Sabin's mouth curled in good-humoured scorn. 'Looks as if you've sunk enough to float a galley.'

''S good wine. You should try it . . .' The lad's head thudded back onto the trestle and he began to snore, saliva drooling from his open mouth.

He was going to have a head like a bell tower on Easter morn when he awoke, Sabin thought with grim amusement. If Simon's mother and stepfather could see him now, they would be furious – as much with him as the boy. Whenever there was trouble, it was so often Sabin's fault that even when he was innocent he frequently got the blame.

Abandoning Simon to his sotted slumber, he returned to Lora. The generous scattering of silver had prompted the landlord to find half a roasted hen, a wheaten loaf and a compote of apples stewed in honey. 'If you have a quieter place where myself and the lady can dine in peace, I will not be ungrateful.' Sabin touched the pouch at his belt.

The tavern-keeper raised a knowing eyebrow and, placing the food on a tray, started for the door. 'This way, sir,' he said.

Sabin caught his sleeve. 'I'll ask you to watch out for the lad too.' He jerked his head in the direction of his snoring half-brother.

'As if he were my own, sir.' The landlord gave a mildly

sardonic bow and, straightening up, led Sabin and Lora to a chamber at the rear of the hostel. There was a large public dormitory on the floor above the drinking room, but the landlord had found it profitable to provide accommodation offering a degree more privacy. His wife had thought him mad when he converted the old hay store. Now she dressed in blue Flemish wool and thanked his business sense.

The chamber boasted a bench against one wall, a central hearth burning charcoal for heat without smoke, a handsome enamelled coffer and, most importantly, a capacious bed with a feather mattress. The landlord placed the tray on the coffer and lit candles in the wall niches either side of the bed. He accepted his payment from Sabin with a murmur and bowed out of the door.

Sabin listened for the click of the latch, then turned to Lora with a bright, incorrigible grin. 'I have been dreaming of this for weeks now. You and me and a bed.' Going to the flagon, he poured two cups of wine.

Lora swayed over to him. Removing the goblet from his hand, she dipped her index finger in the wine, withdrew it, and slowly sucked from base to polished nail-tip. In the candle shadow, her eyes were as black as sin. 'I hope you make it worth my while,' she purred, dipping her finger again, this time reaching up to outline his lips. The sheer eroticism of the gesture made Sabin want to grab her, throw her onto the bed, and take her fully clothed like a common street whore.

'In full measure!' he said in a lust-choked voice. His hand trembled as he pushed down her hood and plucked the golden pins from her veil. Her braids shimmered like the leaves of a copper beech in late summer and she smelled intoxicatingly of cinnamon and roses.

'You do know that poaching the King's game is a dangerous sport,' she cautioned, using her forefinger to collar his throat with jewelled red droplets.

'I'm a dangerous man, sweetheart,' he muttered and set

his hands at her waist, drawing her hip to hip. It was at once a relief and a frustration.

She laughed and rubbed against him. 'That is what everyone says. I have been warned more than once to stay away from you.'

'And obviously paid no heed to the warnings.'

'Oh, I've paid them every heed. But my curiosity is the greater. I want to know how true the rumours are.'

'What rumours?'

She eyed him coquettishly. Her hand went down between his legs and explored. 'About the size of your tally stick,' she said.

Amid flurries of laughter interspersed with lustful urging and gasps of pleasure, Sabin and Lora tumbled on the bed, shedding their clothes with abandon. The cord holding up Sabin's braies was knotted and there were some moments of exquisite torture while a giggling Lora unpicked the tangle with her sharp nails.

She gave a mock pout. 'You just don't want me to see the prize!' Her loose hair curtained her face and twisted in auburn ringlets to cover her lush, freckled breasts.

'Believe me, I want you to do more than see it!' Sabin said hoarsely.

'Then what do you want me to do?' Her voice was a throaty purr. 'Aha!' She prised the knot free and loosened the cord. His braies slipped down and her eyes widened. 'My, my,' she said with admiration.

Sabin grinned. 'I'm a man of deeds rather than words. I'd rather show you than tell you.'

She spluttered, then burst out laughing. He pounced, rolling her beneath him on the soft feather mattress.

Sabin was savouring the first tight, deep thrust when the door slammed back on its hinges and the three soldiers burst into the room, one clad in mail, the others wearing the quilted tunics of men-at-arms.

Lora screamed in Sabin's ear like a fishwife. He was out of her and off her in a single blur of motion, his hand groping instinctively for the sword on his discarded belt.

'Hold!' the mailed soldier bellowed and Sabin found himself cornered and looking down the length of three blades. His chest heaving against the steel points, he stared through his tangled hair at his assailants and lowered his hands. Lust withered more swiftly than a storm-toppled tree. On the bed, Lora whimpered and frantically sought to cover herself.

'What do you want?' Sabin demanded, but thought that he already knew. These weren't thieves out for his purse. These were the King's men. The poacher had been caught with his hand – and more – in the snare.

'If King Henry was less merciful, your cock and bollocks,' their leader snarled, lowering his blade to Sabin's genitals to emphasise his point. 'You have played him for a fool and now you will pay.' He snapped his fingers at Lora. 'Get dressed, slut.'

Whimpering, Lora struggled to don her chemise and gown. An abrupt command and Sabin's arms were grabbed and lashed behind his back. He was forced to his knees in the thick straw of the chamber floor.

'Don't hurt him,' Lora implored, her voice breathless with fear.

Their leader jerked his head at one of his men. 'Christ, Arnulf, get her out of here and put her on the ship.'

A soldier seized her wrist, yanked her from the bed and dragged her sobbing and screaming out of the door.

Sabin held himself rigid but felt his entrails dissolve. He knew it was going to be bad, and could only pray that they did not cripple him permanently.

'Now then.' The leader circled Sabin, his boots crackling through the fresh straw. 'I am authorised to take reparation for the insult you have given your King.' Picking up Sabin's pouch, he emptied it of the remaining coins. A magnificent cloak clasp of English silverwork fell out into his hands.

Sabin lunged and was brought up against a sharpened edge. 'That was my father's!' he burst out and struggled against his bonds. A sword was reversed and the hilt clubbed against his temple. He swayed, seeing stars. A booted foot slammed between his shoulder blades and his cheek hit the straw with bruising force.

'*Was* is right.' The leader tucked the money and the brooch into his own pouch, latched Sabin's swordbelt around his own waist and drew the blade to test the balance. 'Decent, but I've seen better. Still, it should fetch a good price.' Sheathing the weapon, he laid his foot beneath Sabin's jaw. 'Pick him up, Richard. I haven't finished with him yet. In fact I haven't even started.'

Through the eye that was only half swollen shut, Sabin focused on the guttering flame of the candle in one of the niches. Its partner had gone out, and that side of the room was cloaked in darkness. If some parts of his body were not clamouring with pain, it was because they were still numb; the agony would come later. King Henry's men had known their business. Sabin was too high born and well connected to die, but not protected enough to be immune from a severe warning.

'Christ,' he groaned and struggled to sit up. His hands were still tied behind his back and he was naked. A purple bootprint stained his ribs, and his abdomen felt as if someone had been using it as a threshing floor.

The charcoal fire had died to grey and the November chill was seeping into the room. How long had he been lying here? He did not know, save that the candles had been fresh when he and Lora had been shown to the chamber and now he was about to be left in darkness. He struggled to his feet, collapsed, fought his way up again and wobbled to the bed. The effort opened up a drying cut on his lip and he tasted fresh blood. Sabin fell face down on the mattress, turned his head to one side so that he could breathe and let oblivion swallow him.

When next his awareness returned, pallid dawn light was threading through the shutters. He was chilled to the bone, stiff as a corpse, and someone was kneeling over him.

'Is he dead?'

Sabin recognised Simon's frightened voice.

'Not yet, sir,' replied the landlord, 'but I doubt he's in the land of the living either.'

There was a sharp tug at Sabin's back as the landlord used a dagger to sever the cords binding Sabin's wrists.

Sabin groaned. His arms had set in their trussed position and to move them was at first impossible, then agony. His entire body throbbed with pain, sharp and dull, incapacitating.

'Bones of Christ, what happened to you?' Simon came around the side of the bed. His thin adolescent features were puckered with worry and his complexion was sweaty and pale with his own suffering.

'King Henry's hirelings,' Sabin croaked and felt his lip sting and bleed again. 'I was with Lora . . . God, stop boggling at me like a witless sheep. Go away. Let me die in peace.'

Ignoring him, the youth hovered anxiously. 'I said you shouldn't chase her.'

Since he couldn't get up and walk away, Sabin closed his good eye and hoped Simon would take the hint.

'The *Blanche Nef* sailed without us.' The youth's tone was despondent. He had been looking forward to voyaging on the finest galley in King Henry's fleet. 'The other ships have all gone too. We'll have to find a wine transport to take us home.'

Sabin grunted. Practicalities were beyond him for the moment.

The tavern-keeper's wife arrived with a bowl of warm water, a cloth and some salve. A judicious application of leeches reduced the swelling around Sabin's eye and the cut on his lip was treated with some disgusting grease that nevertheless did its job and prevented the wound from splitting open every time he tried to speak.

In pain and discomfort, but not at death's door, Sabin

dressed and shambled into the tavern's main room where he partook gingerly of bread soaked in milk and a cup of watered wine. He missed the customary weight of the sword at his hip and he had to borrow Simon's spare brooch to pin his cloak.

'My mother won't be pleased when she sees you.' Hunched over an almost untouched cup of wine, Simon studied Sabin's battered features. 'There isn't an inch of you that's not black or blue or red.'

'Your mother never is pleased to see me,' Sabin retorted, pushing another morsel of milk-sodden bread between his lips whilst striving to open them as little as possible. His jaw was aching ferociously and at least two of his teeth were loose. 'You know as well as I do that she'd prefer I'd never been born.'

'She's always been fair to you.' Simon's tone was defensive. 'You've never lacked for anything.'

Sabin shrugged and paid for the movement with agony. Simon was right. The lady Matilda, Countess of Huntingdon and Northampton, had always been fair: so even-handed that no one could accuse her of neglecting her duty or shunning her husband's child, bastard-born of a novice nun, begotten on the way home from the great crusade. What was lacking was the warmth that she bestowed freely on the children of her own body. For him the smiles had always been forced; for Waltheof, Maude and Simon, they were wide and joyous. Her offspring could do no wrong. Sabin, by quirk of fate and sometimes a petulant demand for attention, was usually caught out in transgression. It had not mattered so much while his father was alive. There had been the balance of his affection, albeit tinged with guilt, but after he died, that balance had been removed and Sabin had found himself trying to run up a steep and slippery slope. Sometimes he thought that it wasn't worth the battle, and that he should just slide quietly down into hell. Then again, perhaps he had already arrived there.

'Why did you do it?' Simon asked.

'Do what?'

'Chase Lora when you could have had your pick of the court women.' A hint of envy flickered in the youth's blue eyes.

'I like playing with fire,' Sabin said flippantly, pushing his bowl aside, the sops half-finished. 'I might as well ask you why you drank last night until you dropped. You knew it would give you a head like the bottom of a pond this morning, you knew it would make you sick, but you still went beyond enough and into too much.'

'It was good wine' – Simon was still on the defensive – 'and I don't like sailing – even on the best galley in the fleet.'

'Not because your stepfather would disapprove of you getting roaring drunk in a dockside tavern and you felt like defying his rules?'

Simon's throat flushed red above his tunic collar. 'I didn't get drunk to spite my stepfather.'

Sabin said nothing, but his look was eloquent. Two years after her husband's death, the lady Matilda had wed David MacMalcolm, Prince of Scotland: a political match, to be sure, but one from which deep affection had developed. The marriage had been blessed with several offspring, the eldest only six years old. Prince David took his parental responsibilities seriously and that included dealing with his stepchildren. Being the bastard of Lady Matilda's first husband, Sabin was on the periphery and only the most heinous of his misdemeanours were brought to Prince David's attention. However, they were numerous enough to have earned him a reputation and last night's incident was certain to add to it.

Simon pretended great interest in a dubious stain on the trestle.

Manoeuvring his cup to avoid his cut lip, Sabin finished his watered wine. 'I went after Lora because I liked the way she laughed and I wanted to unbind that hair of hers and run it through my hands,' he said. 'She wasn't jaded like some of the women at court. And yes, perhaps I did want to see if I could persuade her to abscond Henry's bed for mine. I admit that I might have overreached myself but—' He stopped speaking as the landlord's wife returned from a visit to the fishing boats, her basket filled with two large crabs and half a dozen flounders. Her complexion was grey and she was trembling as she sat down heavily at one of the trestles. Her husband hastened to her in concern, demanding to know what was wrong.

She looked up at him through welling eyes, then across at Sabin and his brother. 'The *Blanche Nef*,' she said. 'I have just heard that last night she hit the Chartreuse rock and sank.'

There was a brief silence while the three men stared at her.

'You are sure?' Her husband was the first to speak. He gestured at her basket. 'You know that Thomas trades more false gossip than he does fish.'

'I didn't hear it from Thomas,' she said with tearful indignation. 'Emma told me. Her husband was out fishing and rescued a man from the sea at first light. He told them that the *Blanche Nef* had foundered on the reef and, when they tried to prise her off, she sank.' She waved her arm. 'Go and ask for yourselves if you do not believe me. Go and look. They say that pieces of wreckage have been washed up by the Point and at least one body. All those young people . . . all those we entertained last night . . . every one of them drowned, including the Prince.' Covering her face, she began to weep in earnest, rocking back and forth on the bench.

'Holy Christ,' Simon whispered and signed his breast. He gave Sabin an appalled look. 'We should have been with them.'

Sabin stared blankly at the door that the woman had left open in her distress. Raw November air blew into the room. Across the rectangle of pallid light he watched people going about their business and heard the screaming of gulls over the landed catches from the fishing boats.

'Perhaps it isn't true,' Simon said. 'False rumours always spread like wildfire.'

Sabin heaved himself to his feet and moved stiffly to the door. The wharfside was as busy as it had been last night, but now it was filled with clusters of townsfolk, bartering opinion and speculating on the news. As Simon said, it might not be true, but there was a cold knot in his belly that told him it was.

There was a sudden flurry as people began running towards the shore where a fishing vessel was beaching, the master and his lads splashing barelegged and knee-deep in the water. One of the youths was shouting and gesticulating. Thrusting past Sabin, Simon sprinted towards the vessel. Sabin lurched after him, the wind tearing into his mouth, making his loose teeth ache.

The fishermen were lifting something out of their craft and bearing it onto the firm shore above the waterline. Sabin saw his brother crane to look and then abruptly turn away.

'It's Lora,' Simon said, swallowing. 'Dear God, I didn't believe it was true . . . I didn't.' Bending over, he retched.

Sabin pushed his way forward, heedless of his superficial pain, for a far deeper one was gathering inside him – as if someone had seized his soft, vital organs in a fist and twisted.

She lay on her back, her auburn hair spilling over her body like strands of seaweed and her complexion a deathly blue-white. The red lips were pale, the once laughing eyes as opaque as stones. Without his urging and blandishments, she would have been safe with the King. He had as good as caused her death.

Someone brought a litter and Lora was lifted onto it. Grains of sand and crushed shell clung to her hair and sodden gown. The smell of brine and fishing boat rose from her body, replacing the warm scent of cinnamon and roses that had coiled around Sabin's senses last night. He shouldered to the side of the litter and gently stroked a tendril of hair away from her marble-cold cheek.

'I should have died too,' he said and did not know if it was a blessing or a curse that King Henry's soldiers had taken his sword to a watery grave. Had it hung at his belt, he would have been tempted to draw the steel and kill himself. Dazed, hurting, he stumbled back to the tavern. The main room was already filling with locals eager to discuss the news, their faces reflecting a mixture of horror and relish. There was very little wine to go around, but there was plenty of rough cider and people had set to with a will. In the background, Sabin was aware of his half-brother shoving out a drinking horn to be filled.

He hobbled away from the noise and sought the room where he and Lora had sported in light-hearted abandon the previous dusk. Here the scent was still of cinnamon, of burned wax from the guttered candles, of spilled wine. He lifted the flagon that had been knocked over in the initial scuffle and saw, shining among the rushes, a hair ribbon of woven green silk. Picking it up, he twined it around his fingers. The shimmer was like the glint of a drake's head in spring. Fierce heat prickled his lids, adding to the pain of his bruised eyes, but he did not weep. Tears were too easy a release. As a child, punished for mischief and misdemeanour, pride had been the stones and defiance the mortar in the wall that had prevented him from crying. Since then, that wall had been many years in the building and fortifying, so it now stood so vast, so high, so strong, that even if it was damaged, it would not crumble. It kept enemies out, and imprisoned him within.

He lay down on the bed and bent his forearm across his burning lids, the ribbon still woven around his fingers. There would be no wine galleys sailing for England today. Tomorrow perhaps, bearing the unbearable news. Grimly pushing all thought and emotion from his mind, Sabin took refuge in slumber, lightless and fathoms deep; the closest he could come to death without dying.

Chapter 2

Castle of Roxburgh, Scottish Borders, December 1120

A bitter winter dusk was darkening towards nightfall as Edmund Strongfist and his daughter Annais approached Prince David's new keep at Roxburgh. Heads down, their mounts plodded along the muddy track that had been churned by other horses and ox carts into a thick brown sludge. The pack pony bearing their baggage was a hard-mouthed, contrary beast and occasionally, her father's serjeant-at-arms had to yank on the lead rein to remind it who was master.

'Solid defences,' Strongfist commented with gruff approval, his breath whitening the air. Hoar droplets dewed his eyebrows and thick, fair beard. 'There has been a fortress here time out of mind, but Prince David has set his own mark on the place . . . and his Countess too,' he added as an afterthought.

Annais lifted her gaze to the castle rising out of the misty rain, its steep defences sheering down to the spated brown rush of the River Tweed. Lanterns cast a golden glow across the entrance arch beckoning travellers over the bridge and into the courtyard. 'It seems huge compared to the Priory,' she said.

'It is bound to.' Strongfist took his gaze from the walls and fixed it on her. 'Are you having second thoughts?'

Annais shook her head. 'No, Father, I am certain.'

He resumed his examination of Roxburgh's fabric. 'As long as you know your own mind,' he said. 'Inasmuch as any woman ever does.'

The wry look she cast at his back was not unaffectionate. She had spent the past five years in a nunnery, receiving tuition and upbringing while her father was occupied in the service of Prince David. With her mother untimely dead of a fever, the Priory at Coldingham, where her aunt was sacristan, had seemed the best of the few choices open to them. Her father said that an education would stand her in good stead when she came of marriageable age. She had now reached her seventeenth year and thus far, no suitable man had sued for her hand and her modest dowry. Those who were young and handsome had no prospects; those who had prospects were much older men and Strongfist refused to wed her to someone with more years than himself. Since she had no desire to join her aunt and take the veil, and since her father's circumstances had recently changed, she was currently as free as any young woman of her status could expect to be.

Riding into the courtyard behind her father, Annais stared round at the slabs of firelit stone, their sturdy brutality contrasting with the limewashed timber service buildings in their shadow. An appetising aroma of mutton stew wafted through the drizzle, making her stomach growl. She had never grown accustomed to the discipline and sparseness of convent food and had spent her time at Coldingham in a state of permanent hunger. Dismounting unaided from her mare, she shook out her skirts. Although she was wearing her winter cloak of double-lined wool, the moisture had still penetrated the layers and her gown was clammy with damp.

The serjeant led the horses away to the stables with the instruction to bring the baggage pack along to the hall later.

Holding her gown above the mire, Annais followed her

father through the alleyways between the byres, stables and workshops until they came to a fine timber hall with wooden shingles and a solid oak door banded with wrought-iron decoration.

'Soon be dry now,' he said by way of encouragement and stood aside for a soldier who was on his way out. Belatedly recognising him, Strongfist uttered a greeting and clapped him on the shoulder. 'Duncan, it's good to see you!'

The knight half smiled and muttered a response, but his eyes were sombre.

'What's wrong? Have you lost your wages at dice again, or has your mother-in-law been harrying you?'

Duncan waved aside Strongfist's jocularity. 'You haven't heard, have you?' he said.

'Heard what?'

'About the *Blanche Nef*.'

Strongfist shook his head and gestured to Annais. 'I've been away at Coldingham fetching my daughter and the Priory's hardly on the beaten track for gossip. Why, what has happened?'

Duncan shook his head. 'The court was returning from Normandy. The *Blanche Nef* foundered out of Barfleur harbour with the loss of all on board, including William the Atheling. We had the news from a royal courier two days ago.'

'God rest their souls that is terrible!' Strongfist crossed himself, as did Annais.

'Indeed it is,' the knight agreed, 'and I fear that the tragedy strikes closer to home than that. It is likely that our Countess Matilda's son Simon and his half-brother Sabin were aboard too, and that they have perished.'

'Sweet Jesu, no!'

'The household is in deep mourning. If you want to report to Prince David, he is in the chapel with the Countess and her daughter, although if I were you, I would find sleeping space in the hall and leave it until morning.'

Strongfist nodded stiffly. 'Thank you for the warning.' He sought for something positive to say. 'At least the lady has her younger children for comfort, and her other two from the first marriage.'

'Aye, but you know how much store she set by the lad, and him just on the verge of manhood.'

'Is there no chance that they survived?'

Duncan screwed up his face. 'If they were on the *Blanche Nef*, no. It foundered two miles out in pitch darkness. The only one to live to tell the tale was a common butcher who was on board collecting dues owed. I will talk to you later, I'm supposed to be on duty for my sins.' Slapping Strongfist's arm, inclining his head to Annais, the knight squelched on his way.

Father and daughter entered the smoky fug of the hall. A thick layer of rushes carpeted the beaten earth floor and heavy hangings covered the shuttered windows, keeping at bay the worst of the dank and cold.

'Christ have mercy on their souls,' Strongfist muttered as he walked to the fire, extending his hands to the warmth as if by heating them he could banish the knight's words.

Annais frowned. Although her father served Prince David, she had never had much to do with him or his family. She knew that the Prince had married an English widow, Matilda, Countess of Huntingdon and Northampton, and that the lady already had three children from her first marriage. The eldest was in holy orders, the middle one a daughter, and the youngest was the one for whom everyone was mourning and praying. But her quick mind had not missed the mention of a half-brother. 'Who is Sabin?' she asked.

Her father grimaced. 'A scapegrace bastard of the Countess's first husband,' he said. 'Wild, by all accounts, and a bad influence on young Simon. I know him vaguely by sight but our paths have seldom crossed.'

They were joined by several of her father's companions from the Prince's retinue. There were more greetings, more discussion of the tragedy and its implications for Prince David and his wife . . . and for King Henry who had lost his only legitimate son. Finally, when those subjects had run their course, the talk turned to matters more personal.

'So tell us, are the rumours true?' demanded Alexander de Brus, a knight with whom Strongfist often rode escort duty.

'What rumours?' Strongfist widened innocent eyes.

'Oh come on, man, don't be cagey. We hear you're bound for Jerusalem to offer your sword in King Baldwin's service.'

Strongfist folded his arms. 'What of it?'

'What of it?' De Brus laughed. 'It's not the kind of decision you up and make on the spur of the moment – as if you were just riding off for a day's hunting.'

Strongfist planted his feet firmly apart, asserting his own piece of ground. 'It is more than twenty years since I was at the taking of Jerusalem with my cousin Fergus. Beardless lads still lacking our spurs.' He snorted at the memory and tugged his thick, fair beard. 'Fergus stayed to serve, and I would have done so too had I not promised my father that I would return whole and bring him a handful of dust from the roads that Christ himself had trodden. Then I wed the lass's mother and that put an end to my wanderlust.' He thrust one foot forward and looked at the spur adorning his heel, symbol of mature knighthood. 'Now my wife and my father are dead and my older brother has the rule of our family lands. Fergus is a lord of wide estates and writes to me that the same can be mine if I choose to return to Outremer. They are in desperate need of experienced warriors.'

Alexander laid his hand on Strongfist's shoulder. 'No one blames you,' he said. 'It is plain that the reasons for your going are greater than those for you to stay. It is not as if you and your brother have ever been close.'

Strongfist said nothing, but did not bother to conceal the downturn of his mouth. His brother's charity, like his nature, was about as palatable as last night's porridge left out on a cold lintel. While their father had lived, Strongfist had endured, but now it was time to leave.

'What of your girl?' De Brus glanced at Annais who had remained modestly silent in the opinionated masculine company. 'Will you take her with you?'

Strongfist looked at her too. 'Yes. I would not wall her up in a convent for the rest of her days when she has no calling. Nor in all good conscience could I leave her in my brother's care.' His expression was wooden. 'She would not flourish in his household, biddable though she is, and I am not convinced he would select a husband suitable to her nature. I am hoping that with her education she will be given a place within the household of Baldwin's Queen. If God is good, perhaps she will make a match with an Outremer lord.' He gave her a pride-filled smile, and she managed to smile back, dutifully.

She was glad when one of the Countess's maids took her away to the women's chambers on the floor above the hall. It had been disturbing to be talked about rather than included in the conversation – as if she were a prize mare.

Annais was given sleeping space in the maidens' room outside the Countess Matilda's solar and furnished with a cup of hot wine, a bowl of mutton pottage and half a loaf. The Countess, she was told, was still at prayer in the chapel with her husband and eldest daughter and would remain there long into the night.

The younger children had been tended by their nurse and put to bed in a small side chamber. Annais glimpsed them briefly while devouring her bread and stew. There was a sturdy, sandy-haired boy and two fair-haired little girls, the youngest little more than a babe in arms.

Having finished her food, she rinsed her bowl in the bucket provided and helped the other women to lay out the pallets for the night. Under the strict rule at Coldingham, she had grown accustomed to all forms of labour. Despite its prestige, the Priory had not been a haven for gently bred young ladies intent on nothing more serious than embroidery. Annais knew how to stuff both a sleeping pallet and a chicken. She could sew a fine seam and neatly stitch a battle wound. She wrote a fluent hand in Latin and French, but was equally at home daubing a wall in limewash with a hog's bristle brush.

Once the pallets were arranged, the women began preparing for sleep. Annais removed her gown and draped it over a coffer, spreading the muddy skirts the better to dry out the damp. The garment was really in need of a stiff brushing, but there was small point when she and her father were to continue their journey on the morrow to her uncle's keep at Branton.

Unpinning her veil, she took her comb from her travelling satchel and unbraided and groomed her hair until it shone like polished oak. Prayers were next and there were many to say. Annais ran her prayer beads through her fingers, counting off a smooth agate oval with each supplication completed. Her final one was for the missing young men.

Her pallet was close to the door and her sleep was light. When the hinges squeaked, she jerked her head from her pillow and by the fluttering light of the night candle, saw several people enter the room. A striking woman with heavy bronze-red braids swinging beneath her veil was comforting a slender adolescent girl. Behind them paced a man of average height and build, dark-haired and watchful. His cloak was lined with ermine tails and gold embroidery flashed in the candle glow. Annais realised that she must be looking at the Countess Matilda, her daughter Maude, and Prince David MacMalcolm who was King in all but name along the Scottish borders.

Moving quietly, they crossed the antechamber and slipped through the curtain into the Countess's private domain. Moments later, Annais heard murmurs and the sound of suppressed weeping. A whiff of church incense from their garments lingered in the air.

Annais sighed and closed her eyes. She tried not to think about the young men who had drowned – not so much for their sake, although she did say another heartfelt prayer for their souls, but for her own. The way to Jerusalem involved many sea crossings including the narrow channel between England and Normandy that had claimed the *Blanche Nef*. Her father had often spoken of the voyages of his youth. Sometimes, the more garrulous for drink, he had told expansive tales about waves as high as cathedrals and strange fish with huge jaws and teeth like rows of daggers. The stories had frightened her to the point of nightmares when she was a little girl and her mother had rebuked Strongfist severely for telling them. Annais's fears had diminished as she matured, but the notion of the journey itself was like a huge fish swimming through her mind, disturbing her tranquillity.

The main door widened again, softly, and the flicker from the night candle illuminated two male figures. Annais wondered if she should scream, for their tread was careful, almost furtive, and one of them was wearing a sword. However, she decided that to get this far they would have already had to pass several sets of guards, and there was more cause for curiosity than concern.

The one with the sword was fair-haired with features lengthening out of boyhood and a rash of adolescent blemishes at his temple and jaw. His companion was dark and had a face like a gargoyle, swollen of eye, puffy of lip and markedly devilish. He even moved like a creature from the other world, his shoulders hunched and his gait awkward, as if his long cloak concealed horned hooves and a tail. Annais almost started to make the sign of the cross then castigated herself for being foolish.

They had nearly reached the curtain to the inner chamber when the fair one tripped over the pallet of a sleeping maid. The woman jerked awake with a cry, stared up at the intruders and raised the sound to a piercing shriek. The young men's attempt at stealth proved futile, as everyone else was startled from sleep. A child began to cry and a bleary nursemaid stumbled to attend it. The main chamber curtain rattled aside and Annais saw that candles were being hastily lit.

'What is it, what's wrong?' Countess Matilda emerged, a

cloak thrown over her linen shift, her ruddy bronze hair streaming down her back. Then her eyes lit on the two young men and blazed with joy. 'Simon!' Regardless of propriety, she ran to the fair one, flung her arms around his neck and burst into tears. After a moment's uncertainty, the youth returned her embrace with fervour. The dark one stepped back, and although it was difficult to judge his expression because of the state of his face, Annais thought that it tightened, and she could almost sense his mental retreat.

'We thought you drowned,' the Countess wept, relinquishing her hold to pass the youth on to his sister. Wiping her eyes on her sleeve, she turned to the dark one, and drew back with a gasp.

'I fell, my lady,' he said without expression. 'It is indeed true that the *Blanche Nef* sank with William the Atheling on board, but we missed the sailing.'

Prince David joined the greeting, embracing Simon heartily, but clasping the other's hand with more reserve. The family retreated into their chamber and attendants were sent running for food and wine.

Following the initial excitement, a degree of calm was restored. The rumble of conversation came muted through the curtain but the women in the outer chamber could decipher no individual words. The senior maid ordered everyone to go back to sleep and, to emphasise the point, snuffed all the candles, even the thick night one that was usually left burning. A whispered conversation between two of the wenches was silenced by a terse command.

Annais's eyes were gritty with weariness, but she stayed awake for a long time, pondering the scene she had just witnessed. She was of a practical nature, but sensitive to atmospheres, and there had been sufficient undertow in that encounter to drown any but the strongest swimmer.

Prince David of Scotland, lord of Huntingdon and Northampton, rubbed a weary hand over his beard and considered the young man seated before him. On the trestle separating them were the remnants of a breakfast of oatcakes and curd cheese, and half a pitcher of brown heather ale.

'Now,' he said, 'I will have the truth about what really happened at Barfleur.' His tone was pleasant, his French bearing the merest hint of a Scots burr, for he had dwelt most of his life at the English court. 'Much as I am overjoyed to see you and Simon whole, I would know what the price is to me and mine.'

Sabin lowered his gaze from David's piercing dark one and suppressed the urge to squirm. The Scots Prince was scrupulously honest in his own dealings and expected others to extend him the same courtesy.

'The truth is as we told you, sir,' Sabin said. 'We got drunk and the *Blanche Nef* sailed without us.'

'And in your drunken stupor you managed to fall over not just once, but several times?' David arched a slender brow.

Sabin shrugged. 'Does it matter what happened? Without it we would be feeding fish at the bottom of the sea with the rest of them.'

'Your tone borders on the insolent.' Grooves of muscle tightened in David's jaw and his tone was no longer pleasant, although it remained even.

'That was not my intent. I am saying that you have the fabric of the matter. There is no reason for you to examine every single thread in the weave.'

'Let me be the judge of that.' David folded his arms. 'If you won't tell me, then I will ask Simon, but I would rather hear the tale from your own lips. It is your responsibility, not your brother's.'

Sabin sighed. 'There is little enough to tell. Simon drank too much and fell asleep across a table.'

'And you?'

Sabin considered saying that he had been roughed up during a dice game, but he knew that the truth would eventually emerge. If not here at Roxburgh through a slip of the tongue, then at court, where his face, whatever its hue, would be less than welcome. 'I was abed with King Henry's youngest mistress,' he said. 'She persuaded Henry to let her stay behind and sail on the *Blanche Nef*. I took her to a tavern. By that time, Simon was snoring in his wine.'

'I see.' The grooves of muscle deepened and a hint of distaste gave the firm lips a downward curl. 'And your face?'

Sabin shrugged. 'The King was more jealous of his rights than I thought. He set some men to watch over her . . . they interrupted us and this was the result. I am not proud. You are right to look at me in that way. Lora is dead. Without my persuasion she would still be alive.'

David sighed and steepled his hands beneath his chin. 'What am I to do with you? You lurch from one scrape to another. If it's not gambling, it's whores. If not whores, then drink and brawling. Surely you have been raised to do yourself more justice than that? What would your father say if he could see you now?'

Sabin had been waiting for that particular club to emerge from the armoury. Every time he was caught straying from the path, it was used to belabour him. 'Since he is dead, we will never know, and, even if you are married to his widow, you have no right to put words in his mouth.' He jerked to his feet and felt the bench wobble behind him with the force of his movement.

'Sit down,' David said icily. 'I have not finished speaking.'

'You have nothing to say that I want to hear,' Sabin answered. 'I wish that I had drowned on the *Blanche Nef* too. I am sorry for my sake and yours that I did not. Who knows, perhaps we'll both be more fortunate next time.' Turning on his heel, turning his back on the Prince, he strode from the room. The act of standing erect and lengthening his stride sent pain lancing through his ribs and abdomen, but his pride held him straight.

He half expected the Prince to call him back or to send guards after him, but nothing happened, save that the space between his shoulder blades was suddenly very sensitive.

He knew he had been rude and graceless, but that was in self-defence. If Prince David had been less judgmental, Sabin might have been more conciliatory himself. Besides, he was torn. A part of him cared deeply what his father might think about him, but another part remained angry that his father was dead, that whatever he might have felt and said was shut in the silence of the tomb.

The grim speed of his exit brought him from the hall and into the courtyard. A bitter wind was blowing and yesterday's drizzle had become a harder, unforgiving rain. A practice for winter, Sabin thought. It always came earlier to these hills than in the softer south.

One of Prince David's knights was preparing to leave. Sabin knew Edmund Strongfist by sight but had no deeper acquaintance with the man, except to know that he was of English ancestry displaced by the Normans after Hastings and resettled on the Scottish side of the border. Strongfist heeled his horse and turned towards the gate, and Sabin saw that he had a female companion. Heavily cloaked against the weather, there was little of her to see, although as she passed he received the impression of startled doe-brown eyes and a glint of dark braid. The impression was fleeting and gone and Sabin had no time to dwell on it as the couple rode on their way, a man-at-arms and a packhorse in tow.

He stood shivering in the courtyard, undecided whether to go back inside and find somewhere warm and inconspicuous to hide for the rest of the day, or to squelch into the town, commandeer a corner of the alehouse and live down to Prince David's worst expectations. The sight of three off-duty soldiers heading in that direction made up his mind and he followed them across the drawbridge. There was comfort and solidarity in companionship and they would not care what his father might or might not think of his behaviour.

Chapter 3

Sabin was too drunk to be clear who or what started the fight, only that it erupted out of nowhere with the force of a storm wind. It might have had something to do with a jostled elbow and a spilled pitcher of ale, or perhaps an adverse roll of the dice or a look that was taken amiss. There was shouting, some of it his own, raw with drink-fuelled rage, and then the punch in his already tender gut that felled him to the rushes, his knees doubling towards his midriff and his mouth wide open, gasping for air that would not come.

Above him a knife flashed. There were more shouts and a struggle of shapes and shadows. He rolled away from the strike of the steel, became entangled in his own cloak and in a last effort to prevent himself being skewered, lashed out with his feet. His assailant staggered, struck his head on the solid oak corner of the trestle as he fell, and sprawled his length. The knife jerked once in his hand, then fell into the straw.

The shouting grew ragged and subsided. A soldier leaned over Sabin and his assailant. 'Robbie?' He shook the prone shoulder but to no response. When Robbie was rolled on his back, it became obvious why. There was a dimple in his skull the width of three fingers and he was dead. The sound of stertorous breathing came from the living who were staring at the scene in horror. Robbie stared back, unblinking, unmoving. Sabin tried to rise, wobbled, fell, and stayed down.

'What is going to happen to Sabin now?'

Poising her needle, Countess Matilda looked up from her embroidery and fixed her attention on her son. Simon had been aimlessly wandering the chamber for several minutes.

'That is for your stepfather to decide,' she said. As soon as news of the tavern brawl and its fatal outcome had reached their chamber, David had ordered Sabin clapped in manacles and thrown in Roxburgh's dungeon. Matilda had never seen her phlegmatic husband so close to losing his control – fists clenched, nostrils pinched with the effort of containing his rage. She suspected that Sabin had been chained out of sight to prevent a second killing.

The youth folded his arms and scowled. 'It wasn't Sabin's fault, everyone says so.' His voice, recently broken, was rough with challenge.

'It does not alter the fact that a man is dead and all the witnesses so drunk that they could scarcely remember their own names in the morning, let alone what happened the night before. Thank Christ that you were not with him.'

Simon gave the floor rushes a rebellious kick. 'I wish I had been.'

'Then you are a foolish child,' Matilda snapped. Making an effort, she moderated her tone. 'Your stepfather will deal with him justly. He is never unfair, you know that.'

He flashed her a resentful look. 'That's what I told Sabin about you when we were in Barfleur. His mood was sour and he said that you wished he had never been born.'

Matilda resumed her sewing, as if she could order her thoughts through the precise control of the needle. Although her expression did not change, Simon's words had struck a tender part of her conscience. 'Even if I took no pleasure in the circumstances of his birth, I do not begrudge Sabin his life,' she said. 'Although God knows what he is going to make of it. In truth I worry for him.' She worried too at the effect that Sabin had on this son of hers. Her eldest, Waltheof, was studying for the Church and well removed from the dangerous glamour of Sabin's reputation, but Simon was made of a different metal and was at an impressionable age. She could understand the attraction that Sabin's wild ways might hold for a youth beginning to chafe at the parental rein.

'Do you?' Simon kicked the floor rushes again, releasing the expensive scent of cinnamon bark. 'Have you been to see him?'

'Not yet,' she said.

'The guards wouldn't let me near. They said no one was to see him until my stepfather had spoken to him.'

The way he said 'stepfather' was telling. Matilda sighed and pushed her needle into the fabric. 'A day in a cell without company will do him no harm. He needs to reflect on the consequences of his actions.'

'You see, you are blaming him already.'

'It was his choice to visit the alehouse and drink himself into a stupor.'

Simon made an impatient sound. 'Sabin was right, you do wish him unborn,' he said with the unfairness of burning adolescence, and strode from the room.

Matilda tried to return to her sewing, but she had no heart for the task and her concentration had departed in her son's stormy wake.

Sabin. He had been christened Simon after his father, but she had quickly changed his name to the masculine version of his mother's. Simon was an appellation reserved for the legitimate heir to the earldom of Northampton. She had always felt guilty about that particular act. She had stolen the infant's given name. And because she felt guilty, she felt resentful. His father had yielded to her on the matter, a little too easily, she sometimes thought. Perhaps it was to appease her in the wake of his carnal sin, or perhaps to remind him of the boy's mother. She had never probed that particular sore spot too hard. Matilda had only met the mother once: at the convent of the Holy Redeemer in Evreux. Clothed in a nun's habit, Sabina had possessed the grace of a Madonna, and tranquil violet-grey eyes. Her son had inherited her feline grace and owned a masculine version of her features, but his eyes were his father's and they held fire, not tranquillity. He had been born of a single coupling, so both Sabina and her husband had said. A brief slip from the path, before guilt and common sense had returned them to the straight and narrow, but the consequences had already taken root. Sabina had died of a flux when Sabin was five years old, and although Matilda had said the necessary prayers, she had not mourned too hard.

Matilda gazed at her embroidery without seeing it. Dealing with Sabin had been easier when his father was alive. The boy had been less wild then. Into mischief, certainly, but reachable. All that had changed when Simon died. Suddenly it was like dwelling with a wild creature. It had been a relief to send him away to the royal court for training, and an even greater relief when her second husband had shouldered the burden of dealing with Sabin's waywardness on the occasions that the boy returned to their household.

She felt uneasy that she had been shirking her responsibilities. She had promised Simon that even if she could not love his son, she would make sure he lacked for nothing to advance his life. A promise that she had not kept, for Sabin languished in a cell, manacled and involved in a man's death following a drunken brawl.

The thought galvanised her to her feet and caused her attendant, Helisende, to glance up with a blink of surprise. Matilda went to the door and spoke to the guard. The man inclined his head, but looked doubtful.

'Are you certain, my lady?'

Her jaw tightened. 'Quite.'

He bowed and departed. Rubbing her hands, Matilda returned to the centre of the room. 'Put some more charcoal on the brazier,' she commanded Helisende. 'It is cold today.'

Helisende, who had been her maid and companion since they were small children, busied herself with the task. 'Do you know what you're about, mistress?' she asked shrewdly.

Matilda steepled her hands at her lips. 'No,' she said. 'Only that there has to be a way of breaking this circle.' She looked at Helisende. 'What would you do? Would you leave him in the prison to stew?'

The maid considered. 'Not beyond the time he has spent there now.' She dusted her fingers. 'Did you have time in all the upheaval of Sabin and Simon's return to mark the presence of Edmund Strongfist and his daughter? They were passing through on the way to Branton.'

Matilda frowned. 'Wasn't the daughter among the ladies of the chamber?'

'Aye, she was. Straight from the nunnery at Coldingham.'

Matilda winced at the mention of nuns.

'Strongfist fostered her there after the death of his wife,' Helisende said. 'But she's not taking vows.'

'What have Edmund Strongfist and his daughter to do with Sabin?' Matilda asked with impatience. She prayed that Sabin had not gone and debauched the girl. His reputation with women had begun the moment his voice had broken. But then she castigated herself. Such a happening would have come to her ears earlier than this. Indeed, knowing Edmund Strongfist, Sabin would have been emasculated by now and the offending member cast to the hounds.

'They are making plans to go and dwell in Outremer,' Helisende said. 'I heard it from his serjeant when I was fetching you that camomile tisane from the kitchens. If I were you, I'd send Sabin with them. He could atone for his sins at the Holy Sepulchre and you would not have to worry about what he was doing.'

Matilda gazed at Helisende in dawning admiration. 'That is an excellent idea,' she said after a moment.

'I know,' Helisende replied without a shred of false modesty. 'It'll either be the making or breaking of the lad.

Edmund Strongfist is not one to suffer fools gladly. He'll control him.'

There was a knock on the door. Helisende went to answer it, and Matilda swiftly put the eagerness from her expression. It would not do for the young man to see her smiling like a cat that had just eaten a mouse.

Looking dubious, the guard ushered Sabin into the chamber. Stalks of straw adhered to the young man's garments and the musty chill of the cells emanated from him in tangible waves. Beneath the bruising, his complexion was white with cold and tinged with blue. The dark hair lay flat and limp over his brows and the tawny-green eyes were as dull as stones.

A pang went through Matilda and suddenly it was very easy not to smile. 'You look frozen to the marrow,' she said. 'Come, sit by the brazier and get warm.'

Sabin gave her a wary look, but did as she bade. Usually he moved with fluid grace, but now he walked with a hunched shuffle more appropriate to an old man.

'Was I released by Prince David's command, or yours?' He glanced around as if expecting to see her husband.

'By mine.' Matilda poured him warm wine from the jug that stood by the hearth. 'And do not ask me why, because I am not sure that I know myself.' She handed him the cup. He took it and as he drank his teeth chattered against the rim of the cup. There was a red abrasion on his wrist where the manacle had chafed. 'When did you last eat?'

'The day before yesterday, at the dinner trestle . . . I think.'

'I'll bring food,' Helisende said, and whisked from the room. A brief silence followed her departure.

'What will you do with me now?' Sabin asked eventually.

'If you give your word of honour not to leave these rooms, you may remain here,' Matilda said, knowing that she could not send him back to his cell.

Wry amusement curled his lips. 'Surely that is setting a fox amongst all the plump little chickens? Besides, I thought that my word of honour counted for nothing around here.'

Matilda refused to rise to his bait. 'I do not believe that you have ever intentionally acted with dishonour.'

'It is just that circumstances conspire against me,' he mocked.

She went to a coffer standing against the wall and brought out the casket containing her ointments and nostrums.

'I suppose you know the tale of what happened at Barfleur,' he said. 'Do you not think it was dishonourable of me to steal King Henry's mistress from beneath his nose?'

'I think it was foolhardy,' she said. 'And you both paid the price: she with her life and you with your conscience. Hold out your hand.'

Again he hesitated, but then did so. She broke the wax seal on a fresh pot of marigold salve, dipped her finger and lightly anointed the abrasion caused by the manacle.

'Even so, I am a disgrace to the household and the name of my father . . . or so Prince David says.'

'Do you want me to condemn you, or condemn my husband for his opinion?' She wiped her finger on a soft strip of swaddling cloth and then bound it around his wrist, securing it with a silver pin. 'Do you consider yourself a disgrace?'

She released his hand and he withdrew it. 'I think it a little late in the day to seek my opinion,' he said. 'It has never mattered before, so why should it matter now?'

Matilda sighed. He had raised a thorny barrier around himself and she recognised her own responsibility for many of those thorns. And David's too. 'Helisende made a suggestion to me about your future while the guard was bringing you from your cell.'

'She wants to marry me?' The mocking tone was back. Sabin tipped a fresh measure of wine into his cup.

Matilda struggled with her temper. 'How can I help you if you will not help yourself? You stand in danger of being accused of taking a man's life. You could lose your own . . . and while you think that it would be no loss to anyone, most of all yourself, you would be terribly wrong.'

She waited for the bored expression, for the raise of a scornful eyebrow, but something must have reached him, for he lowered the cup and gave her a direct look filled with knowing. 'I suppose you would have failed in your duty,' he said.

'Yes, I would.'

'I am not sure about the loss to myself,' he said, 'but I suppose I owe you for the years you have tried and tolerated.' A self-deprecating smile crossed his lips and was gone. 'So what does Helisende have in mind for me – a gibbet?'

'No,' Matilda said. 'A cross.'

'A what?' Horrified astonishment filled his eyes. 'She wants to make a monk of me? Or a hermit?' He laughed without humour. 'At least if the latter I'd only have my own company to bruise and damage.'

'No, a crusader's cross.' Matilda clung to her patience. 'Edmund Strongfist is leaving to take service with King Baldwin of Jerusalem. As a trained warrior, you will be useful company. You can pray for your sins at the Holy Sepulchre and use your skills in the name of God.'

The astonishment remained and the laughing mouth closed to a straight line. His expression was so similar to his father's that it was like a sharp blow in the soft space beneath her heart.

'It is a clever thought,' he acknowledged after a moment. 'I will be safely out of the way and engaged in business of which for once the Church approves. When folk ask of me at home, you can tell them my whereabouts with pride, instead of looking over your shoulder. I won't be here to be a bad influence on Simon either, will I?'

She thought how vulnerable he looked, how exhausted and young beneath the bravado. 'Indeed that is true,' she answered steadily. 'Do you blame me for such thoughts?'

He shook his head. 'Doubtless in your position I would be thinking them too.'

'Your father took the cross, but he had to turn back at Dorylaeum because of a leg wound,' she said. 'And when he took it a second time, he knew he was dying and his strength only got him as far as Normandy. I thought you might complete the pilgrimage in his name.'

'Purpose upon purpose,' he said, the mockery back in his voice. 'You do not need to pile your packhorse with quite so many riches, my lady. I am already convinced.' He tilted his head. 'I will go willingly, but what does Edmund Strongfist say to this suggestion?'

Matilda had the grace to blush. 'He doesn't know yet.'

'Ah. And if he does not want me?'

'I think it unlikely. Whatever your reputation, no one has ever disputed your talents in the field. He would be mad to turn down the skills of another warrior on the journey.'

'And if I get out of hand, they do not call him Strongfist for nothing.' He finished the wine and set the cup aside. 'If I were him, I think that I might err on the side of madness.'

Matilda sighed. 'You are being given a chance, Sabin,' she said. 'Do not waste it. Here you have been marked by what has gone before. In Jerusalem, they do not know you. You will be just another Frankish face in the crowd with a future and a reputation to mould as you choose.'

The door opened and Helisende returned with a basket of oatcakes still warm from the griddle and glazed with honey. The maid glanced in his direction. 'You have told him?' Sabin smiled at her.

Matilda looked rueful. Helisende had always had a soft spot for Sabin, ever since he had been brought into their household as a swaddled scrap barely two weeks old.

'Indeed my lady has, and that it was your idea.' Easing to his feet, Sabin took the basket from Helisende and lightly kissed her cheek. 'I always knew you wanted to be rid of me the most.'

She gave him an affectionate cuff. 'Sit down before you fall down and eat those oatcakes,' she said brusquely. 'If I want rid of you, it's because I'm ambitious for you. You no more fit in here than a war sword belongs in the kitchens for chopping parsnips.'

This time Sabin's laughter was genuine. 'I would not have put it quite like that.' He began to wolf the oatcakes.

'Well, I would.' Helisende wagged her index finger. 'I expect great things of you, and not the kind that have brought you to this pass.'

Sabin swallowed, rinsed his mouth with the last of his wine and looked at the two women. 'Then I will not disappoint you by saying that you are expecting too much.'

'No, you will not.' Helisende folded her arms with the determination of a battle commander about to send a champion onto the field.

Matilda turned away, knowing her own faith would never match her maid's and that, for once in his life, Sabin was probably right. 'I will go and speak with the Prince,' she said. 'The sooner he is told, the sooner matters can be resolved.'

Chapter 4

Sabin stood in the gateway at Roxburgh and made his awkward farewells. The December morning was hard with frost, good for travelling but bitterly cold. Prince David clasped his hand briefly and gave him a nod that contained both goodwill and warning. 'Your last chance,' he said. 'Use it wisely.'

'You think me capable of wisdom?'

David's lips twitched. 'Are you not travelling to the land of miracles?'

Sabin returned the smile sourly.

From the children there were kisses and hugs. Young Henry had to be stopped from dashing around like a spark on the wind, and upsetting the horses. Countess Matilda embraced Sabin and he returned her clasp. Both of them acknowledged that it was a public duty, but neither drew back. Helisende wept and for an instant clung with maternal ferocity.

'Promise you will send word to us.' She drew her knuckles across her eyes.

'I promise . . . God willing.' He grinned. 'I will send you a bolt of golden silk from the harem of a Syrian emir.'

'I want no gifts. That you are safe will be reward enough.'

Finally, there was Simon. The youth was dressed for the occasion in the blue cloak that had belonged to his Saxon grandfather. Lined with the pelt of an arctic bear, it was a rare garment. His stepfather might be a prince, but Simon was heir to an earldom and royal blood ran in his own veins.

'I'm going with you in spirit,' he said as he and Sabin embraced. 'I wish I was going with you in body too.'

'Don't let your mother hear you say that.'

'She knows.' Simon smiled wryly. 'She'll watch me like a hawk for the next few days to make sure I don't take off after you. I might have risked it, except that Strongfist would tie me across my horse like a parcel of heather and send me straight back.'

He was trying for lightness and not succeeding. Sabin tightened the embrace. 'I will pray for our father at the Holy Sepulchre,' he said. 'And I will send you news, I promise, although I am not so sure about a bolt of golden silk. An emir's head perhaps?'

Simon found a more genuine smile. As Sabin released him, he took the large silver pin from his cloak. It was circular with a fastener in the shape of a thistle; the head was set with a large amethyst. 'Here,' he said. 'Take this to remind you of us. You lost yours on the *Blanche Nef*.'

Sabin looked down at the offering and shook his head. 'I cannot,' he said. 'It is part of your inheritance.'

'And it is mine to give.' Simon jutted his chin. 'If you do not take it, then I will throw it into the Tweed as an offering to God.' He thrust out his hand insistently. After a brief hesitation, Sabin took the brooch. It was as large and solid as a church doorknocker, and so cold from the air that it almost burned in his fingers.

'What choice do I have?' he said. 'It would be a sin to send a second to join the first.' He pushed the pin through his own cloak, which was of heavy green wool lined with marten skins. The existing pin was Simon's too, of good bronze with a pattern of beadwork circles.

'God speed you.' Simon's voice was tight with emotion.

'And keep you,' Sabin responded, feeling his own throat constrict. Abruptly he turned to his dun cob, and swung into the saddle.

Edmund Strongfist had sat his mount silently throughout the farewells. Now he inclined his head in salute to the Prince and his family, and clicked his tongue to his own mount.. Man and horse rode over the bridge at a brisk walk that settled into an easy long-swinging stride. They had a full day's ride ahead of them. Sabin followed, the dun's shod hooves ringing out, the pack pony clopping behind. Although he was tempted to look round, he kept his eyes fixed on the space between his mount's ears.

Strongfist was the one to turn, his light blue gaze fixing briefly on the walls of Roxburgh before settling on Sabin with assessment. 'No doubt you have been told as much about my reputation as I have been told about yours,' he said. He spoke French, but his accent was a peculiar blending of English and Lowland Scots. 'What you have heard of mine is likely true. I am hoping that the opposite applies to yours.'

Sabin raised his brows. 'If you are going to judge me by my past then I am condemned already. I might as well save you the trouble of the journey and jump into the Tweed now.' He indicated the roaring brown water, scummed with white.

The knight's eye corners crinkled with grim humour. 'That would be too easy. Besides, from what they say of you, you would likely float. Nay, I judge men by what I see myself, not what I hear from others.' He made a beckoning gesture. 'Ride alongside me. I'm not an owl to turn my head naturally like this.'

Sabin heeled the dun's flanks and joined Strongfist. They had spoken very little at Roxburgh: all the talking had been done by Prince David. A large bag of silver was now sequestered somewhere about Strongfist's person – expenses that had not been given to Sabin for fear that he might squander them. Or perhaps it was bribery to a gaoler. Edmund Strongfist had been summoned from his winter quarters at his brother's keep at Branton in order to take charge of Sabin, and that was where they were going now to await the pilgrimage season.

'You will find me easy enough company,' Strongfist said. His breath whitened the air and droplets of moisture hung in his fair beard. 'I have rules, but they are simple. I ask nothing of you that I do not ask of myself.'

'Prince David has rules like that too,' Sabin said neutrally.

'Aye, well, I'm not so much of a saint as he is.' Strongfist matched Sabin's tone. 'All I ask is that if you drink, you keep enough wits about you to handle a sword; if you wench, you do it discreetly; if there's trouble you walk away rather than become embroiled . . .' He looked sidelong at Sabin. 'Oh yes . . . and if you go near my beautiful convent-raised daughter, expect to find your bollocks cut off and stuffed up your arse.'

The knight's tone was conversational, but Sabin was in no doubt that Edmund Strongfist would not hesitate to act. Sabin thought of the girl that he had seen riding in Strongfist's wake. The soft glance of an eye, the glint of a dark braid. Forbidden fruit. It had started that way with Lora.

'I swear I have no intention of touching your daughter.' Sabin made the sign of the cross on his breast to reinforce his words.

'As long as we understand each other.'

'I think we do, sir,' Sabin said with what he hoped was convincing sincerity.

Strongfist's grunt of response could have been either satisfied or pessimistic, but Sabin did not pursue the issue to find out.

They continued their journey through a world of frozen grey. Sabin was glad of his cloak and the foresight he had had to don the padded tunic he usually wore beneath his mail. The mail shirt itself had been heavily greased to keep out the rust and rolled in a sheepskin, which was secured behind his saddle. He had heard tales of how hellishly hot the lands of Outremer were, that a man could stew to death within his armour. Today he could not imagine such heat.

'They have weather like this in Outremer too,' Strongfist

said as if reading his mind. 'In the mountains, the nights can be as cold as a witch's tit, and on the high ground there is often snow.' He looked at Sabin. 'But mostly it is the heat that men remember because of the intensity and the days, one upon the other, when there is not a cloud in the sky. The wind is as hot as the fires of hell and the sun beats down on your head like a hammer.'

'And yet you want to go back?'

Smile creases grooved Strongfist's cheeks above the fair beard. 'It is a land of great beauty too. The olive groves are shady at noonday and the houses have courtyards with pools and fountains. The Plain of Sharon is lush and green and there is good hunting. You breathe in the dust and it becomes a part of you. I cannot tell you. You must see for yourself.'

'My father went on crusade, but he never spoke much of it. He had to turn back after the battle of Dorylaeum because he was mortally sick.'

'I know your father was at Dorylaeum,' Strongfist gathered the reins through his fingers. 'I was with him at the battle and a desperate one it was too, with the Turkish hordes assaulting us on all sides. We had to stand firm, hour upon hour while the sun dried our sinews to leather. For a time, I was in the same line as your sire. We knew he was suffering, but he would not leave his position, even when he took a Saracen arrow in his side.' He looked at Sabin. 'He was a *preux chevalier*, your father. You should be proud of him.'

'I am,' Sabin croaked and there was almost a lump in his throat. Usually people spoke of what his father would think of him, not what he thought of his father. 'He always regretted that he had to turn back. He never went to a priest to have his vow rescinded. When he knew he was dying, he set out again, but it was too late . . .' He broke off and clicked his tongue to the dun, urging it to a trot. Its hooves rang hollowly on the frosty ground. He concentrated on the sound, on the surge of its powerful body, on the raw cold burning his face.

After a moment, the grey trotted up beside him. 'It is not too late for you,' Strongfist said and leaned across to squeeze his shoulder, the power in his fingers revealing the source of his nickname.

Sabin forced a smile. 'So I am told, but that the hour draws perilously near.'

Strongfist removed his hand and nothing else was said. In silence, uneasy at first, but becoming more companionable, the two men rode on towards Branton.

The scribe's wall chamber at Branton had room for little more than a stone bench and a lectern, positioned to gain the best from the weak winter light filtering through the narrow window. Having dwelt within a regime of nuns, Annais was accustomed to bodily privation, but still she wondered how Andrew, her uncle's scribe, managed to sit here at his labours without benefit of a brazier. The draught from the window-slit was perishing, yet if she closed the shutters, she would have to light a candle in order to see her writing. The only consolation was the modicum of privacy afforded by the heavy curtain drawn across the chamber entrance, which shielded her from prying eyes.

Annais nibbled the end of her trimmed quill and studied the list she had written on a scrap of parchment. It was an inventory of the items needed for their journey. Whether it would all fit on three packhorses was another matter, and she did not know how much their travelling companion was bringing with him.

Her father had been ambivalent when the messenger from Prince David had arrived with the 'request' that Sabin FitzSimon be permitted to accompany them to Jerusalem. The young man's reputation for wildness and trouble was precariously balanced against that same young man's reputation on the battlefield, although the promise of several marks of silver for expenses had somewhat tipped the scales. It would be useful to have extra protection on the road, her father had said with stoic resignation as he prepared to return to Roxburgh and fetch FitzSimon.

Perhaps four packhorses, she thought. One would need to carry fodder for itself and the others. At least her clothes would not take up much room. There was little call for a vast wardrobe in a nunnery and what she had was serviceable and plain.

There had to be room for her harp. She glanced at the small instrument beside her on the bench. It had travelled with her English grandparents to their exile from England and the boxwood was smoothed by the hands of many generations, their songs blended deep into the grain. She had learned the first notes at her mother's knee, and then later with the nuns; she was skilled in tunes both secular and religious. Her father said that everyone had a God-given talent, and hers was her music. Just to ripple her fingers over the pale horsehair strings soothed her soul and gave her a feeling of inner calm.

A shout from the courtyard below the meagre window distracted her from her thoughts. Turning, she peered out and saw that her father had arrived with Sabin FitzSimon in tow. The young knight rode a solid dun cob and had a tubby Galwegian pack pony on a leading rein. Like her father, he wore a fur-lined cap against the cold; there was a sword at his hip and a large kite shield strapped at his back. The distance was too far for her to see his features clearly. Last time he had resembled a grotesque that one of the stonemasons had been carving for a waterspout at the Priory. She noticed that he moved a deal more easily than he had done at Roxburgh. Annais rolled up her list, put her ink and quill away in the scribe's coffer and went down to greet them.

By the time she arrived in the hall, her father had entered with FitzSimon at his heels. The young knight's gaze was assessing as he folded his fur cap into the satchel hanging from his shoulder. His hair was spiked and tousled from the headwear. Although patterned by a swirl of fading colours, his features were no longer swollen and distorted. He had clear, light eyes of variegated amber-green and bones that remained just on the elegant side of bold. Her stomach wallowed. She was unaccustomed to men and those she did know were family and without dangerous reputations.

'Sweeting!' Her father leaned down so that she could kiss his cheek, and then he folded her arm through his and presented her formally to his companion.

Sabin FitzSimon bowed. 'Mistress Annais,' he said. 'I am pleased to make your acquaintance.'

Trained to music, she appreciated the quality of his voice and wondered how it would sound in company with her harp. 'And I yours,' she responded. His cloak was pinned with a magnificent brooch – a great silver thistle with an amethyst jewel in the head. Beneath the cloak, the hem of his tunic sparkled with metallic embroidery. Annais gazed admiringly. It was as if a gilded figure had stepped out of a stained church window and come to life. Sabin FitzSimon's eyes might be as clear as coloured glass, but they looked through rather than at her. The polite expression and amiable curl of the lips were born of distant courtesy and possessed no substance. A glance at her father showed that the greeting appeared to find favour with him.

The men exchanged looks and Sabin took a back-step. 'You will find me no oath-breaker,' he said.

'You know what would happen if you did,' her father said flatly. 'Come, you must meet my brother. He knows nothing of your reputation or your reasons for being here, other than your wish to make a pilgrimage in respect of your father's soul.' He gestured somewhat brusquely at his daughter. 'Annais, go and help your aunt. I will speak with you later.'

Annais pursed her mouth at the dismissal, but did as she was bidden. She could understand her father's concern. He was like a shepherd inviting a wolf to sup at his hearth and then spending the rest of the night in terror for his sheep. She wondered what the oath was that Sabin FitzSimon had no intention of breaking.

Over the following weeks, Sabin caused a minor stir in the household. Annais watched him charm her aunt, the normally dour lady Wulfgeat, until the woman almost simpered. He was the subject of endless discussion in the women's bower. Rumours abounded, from the almost true to the fantastical. Annais, who could have enlightened the ladies and wiped the approval from her aunt's expression with a single sentence, kept her own counsel.

Not that he had shown any signs of living up to the reputation he possessed. He was polite to all, but unforthcoming. Sometimes he would play dice with the men in the hall, or settle down with her father for a game of chess over a flagon of wine. But she never saw him the worse for drink and if his eyes occasionally strayed over this woman or that, it was in idle perusal. Annais herself might not have existed for all the attention he paid her.

She went to watch him train on the open ground beyond the keep where the garrison and the knights practised their craft. While he did not have the stolid strength of the older men he was unbelievably fast, skilled in the use of his weapons, and possessed the balance of a cat. She began to understand why her father had taken the risk. If her own God-given skill was music, then Sabin FitzSimon's was combat.

He came from the field flushed and sweating hard despite the raw cold of the day. No longer a polite and distant effigy, but a man vivid with life, filled with pleasure and pride. Annais drew a sharp breath and suddenly she was as flushed as he was. He caught her gaze on him and, for an instant, she was trapped like a doe in a hunter's snare. His eyes were woodland gold. It was no more than the briefest engagement, for he immediately changed focus to the middle distance and she was free to hide herself among the other women, her cheeks as hot as wafer irons.

For the rest of the day she avoided the hall and spent her time in the women's quarters, helping to embroider a cloth for the dais table, although embroidery was one of her least favourite pastimes. By the time dusk arrived, her eyes were blurred, her thumb sore where she had accidentally driven a needle into the quick of her nail. She had also reached the conclusion that she was being foolish. Sabin FitzSimon, whatever his reputation, was unlikely to attempt a seduction beneath her father's nose. What had happened was a single unguarded look, caused by no more than the residue of his triumph on the field and her admiration for his prowess. There was no reason to skulk in the purgatory of the bower. Indeed, by skulking she made it seem more than it was.

Setting her piece of the embroidery aside, hoping that her aunt would not notice the small brown bloodspot marring the bleached linen, she went down to the hall. Her father was deep in conversation with several of the household knights. Sabin had been playing a game of merels with one of the older squires but, as Annais arrived, the youth rose, stretched, nodded to Sabin and went off to attend to his duties. Sabin started to put the wooden gaming pieces in their leather pouch. He paused briefly as Annais took her place on the bench across from him, then continued the task with nimble fingers.

'I see that you are trying to get me killed,' he said with a rueful glance in her father's direction. The latter had turned with the unerring instinct of a hound on a scent and although he remained among his companions, it was obvious that his attention was no longer wholly on the conversation.

Annais frowned. 'Have you been told not to speak to me?'

He smiled grimly. 'I have been told that you are a beautiful, convent-raised innocent and that if I so much as loosen a single hair of your braid, your father will mutilate me where it matters.' He tugged the drawstring tight on the pouch and, placing it on top of the little gaming board, pushed it towards her. 'By all means play, *demoiselle*, but not with me.'

She reddened, for the words had a double meaning, and even if she had been raised in a convent, she was not entirely as innocent as her father thought. There had been a couple of women who had turned to God for solace only after living well-rounded lives.

'And if my father wasn't watching?'

He rose to his feet. 'I think the answer would be the same. The match would neither be even, nor fair.' Inclining his head to her, he strode off down the hall.

She felt hot and a little foolish. It had been a rebuff in no uncertain terms. She also felt aggrieved because she had only been attempting to be civil . . . or had she? A small inner voice whispered that there was more. That she had wanted him to stay and play at merels, had wanted to watch his swift, supple fingers move upon the pieces.

Her father's shadow darkened the grainy light from the lantern standing on the trestle. Sitting down, he unfastened the drawstring of the gaming pouch that Sabin had pulled tight. 'You need a partner for merels?' he said.

Annais didn't really want to play but she nodded dutifully. 'You have warned him well,' she said. 'How are we going to be travelling companions if we are not even permitted to speak to each other?'

'I have set no such terms upon him,' Strongfist said, 'nor upon you.' His blue eyes were shrewd as he arranged the merels pieces. 'But when you come from the women's quarters and go straight to him with a high colour in your cheeks, it gives me cause to be anxious.'

'Without reason!' Annais cried with righteous indignation. 'I spoke to him out of courtesy.'

'I am glad to hear it, daughter.' He indicated that she should open the game.

Annais was tempted to shove one of the pieces in temper, but her years in the convent had taught her discipline, and when she made her move it was measured and steady. 'You told him that you would harm him if he touched me.'

'Indeed I did, as I would tell any man who had not the right.' He looked thoughtfully at his daughter. 'Sabin knows my rules and he has agreed to abide by them. I hope you are not going to make them difficult for him to keep.'

Annais stared at him, feeling hurt. 'You do not trust me either?'

'Of course I trust you.' He rubbed the back of his neck in discomfort. 'But men like FitzSimon are attractive to women. I've never seen so many ladies come out to watch battle practice in midwinter before. They see prowess on the field, and when its instigator is young and handsome, the results are inevitable.'

Annais looked quickly down at the merels board as if considering her strategy. What her father said was so true that it was mortifying.

'By all means be civil to Sabin FitzSimon,' Strongfist said in a gentler tone, 'but do not seek his company. I am glad to see from his behaviour just now that he has taken my strictures to heart. All I ask is that you do not hinder him.'

'No, Papa,' Annais said in a chastened voice. In a way, although she felt resentful, she was also relieved. Having rules by which to abide was like having an anchor in a stormy sea. She would not make a fool of herself again.

'Good lass.' He nodded and, dismissing the subject, settled down to consider his strategy. Although he won the first game easily, Annais had recovered sufficiently by the second to run him close, and the third time she defeated him, with a delighted laugh.

The hayloft was filled with the fragrant aroma of summer from golden stalks, fat dried seedheads, faded stems of clover, poppy and feathery Our Lady's bedstraw. His heart thundering in the aftermath of pleasure and exertion, Sabin inhaled the evocative scents of the season, blended with the sweat and woodsmoke exuding from his companion's damp skin.

She was a dairymaid, but since the dairy was not particularly active in the winter months, she had time to spare and was prepared to give generously. She was a widow, unattached, experienced and barren, all of which gave Sabin cause to thank God for His bounty.

Although his much-needed release had felled him like a poled ox, he managed to roll off her and flop on his back. After a moment, he found the strength to pull his braies back up and retie the cord that held them at his waist.

The woman leaned on her elbow and watched him, her loose tawny-brown hair tumbling about her shoulders.

'How long before you leave?' she asked, winding a coil of it around her forefinger.

He flashed her a grin, his chest heaving. 'Why? Was my performance so bad you cannot wait to be rid of me?'

She laughed, her eyes full of candid humour. 'You dined with fine manners despite your hunger,' she said. 'I just wondered if you were going to be a regular guest at the board.'

He shrugged and pillowed his hands behind his head. 'We leave next month, providing we get no more snow.' He closed his eyes, feeling drowsy and replete. A smile curled his mouth corners. 'But I will need to feed myself up for the famine to come.'

'There is Sir Edmund's daughter,' she said slyly and rolled over so that she lay along the length of his body.

Sabin chuckled and did not open his eyes. 'Precisely,' he said. 'There is Sir Edmund's daughter, and I want to live.'

It was late when Sabin finally bade farewell to his companion and they went their separate ways, she to the kitchens, he to the hall. They had slept for a time in their nest of hay, had woken and lazily taken a second appreciation of each other's bodies, by which time dusk was but a memory and outside it was full dark.

The evening meal had been served and finished for some while, but he intercepted a basket of bannocks on its way back to the kitchens and helped himself to a beaker of heather ale from a jug that had been left out on a trestle.

As he approached the dais table, he heard a soft ripple of notes, delicate and sensual as sunlit shallows over warm sand. Having dwelt at the English court, he was accustomed to hearing music, but usually in elaborate arrangements with more than one musician. Here, the single harp spoke across the layers of smoke with a wistful beauty that caught his attention and drew his eyes to follow his ears.

Not for one moment did he expect the musician to be Edmund Strongfist's daughter and he was so astounded that for a moment he checked his stride. Her skill was in the same realms as the bards who played at King Henry's court. The notes reached out and touched him like fingers. It was almost frightening that this slip of a girl with her great brown eyes and gauche mien should have such a luminous talent.

She was thoroughly absorbed in her music, her head bent over her harp in the manner that he might bend over his sword blade as he honed it in preparation for battle. The look of concentration on her face made it quite tender and beautiful. Her audience on the dais was spellbound. Sabin watched from a distance, recognising the danger. *There is Sir Edmund's daughter*, the dairymaid had said and, although she had been teasing, her eyes had been shrewd. How easy it would be to go quietly to the dais, to take his place among the listeners, to look at her and let her know when she raised her head from the beguilement of the music that he had been watching her. He knew how to set a twig so close to the fire that it smouldered and smouldered, gradually becoming so hot and volatile that all it took was one gentle nudge forward to create a blinding immolation. He had done it many times. From curiosity, from boredom, for no more reason than the challenge. Now, because he had made a promise, he held back. For Edmund Strongfist, for the girl engrossed in her music, and for himself.

Turning his back on the dais, on the beautiful embroidery of notes, Sabin walked quietly from the hall, purloining the ale pitcher on his way out.

Chapter 5

Annais opened her eyes and stared at the flapping roof of the deck shelter. There was sunlight behind it; she could tell from the white glow shining through the canvas. The creak of timbers filled her ears, the conversations of sailors, the hiss and slap of the waves beneath the galley's keel.

Gingerly she sat up and pressed her hand to her aching stomach. Over the past weeks she had retched so hard that she had vomited blood. How she could be so sick and still be alive was both a miracle and a torture. While others had been praying for the heavy seas not to boil up and engulf them, she had been exhorting God to end her suffering and let her die.

Apart from crossing rivers on a ferry, her feet had never left dry land. She had been terrified of boarding the pilgrim galley, but determined not to show her fear. No one knew how her mind had dwelt on the wreck of the *Blanche Nef*, of how she shrank from the thought of the green, cold fathoms beneath her, filled with nameless creatures and the white bones of drowned sailors.

The deck heaved beneath the woven rush matting on which she lay. She waited for the familiar and dreaded nausea to begin, but her only sensations were the hollow gripe of hunger, and pain from the constant retching. Her father and Sabin had said that the sickness would pass, the former with anxiety in his eyes, the latter cheerful and unperturbed. Perhaps they were right. Perhaps the worst was over. She had vowed that once her feet touched dry land, she would never sail on the deep ocean again. Several times they had put into harbour along the coast of Spain to take on fresh barrels of water and food supplies, but it had been only for one night and she had spent most of the time asleep. Besides, the ports were not the kind of places that her father would let her go ashore, even if she had been capable of walking along the wharfside.

They were now following the African coast. Her father said the route they were taking was the one used by the crusading English prince, Edgar Atheling. Annais did not care who had used it, only desired that the purgatory of the journey should end.

She could hear the sound of male voices, loud with excitement and laughter, outside the shelter. Crawling to the entrance, she parted the tent flaps and immediately had to squint, for the sunlight was blinding in a sky of lapis-blue. One of the sailors had lit a cooking fire on the ballast stones and the heat from the flames shimmered skywards. An aroma of onions and root vegetables drifted towards her, aggravating the hollow feeling in her stomach. Some headless silver fish were frying in a skillet and the smell of the spitting fat made her mouth water.

Unsteadily, Annais stood up and grasped a halyard for support. There was a slight breeze, enough to flutter her wimple, but not sufficient to fill the belly of a sail and drive the ship forwards. The crew had broken out the oars, but seemed more concerned with their shouting and jesting than with rowing.

Annais made her way slowly to one of the water barrels, dipped the ladle and took a drink. The taste was not particularly pleasant, having a flavour of oak and staleness, but she was thirsty. The crewman tending the cooking fire glanced sidelong at her and murmured a greeting.

She responded politely and asked him what the shouting was about.

His grin deepened the weather creases at his eye corners. 'Some folk acquire their sea-legs long before others,' he said.

'And then they just have to brag about it.' She looked at him blankly.

'Have you ever heard of the Viking sea-reaver Olaf Tryggvasson?' Taking a wooden spatula, he deftly turned the fish in the skillet.

Annais shook her head. She could recite most of the saints who had ever existed, but her knowledge of Vikings was somewhat less detailed.

'The claim was that he could run from one end of his longship to the other along the oars of his men. Yon young fool's wagered he can do the same.' He jerked his head towards the prow of the ship.

Annais took a few faltering steps and hastily leaned against one of the water barrels for support. In front of her, another crew member became aware of her presence and stepped aside, yielding her a clear view of the prow of the ship.

Clad in naught but his linen braies and a dazzling smile, Sabin FitzSimon was playing up to a laughing, sceptical audience. One crewman was taking bets and silver pennies strewed the square of red cloth spread at his feet.

Sabin leaped onto the top strake of the galley and grasped a halyard to steady himself. He drew several deep breaths and although the smile remained, Annais saw that it was fixed and meaningless. His focus was nailed to the line of oars stroking the galley through the water. She saw his chest expand with a final breath. When he made his move it was fluid and without hesitation. He leaped precisely onto the first oar, and, arms outspread for balance, danced lightly along the line, leaving each oar before it could dip with his weight and cast him into the sea. He reached the bow of the galley near her shelter, pivoted, and returned to the prow in the same manner, nimble as a breeze.

The crew and other passengers cheered, clapped and whistled. The sailor holding the bets knotted the four corners of the red cloth and handed it to Sabin, who took it with a flourish and a bow. His success was the signal for others to try their luck, but although some got halfway, no one succeeded in turning and running back. Shouts of encouragement were punctuated by groans of dismay and loud splashes. The deck began to fill with dripping men. When Sabin succeeded in running the oars a second time without mishap to prove that it was more than just good fortune that had kept him dry-shod, the others tossed him into the sea.

Annais watched the sport until her legs began to buckle. She retired to sit on a bench near the cooking fire and accepted the oval of flattened bread that the sailor tending the fire offered her.

'Feeling better, sweetheart?' Her father came to the fire. He had succumbed to the exuberance of the moment and he too wore only his thick linen braies. His head, hands and wrists were a deep sun-weathered brown. Everywhere else was the white of new milk.

'A little,' she said. 'I don't feel sick any more – just sore.'

Sabin sauntered over to the barrels to drink a dipper of water. She watched the movement of his throat as he swallowed, and the way the sea water sparkled on his chest. His braies were made of the finest linen chansil, and because they were saturated, left no room for modesty. He had tied the cloth of coins to the waist cord and the weight pulled the garment down over the point of one hipbone. Annais tried not to look but it was difficult. He finished drinking, fetched his knife from his pile of clothes, and leaned to spear one of the sardines smoking on the griddle.

'You must have learned that trick somewhere,' Strongfist said. 'No man, no matter how good, could do that without training.'

Sabin shrugged. 'When I was a squire we used to do it all the time on the barges on the River Thames. There is no trick to it. All it takes is balance and practice.' He blew on the fish and delicately began to eat it, fiddling out the small bones and flicking them aside.

'Like most things,' Strongfist said, a smile parting his fair beard.

'Indeed,' Sabin answered with a glint of humour. 'The problem is that I have had more practice at losing my balance than at gaining it.'

'Until now.'

'Until now,' Sabin agreed. He sat down on one of the ballast stones. More sardines waited their turn and he tossed a couple into the pan. His glance flickered to Annais and the diminishing morsel of bread in her hand.

'It is good to see you outside the shelter, mistress,' he said courteously. 'Dare I hope you feel improved?'

She murmured that she did, and found herself resenting his enquiry. With the crew members and pilgrims – all men – he was jocular and easy. She had heard his laughter a moment since and watched him run like quicksilver along those oars. But with her he was grave, so correct and polite that his distance was almost a rebuff.

Her father leaned over to squeeze her arm. 'I'll be happier when she's filled out again. She's all skin and bone, like a heifer in a year of famine.'

Annais drew back indignantly as the men laughed.

'Don't you worry,' the cook said. 'I'm sure you'll have plenty of offers from eligible men in the Holy Land to fatten her up.' He patted his belly so that no one could mistake the innuendo.

There was a moment's awkward silence, for the words had crossed the line between good-natured jesting and into tavern-talk. Strongfist stiffened and Sabin stood, his fist tightening upon his knife hilt, its blade edged with shreds of fried fish. For a moment Annais thought that he was going to assault the sailor, but then saw that Sabin's attention was fixed on a point beyond the stern.

'What is it?' Strongfist was alert too, shading his eyes against the hot blue light. Behind them, the rest of the crew was still boisterously engaged in the sport of oar-dancing.

'A ship,' Sabin said. 'She's lateen-rigged.'

The words meant nothing to Annais. She rose and squinted across the sun-dazzled water. There was indeed another vessel on the near horizon and it appeared to have three sails whereas their own galley had one.

'Go inside the deck shelter,' Strongfist commanded her.

'Why, what is it?'

'Never mind. Just go.'

'It's possibly an Arab ship out of Tunis,' Sabin replied, cutting across Strongfist. 'She might be a harmless trader, but she might also be carrying pirates, and with a rig like that, she's capable of running us down. Your father is right. You had best go within the deck shelter. If they see a woman on board, it will increase their incentive to attempt us – should that be their inclination.'

Annais swallowed. 'Pirates?'

'No different to the robbers who haunt the mountain passes on the overland journey. They take their opportunities as they arise.'

'By Christ, shut your mouth,' Strongfist growled. 'Do you want to make her witless with terror?'

'I think you underestimate your daughter, sire.' Turning away, hands cupped at his mouth, Sabin bellowed a halt to the oar-dancing.

'I would rather know, Papa.' Annais raised her chin. 'You are always saying I am descended from warrior stock.'

'Indeed you are, child, but I wonder if I have done you a disservice by bringing you.'

'Never think that. The disservice would have been leaving me behind.' She kissed his sun-hot cheek and tasted dried salt.

He found a half-smile. 'You're a good lass. Now go.'

Annais made her way back to the deck shelter. The cook had already doused the fire and all merriment had ceased.

Ducking within the canvas, she sought among her belongings until her fingers closed around the hilt of an English scramaseax that had belonged to her great-grandfather. She gripped the hilt of shaped antler and drew the knife from its scabbard. The blade was fashioned from numerous bars of steel, hammered and blended so that a pattern seemed to shimmer like snakeskin beneath the surface. Annais gazed briefly into its sinuous mirror before resheathing the weapon. She knew she ought to lace up the flaps of the shelter, but could not bring herself to do so. Her father wanted to protect her by keeping her in ignorance, but Sabin was right – she did need to know.

She felt the kick of their vessel as the rowers took up a hard, steady rhythm in an effort to outrun the other ship. The sea vibrated against the strakes and resonated deep in her stomach where the queasiness of seasickness had been replaced by the queasiness of fear. Through the gap in the tent flap, she saw crew and passengers preparing to fight. Sabin paused briefly in front of the shelter, affording her a view of his legs and lower body, now clad in hose and boots, and a knee-length padded tunic. He had buckled on his swordbelt and drawn the blade. Unlike her knife, it looked like a plain serjeant's weapon.

'I feel so helpless.' She had spoken more than half to herself, but he heard her.

'Then pray for us, *demoiselle,*' he said without stooping or turning. 'If we cannot outrun them, then they might be put off by the notion that we are armed to the teeth and not as soft a target as we look.'

'And if they are not?'

There was a slight stir of the gambeson hem to suggest that he had shrugged. 'Then we fight . . . Of course, I could be wrong and they could be sailing us down just to give us a friendly greeting.' He moved away then, his step light and quick.

Annais fumbled her small gold cross from beneath her linen shift and began to pray.

Sabin watched the other ship gain ground on them. 'We should stop rowing,' he said. 'The men will exhaust themselves and be of no use if it comes to a fight. They are going to catch us; it is but a matter of time.'

Strongfist, who had arrived at much the same conclusion, spoke to the captain. The man shook his head, looking unhappy, but after a moment, bellowed a command. The frantic pace slowed and the galley ceased to shoulder the water.

Sabin moved to the side of the ship, his shield on his left arm, his sword unsheathed in his right hand. Similarly armed, Strongfist joined him. Two mail-clad knights followed him, six footsoldiers, in quilted tunics like Sabin's, and a priest armed with a stout quarterstaff.

In a hiss of white water, the pursuing ship surged within range. Her three sails were the dark brownish-red of dried blood and her deck was lined with turbaned men brandishing weapons.

'That settles the matter of friend or foe,' Sabin said.

'They're common sea-reavers,' Strongfist muttered. 'Not a decent piece of armour among them, although that doesn't make them less dangerous. They'll throw grapnel ropes to try to haul us in and rely on speed and agility to do the rest. If we can beat off their first attack, they'll run.' He spoke swiftly, his eyes never leaving the oncoming dhow.

A rope armed with an iron grapnel snaked across the short gap of churning water between the galley and the dhow. The claws dug into the wash strake and the rope went taut. With mighty heaves, the crew of the dhow began hauling the galley in, causing her to turn in the water like a fly near a drain hole. Strongfist's sword hacked down, parting the fibres of the rope in a single blow, but more grapnels had hissed out, tangling and parcelling the pilgrim galley to immobilise her for devouring.

The ships ground together and bounced apart. The reavers took advantage of the dhow's higher freeboard to leap on to the deck of the galley. Sabin jumped backwards, avoiding the slash of a sword that, had he been slower, would have disembowelled him. He backed again, drawing his assailant onwards. The pirate sprang, landed on the roasting hot ballast stones and screamed. Sabin swiftly despatched him, danced nimbly over the searing rocks and tackled his second raider.

The fighting was furious and brutal. Sabin had seldom fought against curved swords before, and the swift flashes of the blade took all his speed and focus to avoid. A split moment of delay bared him to a downward slice that opened his gambeson like a fishwife gutting a herring and streaked a stinging cut along his ribs. He swore and spun from the blade, got his shield up in time for the next assault and ducked to hack low at the raider's unprotected shins. The man went down, screaming, bleeding. Sabin leaped over him and darted to Strongfist's aid. The latter was under assault from both sides and bleeding profusely from a slash to the browbone. Sabin caught the descending blade on the edge of his shield, thrust sideways and came in hard with his sword. Knowing that the blow was true, not waiting to see the man fall, he pivoted and struck down the other pirate and moved on: fast, balanced, a little desperate but not despairing. The pilgrims were outnumbered, but they had the better fighting skills. Sabin downed another raider. He was breathing hard now, but his movement remained easy. He tried to imagine that it was a morning's battle practice at Henry's court.

Commands were screamed from the dhow in a language that Sabin did not recognise but he could hear the urgency. As swiftly as they had attacked, the pirates retreated, fleeing to their ship and slashing the grapnel ropes to part the vessels.

Open sea swelled between the dhow and the galley.

Strongfist began picking up the pirate bodies and heaving them over the side. The diminished occupants of the dhow brandished their weapons and spat threats, but did not attempt to follow them up. The captain of the galley roared a command, and the crew made haste to take up their oars and pull.

'Christ!' Strongfist staggered over to Sabin. Blood had begun to clot in a black lump along the cut to his brow. 'That was too close for comfort.' He clasped Sabin's hand. 'I owe you my life.'

Sabin shook his head. 'You owe me nothing,' he said. 'You would have done the same for me.' He drew away from Strongfist's grip and, weak-kneed in the aftermath of battle, lurched over to the ballast stones. His first victim had gone over the side, but his scimitar gleamed against the hot, blood-stained boulders. Sabin set his hand to the hilt and turned it in his hand. There was some rust along the blade, perhaps caused by old blood, or the sea air. The man had not cared for it properly. He swept an imaginary blow – and paid for it as the cut across his ribs opened up and pain seared. He gasped and pressed his hand to his side.

'You are wounded?' Strongfist's voice was anxious.

'No more than a scratch,' Sabin answered. 'My gambeson protected me from the full blow.' He set his fingers to the mouth-sized slit in the side of the garment and looked up as Annais emerged from the deck shelter and threw herself into her father's arms. Strongfist's good side had been facing her, and when she saw the clotted mess along his browbone, she drew back with a gasp of dismay.

Sabin thought for an instant that she was squeamish, but revised his impression as she gently touched the cut and said that it needed stitching. She was pale with shock, but her expression was of concern for her father, not herself.

'It's nothing,' Strongfist said with gruff dismissal.

Even if not serious the wound was more than nothing, but Sabin held his tongue. Annais had eyes to see for herself. He noticed that she had a rather fearsome knife thrust through her belt and his lips twitched in amusement. 'Who were you intending to stick with that?' he asked.

Her cheeks blazed. 'I haven't decided yet.'

His smile became a grin. Turning away, twirling the scimitar, he went to talk to the ship's master.

Annais took her father to the deck shelter. She bathed his wound, set in two stitches as Sister Joveta at the infirmary had shown her how to do, and dressed it with a salve made from self-heal and honey. There were other minor wounds for her to tend: cuts and grazes, a splinter from a shield that had to be tugged out with tweezers, broken fingers to be bandaged together.

Finally, as the fire was rekindled on the ballast stones and the cooking pot slung back over the flames to provide the evening meal, Sabin ducked into the deck shelter. He had removed gambeson, shirt and tunic to leave him bare-chested again save for the small crucifix dangling on a cord around his neck. A tang of sweat and salt clung to him and Annais felt suffocated by his scent and proximity.

'What do you want?' The sound emerged as a croak. She tried to back away without making it too obvious.

'Some of your salve for this tear in my hide.' He turned to expose the scratch from the scimitar blade. 'I have a needle in my pack, but the eye has broken. So I thought I might be able to prevail on you for one of those too.' His gaze settled on her hand, which had gone to the sheath at her waist. 'I promise to behave . . . despite my reputation.' He sat down and gestured towards the knife. 'Can I see?'

Reluctantly she drew the scramaseax from her belt and handed it to him, hilt-first.

His touch on the haft was careful and admiring. 'It is a very finely crafted piece of weaponry.' Lightly he traced the pattern welding on the surface and then cleaned his fingerprints with his folded shirt until the steel shone like moonlit water.

'It was my English great-grandfather's,' Annais took her pot of honey salve and, gesturing him to lean to one side, set about cleaning and smearing the scimitar wound. He flinched at the first touch, then held himself still. 'My father has his sword too.'

'I used to have my father's cloak clasp, but I lost it.' He returned the knife. His tone was carefully neutral.

'I thought your cloak clasp was a family jewel,' she said, thinking of the huge penannular thistle she had seen him wearing.

'It is, but given by my brother. He has our father's sword too, and his hauberk for the time when he is old enough to wear it . . . God help him.' He started to rise to his feet before the conversation took him into the murky waters off the coast of Barfleur.

Annais cleared her throat. 'You said you wanted a needle,' she reminded him and pointed to his side. 'It's a sharp cut, but it doesn't need stitching.'

His taut expression relaxed into a smile. 'It's not for my hide, it's for my gambeson. There's a gash in it like a halfwit's grin.'

She wondered whether to offer to sew the tear for him and decided against it. Had he wanted her to do so, he would have asked the boon of her skill rather than the boon of her equipment. She found her small needle case, carved from a goose's wingbone, tipped out a small strip of linen cloth and from it removed the sturdiest of her silver needles attached to a bright strand of green thread.

'I have never been so afraid as I was when I heard the attack,' she confessed in a low voice. 'I thought we were all going to die.'

'I was afraid too,' he said. The hand that took the needle from her was steady and dry.

'You don't look as if you were.' She shook her head. 'Jesu, I am still quaking inside. You were nearly killed and yet you smile.'

He shrugged. 'Once the fighting began there was time only

to act. I wasn't killed, therefore I should thank God and give praise for my life.' He tilted his head to regard her. 'I am holding myself back,' he said softly, 'because I am in a confined space and under obligation to your father.'

She stared at him, an unconscious frown between her brows and her eyes filled with question.

'Usually,' he said, 'I would spend the night after a battle steeped in wine and women. Well, it's never wise to get drunk aboard a ship in potentially hostile waters. Besides, we don't have that much wine aboard, and the only woman is a virgin and out of bounds.'

Annais reddened. 'I thought you spent *all* your time steeped in wine and women,' she said loftily.

He rose to his feet. 'I'm a reformed character, and you should not believe everything that people tell you. I'll return your needle when I have finished.'

'Keep it,' she said irritably. 'I have plenty more.'

For a while she sat and fumed, but she could hear the sounds of conversation from around the cooking stones and smell the teasing aroma of stew. The bread she had eaten earlier had only whetted her returning appetite and now she was ravenous. Pride and chagrin were cold substitutes for food and companionship.

Annais took her harp from its bag and unwrapped the thick swathe of cloth protecting the wood and strings from the salt air. If she played at the fireside she would not have to talk and the men would forget to be constrained by her female presence as they enjoyed the music.

She came to the fire and her father made room for her on his bench with a murmur of approval as he saw the instrument. Sabin was sitting on a ballast boulder, his head bent over the rip in his gambeson. She saw that it was indeed a wide slash, and that he had the ability to sew as neatly and daintily as any woman. Who had taught him to do that, she wondered, or was it another natural skill? Perhaps it went with his feline swiftness and balance.

He glanced up once as she joined the men at the fire. There was a gleam of humour in his expression and wry acknowledgement which she circumspectly returned. Then he lowered his gaze to his task and she made herself busy, first with a bowl of stew, and then with her harp. The soft tones of 'Stella Maris' drifted like incense to mingle with the heat haze, wreathing the listeners' minds and carrying on the wind to join sky and sea.

Chapter 6

City of Jerusalem, Spring 1121

They approached Jerusalem on the pilgrim road that led from the port of Jaffa, and thus the great tower of golden-grey stone rising above David's gate dominated their first sight of the city. They had hired horses and pack mules in Jaffa for what Strongfist declared was an exorbitant sum, but at least they were mounted and did not have to trudge through hammering heat as the sun reached its zenith. Many of the pilgrims sharing their road were on foot. The contents of water bottles frequently swilled sun-roasted faces, but offered little relief.

Sabin's mail was rolled behind his saddle but he was still gently cooking in his mended gambeson. He wore his sword conspicuously at his hip as a mark of his rank and a warning to the thieves and cutpurses jostling among the crowds. Strongfist gazed up at the towering walls and pinched tears from his eyes. 'I have held it in my memory many long years,' he said, 'but at the same time I had forgotten how magnificent it is.' Unlike Sabin, he wore his hauberk, and although he had covered it with a sleeveless linen surcoat, his face was still scarlet and pouring with sweat. 'When the Saracens surrendered that tower to Raymond of Toulouse, we flooded into the city like water through a sluice gate. There was no stopping us.' He looked at Sabin. 'I was younger than you, still a boy.

What I saw on that day . . .' He broke off, his throat working.

Annais pressed her horse forward and touched his arm. 'Papa?'

He forced a smile and shook his head. 'I am foolish,' he said. 'Look with your own eyes, pay me no heed.'

Guards flanked the gateway, leaning on their spears and observing the procession of pilgrims with a bored air. There were guards on the wall walk at the top of the tower too.

Beggars and cripples huddled in the shade of the gate, crying for alms in the name of Jesus Christ. The stench of heat and soiled bodies was as strong as a blow. Sabin looked at outstretched brown hands, at blind eyes and missing limbs. He had come across such sights frequently during his travels in England and Normandy, but seeing them here, under the burning light and in the most sacred city in Christendom, made them more vivid and shocking. One old man sat huddled in a tattered cloak of threadbare grey wool. Stitched to the left side, above the heart, was a ragged cross, the colour an insipid rose-pink, although once it had probably been blood-red. His pupils were milky and the two teeth that remained in his jaw were the same yellow as the tower in whose shade he sat.

Sabin fished in his pouch and withdrew a coin to toss into the old beggar's wooden bowl. He wondered if he had been at the taking of Jerusalem with Strongfist.

Strongfist had some broken silver to distribute among the beggars, and he too spared a pitying glance for the old man. 'There but for the grace of God,' he said and crossed himself.

'And yet you still wanted to come back? Do you not fear that one day you will take his place?'

'Of course I fear it,' Strongfist said, 'but less than the notion of serving under my brother for the rest of my days. I would rather beg at the Gate of David than coddle a bowl of pottage grudgingly given at Branton.' He shook his head and droplets of sweat flew like salty rain. 'No, for better or worse, I am here to live and die for God's honour.' He nudged his horse forward, easing ahead of Sabin.

Two women passed, giggling to each other behind their hands. Loose silk robes flowed around their bodies and they wore leather sandals upon their feet. A glimpse of ankle was shockingly exposed. Their veils were fashioned of cobweb-fine fabric edged with pearls. One of them shot Sabin a look and instead of the liquid darkness he had expected, the woman's eyes were the colour of aquamarines, enhanced by kohl, and her brows were fair. She nudged her companion and numerous dainty bracelets tinkled on her wrists. The other woman darted a glance at Sabin and her gaze too was light – a warm grey like serpentine. The guards accompanying them had the sand-brown complexions and black moustaches of native men, but there was no mistaking that the women were Frankish and of high rank.

Sabin dipped his head to them, feeling intrigued and amused. The women returned his courtesy and moved on. Perfume, heavy with the scent of rose attar, lingered in the air along with their laughter. Strongfist narrowed his gaze on their progress and tightened his lips.

'Twenty years ago such women would have been whipped through the streets,' he growled.

'That would have been a shame.' Sabin stared in their wake, inhaling the fading, delicious smell of roses.

Strongfist gave him a withering look. 'This is Jerusalem,' he said. 'Not Sodom.'

Sabin was polite enough not to argue. Strongfist wanted things to be exactly as they were when he left, and was obviously suffering from disappointment. As usual, Annais's lids were downcast, but he thought that her expression was wistful rather than shocked. Stewing as she was in that heavy woollen gown, she was probably wishing herself robed in layers of cool silk. He knew he was.

They rode on past the Gate of David and, from broad thoroughfares, entered streets that were dark and vaulted and winding with scarcely room for two beasts to pass together. A turbaned man squeezed his donkey through what seemed an impossible gap between Sabin's mount and the wall, his progress marked by the pungent, eye-watering stench of stale fish.

Annais made a small sound and drew her wimple across her lower face. Sabin coughed against his sleeve.

'The fish market's not far away,' Strongfist said, nodding up the narrow street. 'If there's any left at this time of day, it's usually cheap.'

'I wonder why,' Sabin croaked. The stench had lessened, but a miasma lingered.

Strongfist grinned. 'You'll grow accustomed,' he said, and brought them to another covered thoroughfare. If the stench of decaying fish had sounded one appalling, blaring note, then here the smells were a jangling cacophony. On either side of the street cookstalls jostled cheek by jowl for available space. Portable braziers, ovens and griddles belched out searing heat and odours of hot oil and frying meat heady with spices. A woman wearing a white headcloth was selling piles of the laciest pancakes Sabin had ever seen with some kind of honey syrup drizzled over them. There were cubes of lamb, threaded on olive wood skewers and seared over fierce charcoal. There were vine leaves stuffed with wild rice, almonds and shredded goat meat. Pungent cheeses, figs, oranges, lemons . . . and back to the whiff of fish as a villainous-looking individual fried some specimens in a large oval pan.

'Fresh from Lake Galilee!' he shouted hopefully at Strongfist and his party as they rode past. 'Fresh from the water where Our Lord Jesus Christ walked! A descendant of the fish caught by St Peter himself!' He flipped the fish in the pan and used the utensil to swat a fly that had landed on his sleeve.

'Is he quite sure it's the descendant and not the original?' Sabin asked. Annais made a spluttering sound and her father chuckled.

'They call this place the Street of Bad Cookery,' Strongfist said.

Sabin snorted. 'I would never have guessed.'

'It's unfair really,' Strongfist said judiciously. 'Some of it is excellent. The problem is that you take your life in your hands sorting the good from the bad. I ate here frequently when I was here before. We would sleep the night in the pilgrim hostel at St Sabas and then come here for food.'

They came to another cookstall, laid out beneath a striped red and yellow awning. There were no spicy dishes on offer here. Instead, a plump woman in a dress of blue linen and matching kerchief was stirring a cauldron of hearty-smelling pottage. Wheaten loaves were piled high on a stand to one side of the cooking fire and strings of blood pudding cascaded from the awning poles, like strange swollen fruit. A man was taking coins and doling out bread and pottage to a steady stream of red-faced, woollen-clad pilgrims.

'Food from home!' the woman raised her voice to cry in French that bore the heavy accent of England. 'Good honest fare that your mother would be proud to serve!' Glancing up at the mounted men, she gave them a winning, red-cheeked smile.

Sabin laughed. 'They know what they're doing. There's nothing more reassuring than finding a little bit of home in the midst of a foreign land.' Not that he personally was longing to taste the pottage. If the thoroughfare had not been so narrow and busy, he would have reined about and gone to sample the lacework pancakes.

Strongfist was already dismounting at the stall, but instead of producing his wooden eating bowl, he advanced to the man and addressed him by name.

'Wulnoth!'

For an instant the man looked taken aback, then he narrowed his eyes, thrust his face forward to examine Edmund's and broke into an ear-to-ear grin. 'Edmund Strongfist! By the Holy Face of God! Lord Fergus said he had written, but I never thought you would come!'

'Have you no faith? I said that one day I would return.' Edmund gestured to the cookstall. 'What are you doing here?'

'It's our livelihood,' Wulnoth replied. 'I took a Turkish arrow in the thigh, and couldn't follow Lord Fergus no more, so I turned to this instead . . . and it pays our way. Lord Fergus set us up to start off.'

'And Lord Fergus himself?' Edmund squeezed to one side of the queue. 'Is he lodged in the city?'

'Yes, sir. He has a house near the Holy Sepulchre. I'll take you if you'll give me a moment.' Poking his head around the awning, he let out a piercing whistle. A young man clad in a cotton tunic trotted over from one of the other stalls. He wore shoes of embroidered leather with turned-up toes and his hair tumbled around his face in artful disarray.

'Matthew, take over for a while,' he said. 'Yasmina doesn't look busy.' Wulnoth turned to Strongfist. 'I have two stalls, one for those who are homesick and another for those daring enough to sample the local fare. Matthew and his sister Yasmina are my helpers.'

The lad dipped his head like a gazelle and bestowed Strongfist a look out of dark, liquid eyes. Strongfist gave the slightest incline in return, his nostrils flaring. He expected to smell rose attar, but the young man's scent was merely of cooking oil. Sabin's gaze wandered across the way and perused with admiration the young woman who was standing behind a counter of sweetmeats piled high like nuggets of gold. Strongfist saw the direction of Sabin's interest and gave him a warning nudge. 'Not now,' he said from the corner of his mouth.

'But certainly later,' Sabin said with a lazy smile before returning his attention to the matter in hand.

With more competence than his slight frame and dainty manner suggested, Matthew took over ladling out pottage to the queue of pilgrims. Wulnoth removed his grease-spotted apron to guide Strongfist and his group to the house of Fergus MacMalcolm, cousin and former crusading companion of Edmund Strongfist and now castellan and administrator to King Baldwin of Jerusalem. Wulnoth led them to the end of Malquisnet Street and they emerged from the covered walkway and were engulfed by the stench of the fish market in all its putrid, overblown glory.

'You get used to it.' Wulnoth's tone was patronisingly cheerful. 'It's not always this bad, but someone brought in a cartload of fish this morning that was on the turn and should have been used on the fields or for pig fodder. Idiots on the gate should never have let him through.' He bore left and as the stench began to fade, bore left again and brought them to a flat-roofed house built, as all the others were, of warm, golden stone. Wild geraniums rioted over the surrounding wall behind which could be heard a soothing trickle of water and the low murmur of conversing women. A small brass bell with a tasselled pulley dangled beside a heavy wooden door reinforced with bands of exquisite wrought iron.

Wulnoth signalled his charges to dismount and gave the bell rope three vigorous tugs. The sound jangled loudly and faded away. The sun beat down, its rays so hot that Sabin felt as if fire were licking along his shoulders. Beside him, Annais gasped and swayed in the saddle. He turned and saw that she was biting her lip. Her face was burning scarlet and there were wringing-wet patches of sweat on her gown. He took her arm to steady her and felt the swift throb of her overheated blood through his fingers. 'I am all right,' she said.

It was so obviously a lie that he held on to her. Beyond the wall and the door, soft footfalls approached, a latch drew back, and the door opened on a brown-skinned man wearing a long robe of white cotton and a large crimson turban.

'Safed, I've brought some visitors to my lord,' Wulnoth said. 'An old friend from Lord Fergus's crusading days, together with his family.'

The porter dipped his head and widened the door, revealing a cool, dark corridor with rooms leading off it. 'Be welcome,' he said in clear, but accented French. 'If you will enter, I will send for my lord and tell him of your arrival.'

Wulnoth took their mounts. 'I'll bring these round to the stables,' he said.

Annais took two steps towards the oasis of shade and staggered. Her sodden weight slumped against Sabin and he grabbed her. Strongfist turned and, with a concerned oath, took her from the young man.

'It is the heat,' he said as he lifted Annais in his arms. 'If she was a horse or an ox, I would hurl buckets of water over her to cool her skin.'

'I will send for my lady. She will attend to her,' Safed said. He led them to a room and indicated they should wait. Colourful rugs adorned the thick whitewashed walls and rush mats covered the flagged floor. There were several wooden settles pushed against the side of the room with embroidered seat cushions covering the polished wood. On a trestle in the centre of the room stood a large silver bowl piled with citrus fruits.

Barely had Strongfist placed Annais on one of the benches when two women arrived, followed by a maid. One was plump and fair-complexioned and of about Strongfist's age. The other was perhaps ten years younger with raven brows and dark blue eyes subtly outlined with kohl.

The fair one introduced herself as Lady Margaret, wife to Lord Fergus, her companion as Mariamne FitzPeter, and moved swiftly to Annais. She laid a capable hand to the girl's brow and clucked her tongue. 'Come with me, my dear,' she said briskly. 'We'll soon have you feeling better.' She helped Annais to stand and looked at Strongfist. 'Fergus will be here soon. Make yourselves comfortable. Safed will see to your needs.'

Between them, the women drew Annais from the room.

Strongfist gazed around in bemusement. 'Fergus told me in his letter that he had become a man of influence. I do not know why I had expected everything to remain the same,' he said.

Sabin paced the room, studying the rugs, the dyes of which were richer and subtler than anything he had seen before, even at Henry's court: the deep crimson of cultivated roses, the smoky green of sage leaves and a blue that was the hue of cornflowers at dusk. He laid his palm to the weave and discovered that the texture was close and plush.

'Some folk put them on the floor, but my wife's a proud and practical woman, she willna hear of it. She's probably right. I usually have camel shit on ma shoes.' The voice spoke in French but with a heavy Scots accent.

Sabin turned and found himself facing a short, but robust individual. A dandelion puff of red hair fuzzed out from his scalp and there was a spectacular beard to match. He was clad in a long robe similar to that sported by the native Arabs, but his was cinched at the waist by a belt of green silk. Red hair sprouted at the embroidered neck opening of the robe and his huge feet were encased in kidskin boots.

'Whether on floor or wall, they are very fine,' Sabin said diplomatically.

'Oh aye, you'll find nothing like them outside o' a Syrian fortress. Captured that one on the Tripoli campaign.' The apparition flung his arms wide as he spoke. 'Edmund!' he bellowed exuberantly. 'By the saints, man, it took you long enough!' He threw his arms around Strongfist and hugged him ferociously. 'What have you been doing with yourself for a score of years?'

'Paying my family dues . . . raising a child . . . I—'

'And a fine laddie he is too!' Their host disengaged from the embrace to slap an enthusiastic arm across Sabin's shoulder.

'Takes after his mother, does he?'

Sabin's lips twitched. 'I am told that in many ways I do.'

Strongfist scowled at him. 'Fergus, this isn't my son,' he said irritably. 'This is my travelling companion Sabin FitzSimon, son of the Earl of Northampton.'

'Bastard son of the Earl of Northampton,' Sabin qualified with a bow. 'And on pilgrimage for my own good and everyone else's.'

Fergus hesitated while he assimilated the information.

Then he belted Sabin's shoulder again. 'Well, whatever your parentage, you're welcome. Any companion of Edmund's is one of mine too. I assume you're escaping trouble at home, but you don't need to speak of it. Most of the youngsters who arrive here are on the run. You don't get many pious ones, and then they're usually raving mad.'

'I can assure you that I'm as sane as you are, my lord,' Sabin said gravely.

The Scotsman bellowed with laughter. 'That'll stand ye in good stead,' he said and returned his attention to Strongfist. 'You said raising a child?'

'My daughter Annais. She was overcome by the heat. Your wife and her lady are caring for her.'

'Ah, the lassie I passed just now. Don't you worry. Margaret and Mariamne will sort her out. If I had even half a bezant for every newcomer who's dropped o' the heat stroke, then I'd be a rich man.' Fergus clapped his hands and a servant arrived, soft-footed, white-robed. 'Wine for our guests,' he said, 'and sherbet.'

Strongfist glanced around. 'You appear to be a rich man already. When I left for England, all you had were those poxy lodgings in Malquisnet Street and your sword.'

Fergus flashed a smile. 'You should have stayed. Why go home to toil for that ungrateful family of ours when you could have stayed and reaped the rewards? I have estates to administer in the north, fishing villages up the coast near Arsuf, and this house in the city. You could have had the same.'

'I made a promise to my father that I would come home if I lived,' Strongfist said defensively. 'I have never broken a promise in my life . . .'

'I suppose not. You swore you would return to Jerusalem and here you are.' Fergus rumpled one hand through the abundant red fluff on top of his head. 'It's not too late, mind, which was the reason I wrote to ye. Indeed,' he said with a sudden twinkle, 'as it happens, you might just be in time. Mariamne's recently widowed and there are some fine lands lacking a lord and master. What's more, they are in my gift to appoint.'

Lady Margaret unbound Annais's wimple and in its place laid a moist citrus-scented cloth across her flushed brow. 'You need lighter clothing, child.' She plucked at the heavy linen gown, which was Annais's best summer one. 'This might do for an evening when there is a chill breeze, but it is no use in the heat of the day.'

'I have a gown that might fit,' said the other woman. Her voice was cool and light, like pale wine. She moved with feline grace to a painted enamelled coffer standing at the side of the room, unfastened the hasps and threw back the lid.

A serving woman entered the room bearing a tray on which stood three glass goblets decorated with blue swirls. She stooped to Annais, who took one of the goblets and looked with bemusement at the semi-liquid mush floating within, pale dirty yellow against the green and blue glass. The goblet was not just cool but icy in her hands and felt wonderful.

'Sherbet,' said Margaret. 'The wine here is excellent, but it is better to drink such as this in the heat of the day.'

Annais took a sip and recoiled at the assault on her palate – sour, frozen, but with an underlying tang of sweetness. She had encountered lemon a couple of times in her life – once at a banquet at Branton to celebrate her cousin's knighthood where strips of rind had been served in a curd tart, and once in Spain on their journey here when it had been squeezed into honey and water and all that she had been able to keep down. But neither had prepared her for this sharp intensity of flavour.

'You do not like it?' Margaret asked, watching her.

'Oh . . . no. It is wonderful, but strange.' Annais sipped again, relishing the cold on her tongue and the way the little ice crystals melted against the roof of her mouth. 'Where do you get the ice from when it is so hot outside?'

'It is brought down from the mountains by donkey and camel trains and stored in deep pits in the ground, insulated by hides and hay. Of course it is a luxury and Fergus grumbles about the cost, but not so much that he will give it up.' She laughed softly. 'Nor would I let him.'

Annais drank and drank again, beginning to revel in the tastes and the textures. The lady Mariamne closed the lid of her coffer and returned with a gown over her arm. Russet silk, scalloped with gold embroidery, shimmered across her arm. 'We are much of a size,' she said diffidently. 'See if this gown will fit you until you can find something more suitable.'

Annais stared at the fabric. It shone like a still pond at sunset.

No one had gowns like that in England unless they were of the noblest rank. The Prioress at Coldingham would have looked upon the garment with censorious eyes. 'Madam, I cannot. Surely it is your best gown.'

Mariamne FitzPeter looked mildly amused. 'For certain it is not my workaday dress,' she said, 'but I have more and finer. Here in Outremer people dress differently. Robed as you are, you might be mistaken for a peasant.'

The words were spoken with a smile, but Annais did not miss the slight narrowing of the lovely eyes. 'It is very generous of you, madam, thank you.'

Mariamne gave a little shrug that asked what else could she do in the circumstances. 'I am glad to be of help. You will need a headdress too.'

'I have one that will suit,' Margaret said quickly, keen not to be outdone.

Annais found herself stripped of her linen gown and undershift. At first she tried to stop them, but the women were so matter-of-fact about the process and so determined to have their way that it became easier to yield.

'You're not in England now,' Margaret said briskly as she tossed Annais's shift and gown into a basket. 'You will find that people bathe here far more often than they do back at home. It cools the blood and we have enough stenches with which to contend without adding to them.'

'But don't the priests object?'

Margaret snorted. 'Most of them are first in line at the bathhouses,' she said, 'those who don't have baths in their own homes.'

The serving woman brought a bowl of tepid water that had been scented with a few precious drops of rose oil and Annais was lightly sponged down. The feel of the water drying on her skin was heavenly and a slight breeze filtering through the latticed shutters only added to the pleasure of the sensation.

Her hair was unbraided and that too was sponged before being secured again in two plaits.

'I married Fergus after my first husband died of a flux,' Margaret said as she helped Annais to don a light cotton chemise, 'so I did not know him in the days when he and your father were together. He often spoke of his cousin Edmund though, and of Edmund's strength and fortitude.' She tied the chemise at Annais's throat, fingers fussing. 'When Fergus spoke of seeing him again, I humoured him without believing it would come true. Men who leave Outremer for twenty years seldom return.'

'It was always my father's dream,' Annais replied. 'He only returned to England because of his promise to my grandfather. Then he met my mother and I was born. He set the dream to one side, but he never put it away and it was always understood that he was marking the time until he could come back.'

'And what of the young man who is with you?' Mariamne spoke out for the first time as she handed the russet silk dress to Lady Margaret. 'Is he a relative?'

Annais glanced up. The woman's blue eyes held a gleam and the carmine lips were slightly parted. 'No, my lady,' she answered, feeling wary, although she did not know why. 'His name is Sabin FitzSimon and he is kin to the Earl of Northampton. He is here to make a pilgrimage in respect of his father's soul and to offer his sword to the King of Jerusalem for a while.'

'Ah,' said Margaret. 'A boy adventurer.'

Annais did not contradict her for the words described Sabin well. Mariamne FitzPeter said nothing, but the red lips pursed in speculation.

The women dressed Annais in the copper-coloured silk. Margaret tied the cords from armpit to hip so that the dress clung tightly to breast and waist before flaring in extravagant folds to the floor. Annais gazed down at herself. Since the chemise was so light and the fabric of the gown so thin, she could see the outline of her nipples. The Prioress at Coldingham would have fallen down in an apoplexy at the sight of such wanton exposure. She was certain that her father would not approve. It might wring a response from Sabin, but of the sort that would only make her father even more agitated. Yet she could not screech that it was the dress of a harlot because its owner was walking around her, tweaking and adjusting the folds of the skirt.

'It suits you well,' Margaret said with an encouraging nod.

Annais was uncertain. 'Is it not a little too tight?'

'No, it is perfect, although you need a belt. With a waist as narrow as that, it would be criminal not to show it off.' Thoroughly enjoying the moment, Margaret darted away to another coffer, rummaged, and returned with a length of gold braid. She passed it twice around Annais's waist and folded it over. Two weighted fillets of decorated gold dangled at the ends, which hung at the level of her shins. 'I have always missed having a daughter to dress,' Margaret said. 'I bore only sons and they're away squiring. Besides, you know what boys are like – they don't gild the lily as girls do.'

Annais certainly enjoyed gilding the lily, but there had been small opportunity in her life to indulge in such pleasure, and her upbringing had set a restraint on her desires. She ran her palms over the sheer silk, so luxurious, so different from the heavy linen garment she had just discarded.

'My father might think the gown is not modest,' she said

as Margaret floated a veil of golden gauze over her braids and fastened it with exquisite pins of ivory and gold. 'I have been raised in a convent for the past five years and he is accustomed to seeing me in more sombre dress.'

'If he's to stay in Jerusalem, then he'll soon have to unaccustom himself,' Margaret retorted, her lips firming. 'Unless, of course, you are to enter a convent here?'

Annais shook her head. 'I was lodged with the sisters at Coldingham for my education, not because I was intended for the Church.'

Margaret stepped back to examine the finished result. 'Well, then. You will find there is fierce competition for husbands in Outremer. You need to take every advantage that nature has given you in order to snare one.'

Since Annais's immediate goal was not snaring a husband, she said nothing, but looked suitably attentive, a skill she had developed at Coldingham and necessary sometimes when the Prioress was bent on a lecture.

With trepidation she let the women lead her back to the original room, and when she arrived, discovered that her father and Sabin had also been given occasion to refresh themselves. Her father now wore a cotton tunic obviously borrowed from Fergus, and Sabin had removed his gambeson and was wearing his Norman court robe of maroon silk. Both men had goblets in their hands, although the smell was of wine, not sherbet.

Her father's eyes bulged at sight of the russet gown, as she had known they would, and blood darkened the sun-flush across his cheekbones.

'Sir Edmund, I have lent your daughter one of my own gowns,' said Mariamne FitzPeter, stepping quickly into the space where Strongfist drew breath for a tirade. 'I know that the fashion may seem immodest to your eyes, but it is the mode of dress worn by the women of the court, including the Queen. Of course, your daughter would cover herself with a shawl if she went out in public. If you disapprove, then of course you will soon be able to attire her more fittingly from the fabric markets.'

Strongfist opened and closed his mouth as if he were a fish hooked from the water and cast gasping on the bank.

'Aye, the lass looks gey bonny,' Fergus said, his own voice filled with admiration and approval. 'It would have been foolish to keep her in that heavy sack she was wearing before.'

Strongfist scowled. 'Surely no more foolish than exposing her thus?'

Fergus shook his head. 'It is the way of things here, man,' he said. 'You can always tell the newcomers from those who have dwelt here a while by their clothing and their ways. The sooner you adapt, the better you will settle. Look at my wife, look at Lady Mariamne.' He gestured to the other women's attire. 'If you missay your daughter, then you missay them too.'

Strongfist stared at Annais with a mingling of dismay and shock. When he had collected her from the convent, it had been simple to think of her as still little more than a child. The dark, sombre garments had concealed her curves, and her attitude had been demure and grave, giving few overt signals of femininity – or certainly none that had made him think of her in the sense of a blossoming woman. When he had been warning Sabin away, he had been warning him against damaging a child. Now he could not avoid the fact that his daughter was a woman, ripe for the notice of men. In Christ's name how could they *not* notice her in that gown! She had her mother's rich dark hair and doe-brown eyes. Before he would have said that she was pretty as all young women were pretty, but the colour and cut of that gown made all the difference.

Somehow, he drew his wits together from the four corners where his daughter's emergence from her chrysalis had scattered them. 'I mean no disrespect,' he said slowly. 'You are right, Fergus. Matters are different in England. Even at the royal court, the women would be hard pressed to follow such fashions. You must give me some leeway to grow accustomed.' He took a deep swallow of his wine and watched Mariamne move across to Sabin and refill his cup, leaning towards the young man and smiling.

He thought about what Fergus had told him while he was swilling his hot face and changing into a lighter, more comfortable tunic. Here was a huge opportunity if he wanted to reach for it . . . if he could set aside the caution that maturity had laid upon him, and leap to the challenge with a young man's eagerness. After all, it was why he had returned to Outremer.

Chapter 7

'A new king, a new palace,' said Fergus as he led Strongfist, Annais and Sabin among the labyrinth of buildings and corridors that made up the royal residence. The complex stood beside the Jaffa Gate and building was vigorously in progress. Scaffolding fenced the walls and the constant musical chink of a stonemason's chisel punctuated the morning air. 'The King used to occupy Solomon's palace on the north side,' Fergus said over his shoulder for Annais's and Sabin's benefit, 'but Baldwin's given it to the Knights Templar now and moved here. More room, especially with apartments needed for Queen Morphia and the Princesses.'

Vigilant guards were everywhere, some with fair Frankish colouring; others tinted with the warmer tones of the East. Most wore European or Turkish ring-mail, but a few sported the lamellar armour of Constantinople, the overlapping scales of steel almost as thin as shaved wood and shot with gold. Sabin admired these Greek hauberks, but thought that they must cook the wearer in summer heat.

'King Baldwin's not a man to be afraid,' Fergus said as they were halted by yet another set of crossed lances before being permitted to enter the great hall, 'but the danger of assassination stalks him as close as a shadow.' There was humour and irritation in his eyes. 'His advisors would create a cage of swords around him, but he baulks them when he can.'

Sabin gazed around the hall. In many ways, it resembled

the great residences of Normandy and England, but on a grander scale. There was the same sense of purpose and bustle, the same officials and etiquette. The familiarity was like the background to a tapestry on which the foreground had been changed. Instead of the deep and sombre colours of King Henry's winter court, the people wore bright silks that displayed rather than concealed the body. Here, Annais did not look out of place in her revealing russet gown, but fitted seamlessly into the surroundings. The atmosphere was vibrant but with a sensual undertone that hinted at languor.

As in the halls of home, the walls were white, but since the fires were less often lit, there was little blackening. Instead of clay and rushes, the floors were tiled with ornate scroll and leaf patterns. Rich Turkish rugs adorned the walls and covered the dais at the far end where stood a table of white marble arches, striated with gold. Glass hanging lamps burning perfumed oil were suspended above the table on brass chains. Sabin's eyes were wide to the hinges yet he was still unable to take everything in.

'Aye,' said Fergus with pride. 'It's gey fine. Ye'll not have seen anything like this before.' He looked fiercely at Sabin, daring him to contradict his words.

'No,' Sabin said truthfully. 'Never.' He lifted an enquiring brow. 'Is it like King Henry's court where the King deals with business before dining and the entertainment comes after?'

Fergus eyed him curiously. 'You know your way around the court, do you then, laddie?'

Sabin's smile was rueful. 'You could say that.'

Fergus grunted. 'For all the finery that you see, King Baldwin's a soldier first and he doesna suffer fools or flatterers gladly. Remember that and ye'll do well enough.'

Sabin nodded. 'I know the rules,' he said. And forbore to mention how often he had broken them.

Drinking snow-chilled sherbet from a cup of exquisite rock crystal, Sabin decided that he could rapidly grow accustomed to this. The wines of Jerusalem were also excellent, but it was too easy to over-indulge in this heat and then have to pay for it in misery. Sherbet carried no such hazards and was more refreshing. Besides, while he was still such a newcomer, it was prudent to keep his wits about him.

'So, what think you of the Holy Land?' asked the Baron to whom he had recently been introduced. Gerbert de Montabard was a northern neighbour of Fergus's and in Jerusalem on business with the King. He was perhaps thirty years old with curly brown hair and light grey-blue eyes.

'I have not had time to truly judge,' Sabin said, 'but if you pressed me, I would say that everything is more eye-catching and intense than at home. The heat is stronger; so are the colours and the textures. It is as if I have to walk on the balls of my feet with my hand to my sword all the time . . . but it spurs me on rather than making me afraid.'

'Ah.' Gerbert gave a knowing smile that set two deep creases in his cheeks. 'You are of the kind that likes to dance with scorpions.'

'I was hoping to put that aspect behind me,' Sabin said wryly.

Gerbert did not pursue the subject and held out his cup to a passing servant for replenishment. 'Will you offer your sword to the King of Jerusalem like your companion?' he asked instead with a nod at Strongfist who was deep in conversation with Fergus and two other barons. Sabin turned to look. Annais was standing with her father, her posture demure, her manner gently attentive. Sabin was coming to suspect that it was mostly from training and had very little to do with the thoughts in her head. Remembering the knife stuck through her belt on the galley, he almost smiled.

'In all likelihood, yes. I doubt that my family will be pleased to see me return home – without at least doing my part for Christendom.'

'Your family sent you away?'

'Couldn't wait to be rid of me,' Sabin said flippantly.

Gerbert took his full cup from the servant and gave Sabin a questioning look.

Sabin shrugged and tried for nonchalance. 'I'm the bastard of an earl and my family has royal connections. Unfortunately, I have been a disappointment to them – you sow wild oats and you reap tares . . . There was some worse than usual trouble, so they gave me into the custody of Edmund Strongfist and packed me off to the Holy Land. I am to pray for my father's soul and seek redemption for my own. If I do not return, I will be mourned, but more out of a sense of relief and duty than genuine grief – except perhaps by my half-brother Simon.' He looked down into his cup.

'So you have no reason to go back?'

'That depends on what I find here.' Sabin's eyes narrowed with grim humour. 'I am told that finding a wife with lands and wealth will not be particularly difficult.'

Gerbert's smile displayed teeth that were crooked but white. 'Likely not,' he agreed. 'You could have the pick of several in this very room. I can introduce you if you wish.'

Sabin laughed and shook his head. 'Ask me again when I have silver in my beard and I might reconsider,' he said. 'I have no plans to saddle myself with a wife. It makes scorpion dancing difficult.'

'I was thinking more of the silver in your pouch, but if you have good weapons, and you know how to fight, you can almost name your price.'

Sabin considered that. The King of Jerusalem had a core of barons and knights upon whom he could call, but it was a small force and he relied heavily on mercenaries to keep his troops at strength. Given good fortune and a couple of years, Sabin knew he could probably make himself indispensable and thus be offered rich lands in payment. But did he want that kind of burden? 'Likely I will follow Edmund Strongfist when he takes up his new duties,' he said.

'What duties?' Gerbert looked at him in surprise. 'I thought you were but recently arrived?'

'We are but, as you said, there are several widows in this room, and Edmund has the necessary silver in his beard. He has come here in search of lands and titles. It is almost certain that, with Fergus' endorsement, King Baldwin will grant them to him along with the hand of a worthy woman.' Judging by the discussions between Strongfist and Fergus, Sabin knew which 'worthy woman' would be giving her hand. Whether the woman herself was amenable had only been discussed in the most superficial terms.

Gerbert looked thoughtfully towards the group containing Strongfist. 'I do not suppose your desire to stay with him is in any way concerned with the daughter?'

'Dear Christ, no!' Sabin said with horrified amusement. 'If I so much as look in her direction, her father starts fondling his sword and glaring. I would not abuse his trust.' His expression sobered. 'One of the reasons I got into trouble at home was women . . . one woman in particular. She died because of my folly and my lust. It is a mistake that I never want to repeat.' He lifted his gaze to Gerbert. 'Annais has been educated by nuns. She plays the harp like an angel, she has a warrior's courage; do not let those meek looks make you think she is without spirit. She would make someone a fine wife and mother of his children . . . but not me . . . never me.' He looked at Gerbert and saw that the man's eyes were clinging to Annais almost as closely as that russet silk dress. 'Perhaps you, though?'

De Montabard dragged his gaze from Annais and, pushing his hands through his cropped brown curls, shook his head. 'I have a wife,' he said. 'But if I did not . . .'

A fanfare ended the conversation as everyone in the room bent their knees and bowed their heads for the entry to the great hall of the King and Queen of Jerusalem.

King Baldwin, the second of that name, had held the throne of Jerusalem for three years. Prior to that he had been Count of Edessa and had dwelt to the north of the kingdom with his

Armenian wife, Morphia, daughter of Gabriel of Melitene. And before that, he had been one of the bulwarks of the crusade. Sabin had been unsure what to expect. Squat and dour, Henry of England had looked nothing like a king, but knew how to act like one, and the power that emanated from him had been as tangible as a cold wind. In appearance, the tall, angular Baldwin was much more suited to his royal role. He had bright blue eyes, thrusting cheekbones and a thin, firm mouth surrounded by a wheat-fair beard. He wore a tunic of gold silk, stitched with so many pearls and gems that it must have weighed almost as much as a hauberk. His Queen matched him in opulence. She was as dark as he was fair, with smooth, olive skin and the liquid eyes of an icon.

While the trestles were arranged in the well of the hall for the main meal of the day, petitioners were summoned to the white and gold table on the dais. Fergus introduced Strongfist, Annais and Sabin to the royal couple, emphasising the fact that Strongfist had been a knight in the service of a Scottish prince, and that Sabin was the son of an English earl and had received much of his education at the court of King Henry of England. Annais was portrayed as an educated young woman with admirable skills of needlecraft and music.

King Baldwin listened to the eulogies with a polite half-smile on his face and an interested but shrewd expression in his blue eyes. Sabin judged that pulling the wool over them would be difficult.

'You are well commended, messires,' Baldwin said, 'and I have faith in Fergus's judgement. I need every fighting man I can lay my hands upon.' He looked particularly at Strongfist. 'So it is your intention to live out the rest of your days in our service?'

'It is indeed, sire,' Strongfist confirmed. 'If I can find a suitable place to settle down and call home.'

'I am certain that something can be arranged,' Baldwin said smoothly.

'Thank you, sire.' Strongfist's colour heightened but his

voice remained firm, and although he displayed the necessary deference, he still held himself proudly.

'And what of you, Sabin FitzSimon?' Stroking his chin, Baldwin turned to Sabin. 'Do you intend to serve out your days in Outremer, or is your pilgrimage but a passing fancy?'

Sabin raised his chin. 'In all honesty, sire, I cannot say. For the moment, I am willing to give my sword in your service by seconding myself to Sir Edmund.'

'That is, of course, if Sir Edmund will have you.' Baldwin's thin lips curved. He looked at the older knight.

Strongfist smiled gravely at Sabin. 'I was not sure when we set out together,' he said, 'but now I would rather have him beside me in a fight than any other man. He has already saved my life in battle and he has kept his word to me concerning other matters. Of course I would welcome him beneath my roof.'

A surge of affection warmed Sabin's core. He had received praise before for his swift reactions and physical abilities, but this went deeper, and there had been genuine affection in Strongfist's voice as he answered the King's question.

'The King likes you well,' Fergus said to Strongfist as they reassembled in the well of the hall following the audience. He purloined a fig from a bowl on one of the tables and bit into it, exposing the fleshy red interior. 'It won't surprise me to see you set up in your new estates before the heat of midsummer parches the land.'

'Think you so?' Strongfist looked pleased and rubbed his hands together tensely, then, catching himself at the habit, he quickly folded his arms.

'Of a certainty. Once the King makes up his mind, he is decisive.' Fergus's smile was knowing. 'You need have no fears on that score.' He slapped Strongfist's shoulder. 'Lord Edmund of Tel Namir.'

Strongfist gave an embarrassed laugh and shook his head.

Annais looked at him with startled brown eyes. 'Tel

Namir?' she asked. 'Is that not the estate belonging to Mariamne FitzPeter?'

Fergus and Strongfist exchanged glances and the latter coughed. 'Her husband held it in trust for the King, sweetheart,' he said. 'Baldwin needs to find a replacement.'

'But what about the lady Mariamne? What happens—'

Gerbert de Montabard joined them and Strongfist turned with relief to talk to him, abandoning his daughter's question as if it had never been asked.

Fergus laid an avuncular hand on her shoulder. 'All in good time, lassie,' he said. 'All in good time.' He gave her what was supposed to be a reassuring wink, but it left her more disturbed. Convent-raised she might be, but that did not mean she was blind. She had often wondered if her father would remarry, and from the hints that had been dropped since their arrival in Outremer, the possibility had seemed ever more likely. But she had not expected it to be so soon, and although she could live as a fellow guest under the same roof as Mariamne FitzPeter, she was uncomfortable with the notion of calling her mother. Nor did she believe that the woman would make a good wife for her father . . . not the way that she had seen her looking at Sabin.

The latter had been captured by a couple of the Queen's ladies and he was entertaining them with some outrageous tale to judge from the way their hands had covered their mouths to stifle their giggles.

'I am told that you have a gift for music, Mistress Annais.'

She faced Gerbert de Montabard and managed a smile of sorts. 'I play the harp after a fashion,' she said. 'Who has been telling you tales?'

'Sabin FitzSimon said that you played like an angel,' Gerbert answered. There was admiration in his gaze and she did not miss the way that it slipped over her figure. He had the decency, however, not to let his eyes linger.

She flushed at the notion of Sabin making such a remark. He was so circumspect with her, so careful, that the few insights she did receive were often second-hand like this. 'He exaggerates my skills,' she replied. 'It is true that I play, but there are many who have a greater talent.'

'I should like to hear and judge for myself some time.'

Annais made a non-committal sound and de Montabard did not pursue the matter, for which she was grateful. From the little she had heard of him, she knew he was married, but that his wife had not attended the court because she was with child. Annais thought him attractive, but common sense and the rules dinned into her by Church and family led her not to encourage him. De Montabard appeared to be of the same mind for, after the initial flirtation, he drew back. Most proper, she thought. Another glance in Sabin's direction revealed that he was no longer in the room, and neither were his companions. She hoped, for her father's sake, that he stayed within the bounds of propriety and did not cause a scandal on their first day at court.

It was with no small degree of relief that Sabin finally managed to rid himself of the two women. They had fastened on him like a pair of starving leeches, neither one prepared to let go and leave her rival with the victory. Sabin had at last resorted to telling them that he had a mistress waiting for him in the Latin quarter of the town, and that he was woefully late for the assignation. Then he had fled, feeling as if he had narrowly escaped with his life.

For the remainder of the morning, he wandered the streets of Jerusalem, absorbing the holiest city on earth with all of his senses. The dark alleyways of the markets with their roofs of palm fronds and their shops and stalls pressed as closely together as flesh upon bone. Piles of exotic fruits. Grapes as dark as vein-blood. Figs and pomegranates. Olives. He wandered down Malquisnet Street again, taking his time on this occasion and indulging in one of the lacy pancakes he had so admired before. He had admired other things too: honey sweetmeats, stiffened with nuts and sesame seeds and served by a girl with dark doe eyes and perfumed hair, black as midnight. She was willing to flirt with him while he ate, for she had her brother for protection and both she and Sabin enjoyed the frivolous exchange of banter, secure in the knowledge that it could go no further – for the moment at least.

Licking the sweetness from his fingers, he walked along the Street of Palm-bearers. The stench from the fish market was still overpowering, but he had grown more accustomed to it, and could breathe without putting his sleeve across his nose. Beyond the stalls with their marine occupants, stiff and silver if fresh, flabby and dull if not, he came to more stalls. Crudely carved wooden crucifixes were thrust beneath his nose, or others of base metal with a red glass bead at their centre. Crosses woven from strips of palm branch; lead ampullae filled with the water in which Jesus was baptised, or with the dust from the ground he had trodden. Sabin walked between the stalls, admiring the industry and acumen of the sellers and ignoring the exhortations to buy, except to be irritated and amused by their persistence.

An arched colonnade of golden stone led into the courtyard that formed the south front of the Church of the Holy Sepulchre and here the booths were as thick as flies on a corpse. Sabin thrust his way through, using his elbows where necessary, until he gained the open space of the courtyard. Here too traders cried their wares, but their numbers were regulated by the black-robed priests overseeing the stream of pilgrims entering the complex of chapels that comprised the Holy Sepulchre. A few moments since, Sabin had been eating halva and jesting with a native girl, nothing on his mind but the pleasure of the moment. Now his flesh tingled, and although the sun was white-hot on his unprotected head, he shivered at the notion of praying at Christ's tomb, site of the miracle of the Resurrection.

He had attended prayer in the great cathedrals at Westminster, Rouen, Fécamp and Caen. Sometimes with reverence, more often with an impatient desire to be out at weapons practice or flying his hawk. Often he had passed the services in flirtation with women, in jesting with friends, in sleep if he had been short on it the previous night, and even on one occasion in a game of dice at the rear of the chapel. Much of it had been a deliberate rebellion at what he saw as the boring piety of his elders. Now, on the threshold of the holiest point in Christendom, a place that most of them would never see, a place that his father had set out to achieve and failed, Sabin hesitated, aware of his own unworthiness. He felt he had more in common with the greedy huckstering outside than with the sanctity of the awaiting chapels.

Other pilgrims crowded through the arches of the colonnade, shepherded past the traders like flocking sheep and thoroughly fleeced into the bargain. Sabin was jostled by the accents of Tuscany and France, by cries of astonishment, excitement and exultation. He listened, understood some of it, and was confused by much of the rest. He envied their chatter, bright as sun-sparkle on water, and about as deep.

Allowing the main surge of Italian pilgrims to go ahead of him, he steeled himself to follow their fading chatter into the first of several chapels. He was here. He would perform the offices for the souls of those who were not.

Sabin spent the heat of the afternoon in the cool, candle-lit depths of various chapels, and it seemed to him that he was wandering within the heart of some vast, faceted gemstone, with each chapel being a window in the facet, cut and polished, shimmering with celestial tints of light. Crusaders and pilgrims had carved crosses on the wall of the staircase leading to the chapel of St Helena, and Sabin took his knife to make a mark for his father. At the Tomb of Christ, he offered silver and lit candles for his father's soul, for Lora's, and, after a hesitation, for his own. It was strange to bend his head in church and actually pray. All around him, voices whispered and echoed, rising above the tiered arches to the domed roof of the chapel of the Franks. Incense perfumed the prayers. The white smoke rose to heaven and the residue drifted down to permeate skin and clothing.

Sabin knelt for a long time. If there was a well of peace and silence within himself, it was elusive, but he was not disappointed, for he felt that he had found peace for his father, and the lighting of a candle had gone somewhat towards assuaging his guilt over Lora. The debt was still outstanding, but it no longer weighed as heavily. At least two sets of pilgrims came and departed, many of them weeping with a surfeit of emotion at having actually touched the place of Christ's burial and resurrection. Finally Sabin crossed himself, rose from his knees and went to find a priest who would confess him of his sins. An hour later, shriven as white as a new lamb, he emerged into the slanting late-afternoon sun.

The relic-sellers were packing up their stalls and preparing to go home. His cynicism mellowed, or perhaps his compassion increased, Sabin bought a small palm-branch cross from a toothless crone and, with her blessings ringing in his ears, pinned it to his cloak and made his way back through the narrow streets and suqs of the city. He found a bathhouse not far from the Jaffa gate, and he entered it, intent upon cleansing his body to match his soul.

The attendants administered to him with courteous efficiency. He was bathed, scrubbed, pummelled, kneaded and oiled until he began to wonder if he had not strayed into a bakery by mistake. A barber trimmed his hair and shaved his face with a razor of Saracen steel so sharp that it left his skin as smooth as a girl's. He also offered to remove the rest of Sabin's body hair.

'It is the fashion,' he said, placing one hand on his hip and looking put out when Sabin refused. 'All the Franks of the court have it done. Only newcomers and peasants sprout hair like beasts.' His gaze assessed the crucifix of hair on Sabin's chest and followed it down while he thumbed his razor longingly.

'Mayhap,' Sabin said with a smile, 'but I am a newcomer and I will claim that leeway for now. Since I am unlikely to disrobe before the court and they before me, I doubt that my boorishness will be remarked upon.'

With a dramatic sigh, the bath attendant replaced his razor in its tooled leather case. 'If you change your mind, which assuredly you will, I will give you a good price,' he said and presented Sabin with a hand mirror so that he could view the difference that the barbering had made. Sabin stared, slightly startled at his own image. He had seen himself in a mirror before. Although they were very rare at home, Lora had owned one – a gift from King Henry for services rendered. The wavering distorted image had shown him a pale young man with thin black brows and symmetrical features lit by a devilish smile. The barber's mirror revealed a much clearer image. A deep tan had replaced the pallor; his eyes were a clear olive-gold rather than being murkily reflected; and the smile showed self-mockery, not devilment. After a brief glance, he returned the mirror to the barber, face down.

'Ah,' said the man with a grin, 'my lord is afraid of the sin of vanity.'

Sabin laughed. 'Far from it, but a man can become a slave to his appearance rather than being its master. There is a line that one should not cross . . . like the difference between barbering one's beard and shaving off the hair around one's cock.'

The barber widened his eyes at the comment and sucked in his cheeks. 'I have Templar knights who come to me, and priests from the Sepulchre who value my services.' His tone was proud and indignant.

'I am sure that they do,' Sabin said in a congested voice, glad that the mirror was still face down.

The barber continued to boast of his clients while Sabin dressed. His shirt and braies had been washed and dried during his time in the baths, and they smelled of sunlight and sandalwood.

'You will come again?' the barber asked as Sabin latched his belt and laced his sword to it by the scabbard thonging. He was aware of the man watching the movement of his hands with hunger and wariness. Wanting to touch. Knowing that such a move would meet with drawn steel.

'I might.' Sabin gave a non-committal shrug and finished latching his belt.

'You will recommend me to your friends?' An obsequious note entered the barber's voice.

Sabin's smile was dry. 'I will certainly speak of you to them,' he said as he paid his fee. Actually, he was quite pleased with the services, although he could not imagine that Strongfist would take kindly to the mention of some of the commodities on offer.

Stepping into the street, he found that the shadows had lengthened and dusk was only a breath away. The buildings bore a reddish tint in the westering sun, as if all the blood that had been shed over them had soaked into the pores of the stones. There was another bathhouse close to the one he had just patronised, intended for use by women, and, as he turned down the street, he almost collided with a Frankish lady and her maid who were emerging from it.

Sabin bowed and apologised and, as he straightened, found himself gazing into the expertly painted face of Mariamne FitzPeter. The scent of exotic oils drenched the air, making it almost hard to breathe.

'I see you have taken quickly to our ways, messire,' she murmured in her light, cool voice. Amusement curled her carmine lips.

Turning to follow her gaze, Sabin saw that the barber was standing on the steps of the men's bathhouse, watching him leave. 'Some of them, my lady,' he said wryly and offered her his arm. 'May I escort you home?'

Inclining her head, she curved her hand around his wrist and paced at his side. 'I visit the baths at least once a week,' she said. 'I know that Fergus and Margaret have a bathtub at their home and indeed I make use of it, but it does not compare with the services on offer at such places as these.'

'No,' Sabin agreed, having first cleared his throat to speak. He started to imagine Mariamne FitzPeter bereft of clothes, her pubic mound shaved as smooth as a silk cushion, and hurled the notion from his mind as if it were red-hot. He grimly resolved to find out about certain other amenities on offer in Jerusalem. He had a place to sleep, he knew where to eat, where to worship and where to bathe. Now all he needed was a discreet establishment where the women were accommodating.

He wondered how Strongfist was going to cope with a wife who painted her face and frequented bathhouses. Not well, he suspected, and he did not want to exacerbate the situation by the remotest hint of familiarity in her presence. Matching his own stately pace to hers, he held his body rigid and did not respond when she leaned slightly towards him.

'I like Jerusalem,' she said. 'My former husband only visited when forced, which was a great pity . . . God rest his soul.' She murmured the words gently and lowered her lids, but Sabin received the impression that the gesture was for his benefit and less than genuine. He asked her politely about the estates that her husband had managed.

Mariamne flashed him a look in which he saw anger, amusement and what he thought was a hint of gratification. 'You want to know about my lands?' she asked. 'That is wise of you, but not original. You tread a path well-worn in Outremer.'

'My lady?'

She shook her head. 'And why should you be any different? I will tell you what you want to hear. My lands are fertile. They grow vines and olives, lemons in abundance, pomegranates, figs and fields of wheat. One of the villages has a glass foundry and we make perfume vessels to sell in Jerusalem and Antioch and beakers for wine and sherbet. We breed horses famed for their speed and endurance, and hounds that are reckoned to be the swiftest and bravest in all Outremer.' She spoke in a colourless tone, as if repeating a boring list by rote.

Sabin recognised her malaise. He had encountered a surfeit of such women while attending on King Henry. Usually they were brought to court by their baronial fathers and husbands, and for many it was the pinnacle of their lives. The younger ones would twitter like little finches hung up in a sunlit window. He and the other squires and knights would be the recipients of batted eyelashes and blushing giggles. Women more jaded and experienced would watch and plan and wait their moment with sultry hunger. Not for them a swift fondle in the screen passage or an assignation behind the stable block. Their demands were met in taverns such as the one in Barfleur where he had taken Lora, in bathhouses, and feather beds while husbands were away hunting. Back in England, Sabin would have enjoyed playing the game. Older, experienced women had a great deal to recommend them, but since he wanted to live, Mariamne FitzPeter, shaved or not, was out of bounds.

'You are silent,' she said, looking at him thoughtfully. 'Has my tally bored you, or is it not enough? Do you want more?' The last question was suggestive. The hair rose at Sabin's nape and at the same time he felt an involuntary surge of heat at his crotch.

'My lady, you could never bore me,' he said with a courtier's gallantry. The words were formal and meaningless and he made sure that they contained not the slightest nuance of ambiguity. With relief, he turned the corner into David Street. Safed was lighting the lamps outside Fergus's dwelling and he opened the strong oak door and bowed Sabin and Mariamne through to the courtyard.

The others were seated on benches around the fountain, drinking sherbet and discussing their visit to the palace. Strongfist's laugh rang out and was plainly in an excellent mood. Mariamne's expression stiffened and she tightened her grip on Sabin's arm.

Turning, Strongfist's eyes lit on the couple. His smile brightened for a moment like a freshly fed fire then grew tense at the corners as his gaze travelled to their linked arms.

'Where did you go?' he asked Sabin brusquely.

Bowing to Mariamne, Sabin managed to extricate himself from her grasp and immediately set about putting distance between them. 'To pray at the tomb of the Holy Sepulchre,' he said. 'To light candles for the soul of my father and for others in my past who are still with me now.'

'You should have told me,' Strongfist growled. 'I was wondering what had happened to you.'

'I was too busy freeing myself from the grasp of the Queen's ladies,' Sabin said wryly. 'And I could see you had your own business to conduct without interruption from me. Besides, I do not need to run to you with every small detail of my life. If I am discreet, it should not worry you.'

'Well, you do not smell very discreet at the moment,' Strongfist grumbled. 'You stink like the inside of a whore's coffer! I do not suppose for one minute that you got like that through prayer.' His gaze flickered suspiciously between Sabin and Mariamne.

Sabin sniffed his armpit, and was greeted by an aroma of fresh linen and sandalwood. There was also an underlying whiff of incense from his audience with God. 'No,' he said cheerfully, 'I went to a bathhouse afterwards. You have some strange ideas about the coffers of whores.'

Strongfist scowled. 'That clever tongue of yours is so sharp that one day you are going to cut yourself.'

Mariamne took the sherbet offered to her by an attendant. 'I was in the women's bathhouses by St Mary Latina and I met Messire Sabin on his way out,' she told Strongfist. 'I hope you do not think the same of me.'

Strongfist looked as if he might choke. 'Of course not,' he said in a congested voice. 'But is visiting a bathhouse wise?'

She looked scornfully amused. 'Why ever should it not be?'

Strongfist's complexion turned purple. 'I should think that was obvious.'

'Och, man, the establishments here are nae like the stews back home,' Fergus declared, thumping his friend on the shoulder. 'It's true that the city has its brothels like any other, but most of the bigger bathhouses are respectable. The Queen herself is a patron, and the Patriarch too. I go mysel' now and again. You'll get used to it. The Romans used to bathe all the time.'

'The Romans are dead,' Strongfist retorted, but his colour became less congested and from somewhere he found the semblance if not the truth of a smile. 'You must forgive me if I take time to learn the customs that have grown up in my absence.'

'No forgiving to do,' Fergus said brusquely. 'I'll take you on the morrow so that you can see for yourself. You don't have to be rubbed with scented oils, but most men do. The women prefer a man freshly clean from bathing rather than steeped in a week's worth of sweat.' He gave Strongfist a knowing nudge to which the latter responded with an embarrassed shrug. 'Men meet up to discuss their business in such places, and women go there to gossip. It is a part of ordinary life, nothing to get your hose in a tangle about.' He turned to Sabin with a gleam in his eye. 'I suppose they offered to shave you as bald as a eunuch's pate.'

Sabin grinned. 'I didn't let the attendant anywhere below my neck with that razor . . . much as he would have liked.' The horrified expression on Strongfist's face almost made him splutter. Turning his back while he composed his mirth, Sabin went to sit on the edge of the fountain and trailed his hand in the water. He was aware of Annais standing in the lantern-lit shadows, her gaze as severe as a mother superior's. He felt a niggle of irritation, for he had done nothing wrong. Perhaps it was a case of giving a dog a bad name and hanging him. Perhaps, with his reputation for poaching on other men's land, she thought the worst of the way he had spent his afternoon. Well and good. The way he intended to spend his evening would compound her opinion.

Obviously feeling that some gentleness was needed in the atmosphere, Lady Margaret requested that Annais fetch her harp and play for them. While she was gone on her errand, Sabin had a quiet word with Fergus. The Scotsman laughed and raised his brows, but murmured an address in Sabin's ear. 'I'm told that Heloise and Dorcas are the ones to ask for,' he said in a low voice, darting a glance at his wife to make sure she was out of earshot. 'Either of them could suck the end off a spear, if you take my meaning.'

Sabin did. He collected his cloak, made sure that his sword was secure at his hip, transferred his money pouch to around his neck, and headed for the door. Returning with her harp, Annais gave him a startled look as he squeezed past her in the corridor.

He said nothing, even though the curiosity in her gaze demanded a response. She was too well bred to ask him directly where he was going and he had no intention of telling her.

It was late when he returned, his way lit by a hired lantern bearer and the light of a halfpenny moon. His steps were steady, for he had consumed no more than two cups of wine at the House of the Oasis. Excellent though it had been, only a fool drank to a point where he was unable to experience the pleasure for which he had paid, or defend himself on the road home.

Safed opened the door even before he could jangle the bell, then, having replaced the bolt behind Sabin, padded quietly back to his pallet in one of the rooms off the courtyard. Sabin stood for a moment gaining his bearings by the glow of the oil lamp left burning on the marble bench in the hall. The sound of the fountain trickling came quietly to him and another noise, blending with the splash of water, so that at first he was unsure if his ears were deceiving him. They were not. It was definitely the bittersweet strains of a harp parting the night air. He followed the sound into the courtyard, his footsteps soft and cautious.

Annais was seated on the fountain seat where he had briefly sat earlier. Her harp was on her lap and her head was bent over the movement of her fingers on the strings. The notes were softer than the breeze stirring the leaves of the fig trees and they had a melancholic air that reminded him of misty autumn days in England and Normandy. Like the strands of a sparkling spider-web, the music captured him and held him fast.

Annais raised her head and saw him listening, and captivated. Her fingers stilled on the strings.

'It is very late,' he said. 'You must have been playing for a long time.'

'I could not sleep and I did not want to stay in my room,' she said.

A room that she shared with Mariamne FitzPeter. Although she did not mention the fact, he sensed her tension and knew its reason.

He came to the fountain, cupped his hands to the water and drank a mouthful.

'If you did not before, then now you truly do smell like a whore's coffer,' she said. 'I know where you went. Mariamne overheard Fergus telling you, and she was not best pleased.'

Sabin shrugged. 'It is no concern of hers,' he said indifferently and sat on the other end of the stone bench, leaving the width of two people between them.

'Is it not?' Challenge rang in her voice.

'No,' he said, 'nor of anyone else's.' He studied the set of her jaw and the angry glint in her eyes. 'You may have seen us returning together from the baths, but it was no more than coincidence.'

Annais looked neither mollified nor convinced. 'My father is going to make a marriage contract with her,' she said, and her upper lip curled a fraction, revealing what she thought of the prospect. 'He desires her, I can see he does, but she has no interest in him and she dislikes me.'

Sabin rubbed his chin and eyed her shrewdly. 'She gave you a very fine dress,' he said. 'Perhaps you are being hasty in your judgement. Perhaps you have grown too accustomed to women who live as nuns.'

Annais shook her head. 'She gave me the gown because it made her look generous and kind in the eyes of others. All you see is the way she leans close to pour your wine and gaze upon you as if she would eat you alive. I don't know why you bothered going to that place tonight. She would have spread herself for you on a table and bid you feast to your heart's delight.'

Sabin's eyes widened. 'That certainly is not the talk of the convent,' he said, not knowing whether to be amused or angered. 'And your own interpretation is less than perfect. Yes, the lady Mariamne flirts, but it is her nature and not reserved for me alone.' He opened his hand towards her in a gesture of explanation. 'It is her way of obtaining notice and, since men have the power, of gaining approval. Many women behave thus. I do not doubt that she has cast her eyes over me and found me appealing. I find her appealing too, but only in the way that I might look at a fine horse or a good blade. I am not lust-hot for her and neither, I am sure, is she for me. If she was annoyed that I chose to go out this eve, then it is but pique, not ravening jealousy.'

Annais wriggled her shoulders and looked irritated. 'You did not see the way she stalked around the chamber and banged her coffer lid.'

'No, I did not, but there could be a dozen reasons for such behaviour.' He tilted his head and regarded her through narrowed eyes. 'Perhaps you are the slightest bit jealous of her, or worried because she is to be your father's new wife – your stepmother?'

Annais sprang to her feet and the harp gave out a shocked

jangle of notes. 'Of course I am not jealous! Are you blind that you cannot see beneath the surface to what she is?'

'I see a widowed woman about to be married to a man not of her choosing because of the lands her former husband held,' Sabin retorted, holding her furious gaze. 'I see perfectly well what she is . . . and what she isn't. And do not tell me I am blind, for I have had a wealth more experience than you on the matter.'

For an instant, he thought that she was going to collar him with her precious, beautiful harp. The danger trembled like the ending note of a tune, plucked hard for drama and resonating into the distance. As the last echo faded, Annais turned from him and ran across the courtyard, her kidskin shoes making no more sound than the pattering of a fawn across a forest floor. He watched her shadow darken among the other shadows and vanish with her into the dwelling and thought wryly that he could have handled the situation better. As he had said, he had a wealth more experience on the matter. For an extra half-dinar, he could have stayed the night at the Oasis. He began to wish he had taken up the offer.

Chapter 8

'There it is.' Fergus stabbed a freckled forefinger. 'Tel Namir. It means the Hill of Leopards, but there are no leopards left. You have to go further into the hills for that sort of game.'

Strongfist drew rein so suddenly that those travelling behind him had to pull up in an undignified press of startled, bunching horseflesh. Dust enveloped the party in a gritty cloud and men cursed as they hauled on bridles and strove to find space for their mounts. Strongfist heard none of it, for he was looking at the castle of red stone crowning a steep outcrop to their left. The level ground below was populated by the flat-topped roofs of a substantial village surrounded by olive groves and cultivated fields. He felt queasy with pleasure, and his eyes filled with more than just the moisture of his unblinking stare. Ten days ago, in the Church of the Holy Sepulchre, he had been married to Mariamne FitzPeter. He had been given custody of Tel Namir and sworn into service as a knight of the kingdom of Jerusalem. Gazing upon the keep and village that were only a small part of his new bounty, Strongfist's only regret was that it had taken him so long to return to Outremer. All this could have been his years ago. His brother's lands paled to insignificance when compared with these.

'I see ye're lost for words,' Fergus grinned.

Strongfist swallowed. 'Completely,' he said, and nudged

his horse forward. Belatedly he remembered his bride who was riding in his dust, her silk wimple drawn across her face. He beckoned her to his side so that they might ride together into the village, and bade Sabin go before them to carry his banner.

Sabin took the spear, its silk pennant rippling on the shaft and secured to the socket. A formalised golden leopard snarled on a background of shimmering cerulean blue. Sabin wore his mail for the occasion, protected from the sun by a surcoat of blue silk that matched the banner. Bowing formally to Strongfist and Mariamne, he reined the horse and trotted out in front.

Strongfist glanced circumspectly at Mariamne. She had scarcely spoken a word throughout the journey. He knew that he was not of her choosing, but he had been selected for his military capabilities, not his aptitude for pleasing women. It was the way of life in Outremer. A man died, his widow remarried in short order and to suit the needs of the estate, not her own desire. He promised himself that he would make it up to her and she would soon realise that it was for the best. He thought that she might come to be reconciled for at least she had made her vows to him without weeping. In their marriage bed, he had found her not unwilling. If he wriggled his shoulders, he could feel the mark on his back where she had clawed him like a cat. He was not a man given to flights of fancy, but the thought of his new wife as a feline was so apt that he grinned to himself. She was fastidious in her ways, self-contained, aloof, but at the same time demanding of attention.

'I am the most fortunate of men,' he said and reached across the horses to lay his hand over hers and stroke her finger where the new wedding ring gleamed.

She gave him a tepid smile. 'And I am told that I am the most fortunate of women,' she replied. Her gaze met his briefly and then slipped away to consider the landscape before them, a part of which was Sabin, bearing the blue and gold banner.

'Between us we will beget fine sons to rule these lands when we are gone,' Strongfist said, his grip tightening as he imagined young males of their mingled blood riding straight-spined and proud.

She slanted him a look through her kohl-lined eyes, which he took for agreement, perhaps even eagerness. Then her horse sidled and she withdrew her hand from beneath his so that she could control the beast.

Annais too had been rather quiet since her father's marriage. Strongfist might think that mutual affection would develop, but Annais had her doubts. Mariamne had been tight-lipped as the women prepared her for her marriage, and congratulations had been received with a smile so thin it could have sliced cheese. There had been no loss of control, no weeping, no hurling of cups against the wall. If Mariamne was volatile, it was within herself. She had gone to her wedding pale but composed. Annais might feel hostile towards the woman but she admired the control that even the Prioress of Coldingham would have been hard-pressed to match. Certainly, Annais had been unable to match it herself. Although she had embraced Mariamne because it was expected, she had then sought a quiet corner in which to weep. She knew that a condition of her father taking these lands was that he should marry Mariamne, but surely the King had other estates within his gift that came without a widow? She had told herself that she was being selfish. Her father might have silver in his beard, but he was not yet in his dotage. It was natural that he should seek a mate, and the lady Mariamne was very desirable. But the selfishness remained, and the dismay and more than a twinge of jealousy. How they were all going to live in amity, she did not know.

A high, strong wall surrounded the village and was pierced by an entrance way of two solid wooden gates protected by a ditch and towers. Villagers emerged from their dwellings to watch the cavalcade ride through on its way to the castle.

Women shaded their eyes, their arms curved protectively around slender brown-skinned children. The potter turned from the flat-bottomed amphorae and glazed cooking pots he had been placing in his kiln and, wiping red-stained hands, bowed to them. At the water cistern, more women stopped to point and chatter.

Strongfist delved into his pouch and flung a handful of coins. Fergus did the same and the bolder children broke from their mothers or came running from their tasks to pounce on the largesse like birds upon grain. The party paused at the small round-domed church where the priest was told of the marriage and bidden to join them at the castle. Strongfist announced that he would provide a feast for the villagers to celebrate the arrival of the new lord.

Annais watched her father assume the mantle of command. He sat straight and proud in the saddle wearing what she called his 'dignified' expression. The people crowded around the church, drawn by curiosity and expectation. Among the handsome, dark-eyed folk, chattering in their native tongue, she saw a handful of Frankish faces, including those of women: pilgrims and crusaders who had come to the Holy Land and stayed to farm and fight.

While her father was playing the benevolent lord, she saw that Sabin had abandoned his own pride to scoop a skinny black-haired boy up on his saddle. Another lad, heavily freckled and blond of hair, revealing his Frankish parentage, was standing by his bridle, talking earnestly and holding the spear with its flaunting blue banner. Sabin smiled and said something in reply. He let the boy on the horse try on his helm and used the moment to draw back his hauberk sleeve and wipe the cuff of his tunic across his wet brow. In mid-action, he caught Annais looking at him and his smile transferred to her along with a slight shrug, as if asking what else he could do.

Annais's own lips curved and before she could think better of the impulse, she nudged her mount over to his.

'You are undermining my father's dignity,' she murmured.

'Nay, I am increasing his popularity. This is Hakim.' He rapped his knuckles on top of the helm and the child beneath it giggled. 'His father breeds horses in the village and he informs me that I am riding a worthless nag. And this' – he indicated the fair boy – 'is Amalric, whose family are part of the castle's garrison and who very much desires to be a squire.' Sabin grinned at her. 'What do you think? Will your father give him to me for training?'

'That depends on what skills you intend teaching him,' Annais replied with mock severity. 'I think he is too young to learn some of them.'

'You are never too young,' Sabin retorted. The boy at the bridle had been listening and had drawn himself up, his dark grey eyes bright with indignation at the suggestion that he might be considered too young for training. 'Have no fear. I will not corrupt him beyond the measure of Christian decency.'

She eyed him with curiosity as he retrieved his helm from Hakim and slid the youngster down the nag's withers to the ground. 'You are fond of children?' She phrased the statement as a question.

Sabin gave her a sardonic half-smile. 'It is more that they are fond of me,' he said. 'They seem to adopt me as one of their own.'

She thought of him dancing along the oars of their galley, and the trick he had of twirling his sword hilt in his hands. She remembered him juggling half a dozen lemons in Fergus's pleasance in Jerusalem.

He winked at Hakim and leaned down to retrieve the spear from Amalric. 'Children are much simpler to deal with than adults,' he said. 'They might not all be innocent flowers, but there are far fewer stings and thorns to look out for.'

That was very true, Annais thought, with a glance at her stepmother who was sitting her horse with the patient expression of a madonna while she listened attentively to Strongfist and the priest. The picture she presented was marred by the whiteness of her knuckles on the reins.

'Yes,' Sabin said softly. 'Your stepmother is a rose at the peak of its beauty. And the bloom of her complexion is dependent on her thorns. Buyer beware.' Unslinging his shield from its long strap, he turned again to the fair-haired boy. 'Here,' he said. 'Join the men and carry this to the castle for me. If you do a good job, who knows, I might make you my squire.'

His expression flushed to the point of incandescence, young Amalric took the shield across his own shoulders. It was no small weight, being made of linden wood planks, edged with rawhide, overlaid with painted linen canvas and bossed with steel. Amalric, however, was a large, sturdy child, promising to make a tall and powerful adult. Sabin watched him adjust the shield and bear its weight, saw that it would not encumber him beyond bearing, and gave a nod of approval. 'You'll do,' he said and turned to Hakim who was looking disgruntled.

'From you,' he said, 'I want proof of your knowledge of horses. Choose me one from your father's herd and I will come and see it as soon as I have the time.'

Annais watched him with the boys and thought about what he had said of Mariamne. 'You should have sued for lands of your own,' she said. 'You are wasted following in my father's entourage.'

Sabin laughed and shook his head. When she continued to look at him, he sobered and lowered his gaze. 'But then my responsibilities would be much greater,' he said. 'I am happy to travel lightly, not be burdened down like those donkeys you see in Jerusalem, bearing so much kindling that their knees buckle beneath the weight. There is a world of difference between having to look out for a squire who will polish my harness and scour my mail, and bearing a duty of care to a place like this.'

'It is fortunate, then, that you were not your father's heir.'

'Strangely enough, that is what everyone always told me at home.' The remark was flippant, but sharp too, warning her off. 'Your father is ready to leave.' Gathering the reins, he swung the horse and nudged it out into the road. A gesture sent the boy to stand in the line of footsoldiers. He did not make a similar gesture to Annais, but she felt herself dismissed in the same wise.

Her father prodded his mount away from the priest and the knot of villagers. He was flushed and smiling and Annais did not think that she had ever seen him look so happy. Cool as a dew-fresh rose, Mariamne rode at his side, her thorns concealed. Feeling as dusty and neglected as a weed at the roadside, Annais tugged her mare into line.

'I thought you might like this room for your own,' Mariamne said with a languid wave of her hand. 'It belonged to my former husband's widowed sister when she was alive. Unless, of course, you would rather sleep in the antechamber with the other women?'

Annais shook her head. 'No,' she said huskily. 'I will have this one.' The antechamber, to which Mariamne was referring, led directly into the main bedchamber where the lord and lady slept. Annais had no desire to lie on her pallet within hearing of her father and his new wife – whether they were breathing in sleep, discussing the day's strategy in soft murmurs, or making whatever sounds men and women made in the act of procreation.

'What happened to her?'

'Who? Oh, my husband's sister?' Mariamne moved around the room, each silken rustle of her gown releasing a waft of attar of roses. 'The heat took its toll on her and she was never strong. She died of a fever within a fortnight of Henri's death.'

'I am sorry. It must have been hard for you to bear.'

Mariamne lifted her shoulders. 'She and I were never fond of each other, and as to Henri . . .' She finished the shrug and changed the subject. 'Your taste is likely not Hodierne's. Do as you will with the chamber. The walls need another coat of limewash. I suppose you will be at home with her crucifix. She spent many hours on her knees in prayer – a most proper and devout lady, God rest her soul.' Mariamne's voice was cool and pitying.

'I may have been educated in a nunnery, but that does not mean I have a particular vocation,' Annais said. She could feel the corners of her mouth pursing with tension. She thought the crucifix was horrible. The dark wood emphasised the cadaverous rib cage of the suffering Saviour and the crude way it was carved only made His agony appear more brutal.

'I did not say that you had.' Mariamne laid a compassionate hand on Annais's sleeve. 'I hope you do not resent me too much. I know that I can never take the place of your own mother, but I am your father's wife and I would like us to be friends.'

Her speech made Annais feel guilty and defensive. Of course she resented Mariamne. And she was fearful too. 'You did not want to be my father's wife,' she said. 'You were forced to it by decree.'

The hand remained on Annais's sleeve. She could feel the outline of palm and fingers through the thin silk. 'Did your convent not teach you that what you want you cannot always have?' Mariamne said. 'Rather you should make the best of what you are given.'

Annais bit her lip. 'My father is a good man. You have been given more than you know.' She removed her wrist from Mariamne's touch.

Her stepmother arched her thin black brows. 'I know exactly what I have been given,' she said. 'I do not underestimate its value, but neither do I view it through a glass of golden light. I will temper myself to your father's hand, but he must learn to adapt.' She moved to the door and flicked her glance to the crucifix dominating the wall beside it. 'Husbands are hard to come by in this land for a girl without prospects, although doubtless your father will furnish you with some sort of dowry from the revenues of Tel Namir. It may be that you will find a vocation after all.'

Annais did not follow Mariamne from the room. It would have been too much of a temptation to push her down the steep turret stairs. Clenching her fists, she went to the window. Her lips twitched at the sight that met her eyes. Poor Hodierne FitzPeter might only have had a crucifix for solace in her chamber, but when she turned her gaze upon the outside world, she had a fine view of the training ground where the men would come to hone their weapon skills. Not that there were any soldiers practising today. The archery targets stood unquilled and the sack of sand on the quintain post had been unhooked and laid at the foot. A fleece-stuffed dummy used for spear practice was propped against the wall and some jester had put a cup in its mittened hand.

Still smiling, Annais turned back into the room. It did indeed resemble a nun's cell. The bed was covered by a plain blanket of dark wool, albeit that the wool was as soft as coney fur to the touch. The single coffer was plainly wrought, but made from cedarwood so that when Annais threw back the lid, the air was filled with a glorious, resinous scent. It was empty, awaiting the possessions of the chamber's next occupant . . . or almost empty. In the bottom, lodged at the side, something gleamed. Kneeling, Annais leaned over and pinched up a wimple pin between finger and thumb. It was made of gold with a scrollwork head the size of a small pea. Here was no nunly accoutrement. This belonged to the world of the court, of bathhouses and bustling society.

Annais rose from the coffer and thrust the pin through her own wimple, adding to the daintier one of silver currently doing service. Mariamne might want her to become a nun, but the find in the coffer was a portent and had fixed Annais's decision on the matter.

The bed blanket would do for now until she could obtain one more colourful to replace it. Crossing herself, apologising to the image of Christ on the wall, she unhooked it from its nail, placed it at the bottom of the coffer and firmly closed the lid. Exchange, after all, was no robbery.

'Your daughter is finding it hard to accept that you have another wife,' Mariamne said, smoothing her naked thigh over Strongfist's hairy one and raising her leg so that her knee just nudged his softening genitals.

'She will come around,' Strongfist answered somewhat breathlessly. Droplets of sweat sparkled in the coils of his chest hair. 'And I think she minds less than you believe.'

'Do you? I have not gained that impression.'

'It is early days yet. Give her time.'

Mariamne licked her lips. 'Annais was very taken with Hodierne's chamber,' she said. 'I think it reminded her of the convent where you said she was educated. Perhaps in Christ's own land she will find a vocation after all.'

Strongfist eyed his wife in the grainy light from the oil lamp at their bedside. 'I could almost think you want to be rid of her.'

Mariamne's raven hair cascaded around her shoulders as she shook her head. 'Of course not!' Her tone was indignant. 'Did I not offer her my second-best gown when you arrived? Have I not shown her how to dress and comport herself among Jerusalem society? Why should I want to be rid of her, when she is company for me in this—' She bit her tongue on whatever else she had been going to say and leaned over him. 'I want what is best for her. It matters not save that she is content. I am sorry that you doubt me.'

'I am sorry too . . . I am not accustomed to the ways of women. They seem to play by different rules to men.' Strongfist's tone was rueful. He ran his hand over Mariamne's silken shoulder and cupped her breast. Full, firm, delicately veined with blue. The gesture was languorous on his behalf, for they had made love but a short while since. 'And you . . . are you content?'

Her lips curved sweetly. 'Not yet . . .' she said and rubbed herself against his exploring hand.

Strongfist's first wife had been accommodating, but unconcerned if he chose not to exercise his marital rights. Mariamne was a different prospect entirely: predatory, voracious. He had swiftly discovered that taking his pleasure and rolling over to fall asleep was a cardinal sin in her eyes. She expected to be satisfied, and usually more than once.

'You will kill me!' he laughed as she leaned over him, licking, nibbling, arousing. When she took him in her mouth, he almost came off the bed with mingled shock and pleasure.

'It is a sin against God!' he gasped, but made no attempt to push her off. Instead the veins stood out like whipcords in his throat and he experienced a rush of lust the like of which had not visited him since adolescence.

'I am sure the priest will absolve you.' Her response was muffled by his burgeoning flesh. 'He always absolved Henri.'

Chapter 9

'See, messire, I told you no lie.' Hakim pointed to the complex of stables and paddocks running back from the road and standing opposite the church. 'This is where my father looks after the horses of the lord of Tel Namir.' His mouth widened in a gap-toothed smile. Beside him, Amalric shared his pride by folding his arms and looking manly.

Sabin stood and stared. Mares with foals at foot occupied several of the enclosures and it was like looking upon a sea of glittering, shimmering metal for almost every animal was the colour of bronze or copper or gold, with the occasional glint of silver flashing amongst the shoal.

Sabin's mouth began to water. He had always had an eye for good horseflesh, but usually what he rode was borrowed from his family's stable or hired – always the latter since arriving in Outremer. He had not had time to go hunting for the necessary animals. Every knight should have access to a strong riding mount, a warhorse and a beast of burden. One for hunting would not come amiss either. Thus far he had made do with the hard-mouthed bay that Hakim had called a nag, and an evil-tempered pack mule that pretended every shadow was a lion waiting to pounce and kept up a constant braying that strongly tempted Sabin to cut its wretched throat.

'They are Nicaean horses, sir,' Amalric said, eager to show off his own knowledge and prove himself useful. 'The old lord brought them with him from the north when he captured a Turkish caravan.'

Sabin gazed at the polished satin flanks. Nicaean horses. The mounts of kings and emperors. Even Henry of England did not possess a Nicaean, but had to make do with Spanish stock. The animals he was looking at were justly famed for their speed, their endurance and their ability to live on the sparsest of fodder without suffering. Perhaps not stout enough for a Frankish cavalry charge unless blended with colder blood, but superb riding mounts.

'The village has to present a mare and a colt foal to the King of Jerusalem each year,' Hakim said. 'That one is going this time.' He pointed to a mare with a hide the colour of Roman gold, and beside her an inquisitive copper-red foal with raven mane and tail.

Amalric nudged the younger boy. 'Sir Sabin doesn't want a mare and colt,' he said scornfully. 'Show him the stallions.'

Sabin wouldn't have minded a mare and colt in the least but followed Hakim to a long stable block facing the largest olive grove. Here Hakim's father, a native Christian named Yusuf, greeted him. He wore a loose white cotton shirt stuffed into Frankish-style braies and hose.

'Hakim has been showing you our horses.' Father and son shared the same quick smile. 'What do you think?'

'I am overwhelmed.' Sabin spread his hands. 'We have nothing like this at home, even at the courts of kings.'

Yusuf looked pleased and a little smug. He gestured Sabin to walk along the row of stalls. 'We do not keep many stallions,' he said. 'Those used by the garrison are stabled at the castle, of course. The ones we keep here are either for breeding to the mares, or waiting to be trained, sold, or gelded.' He smiled at Sabin's raised brows. 'I know that Frankish lords prefer to ride stallions, but other buyers would rather have their beasts castrated. It makes them more amenable, especially around mares.'

'You mean like eunuchs around a harem?' Sabin said.

Yusuf laughed. 'Exactly like that, messire.' He tilted his head. 'My son tells me that you are in need of a horse.'

'Apparently so. It seems that I rode from Jerusalem on a nag.'

Clucking his tongue, Yusuf cuffed Hakim around the ear and reprimanded him for his lack of manners, but playfully.

'He was right,' Sabin said. 'It was a nag, but the best I could find in the time. Let the boy speak his mind. It is easier to hear the truth than spend time sifting through tact for the meaning. Show me what you have available.'

Presented with a dozen Nicaean stallions, Sabin felt like a glutton arriving at a groaning table. In England, if someone had offered him one such horse he would have been ecstatic. To have the choice of twelve was almost too much. He ran his hands down strong legs, slapped rippling muscles, peered in mouths, allowed Yusuf the privilege of handling and expounding on the excellent state of the genitalia, stood back to study general conformation.

He was much taken by a gold-coloured five-year-old with black points, not saddle broken, but trained to the halter. Indeed, he had almost made up his mind when a pealing neigh issued from a stall at the end of the block. Hooves smacked solidly against wood as the horse within lashed furiously at the closed door. Sabin looked enquiringly at Yusuf.

The horse-keeper shook his head and looked sombre. 'That one is already spoken for,' he said. 'And you would not want him.'

His words immediately piqued Sabin's curiosity. 'Why would I not want him?' he asked. 'And who has spoken for him?' He began walking down the line of stalls towards the end one where the sound of banging shoes was becoming increasingly frenzied.

'That animal bucked Lord Henri off against a wall and cracked open his skull,' Yusuf strode out beside Sabin, gesturing the boys to stay back. 'Three days later my lord died. Because he has caused a man's death, the horse has been given to the Church, as is the rule. Father Andrew is the official custodian now and it is up to him what he does with the creature.'

Sabin could hardly imagine the portly little priest doing his rounds on the horse trying its best to kick its way out of the stall.

'There was talk of him donating it to the Templars,' Yusuf added as they arrived at the shuddering door, 'but nothing has been decided yet. Father Andrew wanted to consult with the new lord.' Yusuf shot back the bolt on the top half of the door and pulled it wide. A black tail lashed and a dappled silver rump bunched and kicked.

Yusuf made huffing sounds through his teeth that sounded like 'Hoa, hoa' and moved to one side so that the horse could see him. In a swish of straw, its hooves echoing hollowly in the confines of the stall, the stallion plunged around and thrust its head out of the opened top door. Eyes rolled, showing their whites. The arched neck was streaked with foam, and it frothed at the muzzle too, making the horse look as if it had just sprung from a breaking wave at the head of Neptune's chariot.

'Wild,' Yusuf said. 'Lord Henri wanted an unusual colour so that he would be remarked upon and admired when he rode past, but he had no notion of how to control an animal like this. Wouldn't have him gelded either. Said that geldings were for infidels and priests.'

'And now a priest has him.' Moving on soft feet, Sabin came to stand at Yusuf's side. 'Clear the yard,' he said, 'and unbolt the other door.'

Yusuf hesitated.

'He can be no worse in the open,' Sabin argued. 'If you leave him confined now, he will work himself into a true frenzy. If he casts himself, he could twist a gut, and then the Church will have nothing but the price of a carcass.'

Yusuf frowned, then opened his hands and shrugged. 'It is your responsibility,' he said.

'I take it in full.'

Yusuf turned and began shouting commands. Within seconds, the yard was clear and Hakim and Amalric ordered off the wall where they had been sitting, swinging their legs.

Sabin drew back the heavy bolt and swept open the door. A fury fashioned of iron and gleaming quicksilver surged out of the stall and careered around the yard, black tail flagged high, crest arched, teeth bared. Sabin was captivated. He had often scoffed at the notion of love at first sight, but now he knew it was true, for it had struck his heart like a smith's hammer on an anvil and moulded it into a new shape. '"He swalloweth the ground with fierceness and rage",' he quoted softly.

Although his eyes never left the stallion, Yusuf smiled through his concern. 'The book of Job,' he said. '"He paweth in the valley, and rejoiceth in his strength".'

The grey galloped towards the men as if he would attack, but shied away at the final moment, sending a spume of dust into their faces. Bucking, kicking, he pounded up to the wall, surged, turned, and slowed to a high-stepping trot. Sabin relaxed the muscles that had been prepared for flight. Yusuf exhaled and wiped his brow.

'This is probably the best horse in the stable, and the most untrustworthy,' he said. 'I would not breed him to any of the mares for fear that the foals would inherit his traits rather than his conformation.'

Sabin shook his head. 'He will suit me well,' he said. 'I have been called untrustworthy myself.'

'But he has killed a man, messire . . . even if it was without intent.'

Sabin smiled grimly. 'So have I.'

Once the grey had expended the first excess of rage and nervous energy, Sabin quietly instructed Amalric to return to the castle and fetch his pack mule. The next step was to put the mule in with the stallion.

'If I am fortunate,' Sabin said, 'the mule will steady him and I will be able to halter him and bring him up to the castle.'

Yusuf nodded, looking doubtful, but prepared to try the trick.

'Does anyone know why he threw his rider?' Sabin asked. 'A burr under his saddle, perhaps, or the sting of a hornet?'

Yusuf shook his head. 'I do not think we will ever be entirely certain, but in my heart I believe it was the whip.'

'The whip?' Sabin looked curious.

'Men impose discipline on their horses in different ways.' Yusuf's expression was impassive. 'Lord Henri used whip and spur with perhaps more vigour than was necessary. He found it hard to master the grey . . .' He made an eloquent gesture.

Sabin could guess what had happened. Some horses would cower when whipped, but in others, fear turned to rage until they became unridable and fit only for dogmeat.

'Let us hope,' he said, 'that whatever damage has been done can be rectified.'

Annais had hunted through her father's baggage and finally found what she was seeking: a woollen blanket of Scots plaid, woven in hues of woad and madder. She fancied she could smell sheep and heather and misty autumn days in its folds. It gave her a pang of homesickness amid the pleasure as she spread it on her bed to replace Hodierne's plainer covering.

Instead of the horrible crucifix, the wall now boasted a glowing Byzantine icon, liquid of eye and haloed in gold. She had found a cloth of embroidered red silk to throw over the coffer and had hung a curtain of heavy gold cotton across the doorway. The fabric, so she had learned, came from a Muslim city called Damascus where dwelt highly skilled weavers. It amused her to think that all these touches would be viewed as the height of luxury on the Scottish borders where silk, even for the wealthiest in the land, was a rarity and saved for the highest feast days.

A cry of greeting floated up through the latticed shutters and was noisily answered. Annais went to the window, unfastened the latch and gazed out on the practice ground. The garrison soldiers had been at spear drill, but had stopped to watch Sabin ride through the postern gate. He was straddling a pack mule without a saddle, and using his left hand on the bridle. A lead rope attached to a prancing grey stallion occupied his right. At a safe distance well to Sabin's rear came the boys, Hakim and Amalric, walking as if they had a serious purpose.

Annais watched Sabin dismount from the mule and walk quietly back to the grey. He stood for a long time, just stroking the horse's neck and fondling the curve of its cheeks. Then he offered it something on the palm of his hand. The mule immediately turned to claim its share, and for a moment he was almost crushed between the two animals. She drew a sharp breath, but he emerged grinning and gave the mule's rein to Amalric. As the boy led the beast away, Sabin pressed his hands to the horse's withers and in one lithe motion straddled its back. The stallion stiffened as if petrified. Annais was convinced that the grey's stiffness would shatter into bucking, plunging destruction and that Sabin would be thrown and trampled to death. But the point of crisis came and went in a single dance of motion that triggered a rush of fluidity through the stallion's limbs. Crest arched, tail flagged, muscles flowing like wind through silk, he high-stepped after the mule. Sabin rode straight-legged, one arm down at his side, the other holding the reins high.

'Ah, now I see why you spend so much time here,' said Mariamne.

Annais whirled with a gasp of surprise. Her stepmother's footfalls had been so soft that she had not heard them.

'There is a fine view of the tilting ground, is there not?' Mariamne stopped at her side. 'All those strong young men . . .' She smiled knowingly.

'I was watching the sunset,' Annais said coldly.

Mariamne leaned out into the light, her long wrists braced on the sill. 'Hodierne used to do that too, or so she said.' Her own gaze travelled along the parade ground, taking in what Annais had been observing. Her breathing stopped on a catch, then recommenced at an increased rate and a flush mounted her cheeks. 'So,' she whispered and moistened her lips. 'He has taken the grey. I thought he might.'

Annais felt the small hairs prickle at the back of her neck. She wanted to cross herself. 'Why should you think he would choose that one?'

'Because of its nature and his.' Mariamne went to the coffer and picked up a ripe fig, running her thumb over its waxy green surface. 'Ferraunt was Henri's mount until he whipped the beast once too often and it threw him against the wall and spilled what wits he had.' Her sharp thumbnail dug into the fig to emphasise her point. 'He was useless at riding anything – be it horse or woman.'

Annais made a small sound in her throat, and Mariamne fixed her with a hard stare. 'It is the truth,' she said. 'Why hide from it?'

'Is it not also disloyal? Will you say similar things about my father when he is not present to defend himself?'

Mariamne split the fig to expose the fleshy red interior dotted with tiny seeds. 'I thought perhaps that you were old enough to be a friend and confidante,' she said in a voice that managed to be gentle and scathing at the same time, 'but I see I have misjudged your maturity.'

Nibbling the fruit, Mariamne left the room on a waft of rose attar. The smell curdled Annais's stomach. It was with tremendous fortitude that she managed not to hurl the bowl of figs in her stepmother's wake. 'Bitch,' Annais said through bared teeth. Uttering the word made her feel a little better. The icon watched her sadly from the wall with its great liquid eyes. She faced it with raised chin. 'Mariamne's a bitch,' she repeated without apology. 'And I am not the one who is immature.'

*

Sabin led the grey into an empty stall knee-deep in straw. He waved away the attention of the groom, who looked mightily relieved at not being called upon to deal with the horse. Amalric tethered the mule in the adjoining stall where the stallion could see it. Sabin sent the boy to the kitchens to fetch food and drink and set about grooming his new possession, his movements slow and measured and his voice a soothing murmur. He had to gain the stallion's trust, and that involved spending time in its company. Tonight he would sleep in the stall, and the horse would grow accustomed to his presence – either that or kick him to death, but he thought the chance worth taking.

The sun had almost set, but sufficient light filtered through the door for him to see to kindle the oil lamp standing on a shelf a little above head height. The green aroma of warming olive oil began to layer the stall. He piled straw to make a bed for himself, placing his saddle at one end for a pillow.

A shadow obscured the deep glow of dusk from the doorway, leaving his vision dependent upon the small flame of the oil lamp. At first he thought that it was Amalric returning with his food, but then silk rustled seductively, and above the peppery notes of olive, he inhaled the sweet aroma of attar of roses. Definitely not Amalric. His spine tingled and the horse ceased tugging at its hay net and swung its proud grey crest to stare at the intruder.

'I met your "squire" on his way back with your supper.' Mariamne's voice was gently amused. 'I take it that you are not dining in the hall with everyone else.' She set down a platter and a jug on the stool.

'No, my lady.' Sabin gestured to the food. 'There was no need. Amalric is competent and he takes his duties seriously.'

'So do I.' She came to his side, and now the smell of her perfume was overpowering. The blue of her eyes was swallowed to darkness in the dim light; all he could see was their gleam. She reached out and touched the stallion's powerful shoulder. Beneath her long fingers the silver-grey hide shivered as if at the touch of a mosquito and the horse stamped its forehoof.

'His name is Ferraunt,' she said, 'and I suppose you already know that he is forfeited to the Church because of what happened to Henri.'

'Master Yusuf did tell me, yes.' He gave a wry smile. 'Indeed, he tried to dissuade me from choosing him. The horse was shut in a stall so that I would not see him, but after he tried to kick his way out, there was little Yusuf could do, save yield to the will of God.'

She returned the smile. 'Or the will of the man. I thought you would choose Ferraunt. Your natures are suited.'

Her voice had dropped a note and grown husky. Sabin recognised the game. It was not an invitation as such, but an overture to an invitation. She was tempting him. Displaying the goods that might be his if he played well and showed that he understood the rules. Sabin swallowed, aware of how dangerous this was. 'Ferraunt is a word for his colour,' he said. 'Does he have no other name?'

Mariamne laughed throatily. 'Many,' she said, 'but none that you would want to shout across a tiltyard or mention in polite company. Henri would sometimes call him Lucifer . . . which is fitting in a way since the horse was responsible for sending him to the devil.'

Sabin laughed too, but through his mirth ran a strand of unease. Her tone was acrimonious and it was plain that she bore no fond memories of her former spouse. He wondered if Strongfist knew how much he had bitten off.

'I am but teasing.' She touched his arm. 'But it is a good name, don't you think?'

'Admirable,' Sabin said, his breath a little short. 'Are you intending to stay and share my dinner, my lady?'

'Do you want me to stay?'

'Nothing would please me more, my lady,' he said, inclining his head, 'but will they not miss you in the hall?'

'I suppose they will.' Mariamne sighed and reluctantly

took her hand from his sleeve. 'My stepdaughter could, of course, take my place at the high table, but they would still send someone to look for me. Besides, I am not certain that the girl is capable of performing the duty of chatelaine. She needs much guidance, and her moods are strange.' She glinted him a sidelong look. 'I sometimes wonder why her father did not leave her in the convent instead of bringing her with him. I am sure she would have been much happier with nuns.'

Sabin looked thoughtful. 'I do not think that she has a vocation,' he said tactfully.

'Do you not? She keeps to her chamber like a nun and spends much time praying to that icon she has hung on her wall.'

'You surprise me.' He felt driven to defend Annais. 'She prayed a lot when we were on board ship, but that was when she was seasick. Once she recovered, she was no more devout than anyone else was . . . although she would sometimes wake during the night at the times of the holy offices.'

Mariamne tilted her head. 'You like her, don't you?'

'Yes, I do,' he said, 'but I have no desire to take advantage of that liking. Nor is liking the same as lusting.'

She absorbed the information with cat-narrow eyes and ran her tongue over her lips in a frankly sensual gesture. 'You know the difference then?'

'Oh yes, my lady. I know the difference well indeed.' His body was telling him the difference in a very loud voice. His body was telling him that there was a convenient bed of straw right by his feet. Once, not so long ago, he would have followed the urgent sensations to their hot, shameful conclusion. Now, he held back, knowing that there was a line he would not cross, no matter how much she dared him and his body demanded. All he had to do was think the word 'Lora' and resistance was easy. He turned away to the horse and rubbed the sleek grey neck. Rings of dapple like links of mail shone in a steel-dark pattern over the base colour and the mane was as silky black as a Saracen girl's tresses.

'And I wonder which it is that you feel for—' She stopped abruptly and turned around as Amalric appeared in the doorway. The youth's gaze flicked between Mariamne and Sabin with a knowing that was beyond his years.

'My lady, Lord Edmund sent me to find you and say that the dinner horn is about to sound.'

'Thank you, child.' She patted his cheek like a cat patting a mouse and smiled. Sabin thought that she concealed her irritation well, but then perhaps she had had much practice. He doubted that he was the first. 'I will come directly.' She looked at Sabin. 'I hope we can continue our conversation another time.'

Sabin tightened his fingers in the satin-black mane, but before he could answer she was gone in a rustle of silk and a swirl of heavy perfume. Sabin breathed out and pressed his head against the stallion's warm grey neck. The horse sidled, but at the same time swung its head to nudge his hair. Its hay-scented breath gusted over him, replacing the smell of roses. He looked at Amalric and grimaced.

'I should thank you for saving me,' he said. 'As much from myself as her.'

'I know what my lady is like,' Amalric said. 'There was a knight of the garrison before . . . and Lord Henri had to send him away.' He looked anxiously at Sabin. 'I don't want you to be sent away too. My father would never let me follow you and I'd miss my training.'

Sabin gave a bleak laugh and tousled the lad's blond head. 'I'll do my best to avoid temptation,' he said, thinking wryly that the temptation in the meantime would be doing its best to hunt him down and pin him in a corner.

Annais was late to the hall and the dishes of spiced roast lamb were already being carried in. Her father sat in his chair at the high table with the senior members of the garrison. There was an irritated frown between his eyes as he looked at the empty chairs that should have been occupied by the women.

Annais quickened her pace and since her attention was on the dais, did not see Mariamne hastening from the side entrance until they collided.

The desire to snarl, 'Watch where you are going,' was on both women's lips, but each managed the grace of a stiff apology instead. Annais stepped back allowing her step-mother to go in front, and noticed, as Mariamne swept ahead with high colour and glittering eye, the stalks of straw clinging to the hem of her gown.

There was a third empty place on the dais table, but Sabin neither came to dine nor arrived to play dice or merels after the meal had finished. Having discovered his whereabouts from one of the garrison who had been in the tiltyard when he returned with the horse, Annais hoped that she was wrong, and kept her thoughts to herself.

Chapter 10

Jerusalem, Autumn 1121

Sabin watched with amusement as the bathhouse barber approached Strongfist with his shears, emollients and depilatory unguents.

The latter waved the man away with an expression caught between alarm and revulsion. 'I'll keep all the hair that God gave me,' he growled. Water rippled at his waist, tinted pale green by the Roman tiles lining the bath and flowing with gold from sunlight diffused through the fretwork shutters.

'If you are to stand before the King, then you will need a trim at least,' Sabin said, grinning. 'What you have at the moment is a pair of eyes peering out of a thicket.'

Strongfist ran a hand through his wet hair. 'It's not so bad.'

'Not when it's soaked, I agree, but wait until it dries. You'll look like a sheep on the day before shearing. I heard your wife remark to her maid that she was considering doing what Delilah did to Samson and cutting it all off while you slept.'

'Oh very well.' Strongfist gestured the barber to attend him, but wagged a warning forefinger. 'But only the hair and beard, and only a trim. You make me look like a Turkish bath boy and I'll shave your bones with my sword.'

The attendant looked affronted while Sabin spluttered on his mirth. Gesturing rudely, Strongfist left the pool and padded off to be shorn, leaving broad wet footprints on the tiles. Sabin lazed in the water, enjoying its cold lap against his body. There were no baths in Tel Namir, although the castle did have tubs and there was a stream running through the village that even in the height of summer did not dry up. Still, neither could compare with the luxury of the bathing facilities available in the cities.

The lady Mariamne had been in high spirits ever since her cajoling had finally persuaded Strongfist into bringing his entourage to Jerusalem. He was to report to the King's officials on the first summer of his tenure and present the rents owing from the harvests. Strongfist could have sent representatives and remained at Tel Namir, but his wife had persuaded him otherwise. Being seen at court now and again was important, she said. Paying a fleeting visit to the Patriarch's palace in Antioch was simply not enough.

Sabin had tried to keep his distance from Mariamne. She teased him with little touches, batted eyelids, and knowing, sultry looks, wanting, he thought, to see how far she could push him. He pretended to be impervious, but he wasn't. He stayed away from the hall and the places that were her domain, spending his time in the male company of the garrison. He took out patrols amongst the foothills to the east. He lingered with Yusuf, absorbing horse lore, broadening his riding skills by learning how the Saracens rode into battle, their stirrups shorter and their bodies attuned to the movements of their mounts. Yusuf was teaching him Arabic too. When he had to spend time in the castle, he made sure that he was never alone. But if anything, his avoidance seemed to have whetted Mariamne's appetite. She treated his behaviour with pitying amusement, as if he were a recalcitrant child whose measure she had down to the last grain.

Strongfist was oblivious of his wife's behaviour. Like so many barons that Sabin had known before at the English court, providing that his household was well ordered, his bed occupied, and rules seen to be obeyed, he thought that all was well with the world . . . even if it wasn't.

Sabin sighed and splashed his face. At least in Jerusalem there were establishments such as the Oasis where he could vent the heat generated by the dry frictions at Tel Namir and not have to worry about repercussions.

A customer descended the steps into the pool. The exposure of new white skin above the tan line on his neck revealed that he had already undergone the ministrations of the barber. He had short brown curls and grey-blue eyes, heavily seamed by staring at the sun. 'Gerbert de Montabard,' Sabin said.

The man turned, looked puzzled, and then smiled in dawning recognition. 'I have a poor memory for names, but I surely know your face.'

'Sabin FitzSimon.' They clasped hands. A bath attendant brought them cups of frozen sherbet and bowed out of their presence. The men exchanged pleasantries. Sabin told Gerbert about life at Tel Namir. Gerbert listened attentively enough, but when there was a lull in the conversation addressed a subject that had obviously been on his mind.

'And your lord's daughter, the lady Annais – how does she fare?'

'Ah,' Sabin chuckled. 'You remember *her* name then, if not mine?'

Gerbert made a gesture with his hand. 'You would look at me more than askance if it were the other way around,' he said. Reaching to the side of the pool, he took his goblet of sherbet. Light flowed through the pale Tyrian glass and settled in the heart of the frosted lemon juice. 'I remember her skill with the harp,' he said. 'Truly she played like an angel.' For a moment his eyes were distant with memory, and even looked a little sad.

Then he rallied. 'Is she yet unbetrothed?'

Sabin looked at Gerbert. 'For the moment.'

Gerbert flushed. 'I know you told me that you had no interest, but I thought you might . . .'

Sabin laughed ruefully. 'Her father would burst his hauberk at the notion of such a match and it would scarcely suit me.

Strongfist will likely beget sons to follow him at Tel Namir and Annais will only have a small portion for her dowry.' He shook his head. 'I have no desire to take any wife for the moment.' He emphasised his final words. People seemed to find it important to tie him down and, rather like his grey stallion at the sight of a whip, it made him skittish.

'Begetting sons to inherit is more easily said than done,' Gerbert said. 'Even when a child has been conceived, it may be miscarried, or die soon after birth.' He looked down at his sherbet, his expression sombre.

Sabin recalled Gerbert saying last time they had met that his wife had been with child. He made a hesitant enquiry.

Gerbert drew a deep breath. 'My son died at birth,' he said, 'and my wife a week later of the childbed fever.'

'I am sorry.'

Gerbert shrugged, dislodging water droplets from his shoulders. 'It is a common tragedy,' he said. 'We even employed an Arab physician, but there was naught he could do. The child emerged feet first and tore Odile badly.' He gave Sabin a steady look. 'I am in mourning for my wife and infant, but in Outremer life does not stand still. It is my duty to wed again as soon as I may.'

Sabin nodded. 'And you were wondering if there were any obstacles in your path should you choose to court Annais?'

Gerbert rubbed his palm across his face. 'Yes.'

'Not from me,' Sabin said. 'I would be no good for her.' He studied Gerbert thoughtfully. 'I am sure her father would be delighted.'

Gerbert lowered his hand. 'What of Annais herself? Do you think she will object?'

'I doubt it,' Sabin replied. 'She and her stepmother are not fond of each other and the situation is awkward at Tel Namir. I believe she looked kindly on you when you met at court.'

The cynical part of Sabin was amused that Gerbert should be seeking the advice of someone of his reputation. Prospective husbands had never sought his counsel before – although one had once asked Sabin outright if he had bedded his betrothed. Not that Sabin could imagine bedding Annais. There had been a moment when he saw her in that russet silk gown when the notion had burned rather brightly, but since he had forsworn playing with fire, he had quickly smothered it. He did his best to view her as a sister, and most of the time he succeeded. He thought that she and Gerbert would suit each other. She would fall for his decent honesty and admiration. He had already fallen for her wholesomeness, her harp playing, and doubtless would be captivated by her formidable domestic skills. 'You do not need me to smooth your path,' Sabin said, 'for there are no obstacles . . . unless your overlord has an interest in where you remarry?'

Gerbert shook his head. 'I have paid an indemnity to marry whomsoever I choose,' he said, 'and I have no relatives in Outremer with opinions to please.'

'Then your road is open.' Finishing the sherbet, Sabin heaved himself from the pool. A bath attendant came forward with two soft linen towels. Sabin folded one around his hips and used the other to dry the sparkling beads of water from his body.

Strongfist returned from his experience with the barber and Sabin regarded him with gleaming eyes. The former still sported a full head of hair; it had only been trimmed into shape at brow and nape, but the beard had been closely shaved to hug the jawline and showed Strongfist's firm bones to advantage.

'I never realised what a handsome man you were,' Sabin remarked.

'You needn't start realising now either,' Strongfist growled.

Sabin chuckled. 'Marianne will like it.'

'She had better, since I've done it for her.' Strongfist entered the pool and ducked his head to swill off the loose hairs. 'I haven't felt this exposed since I was knighted.' Belatedly noticing Gerbert, he held out his hand. 'Good to see you again.' He cleared his throat in mild embarrassment.

'I still find it passing strange to conduct talk in a bathhouse mother-naked.'

Gerbert smiled. 'It becomes easier with time.'

The attendant brought more sherbet and offered another cup to Sabin who shook his head. 'I have to be on my way.' He nodded to Strongfist and de Montabard. 'Besides, you have matters of importance to discuss.'

Strongfist raised his brows in surprise and the back of Gerbert's neck reddened. Grinning, Sabin left them.

In the women's bathhouse, Annais lay upon a towel-covered table, head pillowed lazily on her hands as the attendant worked scented oils into her flesh. The feelings of sensuous lethargy engendered were so wonderful that she was sure it must be a sin. Briefly she thought about the strict regime at Coldingham, and what the nuns would have thought if they could see her thus prostrated in God's own city, then she banished the image from her mind. She was not going to spoil the moment by magnifying a prickle of guilt into a gigantic thorn. If she had to pay for this bliss later, then so be it. She would go to confession and say the requisite prayers.

Mariamne had opted to have all surplus body hair removed, and lay on her own table like an effigy of perfectly proportioned gleaming marble. Her black hair was twisted high on her head, revealing the graceful column of neck and the exquisite line of her jaw. She had been married to Strongfist for almost five months and her belly was still as flat and firm as a virgin's. Below it, her pubic mound was a hairless cleft. Annais could imagine what that would do to a man, and the path of her thoughts made her bury her hot face in her folded arms. The attendant had offered to shave her too, but Annais had refused.

'She is a virgin,' Mariamne had said with amusement. 'Best to break her in slowly. Besides, she may consider taking the veil, and although nuns must crop their hair in obedience to God, I do not believe that they shear other parts.'

Annais had thought about walking out, but that would have been failing the challenge. She had almost insisted on being shaved too, just to prove she was bold enough, but then had wondered if she really wanted to compete with her step-mother. If she yielded to the goad of the woman's words, then she had lost before she started.

Pampered, oiled, soothed and invigorated, the women returned to Fergus's house, where they were lodged for their sojourn in Jerusalem. The men had already returned from their own visit to the baths and Annais saw that they had added Gerbert de Montabard to their company. She felt a surge of pleasure, and her smile of warmth was genuine when she greeted him.

He seemed flustered, almost stammering his words, and beneath his tan his face had a high colour. Her father was full of bluff bonhomie, slapping Gerbert's shoulder, making sure his cup was filled, rubbing his hands together as she had not seen him do in a while. Sabin held back, looking wary but also amused. There was a conspiracy here, she thought, and the way the men kept throwing glances in her direction, Annais knew that she must be the subject.

Mariamne had noticed too, for her lips tightened, and after a moment, she made an excuse to take Strongfist on one side. Whatever she asked and whatever he answered set her mind at rest, for she nodded and even began to smile a little. Annais bit her lip and tried to make polite conversation with Gerbert by enquiring after his wife.

Gerbert straightened his shoulders as if bracing them to receive a blow and gave her the tidings, but it was Annais who recoiled. 'I am sorry . . . I did not know.'

'There is no reason that you should,' Gerbert said. 'The news is recent and I have not bandied it abroad. It is indeed a great sorrow.' He broke off and looked at her. 'Your father . . .' He swallowed. 'Your father was kind enough to invite me to dine here tonight.'

It was not what he had been going to say, she was certain

of that. Remembering the swiftness of her father's marriage, and what she had learned of life in Outremer in the few months since her arrival, realisation was swift to dawn. 'I think it was more than kindness,' she murmured.

He made an awkward gesture. 'I . . . I was hoping that you would . . . that you would play your harp. The sound has haunted me ever since I last heard you.'

That had been when his wife was still alive, she thought, remembering the moment of attraction that had sparked between them. But he had drawn back and so had she. Now there was no barrier, should they choose to kindle the flame. From the looks her father was sending their way, she could see that he was willing the lightning to strike the timber. Her stepmother too.

'Yes,' she heard herself say, 'I will play my harp if that is what you wish.' She gave him a tentative smile and, because smiling had been difficult of late, felt a glow of warmth at her core. Was it a spark? Perhaps. It certainly lit an eager reaction in Gerbert's eyes.

'Nothing would please me more,' he said. 'Well, almost nothing . . . and I think you can guess what the other would be.'

That night, Annais played her harp for the gathered company. Gerbert sat in a place of privilege beside her, not quite touching but close enough for the delicate hairs on her wrist to rise and draw towards him, close enough to feel his warmth as the cool of the evening settled upon the garden and Safed lit the oil lamps and moths blundered into the pools of hot light and singed their wings.

Sabin listened for a while, studying the couple. Nothing had been openly broached. All was being conducted with the utmost delicacy but it was clear that the match would progress apace. Gerbert's expression was gentle and fully prepared to fill with love. Annais's was shy and modest, a little unsure. But she played her harp with certainty, and the curve of her lips was genuine. Tenderness filled Sabin's own heart, and pride and affection. When it became too much, he quietly left the gathering. With downcast eyes and blank expression, Safed let him out into the street.

This time Sabin spent the extra half-dinar and remained the night at the Oasis.

Chapter 11

Annais's wedding gown was fashioned from a bolt of ivory silk. Tiny seed pearls peppered the neck of the tunic, the edges of the hanging sleeves and the full hem. Seed pearls also decorated the braid belt encircling her waist and glimmered along the fluted edges of the veil pinned to her braids.

By holding up and angling Mariamne's small Saracen mirror, she could see portions of herself and was both startled and delighted by her reflection. Until arriving in Outremer, she had never seen a mirror, and the only notion of her own features had come from hazy images in ponds and the remarks and responses of others: 'You have your mother's brown eyes,' or, 'When you frown you look just like your father.' Priests were always cautioning against the sin of vanity, and she could well understand why when there were objects like this to offer temptation. She began to make a face at herself, but stopped before she had done more than wrinkle her nose, aware that her stepmother was watching her with superior amusement.

Mariamne took the mirror and studied her own reflection, lightly running a forefinger over her subtly reddened lips. She had drawn a fine dark line beneath her lower lashes to enhance her eyes. Annais herself was unpainted. What was seemly in Outremer for a married woman was not seemly for a virgin bride.

'I doubt that you will have need of such finery when you reach Montabard,' Mariamne said. She compressed her lips, rubbed them together, and then parted them, checking that there were no red stains on her teeth. 'Still, every woman should have a rich gown for her wedding day. It is a pity that your father did not choose to hold the nuptials in Jerusalem or Antioch.'

'Tel Namir is his own territory.'

Mariamne made a small, contemptuous sound, but said nothing.

Annais strove not to be angry. It was her wedding day and she would not let Mariamne spoil it. 'Why do you say I will not need my finery once I arrive at Montabard?'

Mariamne set the mirror down and smoothed the folds of her exquisite blue gown. 'Because it is far from Jerusalem, and even Antioch. Gerbert will not expect to bring you every time he has to attend the court. It stands in the foothills in an area of strife. You should be thinking in terms of bandages and cauteries, not silks and pearls.'

Annais raised her chin proudly. 'I dwelt in a convent for five years, and I have lived on the borders of Scotland. That too is an area riven by constant strife and far from the court. I am bred to such conditions and not only will I survive, I will thrive.'

Mariamne sighed. 'Truly you are as prickly as a desert thorn,' she said. 'But I am glad that you feel it is no hardship to go to Montabard.' She folded her arms and her expression softened into something more genuine. 'If I say things to you that seem harsh, it is for your own good. I wish that someone had told me about life's realities when I was your age. Let me advise you on one matter at least, because I know I have more experience than you and you may have need of it.'

Annais wondered what Mariamne could possibly advise her about that she might find of value, then reddened as the answer dawned. She was indeed ignorant, but she did not want tuition from the woman who shared her father's bed. She opened her mouth to say so, but Mariamne must have seen the denial in her eyes.

'Oh, do not be so foolish,' she snapped, but with impatience rather than unkindness. 'That aspect of marriage you can discover for yourself. Gerbert is neither old nor ugly and he's smitten by you. If you cannot make something of such bounty then you are a complete ninny. But there are other things you should know.'

Annais raised her brows.

'Gerbert desires children,' Mariamne said. 'He is still a young man, but time is always short in Outremer. I know that as a loyal and dutiful wife you will do your best to give them to him.'

Annais waited for her stepmother to whip out a phial of aphrodisiac or present her with a charm to wear around her neck to promote fertility. But Mariamne did neither.

'God willing, you will have no problem in providing him with many sons and daughters . . . but such toil is easier and safer to bear with a little respite.' Going to her personal coffer, Mariamne brought out a handful of foamy washed wool and a Saracen glass bottle with a stopper.

'If you wish to protect yourself from bearing a child when a man is inside you, you must soak a piece of wool or moss in vinegar, or sour milk, and push it deep inside your woman's place. It means that his seed will not mix with yours and curdle to form a child.' She presented a stunned Annais with the items. 'Take them,' she said. 'Consider them my personal wedding gift to you.'

Annais clutched the fleece in her right hand, the hard glass bottle in her left. She was fascinated, and a little disturbed. 'Does my father know you use this?' she asked.

Mariamne laughed sourly. 'Do you think I would give a man such knowledge?' she said. 'Of course he does not know . . . but I have not cheated him. Since wedding your father, these things have lain unused in my coffer. Why should

I use them when to bear a child – hopefully a son – would increase my standing tenfold?'

'Then how do you know that they work?'

Mariamne shrugged. 'When I was first married to Henri, I miscarried of infants thrice in swift succession. On the last occasion I lost so much blood that I almost died. A midwife advised me what to do and it worked. I gained the respite I needed.' She removed the wool and the vial of vinegar from Annais's hands. 'I will put these in your travelling chest. I know you can obtain what you need at Montabard, but to have them already will serve as a reminder.' Her tone was brisk and practical and it was obvious that she wished to close the subject.

Annais murmured a weak thank you, more from habit of manners than from genuine gratitude. She wondered if Mariamne's miscarriages were as much connected with her current tardiness to conceive as with the preventative measures. One of the lay workers at Coldingham had been thus afflicted and she certainly had no lore of fleece and vinegar at her fingertips. However, she said nothing to Mariamne. Whereas her stepmother appeared to have no qualms about sharing intimate confidences, Annais certainly did. Indeed, despite her nervousness, she was almost looking forward to the morrow. Even if it did lie on the other side of her wedding night and meant parting from her father, at least she would be a chatelaine in her own right and free of Mariamne.

The wedding feast, like the wine, was in full flow. Sabin gazed into the bottom of his cup, surprised to see that it was empty again. Henri FitzPeter had been keeping back some barrels of superb tawny wine in his cellar, and although they were supposed to be for the Patriarch's table in Antioch, Strongfist had broached them in honour of his daughter's marriage.

'More, sir?' Amalric appeared at his side, the flagon already tilted towards the rim of the cup. Having been given the duty of ensuring that no one ran dry, the lad was being very diligent.

'Why not?' Sabin said. His words were still clear; he had not yet reached the stage of slurring, but knew it wasn't far away. He had not drunk this much since . . . since the night in the tavern at Roxburgh, a night he could not remember except in nightmare flashes of steel and unwieldy firelit motion. A man had died then, sacrificed to the wildness unleashed by drink. And before that, it had been Lora . . . although the intoxication then had been more of lust than wine.

He took a sip from the refreshed goblet and rolled it around his mouth, appreciating the blend of sharp and mellow, the softness of the fruit, the astringent tang of stone. Amalric moved along the high trestle, murmuring and pouring, his fair hair gleaming in the light from the sconces. Robed in silks, glittering with jewels and metallic thread, the company resembled a triptych. Sabin felt as if he were seeping into the colours and gold. There was an unreal quality to the scene, not as if a painting had come to life, more that life was becoming a painting.

He watched Annais laugh as Gerbert raised the marriage cup of rock crystal for Amalric to refill. There was a flush to her cheeks, a dark sparkle in her eyes that told Sabin she had lost sufficient sobriety to forget to be a nun. Jesu . . . if she had come to court in the days when he had prowled the corridors in search of prey, she would not have stood a chance. But that was when he had hunted for the thrill of the chase; to enhance a reputation already blazing with notoriety. He smiled bleakly into his wine. Perhaps now it was he who did not stand a chance. He had kissed her in congratulation after the marriage ceremony in the castle's small chapel, one of many to set his hands to her shoulders and briefly claim her lips. Her skin had been soft and delicately scented with floral oil – although not the attar of roses of which Mariamne was so fond.

'I am glad for both of you,' he had said with lightness but genuine warmth. 'And I will quite understand if you do not wish me to stand godfather to your firstborn child.'

That had made her blush and he had grinned to see it before yielding his place to the next guest in line, his departing gesture an irreverent tweak of her dark braid. He admitted to himself as he took another drink of wine that he was going to miss her. Not so much that he would pine, but enough to notice – like a cold draught in the side when a lover rolled away in the night . . . 'No, not like that,' he said aloud to his cup, both amused and horrified at the image his mind had conjured out of nowhere.

'Did ye speak, laddie?' Fergus leaned towards him. The Scots lord's complexion was almost as red as his hair and his words ran together like sea hissing on shingle.

Sabin shook his head. 'Foolish thoughts aloud,' he said. 'I need to piss, and I need some air to clear these fumes from my head.'

Fergus nodded and waved a floppy arm. 'I'd come wi' ye,' he said, 'but I dinna think my legs'll carry me.'

As Sabin left the crowded hall, the musicians struck up a lively tune: Frankish with eastern overtones. He recognised the sound of an oud. Moments later, voices rose above the music, chanting in the native Aramaic tongue.

'Sir?' Amalric said.

Sabin turned to the youth at his heels. 'Go back within, lad,' he said quietly. 'I'm not going anywhere that needs your company.' His lips twitched. 'I'm capable of going for a piss without falling in the midden, you know; I haven't quite reached the stage of being blind drunk.'

Amalric reddened to the ears and went away. Sabin shook his head. The lad was suffering from a hefty dose of hero worship and dogged Sabin's every footstep. It would pass, but for the moment it was like training a young and troublesome pup.

He walked out to the midden pit, attended to his business, then, not being ready to return to the feast, climbed to the wall walk. The sky was a deep starlit blue, and hung with a huge moon like an opalescent sanctuary lamp. Among the olive trees a nightjar croaked, and he saw the slender shadow of a jackal slip along the village wall and vanish into the deep shadow of the groves. He leaned on the merlon and listened to the faint thrum of music from below, glad of the space between it and him. A year ago he would have been in the thick of the celebration and the last one to leave, but now such a prospect left him feeling despondent.

The aromas of oil and cooking that had drifted to the battlements with the music were suddenly overlaid by a stronger, sweeter scent – one that set his stomach churning and tightened his fingers on the gritty stone.

'Ah, I have found you.' Mariamne's voice was pitched low. She tapped him playfully on the arm and stood closer to him than was proper. 'Your squire said you had gone to the latrine pit, but you have been missing a long time.' There was wine on her breath and her eyes were as wide and dark as Annais's. They sparkled too, but with considerably less innocence.

'I did not realise that my absence was so disturbing that you should feel the need to seek me out,' he said indifferently.

'Indeed I find you greatly disturbing,' she said with a smile in her voice and moved closer until the side of her breast grazed his forearm.

He tried to slide away, but she had him trapped against the stone. 'My lady, this is not wise.'

'This is not a night for wisdom,' she whispered. 'It is a wedding night, a time for ploughing furrows and sowing seed.' She licked her lips and the moonlight glistened on their moistness. 'Will you be churlish enough to refuse a gift when it is offered without obligation?'

He drew a breath to say that he would rather be churlish than dishonourable, but she stole the words from him by taking them in her mouth and pressing herself against him, shockingly length to length. Her perfume engulfed him; her hips undulated against his with instant results. Had he been totally sober, he would have shoved her away, but there was enough wine in his blood to make him hesitate, to yield for a moment to the burning wire of lust. He set his hands to her waist and then lower, to the smooth curve of her buttocks.

She gasped and her hands gripped his upper arms. He felt the bite of her fingernails through his tunic, incising his flesh. Then one hand slipped purposefully downwards. Sabin closed his eyes and swallowed a groan as her fingers enclosed and manipulated.

'There is no one to see. The guards are all elsewhere. No one will know.' Her voice was husky and her hand exquisitely busy.

With a supreme effort of will, Sabin forced her away. 'I will know,' he said raggedly. 'You will know. So will God.'

'Hah, it is a little late to develop a monkish conscience,' she hissed. 'You cannot deny that you want me.' She pressed herself to him, finding her goal again and stroking with a firm, skilled grip.

'As a stallion to a mare or a dog to a bitch,' he gasped as he captured her working hand. He felt raw and sick with lust. 'I could use you on that level and you could use me, but where would that leave us when it was done? Sir Edmund is your husband and my lord . . .'

She gave a scornful laugh. 'I have heard tell that such sensibilities have never prevented you before.'

'What went before is not the same as now. I cannot do this. It should never have come this far . . .'

'But you let it, because you desire my body.' Her lips parted in a feral snarl, part lust and part anger. 'Why don't you show me just how much of a stallion you are?'

A small sound from the walkway alerted Sabin. He turned his head and saw Annais standing on the wooden boards, one hand to her mouth and above it her eyes as wide as cresset lamps. Her complexion was as pale as the silk of her wedding gown. She swallowed and swallowed again.

Sabin swore softly and released Mariamne's hand. She followed the direction of his gaze and stiffened. Then she drew back her arm and swung it full force. The crack of her palm across his cheek was as sharp as a snapped twig. She stalked away from him, thrusting past Annais with sufficient force to send the girl staggering against the wall.

Despite being on the receiving end, Sabin had to admire Mariamne's quick thinking. She was making it appear as if he were the one who had gone too far.

Rubbing her arm, Annais regained her balance. 'How could you?' she hissed at him, her eyes swimming. 'You and she . . . Jesu, how long have you been cuckolding my father?'

'Never!' He held out his hands to her in supplication. She raised her own to fend him off and reject him, her expression one of utter loathing. 'I swear to you I have not touched her.'

'Why should I listen to the word of an oath-breaker when I have the proof of my own eyes and ears!' she spat. 'What were you doing here if not intending a tryst?'

'I came to the wall walks to breathe some fresh air, and she must have followed me. It is not what you think.'

'No? Then what is it?' She was trembling. He could feel her hurt and rage beating about them like a creature with wings and talons. Tearing, plucking, thirsting for blood.

He rubbed his face. 'A mistake,' he said wearily. Images of a bitter November night flooded his mind. A door bursting open, armoured men pounding into the room. Lora screaming. Pain, humiliation . . . and a price that had beggared him. He had nothing left to pay what was owed this time.

'Like all your "other" mistakes?' she scoffed.

'Yes.' He bared his teeth. 'Like all the others. Another lead ingot to drop in the sack I drag at my heels.' He let out an angry breath. 'I do not deny that you caught me and your father's wife in a compromising position, but I had called a stop – you must have seen that.'

'Do you expect me to applaud your late burst of conscience?'

'No. I expect nothing of you but your anger. I admit the blame for letting it get so far. It is my shame that I did not stop her at the outset.' He drew a steadying breath. 'Will you tell your father?'

The pearls gleamed on her dress with each rapid breath she took, and tear tracks stained her cheeks. The contempt in her expression was blistering. 'Are you asking me to keep silent?'

'No,' he said with a grimace, 'that would be setting one calumny on top of another. You must do as your conscience bids.'

'And what of your conscience?' she demanded. 'If I hold my tongue, will you hold yours and pretend that nothing happened?'

'Which is better – to remain silent or speak out? Will your father thank me for putting this matter on his trencher? Shall I tell him that his wife is a whore, his knight a knave, and his honour compromised?'

'You should have thought of that before.'

Sabin shook his head. 'Believe me, I did. If not, you would have stumbled upon a scene far more intimate and shocking and there would have been no choice between speaking out and holding silent.'

Her gaze was searing enough to melt steel. 'I once saw her come from the stables where you were tending your horse. There was straw on her gown and she had the look of a cream-fed cat. What would have happened had I walked in on you then? Would there have been a choice on that occasion?'

He sighed. 'You will not believe me, but yes, there would. I have parried most of her overtures. If I did not parry this one it was because I had drunk one cup too many and she had waited her moment well . . .' He broke off and made an open gesture with his hand. 'Annais, I know I have spoiled your wedding day and I am sorry. That was never my intention.'

'As swiving my stepmother was never your intention.' She glared at him and unconsciously turned the gold wedding ring on her finger.

'No, it wasn't – whether you believe me or not. I will leave Tel Namir at first light. I think it will be best for all.'

Her eyes flashed. 'Do not be a fool! That will only increase the scandal. My father will want to know why and you will have to give him a reason. The wedding guests will come to hear of it and he will become a laughing stock.'

'So you believe that it *is* better to say nothing?'

'For my father's sake.' Her lips tightened. 'I do not care about your soul or your conscience. You have proved how unreliable you are, but I care about my father . . .' Her voice wobbled but she won her fight to control it. 'I will ask Gerbert to request your company as escort. He is short of knights at Montabard. I am sure that my father will spare you from Tel Namir.'

He searched her face. Although he had half expected her to turn away, she held her ground, her chin dimpling, her eyes bright with tears. 'Gerbert will do that for you?' he asked.

'Yes,' she said. 'Gerbert is honourable and decent. He will no more want to have our wedding remembered for a scandal than my father or I.'

He winced.

Annais turned from him. 'I am going now,' she said. 'Otherwise the guests will wonder why I have taken so long, and then there will be another scandal to add to your tally. I will see you in the courtyard on the morrow. Be there and ready to ride.'

He heard the swish of her silk as she left him, and watched her pale figure walk with ghostly grace along the wall walk and melt into the dark shadows of the tower at the far end. 'Jesu,' he groaned and, feeling utterly wretched, pressed his forehead against the cold stone of the merlon.

Gerbert studied his bride with concern. He had just bolted their chamber door on the last of the well-wishers and, for the first time that day, they were alone. She sat in the great bed, her face almost as pale as the sheets of bleached linen, her eyes dark and wide. Throughout the long wedding day and the feast that followed, she had seemed content. The abundant wine had loosened her usual air of modest restraint and made her sparkle until Gerbert was hopelessly besotted. Had they not had to observe propriety and sit throughout the various courses of the feast, he would have taken her to bed hours ago.

Towards the end of the evening, when the entertainers were in full song, she had excused herself, saying that she had to visit the garderobe. Others had had the same notion, for there were several empty spaces on the dining benches. A short while later, Mariamne had returned to her place, smiling tight apology at the guests and seeming somewhat distracted. There was no sign of Annais, and as the time stretched from a crack to a chasm, Gerbert began to worry. He was about to go and search for her, when she returned. His slightly tipsy bride had left the hall with a smile on her lips. Somewhere outside she had lost it, and all the laughter in her eyes. Pale, preoccupied, trembling, she had sat through the remainder of the feast, insisting that nothing was wrong, now and then casting narrow looks through her lashes at her stepmother, occasionally looking over her shoulder as if expecting to see someone else enter the hall. Gerbert's own glance around had shown him that Sabin FitzSimon was missing from the company on the dais table. Was she looking for him? Gerbert rather suspected she was. He promised himself that he would get to the bottom of whatever was troubling her. If it concerned Sabin FitzSimon he would have words – or perhaps more than words with the young man.

Coming to the bed, he threw back the cover and climbed in beside Annais. She was naked, for she had been stripped to prove before the witness of the wedding guests that she came to him unflawed. His gaze dropped to the curve of her breasts. They were small, but shapely and crowned with tender rose-brown nipples. Her waist was slender, yet her pelvis was wide enough for childbearing, wide enough to cup the narrow points of his hipbones and welcome his ride in the act of love and procreation.

The heat of his thoughts must have shown on his face, because he was entranced to see a blush spread from the tops of her breasts, over her throat and mantle her face. She looked like a figure made of almonds and sugar, good enough to eat, and he was ravenous. Yet, he held off. A few moments would make no difference, and they had all night before them.

'Will you tell me what is troubling you?' he asked. 'If it is the thought of what is to come, then I promise I will try not to hurt you.' Reaching out, he twined a tendril of her hair around his forefinger and watched the light gloss on the deep, dark brown. A herbal scent rose from the strands and they were slippery from recent washing.

Annais opened her mouth, drew a breath, let it out, hesitated.

Gerbert waited, his external patience no indication of his inner turmoil. She drew another breath and tried again. 'On the morrow, I want you to ask my father to lend you Sabin as part of our escort,' she said.

Gerbert looked up from the coil of hair and into her face. Her heart was pounding so hard that it was making her body jolt, and her flush had deepened, giving her eyes the luminosity of brown Tyrian glass. The pang of jealousy that had been poised above his heart now stabbed and twisted. Sabin had professed no interest in her, but that did not mean to say that the feeling was mutual, or that the young man had been telling the truth. Sabin had not attended the bedding ceremony, and there had been a period during the celebrations when both he and Annais were absent from the hall. Despite his better nature, the notion crept into Gerbert's mind that his bride and Sabin were lovers. They had had plenty of opportunity. Perhaps she could not bear to be parted from him, and the duty of bedding with another man was what had turned her mood.

'And why should I do that?' he asked in an expressionless tone.

She bit her lip and stared at the coverlet.

'No, look at me.' Gerbert shot out his hand and forced her chin up, pinching her to the bone. 'I will have you meet me eye to eye when you speak. Only liars and cowards look elsewhere, and I hope you are neither of those.'

She had gasped at his movement and the fear and pain in her eyes almost melted him. Almost, but not quite. Controlling himself, he lowered his hand. 'Why?' he repeated.

Her throat worked. 'Because tonight, I went to the wall walk to compose my thoughts, and found my stepmother and Sabin embracing there. She had her hand under his tunic and it was obvious what she was doing. He was fending her off but she was taunting him to take her and, if I had not appeared, he might have succumbed. When she realised I was watching, she slapped his face and tried to pretend that the blame was his.'

Gerbert was not particularly surprised. Mariamne FitzPeter had a certain reputation among the Franks, and there had been rumours before. From what little he knew of Sabin's past, he too had a dubious background in that area. His anxiety diminished but did not disappear. 'That does not explain why I have to take such trouble into my own entourage,' he said curtly.

'To separate my stepmother and Sabin without causing a scandal,' she said. 'Sabin told me he would leave on the morrow, but if he goes without giving a reason, there will be speculation and gossip. I do not want my father to wear the cuckold's horns for all to see. If he finds out, he will kill Sabin . . . and I do not believe that Sabin will defend himself very hard.' She gave him a pleading look. 'If you bring Sabin with us, it will give a valid reason to his going.'

'I see.' Gerbert frowned at her. 'So this is for your father's sake?'

She nodded and kept her eyes on him. Not once did they flicker. 'And for Sabin's too.'

'You are remarkably protective of Sabin FitzSimon,' Gerbert said. 'If I were a less reasonable man, I might be jealous.' He almost laughed at his own words. Of course he was jealous. The demon was perched on his shoulder, its leathery wings brushing his cheek.

'You would have no cause,' she said quietly. 'I would have to be mad to take up with him. Nor, for all the stew he is in at the moment, would he attempt to lay a finger on me.'

'You sound very certain of that.'

'I am,' she said. 'Sabin may have difficulty keeping his braies tied, but he will not play where he is not invited.'

Gerbert shook his head. 'I do not know what to say.'

'I will understand if you refuse, but I am asking you as a boon, please.'

His lips twitched. 'And if I say yes, you will wash my feet in scented water, and dry them with your kisses and your hair?'

She did not return his attempt at humour. 'I know that my stepmother will not stay faithful when Sabin has gone. Eventually my father is bound to discover, but it will be someone else.'

Gerbert frowned. His instinct was to refuse. Left to his own devices he would have done so, but faced by the wide, anxious eyes of his bride, he hesitated, and, while he paused, it occurred to him that if Sabin left on his own, some might attach the wrong woman to the scandal. He sighed heavily.

'Very well,' he said. 'You can count it part of your morning gift – and the greater part at that. But you must do something for me in exchange.'

'What?' She raised her face to his and looked anxious.

He cupped her face, gently this time, and kissed first her cheek, then the corner of her mouth. 'Forget everything for the moment.' He kissed her again, above her top lip, on her chin, and then, softly, fully on the mouth. 'Everything, that is, but me.'

Chapter 12

Strongfist looked askance at Gerbert. 'By all means you may take Sabin if he agrees,' he said with a question in his voice. It was early morning and the men were standing on the battlements of Tel Namir to watch the sun rise over the hills to the east.

'I am grateful,' Gerbert said. 'I am short of good men for my own garrison. I can and do hire mercenaries, but Sabin will be a boon to me.' His tone was level but his face wore an unconscious grimace. He hated telling lies. Anything less resembling a boon he could scarcely imagine, but he had promised Annais, and she had held him to it with a soft murmur as he had left their bed in the first stealing of dawn.

'Still, I am not sure that it is honourable of you to use your wedding feast to poach my best knight.' Strongfist mitigated the words with a smile to show that he was partly in jest.

'My lord, if you would rather I—'

Strongfist quickly raised his hands. 'No, no. I was but teasing you. I am sure that you did not have to persuade him very hard. I am aware that he is less than stretched at Tel Namir and it will not harm him to broaden his horizons. Indeed, I have sensed a restlessness in him of late.'

Gerbert folded his arms and tucked his hands against his ribs in a gesture that was almost defensive. 'I am sure I can do something about that,' he said, thinking that if Sabin displayed any of the kind of restlessness shown at Tel Namir, he would very quickly have an accident over a precipice.

'You'd not guess his prowess from the amount of meat on him,' Strongfist said, 'but I've been with him in battle and I have never seen anything as fast or as sure.'

'In all likelihood, I can promise him several skirmishes. The Saracen leader Balak of Khanzit has been a sharp thorn of late.'

When Strongfist looked dubious, Gerbert unfolded his arms and said quickly, 'Montabard is strong and well defended. I would not have you think that I am endangering your daughter. She will be well protected.'

'I know that,' Strongfist said gruffly. 'If I did not trust you to look after her, whatever your wealth and prestige, I would never have allowed this marriage.' He cleared his throat. 'I hope . . . er . . . I hope you were satisfied with . . .' He made a gesture, his complexion reddening.

'Very.' Gerbert gave an embarrassed shrug of his shoulders. 'Annais is everything I could want in a wife.' He looked into the distance. It was easier than speaking eye to eye. 'She was rising when I came out, but I left her to her women. I thought she might be grateful for some time to herself.'

'Harrumph, yes.'

Proof of Annais's virginity and Gerbert's virility would be shown to all when the bloody sheet from their wedding night was displayed in the hall. No more really needed to be said, but Gerbert recognised and was warmed by Strongfist's concern for his daughter's wellbeing. That in turn fuelled his anger at Sabin and Mariamne. How could they cuckold such an honourable and decent man?

Murmuring an excuse, Gerbert left his father-by-marriage and went in search of his new knight.

He found Sabin in the stables, grooming the grey while it breakfasted on barley and lucerne. Amalric was toiling over the mule, his fair complexion flushed with the exertion he was putting into making the brown hide shine.

Sabin's tunic and belt lay on a pile of straw and he was working in his shirt and hose. The sleeves of the former were pushed back to his elbows, revealing sinewy brown forearms with a dusting of dark hair. He was currying the grey with smoother, stronger strokes than his squire, but the same amount of effort.

When he saw Gerbert standing in the doorway, Sabin blotted his brow on his arm and lowered the comb. 'They say that toil is a good remedy for trouble of the soul,' he opened before Gerbert could speak. 'It would be much simpler if I could change places with the horse.'

'Mayhap, and if I were your owner, I would geld you,' Gerbert said. He noticed other items in the stable: a satchel; a packed baggage roll including a mail shirt and helm; a kite shield and spear. FitzSimon must either have fetched his gear very early, or spent the night here. 'My wife told me what happened, so you need not beat around the bush with me.'

The olive-gold eyes were wary. 'I am sure she told you her version of what happened,' he said.

'And a fair one it seemed to me. I think you are God's greatest fool to let yourself be led by your cock, especially by a woman like the lady Mariamne.'

'You can say nothing to me that I have not already said to myself.' Sabin resumed running the currycomb over the grey's already sleek silver hide. 'I suppose that you are here because Annais told you everything.'

'I would not be otherwise,' Gerbert growled. 'It is only for her sake and her father's that I am doing this. If it were my decision, I'd let you rot in your own dung.'

'In your position I would feel the same. When we are free of Tel Namir, I will leave your entourage if you wish it.'

Gerbert shook his head. 'Ah no,' he said with a bleak smile. 'You do not escape that easily.' He rubbed the point of his chin where bristles were in need of a barber. 'If I am to have you, then it will be on my terms. You will commit yourself to my garrison for a year and a day – on wage-fief terms. After that, I will consider your debt paid and you may do as you wish.'

Sabin inhaled sharply. A wage-fief meant that he would be honour bound to serve Gerbert as his vassal.

'What did you think I was going to do?' Gerbert said. 'Wave you on your way with a smile? You owe me and you owe my wife. I am going to work you harder than a Jerusalem donkey. And at the end of it, you will either be strong enough to bear the burden, or you will be on your knees and I will cut your throat.' Gerbert thrust out his chest to show that he meant what he said. 'Edmund thinks that you and I are in complete amity and that I am as eager to have you in my garrison as you are to come with me. I am not the best dissembler in the world . . . but I am sure that you will have no difficulty. Now, I have wasted enough time on you, and I have other business to attend.' Turning on his heel, he strode out.

Sabin gazed after him. He felt raw with anger and shame, but most of it was directed at himself.

'He does not like you very much,' Amalric ventured.

Sabin glanced at the lad whose presence he had forgotten. 'In his position, I would not like me very much either,' he said.

'Well, I would rather be your squire than his,' Amalric said loyally.

Sabin bared his teeth in a humourless smile. 'And doubtless Gerbert would say that I have corrupted you already for you to think thus.' He set down the currycomb and attended to braiding Lucifer's black mane. 'All I can do is take up the burden and try to stay on my feet. I've made enough of an ass of myself to do so!'

'Your stepmother is not feeling well this morn, so I've taken over her duties,' Fergus's wife said in a voice that managed to be both soothing and brisk.

Annais had already risen from the bed, leaving the maids

to strip the blood-stained sheet. Before being washed, the linen was to be paraded in the hall as proof of her virginity and the success of the wedding night. Robed in her chemise, her dark hair loose and sleep-tangled, she was seated on a cushioned window-seat, watching the sun rise over the hills. 'I would rather it was you anyway,' she said. 'What is wrong with her?' She knew full well why her stepmother was shirking her duties, but it would have seemed strange not to ask.

'Headache and sickness,' Lady Margaret replied with an amused sniff. 'The same as half the folk in the castle. You should see Fergus . . . or perhaps not.' She looked at the red smears and streaks on the linen. 'I have some salve if you are sore.'

Annais began to shake her head, but changed her mind. She had a journey to begin, and sitting a horse was going to be uncomfortable after a few miles. 'Thank you,' she murmured.

Margaret looked at her shrewdly. 'It will become easier,' she said. 'When I married Fergus, I couldn't sit without a cushion for a week! Mind you, he was as impetuous as that hair of his and had about as much gentleness as a charging bull.' She wrinkled her nose. 'He had the speed of one too, so at least it was over soon enough.'

Annais gave a small grimace, knowing exactly what Margaret meant. The place between her thighs was raw and burning. Gerbert had tried to be gentle with her, but she had been tense, and he had been brimming with his need. In the end, when he had forced forward, she had pressed her face into his shoulder and buried her scream of pain against his taut muscles. His weight had pressed her into the mattress until she could not breathe, but as she started to panic, he had lifted off her, and she had gulped air into her starving lungs. He was still rigid as he pulled from her body and the agony had caused her to arch like a bow.

He had stroked her hair and apologised, had told her that it always hurt the first time, but that soon the pain would ease. Then he had pulled her into his arms and fallen asleep. All she had wanted to do was crawl to the other side of the bed and hug her hurting body. Unable to do that, trapped within his warm, breathing bulk, she had done her best to cry quietly and not disturb him. But Gerbert had woken. Clumsy, groggy with sleep, he had nevertheless dried her tears, kissed her softly and murmured more reassurances. He had promised her that they would not do it again until she was ready.

'When does it become easier?' she asked as a serving woman, eyes downcast, brought her a bowl of scented water for washing and a freshly laundered chemise with green silk ribbons at neck and sleeve.

Margaret shrugged. 'When to the man it is less of a novelty,' she said, 'and when the woman is more experienced.' She studied Annais. 'Of course, you can always help matters along.'

Annais raised an enquiring brow. Shortly thereafter, armed with enlightenment, she found herself stowing a flask of olive oil in her coffer alongside the fleece and the vinegar.

By the time she had strategically applied the salve, washed the blood from her thighs and been helped into the fresh chemise and a gown of deep green silk, Gerbert had returned from his various errands. His expression warmed at the sight of her, and he strode across the room to wrap her in his arms and kiss her soundly. The serving women cooed over the gesture and Margaret beamed in a proprietorial fashion.

'A moment alone with my wife, ladies, if you please.' Gerbert smiled round at the women. 'I have things to say that are for her ears alone.'

'I imagine you have.' Margaret raised a knowing eyebrow. 'But do not be too long about it. You've a journey to make.' Arms outspread, she ushered the maids out of the room and closed the door behind them and her.

There was a brief silence. Gerbert touched her cheek. 'You are well?'

Annais nodded. The salve had numbed the soreness between her thighs. 'Yes, my lord,' she replied and was able to give him a genuine smile.

'I am glad. I do not like to see any woman weep, and when I know I have caused it . . .'

'Give me a little time and I will adjust.'

'As much time as you need.' He kissed her again, and Annais responded, thinking, even after last night, how strange it was to have a man's lips on hers, to smell and taste another person in such proximity. Prior to this her father had been the only man who had kissed her – and then no more than a peck on the cheek or a swift paternal salute on closed lips. This husbandly embrace was very different indeed . . . even without the carnal demand.

Gerbert drew away and inhaled a swift, shaken breath. 'You have no notion of what you do to me,' he laughed. 'Giving you time is one of the hardest things I will ever have to do.' He dug his fingers through his cropped brown curls in a steadying gesture and went to sit on the bed, bereft now of its bloody sheet.

'I have spoken to your father about FitzSimon,' he said, 'and although I would say he is a little annoyed that I am taking away a trained fighting man, he has agreed to let him go.'

Annais clasped her hands at her waist. 'Thank you,' she said. 'I know I have asked much.'

Gerbert gave a wry smile. 'Indeed you have. It is certainly not a request I would have made of my own accord, but perhaps it will be to my advantage in the end. Your father emphasises FitzSimon's warrior skills. I can keep him gainfully employed and well away from trouble with women.' His lips compressed. 'Indeed, I intend to make sure that he has neither the time nor the energy for dalliance of any kind.'

'Have you spoken to Sabin?'

'Yes. He was in the stables grooming his horse and looked as if he had spent the night there.'

'What did he say?'

Gerbert shrugged. 'Little enough. Admitted that he had been a fool and offered to leave the moment we were out of sight of Tel Namir. I refused and told him that if I had perjured myself for him, the least he could do was repay me in service.'

'And he accepted?'

'If he hadn't, his honour would not have been worth a grain of dust. Not that I gave him much choice,' Gerbert added with grim satisfaction 'I told him what I wanted and I left him no space to disagree. Of course, he might have taken the coward's way out, and already have left behind my back, but I doubt it. I saw anger in his eyes, my love, but it was directed at himself, not me. If I were a gambling man, which I'm not, I would wager that he'll fight out of his skin to prove himself.'

'I would wager it too,' Annais said. 'It will truly be his last chance.'

Gerbert gave her a keen look. 'He told me when I first met him at court that he had fled some kind of tragedy at home – one concerning a woman. Is that true?'

She nodded. 'He was caught abed with one of King Henry's young mistresses. He was given a beating and she was sent home in disgrace aboard the *White Ship* . . . only it sank not long after it sailed and she was drowned. Then he was involved in a tavern brawl and a man died. His family reached the end of their patience. It wasn't the first time he'd been involved in scandal and fighting. He was entrusted to my father's keeping and sent to Outremer.'

Gerbert cupped elbow and chin. 'And yet you asked me to intervene?' There was surprise bordering on censure in his tone.

Annais made a small gesture. 'Not all of the trouble laid at his door was his fault,' she said.

'Like the most recent incident was not his fault?' Gerbert said with a flare of sarcasm.

She reddened. 'Exactly like that. I am trying to be fair.'

'So am I. He is to serve me for a year and a day as a

wage-fief vassal. After that he is free to do as he chooses – and that to me seems decent recompense for my intervention.'

'It does,' Annais said, but without enthusiasm. She hoped that Gerbert would keep him busy and out of her sight. Being fair was a duty, so was forgiving, but the latter came much harder.

'I have seen nothing of your stepmother this morn,' Gerbert said as he rose to his feet.

'She is unwell,' Annais replied stiffly, 'and likely to remain so, I expect, until we leave. I have called her *nithing* and put her from my mind.'

'*Nithing*?' Gerbert raised his brows.

'In English, it means a person who is worthless, who through their own actions has no place in the world. I know that Sabin does not think of my stepmother as nithing. He thinks of her as he used to think of the women of King Henry's court. I . . .' She turned her head as from outside the door came the sound of Lady Margaret discreetly clearing her throat to remind them of the passage of time.

'You are right.' Gerbert caressed the side of her cheek with his thumb and followed it with a kiss. 'Put it from your mind. Let it rest, even if it be in an unquiet grave for now. Come, we have our guests to attend and a journey to make.'

Sabin waited in the castle courtyard for the bridal party to emerge from the hall and mount their readied horses. He checked Lucifer's girths for the third time and performed a swift inventory of his own equipment. Beneath the blue silk surcoat, his mail had been scoured and oiled until it shone like black snakeskin, and his spurs, his scabbard mountings, the hilt of his sword, the decorated silver badges on his sword-belt winked with sunstars in the strengthening daylight. Last night he had cleaned them all, and cleaned them again, as if the oiled rag that wiped all trace of stain from his armour could do the same to his smirched conscience. It had helped a little at the time, but the effect had almost worn off now, and the waiting was beginning to make his skin prickle, as if tiny thorns were growing out through his pores.

Amalric was tending to the pack mule. That he had been permitted to go with Sabin owed much to the fact that his father had been assigned escort duty to the wedding party. Propped on the ground at the boy's feet were Sabin's shield and spear. Sabin would shoulder the former when he rode out; Amalric would bear the latter, his face shining with the pride that Sabin was doing his best to recover.

Sabin glanced along the waiting line towards a knot of soldiers. He heard a burst of laughter as one told a joke and saw the playful punch of camaraderie. Two more came from the trough where they had been filling their water costrels and joined the group. He found himself wishing that he were one of their number, a common soldier with simple cares. But in such a position, a simple care might seem the most difficult thing on earth.

Sighing, Sabin squinted at the sky. The rags of dawn cloud had burned off, leaving a clear, fine blue. It was going to be hot at the zenith. Wearing armour would be uncomfortable . . . but a necessity on the road where every outcrop and turning might hold an ambush.

A solitary figure emerged from the forebuilding and walked towards the waiting train of soldiers and baggage beasts. The thorns prickling Sabin's flesh seemed to become the size of spearheads and suddenly he felt nauseous.

'My lord.' He bowed his head, acting in proper and formal fashion because it was all he could think of to do. How would he have reacted if Strongfist had caught him and Mariamne on the battlements last night? Bow and address him politely? It was such a ludicrous thought that amidst the feelings of shame, he felt a sickening desire to laugh.

Strongfist halted on the opposite side of Lucifer and stared over the decorated saddle cloth and padded high saddle. 'So, although you have not seen fit to address me on the matter,

I understand that you desire to leave Tel Namir.' The morning light filled his eyes, turning them to the guileless bright blue of a child's.

Sabin gripped the bridle close to the headstall, taking comfort from the champing of the horse against the bit, and forced himself to meet them. Stare upon stare. Matching. Measuring. He drew breath to speak, but Strongfist raised his hand and forestalled him.

'I may look like an old fool and sometimes behave like one, but you should all credit me with at least a little experience. For your sake and my honour, it is for the best that you say nothing and that you leave. That way the illusion is preserved.' He walked around the front of the horse and thrust out his hand, the fingers strong, square and thick-skinned. 'I wish you Godspeed.'

After a hesitation, Sabin reached to take it. 'And may God keep you.' He made the formal response through a throat so dry that his voice cracked. Never again, he swore to himself grimly. Never again, even if all the carnal temptations of the world were heaped before him on a gilded trencher. 'I did not—'

'No words,' Strongfist said through clenched teeth. 'I expect you to guard my daughter and her husband with your life.'

'That is understood without words too,' Sabin said.

Their hands parted, although the imprint of the other's sweat remained on each man's palm.

The rest of the bridal party was emerging from the keep, booted and cloaked for the journey. Gerbert wore his mail, lighter in colour than Sabin's and ringed at the lower hem with a decorative edge of black rivets. His sword hilt protruded through a slit in the side of the mail, and his left hand rested lightly on the pommel. His right was given to Annais. Her dark braids were hidden beneath the full wimple that a married woman would have worn in England, but more, Sabin thought, for travelling than for modesty – unless of course it was a visual statement brought on by last night's incident. The last to emerge from the hall into the growing sunlight was Mariamne. Although pale and heavy-eyed as befitted someone suffering from a drink megrim, she bore no other outward signs of discomfort. If she did not kiss the bride in farewell, it was understood by all that the women had never been more than tepid with each other. After a single glance over the baggage train and its guardians, she lowered her gaze and stood in modest silence a little back from her husband. Sabin busied himself mounting Lucifer and accepting his shield from Amalric. The boy was all too prepared to stare at Mariamne until Sabin nudged him with the shield edge and hissed a warning through his teeth.

Strongfist squeezed his daughter in a bearhug. 'Have a care,' he said and, more gently, touched her cheek. His smile was broad and genuine, but there was a moist glitter in his eyes.

'And you,' Annais responded and for a moment she laid her head on his breast. His broad, scarred hands touched the top swathe of her wimple in benediction. Then she stepped back and her husband's squire assisted her to the saddle. Surreptitiously she ran her knuckles beneath her eyes and sniffed.

'You must visit us soon,' Gerbert said, clasping Strongfist's arm.

Strongfist nodded vigorously. 'I promise I will.'

'My lady.' Gerbert performed a stiff and formal bow to Mariamne, his expression stony. She inclined her head, her own eyes devoid of warmth. Gerbert swung to his horse – a powerful bay and unusually tall, standing at almost sixteen hands. As he gathered the reins, he glanced at Sabin and a look passed between them: on Gerbert's part a silent statement of duty performed and debts that were now owed; on Sabin's, acknowledgement of those debts and determination to see them paid with interest.

The party rode out of Tel Namir and took the road north,

towards Antioch. Glancing back, Annais waved to the diminishing figure of her father before resolutely drying her eyes and facing her new life. Although Sabin felt the urge to look over his shoulder, he paid it no heed, for there would have been no point except to fuel his guilt and regret.

Chapter 13

Annais's first glimpse of Montabard was through the teeming rain of a thunderstorm. Milky purple lightning sheeted the sky behind the hills and was split by jagged whips that cracked from air to ground. The rumble of the thunder seemed to come from above and below, as if the mountains and the clouds were a part of each other and straining to touch. So loud was the noise, so full the vibration, that even had she screamed she would not have been heard. The gullies at the roadside had become gushing silver torrents and the road itself was fetlock-deep in mud.

Her cloak of light wool now weighed like a hauberk as the rain saturated through the fibres. Water streamed down her face. She felt it pooling in the hollow of her throat, running down the back of her neck and seeping into her garments. Gerbert had told her earlier in the day that they would reach Montabard in the late afternoon. It was that now, she thought, although the force of the storm had sucked all the natural light into its dark heart and they were riding by the eerie glow flickering through the clouds. She was awestruck and a little cowed by God's mightiness, her eyes stretched wide and her heart pounding with fear. But she felt the merest touch of exhilaration too.

Gerbert, who had been ahead with the scouts, returned to her, his large bay splashing through the downpour with a high, dished gait. Water dribbled steadily off the nasal bar of his helm, and his surcoat clung in sodden transparency to his mail.

'Just ahead!' he bellowed in between the growls of thunder. 'We have to climb! Shall I put you on a lead rein?'

She shook her head and motioned to say that she was all right. He nodded approval and, with face screwed up against the downpour, continued down the line.

Moments later, Sabin rode up and paused at her bridle. The grey shone like molten silver in the weird light, and Sabin's expression was blazing with joy.

'Is it not glorious?' he yelled.

Annais blinked at him through water-spiked lashes. 'Indeed!' she cried at the top of her lungs, but in order to be heard rather than out of elation. She blew a spray of rain from the crevice between her upper lip and her nose.

He laughed and dug in his heels. She watched the grey disappear into the deluge, like a creature created from cloud and rain. The path grew more slippery and treacherous as the ground began to rise, becoming increasingly steep. Hooves slithered in the mud. Small stones bounced away down the mountainside and the path became narrower, with no room for anyone to ride abreast and give her reassurance. Annais stared straight ahead. Although the rain obscured much of the view, she still did not want to look down and thanked God that her mare was placid. The thunder had made some of the horses skittish and difficult. As they continued to climb, Annais thought that she could see blocks of quarried and mortared stone rather than rough gouges of natural rock. At first, she thought it was an illusion of the rain, but, narrowing her eyes, found that she was indeed staring at a castle wall. It was so high that she had to crane her neck to see the battlements. It made Tel Namir look like a child's toy.

The sheet lightning flickered dementedly and a bird flew out from a niche in the stone, a dark shape against the swollen purple and silver. A rock dove, she thought, but the wings were like scythes and she realised that it was some kind of falcon. The sighting was brief, for the bird was swallowed up in the downpour and she had to concentrate on guiding the mare as the path narrowed yet again to what seemed no more than a goat track.

That this place was to be her new home filled her with apprehension bordering on panic. She had told Mariamne with pride that she was accustomed to life in a border fortress, but not one like this . . . She was briefly overwhelmed by tears, but they were lost among the raindrops streaming down her face, and by the time they came to a narrow postern door recessed in the wall between two watchtowers, she had control of herself again. She heard the slide of a draw bar and the door swung open on oiled hinges to admit the party to a large lower ward, dotted with flat-roofed buildings. Gerbert joined her again, taking her mare's bridle in his wet grasp and bearing to the right where another huge wall loomed out of the rain. There was another entrance, this one a narrow archway over a gatehouse protected by two portcullises. She was aware of a door opening in the gatehouse and a guard emerging to salute the party through. Beyond lay another ward with more buildings, among them one constructed of smaller, finer stones than the wall and roofed with tile. Gerbert rode up to it, dismounted at the door, and lifted her down. They squelched against each other.

'It is not the homecoming I would have desired for you,' he said, 'but welcome to Montabard.' He set his hand to the latch ring, thrust with his shoulder, and opened the door to the great hall. The sound of lashing rain faded into the background as she stared around the long room with its white walls and brightly adorned pillars. Instead of the usual central placing, the hearth had been set in the wall, and the smoke escaped up a chimney with a stone canopy. Trestles were stacked along the side of the room, but some had been left assembled and men were hastily rising from them to greet their lord.

In a flurry of faces, Annais was introduced to Gerbert's

household stewards, to his marshal and constable, to the senior knights of the garrison and household. To memorise their names was beyond her for now and she knew she would have to ask Gerbert to repeat them all later. Water dripped from every portion of her and soaked into the rushes. Her teeth began to chatter and suddenly it was all she could do to remain on her feet. The rest of Gerbert's men were piling into the hall and a pungent aroma compounded of wet wool, horse and sweat began to pervade the air. Nausea unfurled in her belly and she swayed where she stood.

'Here, I've been saving it, but you look more in need than me.' Sabin pressed a horn cup filled with a pale liquid into her chilled hands. Amid the other smells rose one redolent of her former home. She held the cup closer to her face, drawing in the tang of peat streams and smoke and looked over it at Sabin. He had removed his helm and arming cap. Although curling at the edges with moisture, and flattened on top by the weight of the steel, his hair was mainly dry even if the rest of him was dripping. 'Go on,' he said with a gesture, 'before I change my mind.'

She raised the cup and, as she had seen men do in times of need and extremity, took a swift gulp. The usquebaugh hit the back of her throat like liquid fire. She gagged, but it was too late and it was already flashing down her gullet to her belly. 'Mother Mary!' she wheezed.

Sabin gave an incorrigible grin. 'It'll kill or cure,' he said cheerfully and refilled the small horn measure from a silver pilgrim flask whose original purpose had been to hold water from the River Jordan. 'Another of these and you'll be ready for anything.'

Gerbert emerged from a low-voiced conversation with his constable. A worried frown pleated his brow and it increased at the sight of his wife flushed and gasping with Sabin standing solicitously over her.

Sabin glanced up at Gerbert's approach, but neither drew away from Annais, nor acknowledged the other man's superior right. 'Can you not see she is near the end of her endurance?' he said in a brusque tone.

'I am all right,' Annais said indignantly, her voice emerging as a hoarse crow from the ball of fire in her throat. The usquebaugh was working rapidly on her empty stomach. Even if she did not feel fit to tackle all comers, she was no longer in a state of collapse. She returned the cup to Sabin and the motion sent rapid drips of water from her sleeve to the rushes.

'It is like drinking lightning,' Sabin said, 'and lasts for about as long.' He looked again at Gerbert. 'She needs dry clothes and food.'

Gerbert rubbed his forehead and looked chagrined. 'I am ashamed that you need to remind me of my duty. Come, sweetheart, I'll get one of the women to take you to my chamber.' He set a concerned arm around his wife's shoulders and turned her firmly away from Sabin.

Tightening his lips, Sabin strode across to a corner of the hall where one of the stewards and an attendant were doling out linen and cotton towels and the saturated soldiers were stripping and drying themselves. There was also a pile of blankets and robes so that those whose baggage was soaked could have something dry to wear. Dragging off his clinging silk surcoat, Sabin wrung it into the rushes. One of Gerbert's escort knights, whose name was Durand, helped him remove his mail. At least the amount of grease in which he had slathered the rivets before setting out had prevented it from going too rusty, and there were only a few specks for his later attention. Next came the sodden gambeson, streaked with grease and black filaments of iron, then the tunic, damp, but not saturated. His shirt was almost dry, so he left that on, but removed his hose.

'I suppose you heard the news?' Durand said as Sabin flung on one of the dry robes. It was made of striped wool and Saracen in style with a deep neck opening and loose sleeves.

Sabin shook his head. 'What news?'

The knight's eyes were a piercing dark brown, set under

sloping lids. 'The Saracen lord Ilghazi agreed a treaty of peace with King Baldwin, but his nephew Balak has other notions. There have been raids along our borders and Christian villages have been attacked. Thierry, the constable, told my lord soon after we arrived.'

'Ah,' said Sabin. That would account for Gerbert's frowning preoccupation. A wife, no matter her discomfort, could wait when the security of the demesne was at risk. 'And are the raids mere fleabites, or indicative of something more serious?'

Durand shrugged. 'They are likely testing our strength,' he said. 'And even fleabites can become serious if enough blood is sucked from the victim. Since we are supposed to be at peace, I do not expect to see a siege army riding up to our gates, but they are not the kind of tidings to please my lord in his honey month with his new bride.' The knight gave Sabin a shrewd look. 'Are you still glad you had left the soft comfort of Tel Namir for a border fortress?'

Sabin shrugged. 'Believe me,' he said, 'life here can be no more dangerous than it was at Tel Namir.'

The chambers above the hall consisted of a workroom laid out with tapestry frames, sewing benches and a couple of upright looms. Beyond this, through a heavy curtain, was a room for the servants with sleeping pallets arranged along the wall. This in turn gave access beyond a solid wooden door to the largest chamber, which consisted of an integral solar and bedchamber. A smaller chimney was set into the wall with chairs before the fire. Beyond the flame's light, a large bed with embroidered hangings filled the shadows.

The fire had only recently been lit and the apartments had a musty smell that spoke of little use. A chill struck through to Annais's bones and her teeth clacked together.

'Usually my lord would have sent word ahead and we would have been able to prepare a fitting welcome, my lady,' said the woman who had escorted her to the chamber. Her name was Letice and she was a widow in early middle age with a round face and eyes of quick, intelligent hazel. 'But it is too dangerous for a man to ride fast in this weather.' She rummaged in a coffer at the side of the room and emerged with two folded towels. A couple of serving women had come forward and she directed them to strip Annais's wet garments. 'You are not seeing us at our best or most prepared.'

The maids pummelled and rubbed Annais with the towels until cold was replaced by a red, tingling warmth. From the waxed leather travelling chest, the women drew a dry chemise and, at Annais's indication, her woollen gown that had come from Scotland. 'How long have you dwelt here?' she asked Letice.

The older woman raised her eyes heavenwards while she considered the matter. 'I came from France . . . let me see . . . ten years ago with Walter, my husband. We arrived as pilgrims and stayed. He took up service with Lord Gerbert's father and became his constable.' Her voice rang with pride to which there was an edge of sadness. 'Walter died last year of a flux, God rest his soul – and we had no children.'

Annais murmured an appropriate response and made a note to tread gently around Letice. Ten years and a high position in the keep were likely to be defended against the intrusion of a new young bride, especially when Letice's status was no longer bolstered by a high-ranking man. As she shook out the creased folds of the gown, Annais wondered about Gerbert's former wife. He had spoken very little of her and Annais, out of sensibility, had not asked. This room would have been hers, but there was small indication of her presence or character. At Tel Namir, Henri FitzPeter's sister had left behind her crucifix, her plain blanket, a worn place at the shutters where she had watched the men at their drill, and a gold wimple pin in the bottom of a coffer. Here the walls were without decoration, save for a painted frieze of vine leaves swirling the top of the walls. Rushes strewed the floor and the furniture consisted of the usual coffers and settles. But there were no combs, no perfume vials, no sewing box or trinket bowls for holding the small fripperies of a woman's life.

Another maid entered the room bearing a cup of hot wine flavoured with cinnamon and cardamom seeds. There was also a loaf of flat bread and a dish of aromatic lamb stew. Annais's stomach growled like a hungry lion and Letice laughed.

'I know Lord Gerbert when he is on the road,' she said. 'He doesn't think that lesser mortals need sustenance.'

'I doubt we could have eaten anything in this weather,' Annais said to defend her husband. She had noticed that he was indeed a swift traveller who spared little time on the journey for stops to eat – or indeed even to piss behind a bush. She had recovered from the discomfort of her wedding night, but only to have it replaced with saddle-chafe.

Outside the thunder was still rumbling, but with less ferocity than before. The rain continued to tip down as if poured out of buckets. Sitting down on a folding stool before the fire, she devoured the food and asked Letice about her predecessor.

Letice pursed her lips in thought. 'Odile was about your own age,' she said. 'She was quiet and timorous and not very strong. Her marriage was arranged to my lord while his father and hers still lived. It was not a love-match – few are, but they managed well enough together.'

Annais nodded with empathy. She did not have a soul-burning passion for Gerbert, but she liked him and there was potential for her feelings to grow.

Letice folded her arms. 'After she miscarried of two infants, my lady went into a decline and kept much to her chamber and Lord Gerbert spent a deal of his time elsewhere. He was tender of her welfare and he wanted her to regain her health.' Letice sighed. 'She carried her last child for the full nine months but it was the death of her, God rest her soul.' She looked at Annais, who was mopping up the last of the stew with the bread. 'We all pray that this marriage will prove more fortunate.' Her expression said that the way Annais had devoured the food, she was sure it would.

Annais licked her fingers. She hoped it would prove more fortunate too. Perhaps she was already with child and her feet on the start of the path that Odile had trodden. It was a disturbing thought. Sipping her wine, she rose to walk around the chamber. There was dust on the coffers and the hangings although the bedsheets and coverlet were clean. She supposed, with a shiver, that after Odile had died, they had stripped and replaced the linens.

As if reading her mind Letice said, 'We left this room much as it was until my lord should give us instructions what to do. Lady Odile had been unwell for some time and she had no interest in her surroundings.'

'I am sorry for her,' Annais murmured. 'But content for myself. It means that I have an open hand to do as I wish and not feel that I am treading on the hem of a ghost.'

'So you are not displeased with Montabard?' Gerbert asked from the threshold.

She turned with a surprised start to face her husband. Unlatching his swordbelt, handing it to his squire, he advanced to the hearth and extended his hands to the warmth. 'I thought you might wonder what kind of prison I had brought you to.' He glanced towards the rumble of thunder outside the shutters. 'The weather has not played its part either.'

She came to him and stood to one side while his squire helped him unarm. 'But it is an arrival that I will remember for the rest of my life,' she said, smiling. 'A fanfare of trumpets could not compete with this.'

'No,' he agreed wryly and dismissed the squire. The young man staggered out, his arms laden with the sodden weight of the gambeson and the iron heaviness of the mail. Letice made her own unobtrusive exit, taking the maids with her, and softly closed the door.

'So you are truly content to be here?'

Hearing the need for reassurance in his voice, Annais set her reservations aside. 'I am very content to be here,' she said. 'I could not have endured that storm for much longer.' Then she shook her head as she saw his misgiving, and was bold enough to reach on tiptoe and touch his cheek. 'In truth, I am overwhelmed, but that will pass. I know I can make my life here.' A smile filled her eyes. 'If I had been told last year in Scotland that I would soon be wed to a lord of a great castle in Outremer, I would not have believed it . . . I am still not sure that I do. Perhaps this is all a dream.' She ran her hand down his arm. His tunic was damp and puffed with moisture and, beneath it, his muscles were as firm as carved wood. 'Although it doesn't feel like one.'

His breathing caught. 'If it is, I don't want to wake up.' He drew her to him, one hand at the back of her head, fingers meshed in her damp, tangled hair as he lowered his mouth to hers. The kiss was hard and demanding, taking her breath, shocking her with its sudden assault. She made a sound in her throat, half yielding, half fearful protest.

Gerbert released her, but only to remove his damp tunic. The bulge in his braies was mute indication of what was going to happen next. Annais braced herself. It was three days since their wedding night and this was their first one beneath their own roof. She should not have expected the weather and the travails of the journey to convey immunity.

He lifted her in his arms and took her to the bed, with its clean cold sheets, deep feather mattress and pervading musty smell. He told her that it was all right, that he wouldn't hurt her, that she needn't be afraid, that he just needed to . . .

She endured the storm as she had endured it outside. He lied when he said he would not hurt her, but she wasn't afraid, merely discomforted. He did not take long; within seconds, his body was shuddering against hers. Annais raised her hand and ran her fingers through his short brown curls. She could feel the hammering of his pulse in his throat and the small twitches of aftershock rippling down his spine. It had been perhaps a little easier than last time, and there was a certain satisfaction in being the source of her husband's pleasure, but still she thought he had the better part of the bargain and wished she could change places with him, feel what he felt and let him be the recipient of the storm.

Gasping harshly, Gerbert withdrew from her and rolled onto his back. 'I needed that,' he said.

Annais bit her lip. She hadn't, but he was hardly going to ask her opinion. She tried not to feel resentful. Leaving the bed, she shook out her gown and went to pour a cupful of the hot wine. The place between her legs stung and throbbed. There hadn't been time for Margaret's oil, but at least she had the pot of salve in her coffer. She brought the wine back to the bed, took a long drink, and offered the rest of the cup to Gerbert. Heavy-eyed, he took it from her and stroked her face. 'Did I hurt you?'

Had it shown so much on her face? 'No.' She shook her head and forced a smile. 'I am tired, nothing more.'

He nodded and seemed relieved to take her reply at face value. 'It has been a long journey in bad weather. Lie down and rest.' Rising from the bed, he rummaged in one of the coffers for a dry tunic and belt, attached his dagger sheath and headed doorwards.

'Are you not staying?' she asked. 'What of your own rest?'

He paused, spun on his heel and returned to kiss her. 'Presently,' he said. 'I have matters to discuss with the garrison. I've been absent a while and there are changes to be made to the patrols.'

'Tonight?'

'What's done now won't be waiting tomorrow.'

The reply was light enough, but Annais did not miss the lines of anxiety furrowing his brow and the thinning of his lips that only moments ago had been full with desire. She did not ask him for reassurances. He would have given them without a second thought and they would not have been the truth.

Chapter 14

'Why is Gerbert so worried?'

Sabin shrugged his way into his hauberk, jumping up and down until the mail shirt slithered over the quilted under tunic. All about him, harness and weaponry jingled as a detail from the garrison prepared to ride out on patrol. Horses pawed and snorted, their breath emerging as white vapour in the early morning air. Winter sunrise had blazoned the keep walls with red light, not warm as yet, but deep as fireglow.

Having settled his mail, Sabin considered Annais, who was patiently awaiting an answer to her question. She was wearing her woollen Scottish gown, the one Sabin privately called her 'nun's weeds'. A wimple of heavy linen enveloped her hair and throat. He did not blame her. The climate here was cooler than the plain and yesterday's rain had chilled the land so that it was almost like an autumn day in England or Normandy.

'Because it is in his nature to worry,' he said with a shrug. 'And because he has the responsibility for Montabard on his shoulders.'

Her gaze, steady and clear as a peat pool, demanded more of him. He sighed. 'Some of Gerbert's villages have been raided when there is supposed to be a truce between Christian and Saracen. In the lord's absence, enemies have grown bold, and it is necessary to put on a show of readiness and strength.' He checked that his scabbard was securely latched to his swordbelt. 'It is the same as on the Scottish borders, or the Welsh Marches, or the lands of the Norman Vexin. You patrol your territory; you keep it clean.' He looked up at her from his equipment. 'Did Gerbert tell you nothing?'

'Nothing except to rest and not to worry my head. I knew if I asked you I would get the truth, since you are less tender of my welfare.'

He gave a short laugh. 'I never thought I'd hear you say that you believed in my integrity.'

Her look told him without words what she thought of his remark. Grinning, he turned to mount Lucifer. Gerbert emerged from the forebuilding where he had been having last words with the captain of the garrison. His stride was long and purposeful and the frown was deep between his eyes. Seeing it made Sabin even more determined that he was never going to adopt a position where the responsibility dwelt so heavily on him that bearing it brought lines to his face. Discreetly, he reined Lucifer away from Annais lest Gerbert should see and misconstrue their proximity.

Gerbert glanced around at his waiting men, kissed Annais and mounted his powerful bay. 'We'll be back sooner than dusk,' he said. 'Captain Aymer knows the route we have taken should there be need.'

'God keep you safe, my lord,' Annais said.

'I put my trust in Him.' Gerbert gave her a preoccupied smile and swung the bay towards the first of the castle's defensive gateways.

Riding behind Gerbert and Thierry the constable, Sabin gazed around the immensity of the walls of Montabard. Yesterday the driving rain had obscured the half of it, but today, glistening in the sunshine, he realised how huge the place was. 'Some of it was built by Lord Gerbert's sire and some by Lord Gerbert himself,' said Durand, joining him. 'But it was a Saracen fortress before that and a Greek one before the Saracens came.'

And now it was theirs for whatever span they could hold it.

Sabin thought of the courts and keeps and palaces back in England and Normandy. Even among kings, there was little on this scale.

This time, instead of leaving through the concealed postern gate and winding their way down a precipitous goat track, they departed through the main entrance and rode two abreast across a timber bridge spanning a rock-cut ditch. In times of war the bridge could be destroyed, leaving an enemy faced with sheer, vertical walls.

Beyond the ditch was an outpost of the main keep, manned by two guards, and after that, their way was clear to descend the spur of rock to the flat land below. A flash of scythe-blade wings caught the corner of Sabin's vision, and he turned in time to see the final moments of a hunting shahin's stoop upon a rock dove. There was a violent explosion of soft cream feathers and falcon and prey plummeted to a ledge in the rock side. Sabin had seen such sights before. Travelling with King Henry's court it had been almost a daily event with the trained hawks from the royal mews, but this was wild and elemental . . . and stirred his blood beyond the common surge.

'Aye,' said Durand, who had noticed his response. 'The falcons of Montabard are famed. Lord Gerbert has to present one every year to King Baldwin as part of his feudal obligation. If you ask me who is the bravest man in the fortress, I would say the falconer who has to scale the rock face on a rope and collect the young birds from the nest.'

Sabin nodded in heartfelt agreement.

'There is a legend that as long as there are shahins at Montabard, it will remain a Christian fortress.' Durand shrugged. 'It's a fine story, but I think the birds have been here through every rule, and will still be so when we are long gone . . .'

The River Orontes gleamed in the distance but, rather than reflecting the blue of the morning sky, was a swollen brown torrent. Beyond its banks, the flood plain spread to Sabin's view, lush and green, dotted by grazing animals and arable fields. 'Montabard grows cotton and grain and sugar cane,' Durand said. 'There is good hunting along the riverbanks, and plentiful fish in the river.'

Sabin's lips twitched. 'A veritable land of milk and honey.'

Durand returned the smile. 'Those too, if you do not mind scorpions.'

'How bad were the raids?'

'Several grain stores raided in a Christian village and a herd of cattle driven off. Two men killed and an aborted attempt made to burn down the sugar mill.' The knight shrugged. 'There is little we can do to prevent them except maintain constant vigilance. We do not have the numbers to take the battle to them. Ours is ever a defensive game.' He looked at Sabin. 'Have you ever fought the Saracen?'

'No, save on board our ship when we were attacked by Arab sea-reavers, but my father has told me of their methods – that they swoop in, attack and dart away. They are excellent horsemen and accomplished archers and spear-throwers, but they cannot stand up to Frankish cavalry.'

Durand nodded. Unfastening the hook at the top of his hauberk and tugging down the neck of his gambeson, he showed Sabin a jagged pink scar that began at his collarbone and disappeared beneath his clothing. 'I took this last year in a skirmish near Kafartab. Bastard put a lance over the top of my shield. A fraction higher and it would have been in my throat. They're fast, I tell you, faster than you would ever think, until it's too late.' He made sure that Sabin got a good look at the slick pink scar and refastened his mail. 'Some men keep a tally of how many Saracens they have killed. They say that each one is like a stepping stone on the path to heaven.'

'Are you one of them?' Sabin asked.

Durand laughed darkly. 'I was going to ask that question of you. No, I am not one of them, although I was ten years ago when I came to Montabard. Then we raided a Saracen caravan filled with women and children.' He lifted his gaze to Sabin. 'There are some things that a man should not do, even to infidels. I know that we massacred them in Jerusalem when we took the city, but I was not there on that day. I can kill a man in the heat of battle or to save my own skin. I can hunt down raiding parties and kill without mercy. But to cut the throat of a woman, or a small child . . .' His upper lip curled and an expression of utter loathing crossed his face. 'Men who can add such "stepping stones" to their tally must surely be damned.'

'Is that what happened?'

'To some of them before Lord Gerbert's father put a stop to it. Some were ransomed; others were sold.' His eyes were angry with guilt. 'One of our serjeants was intent on butchering a woman and her infant son, but I stopped him and claimed them for myself. She converted to Christianity – although I suspect she pays her devotion with lip service – and for the past four years we have been husband and wife.' He glowered defensively at Sabin as if daring him to pass judgement on the fact.

'So if I said I had come to a border post for the glory of killing Saracens, you would withhold your comradeship?' Rather than rising to the bait, Sabin pushed the issue sideways.

'It is the reason that most young men take up such positions. There are less dangerous livings to be made in Jerusalem and the softer south. Only the truly committed or the very well paid come to border castles like this.'

Sabin smiled. 'And what of renegades and rebels seeking a bolt hole?'

Durand snorted. 'You consider this a bolt hole?'

'Of sorts.' Sabin drew in the reins. 'Perhaps not for ever, but sufficient for the moment. And to answer the question you would have asked . . . No, I too have given up keeping tallies and for the same reason as you.' Durand raised his brows.

'Her name was Lora,' Sabin said, and heeled Lucifer's flanks, urging him forward, and leaving Durand frowning in his wake.

The villagers came from their fields and their houses to greet Gerbert, clamouring around his saddle. They were mostly dark-skinned and dark-eyed, but here and there a child with light eyes or fair hair spoke of Frankish blood. Their dragoman was fluent in French and Gerbert questioned him about the raids while the troop was served with dark wine, flat bread and olives.

The session was short. The villagers, although vociferous, could tell Gerbert little enough save that the raiders had come from the north, from the direction of Aleppo.

Gerbert turned to ride with Sabin. 'Now comes your service to me,' he said. 'I cannot be everywhere at once, so I charge you with the task of preventing raids from the north. I want you to take out patrols. I want you to know this land as if you were born in it. You can borrow guides from the village, and take such men as you need.' His lips curved in an arid smile. 'I do not expect to see much of you at Montabard. There are more than fifty miles of territory to guard and some nights you will need to camp out. You will find the hunting good . . . although it is always wise to beware of leopards and lions.' A trace of hostility coloured his tone. Sabin decided that Gerbert had seen him talking to Annais that morning and had not been pleased.

'As you wish, my lord,' he said with bland courtesy.

Gerbert studied him, then grunted. 'Good. I will show you the rest of the territory. If we ride along the top, you can see for a distance.' He gestured up the valley. 'I leave it to you to explore in detail.'

Although Gerbert's manner was curt, Sabin still felt a surge of pleasure. Literally, he had pastures new to explore and sanction to do as he chose. What more could he want?

Annais spent the day familiarising herself with her surroundings. It was an enormous task, for Montabard was almost twice the size of Tel Namir. The great wall clinging to the precipice surrounded a complex that was in effect a small and almost self-sufficient village.

Letice showed her the bins that housed the grain store, its environs patrolled by sleek, feral tabby cats. Stretched in the sun, washing ears and paws, they watched her through indolent leaf-gold eyes. 'We have little problem with rats,' Letice said. 'When times are lean the cats are fed scraps from the kitchens, but mostly they fend for themselves. There is enough grain stored to withstand a year-long siege – not that it has ever been necessary, but living so close to the border of Frankish territory, it is best to err on the side of caution.'

Annais followed Letice to the amphorae of wine, the jars of olive oil, the crocks of honey and barrels of pickled fish. They came to the kitchens. Although wheaten bread for the castle had been baked earlier in the day, the heat from the ovens was still like a hot wind on Annais's face. The cook and his assistants were preparing a spicy broth into which balls of minced pork coloured and flavoured with saffron were to be cast. Annais was offered a taste, and nodded her approval, even if the heat of pepper did explode in her mouth. More to her preference were some small raisin pasties, bursting with fruit and flavour. With a disarming smile for the cook, she filched a couple from the serving platter on her way out.

Letice took her to every part of the keep. Eating her pasties, Annais followed her guide through dark cellars containing indeterminate shapes that resolved themselves in torchlight to more barrels and sacks of supplies. Here too were the cisterns of the castle's water supply. The hem of her robe powdered with dust, a white net of cobwebs clinging to her bosom, Annais left dark for light and climbed the stairs to the battlements, her lungs heaving and her legs burning under the effort. From here, once she had recovered her breath, she could walk the perimeter of Montabard and gaze for miles upon a terrain of fields, mountains and water meadows. Such was the feeling of possession that she wanted to strike a pose and place her hand on a nonexistent sword.

Letice watched her with amusement. 'Yes,' she said, 'that is how I felt when I first arrived here – as if the world was mine.' Lips parted in a smile of pure delight, Annais wondered how many others had stood like this down the ages. Perhaps these battlements had existed at the time when Christ walked the earth. A shiver rippled down her spine.

'You are not afraid of heights?' Letice asked as they progressed along the wall walk.

Annais shook her head. 'When I was a little girl I used to slip away from my nurse, climb to the top of my uncle's keep and sit in the crenel spaces. It wasn't as high as this, but I would send my nurse and my mother frantic. They needed eyes in the backs of their heads too, for I was cunning and determined. The slightest chance and I was off.'

Letice chuckled. 'Not a seemly way for a girl child to behave,' she said.

'Indeed not,' Annais said with a reminiscent grin. 'The first time I did it, I wanted to see over the battlements like any curious child. I loved the sight of the hills in the distance and how all the people and animals below looked so small. Also the crenels were exactly the right size for me to sit in.' She patted her haunch ruefully. 'It would be more of a squeeze these days. After I was scolded and warned how dangerous it was, it became a challenge. The more I was chastised, the more I wanted to go there.'

'You have a wild and stubborn streak then,' Letice said with a sly smile.

Annais drew breath to deny the statement, then realised she was condemned out of her own mouth. 'Tempered, I hope, by experience.' She laughed. 'I would hate it to become common knowledge in certain quarters.' She could imagine the sardonic glitter in Sabin's eyes should he learn of her escapades.

'My lips are sealed,' Letice said.

They walked on, pausing at intervals to study the different angles of the scenery. Above their heads, a falcon flashed in the blue air, its flight so graceful and swift that it took Annais's breath.

'What did Gerbert's first wife think of this?' she asked.

'She seldom came up to the battlements,' Letice answered in an expressionless voice. 'She was afraid of heights and she did not think it a woman's business to roam far beyond the bower.'

From other things that had been said, Annais was receiving the impression that her predecessor had been a timid creature, incapable of fulfilling her role as lady of the keep. 'So the burdens have fallen to you in the meantime,' Annais said, wondering how to approach the delicate question of authority. She needed Letice to be her ally, not her rival.

'My shoulders are wide.'

'I am glad,' Annais said. 'For there is much I do not know, and I will need your help and friendship.'

Letice looked pleased. 'I will do whatever I can, my lady.'

They had reached one of the towers with steep stairs winding down to the outer bailey. Pausing, Annais looked at Letice. 'I thought that, with the men absent, we could spend the rest of the day engaged in personal business,' she said.

The woman raised her brows in polite question.

'The bedchamber,' Annais said. 'I desire to make it truly mine, instead of a musty place of limbo.'

Letice's hazel eyes brightened. 'That seems like a fine notion,' she smiled.

'It does, doesn't it?' Annais gave a sigh, replete with anticipation.

Chapter 15

Spring, 1122

Sabin cocked an eye to the sun and wondered whether to ride for Montabard or make camp. They had been on a hard patrol and out in the field for more than a week, hunting Arab raiders. A Saracen army was active to the north around the town of Zerdana, and skirmishing parties were as numerous and irritating as the flies that came to drink from every exposed human and animal orifice.

Sabin shaded his eyes against the sun. It was late spring, hot by the standards of England and Normandy but a mere lizard-basking pleasantness in Outremer. Black buck and gazelle grazed the lush grass, their tails switching vigorously. It was deceptively peaceful, but all the time Sabin was drinking in his surroundings, he was also listening and watching for that shadow out of place, for the sinuous line of a leopard's back as it wove noiselessly through the grass, for the flash of harness or armour.

'Do we make camp, my lord?'

'No,' Sabin said. 'Montabard is within reach and there is a full moon tonight. We take a respite and then we patrol again. After that we go home.'

The serjeant, a Syrio-Frank named Malik, said nothing, but Sabin sensed his relief. It had been a gruelling week. Sabin asked nothing of the men that he did not ask of himself, but since he was out to prove that he was of sufficient calibre to lead them and not just a soft newcomer, he had pressed them hard. A shred of common sense and a spark of empathy with the men, however, meant that although he held them on the edge, he had not pushed them over. They thought him a severe taskmaster, but he had earned a degree of respect.

'Sir Thierry and Lord Gerbert have little success when chasing raiders too,' Malik sympathised as Sabin reined around from the knoll where he had been studying the lie of the land. 'Such men have the art of disappearing like ghosts.'

'While we stand out like sore thumbs.' Sabin glanced around at the soldiers in their quilted tunics and rivet-mail. 'We are targets for them either to attack or avoid.'

Malik nodded. 'One of the reasons they do not attack us except by ambush is that we would flatten them with our heavier armour and weapons. If we take to their ways, they can outfight us because they have the skill and we do not.'

The sun slipped westwards, lighting the flanks of the hills so that they shone crimson as if in bright firelight. The deep green of the cypress and cedar trees shimmered with gold in the evening wind, tranquil and fierce at the same time. Sabin felt a longing deep within him, as if he was drawing both sustenance and pain with each breath.

Lucifer quivered and stopped so abruptly that Sabin's spine was jarred. He had been riding the stallion on a relaxed rein, but now he drew the leather tight and raised his right hand to halt the troop. Rapidly he scanned the shadow-washed ground for snakes or scorpions, but there was nothing. Still the horse baulked and snorted, threatening to rear, plunging aside when Sabin tried to heel him forward. 'Weapons drawn,' he snapped and drew his sword. Even as the westering sun flashed on the metal, a second shard of light dazzled out of the darkness and had Lucifer not danced sidelong, the arrow would have sunk shaft-deep in Sabin's breast. Instead, it skimmed past him and lodged in the ground.

'Shields!' Sabin snarled, swinging his own down and

forward. His men rapidly followed suit and closed ranks. The manoeuvre took seconds, and in those seconds that first arrow, loosed from an over-eager bow, was followed by a shower of hissing deadly rain, and the horsemen came galloping in, fresh arrows nocked, tasselled lances piercing the sunset.

'Hold firm!' Sabin roared with a swift arm signal to the troop. 'Don't chase them!'

The Saracens released their second volley of arrows and, whooping, sped away. One soldier was hit in the arm and a horse was struck in the shoulder but not killed. Sabin saw the enemy wheel and turn, watched them come galloping in and fretted Lucifer, holding, judging the precise moment. 'Now!' he bellowed and spurred the grey. His target was an archer, crouched over his mount's shoulders and withers, his loosened turban streaming in the wind as he approached at speed. The arrow flew from his bow but the shot went awry and low, the very tip slicing into Sabin's tough calfhide boot. The blow did little to slow Sabin's impetus and, before the Saracen could rein away, Sabin had him. The last rays of the sun gilded sword and scimitar as they clashed, but the sword was faster, the backswing more efficient. The Saracen tumbled from the saddle, his turban ribboning down with him like a long strip of bloodied winding sheet. Sabin reined about, seized a tasselled lance that was quivering upright in the ground and spurred to join the fray.

The battle was brief but fierce and bloody, with no quarter given on either side. Once the Franks closed with the Saracens, their heavier, superior armour tipped the balance, but not without the cost of several deep wounds and one death. There was a single escapee among the Saracen ranks. A youngster who had been tending the stolen horses fled on one, and cut the others loose. They milled, whinnying and distressed at the scent of blood, but drawn by the herding instinct to stay with the saddled animals.

'Let him go,' Sabin said. 'Round up the horses and bring them with us.'

'What of the dead?' Malik asked. One-handed, he was binding a scimitar cut to his forearm; it was not mortal, but in need of stitching.

Sabin had dismounted to tug the arrow from his boot. A sawing pain and a hot trickling feeling told him that the edge had sliced flesh as well as leather. 'Bring them with us,' he said. 'There are horses enough to carry them.'

By the time Sabin and his patrol arrived at the gates of Montabard, it was full night, although a brilliant white moon lit their way. When they entered the middle courtyard and came to the stables, they found the stalls occupied by the mounts of strangers and they had to take their own to one of the open-sided overflow barns.

Sabin's foot was throbbing painfully and it was difficult to walk. Using one of the tasselled spears to lean on, he saw to it that the more seriously wounded were given immediate succour and the dead man was borne to the chapel.

As the news of their return arrived, Gerbert hastened from the hall, accompanied by a tall, powerfully built man in early middle age. The latter gazed with interest on the bodies heaped across the Turkish horses.

'A fine haul,' he said in a voice that was husky, as if he shouted a lot.

'We were lucky,' Sabin said with a shrug.

The stranger's smile revealed several missing teeth, although those he had left were large and strong. 'Give me a lucky man every time,' he said. 'Your name, sir?'

'Sabin FitzSimon . . . my lord.' Sabin bowed and used formal address, for he could tell from the man's rich garments that he was more than an ordinary knight. The amount of horseflesh cramming the stables suggested at the least a baron with a large entourage.

Gerbert said, 'Sabin, this is Joscelin de Courtenay, Count of Edessa and cousin to King Baldwin.'

Sabin bowed again, more deeply this time – as much in

honour of the man's reputation as his rank. Joscelin of Edessa was one of the foremost warriors in the kingdom, but also known as a man of wide vision and tolerance.

Gerbert said, 'Sabin is here on pilgrimage, sir, and spending some time in my service. His father was an English earl and he has been fostered in the households of King Henry and Prince David of Scotland.'

'But just now I look more like a brigand who has been dragged through the mire,' Sabin added lightly with an irritated glance at Gerbert.

Count Joscelin looked amused. 'You do indeed,' he said. 'Although not in as bad a case as those you have brought back.'

Sabin grimaced. 'Not quite,' he said, 'but few of us have come away unscathed.'

Joscelin regarded the corpses heaped across the Saracen mounts. 'Common bandits do you think, or outriders from Balak's army?'

'If you were to press me, I would say that they were bandits, but perhaps in the pay of a greater lord for the time being. They stole horses and made petty raids on several homesteads, but we found them close to Montabard and I think that they had been told to spy. Otherwise why risk themselves? Why not melt away with their spoils?' He rubbed a weary hand over his face, feeling light-headed with the aftermath of battle and the cumulative fatigue of several days of travelling rations and little sleep. His foot was throbbing as though there was a large drum lodged in his big toe.

'They will find no weaknesses at Montabard,' Gerbert said grimly.

'God help you if they do,' Joscelin replied. 'It is never wise to be complacent, but from what I have seen, you have strong defences and fine men to guard them.' He gave Sabin a soldierly belt on the shoulder. 'I won't keep you,' he said. 'I know you have duties to attend to and you look as if you're almost asleep on your feet.'

Sabin straightened. 'I can manage, my lord.'

The Count's full beard bristled as he smiled. 'No doubt, but every man should know his limits and when to let go . . . and I say that as one who is frequently castigated for not doing so.'

'Then if you will excuse me, my lords.' Sabin bowed again. His injury had set while he stood and it was agony to walk, but pride made him put one foot in front of the other. There was still much to do. Comrades to tend, a dead man in the chapel to be prayed for. Had he not been so tired he would have laughed at the notion that he thought he could ever flee responsibility. It had flung itself over his head like a kidnapper flinging a sack over a victim and it wasn't going to let him escape.

It had been moonrise when he arrived at Montabard. It was dawn by the time he dragged himself up the guardroom stairs, tottered to his pallet, and fell face down on it in a stupor.

Annais laid down her sewing and pressed her hand to her belly. There it was again, that tiny quiver of motion, not sufficiently strong to be seen or felt externally, but a distinct fluttering low down inside her. 'It moved again,' she said in a wondering voice.

Letice smiled. 'Aye, first babes usually do quicken in the fifth month,' she said. 'You are carrying well, my lady.'

Annais returned her smile. She had been swift to conceive; her flux had come once and then not again. Although she had heard that women suffered terrible sickness in the early months, her own experience had been of mild nausea. Indeed, if anything her appetite had increased, and she had already abandoned wearing the fitted gowns she had brought with her to Montabard. Her skin glowed, her hair was as glossy as satin and after initial feelings of tiredness she now possessed a boundless energy. Her air of wellbeing astonished Gerbert. His first wife had retired to bed at the missing of her first flux and had been desperately ill throughout her pregnancy. He had expected similar behaviour from Annais and when he found her turfing out coffers and supervising all manner of domestic sprucing he tried to make her rest. She might do herself harm, he said, she might miscarry. Sensible of his earlier experience, Annais indulged him to a degree, but could only sit for so long without becoming bored. Her sewing skills had improved beyond measure and the infant, when it was born, would have enough swaddling bands and cradle linen to see it through a dozen changes. She had devoted time to her harp playing and even composed several tunes with which she was well pleased. But in between humouring her anxious husband, she had employed herself with a couple of projects. 'Nest building' as Letice had said.

The bedchamber now boasted hangings of heavy Damascus cloth. The walls had received a fresh coat of limewash and Bedouin rugs in opulent colours relieved the whiteness. The plain coffers were mellow with beeswax polish and a colourful enamelled bridal chest stood beneath the window, its lid strewn with silk cushions. The original dinginess had yielded to a room that was bright and welcoming. She had recently set about doing the same for the guest hall, which had received no attention at all during the reign of her predecessor. Here too she had repeated the pattern of limewashed walls and rug hangings. When Gerbert questioned her bustle, she had told him that since she was overseeing, and not actually toiling, there could be no danger. The danger was that she would go mad with naught to do but contemplate her thickening waistline.

She was glad that she had taken a stand, and so was Gerbert after yesterday's visit. Joscelin of Edessa was a great lord, and at least they had had a guest hall worthy to house him. He had ridden out this morning with his entourage of Frankish and Armenian knights – after the corpses of the raiders had been hung in chains from the west wall of the castle. Annais had a strong stomach, but had preferred not to watch the bodies being strung up. Even so, the kites circling in the arches of sky through the open shutters were a grim reminder of what dangled there. By God's mercy and the birds' hunger, not for long. It had to be done; she understood that in a harsh land harsh measures were necessary, but still her heart was soft and she flinched. While Gerbert and Joscelin supervised the grisly duty, she had busied herself amongst the wounded. They had all been tended the previous evening when the patrol had ridden in, but there were bandages to change, stitches to check, tisanes to be administered. There had been no sign of Sabin, which was strange. She would have expected him present to witness the hanging of raiders . . . unless like her he had no desire to see the bodies dangled for the kites to pick clean.

She resumed her sewing. Within her womb, the child fluttered again. 'Gerbert thinks that there is going to be trouble,' she said. 'He tries to keep it from me because I am with child, but I have seen the way he bites his nails when he thinks I am not looking.'

'I have heard nothing.' Letice focused intently on her own piece of sewing but Annais was not fooled.

'Oh, come now.' She tossed her head. 'The knights talk freely in your presence . . . more freely than they do in mine.'

'Naught but rumours,' Letice said firmly. 'There is always trouble of one kind or another on these borders. You know yourself that Lord Gerbert worries small hills into great mountains.'

Annais frowned. 'Indeed he does, but I would like to know what manner of small hill he has worried into a mountain this time?'

'The Emir Balak has broken the truce made with King Baldwin earlier this year. There has been fighting around Zerdana which lies just outside our territory.'

'Is that why Count Joscelin is here?'

'Part of the reason. The other is that he is genuinely passing through on his way elsewhere.'

Annais continued to sew and tried to stem her irritation. It was not Letice's fault that Gerbert saw fit to leave his wife in ignorance. It was useless telling him that she worried more for not knowing, because he wouldn't listen. 'So that is why those men were hanged from the walls – as a sign to others of the fate of all who raid Montabard's lands.'

'I think so,' Letice said. 'And it reassured Count Joscelin. He needs to know that his allies have the strength and stomach for war if it comes.'

'I . . .' Annais glanced up at a loud knock on the door. Soraya, Durand's wife, went to answer it and found Sabin's young squire Amalric standing on the threshold. His fair hair stuck up in spikes as if he had just risen from his bed and his tunic was festooned with stalks of straw. Obviously he had been sleeping in the stables.

Annais beckoned him into the room and, when she saw the look on his face, was filled with concern. 'What is the matter?'

The youth shuffled his feet. 'My lady, could you look at Sir Sabin? I think he is sick. I brought him a cup of wine to waken him, but he would not rouse, and he was hot to the touch.'

The women exchanged glances. 'I'll come at once,' Annais said, beckoning her women and directing Letice to fetch the satchel of nostrums. As they left the bower and descended the stairs, Annais questioned the youth.

Amalric screwed up his face. 'Sir Sabin was very tired when he returned last night, and, yes, I think he was injured because he was limping. He left me to tend to Lucifer and said he had to speak to some of the men. When I went to rouse him this morn, I could not.'

'Mayhap it is just exhaustion,' said Letice. 'He constantly pushes himself to his limits.'

'I hope you are right,' Annais replied grimly.

She was panting by the time she had climbed the stairs to his chamber. Amalric had left the door open and the shutters wide to admit light and air to the room. Clutching the stitch in her side, Annais walked slowly to the bed. Sabin was sprawled face down and head turned slightly to one side on the heavy cotton coverlet. His tanned skin was flushed and sweat gleamed in the hollow of his throat. He had not shaved while on patrol and thick beard stubble outlined his jaw, chin and upper lip. He was still clothed in his gambeson, although swordbelt and mail had been removed and draped across his coffer. The smell of sweat and clothes that had been lived in for far too long rose from him in miasmic wafts – as did the heat. Amalric was right: Sabin was feverish.

She shook his shoulder and called to him. At first, he did not respond, but, finally, she was rewarded with a groan and a fluttering of groggy lids. It was pointless asking him if he was all right, for it was obvious he wasn't. His eyes, which were usually a clear green-gold, were now as opaque as muddy stones.

'Let me be,' he growled.

'You are sick; we have come to tend you.' She laid her palm to his brow, then felt the beating of his pulse, steady but as swift as a hurrying river.

'Tend or torture . . . both the same.' He rolled on his back. Blood had saturated the right cuff of his gambeson and dried to a dirty brown almost as far as the elbow. Horrified at the sight, she took his wrist and examined it for a deep cut, but, although there were bruises, the skin was unbroken.

'Not mine,' Sabin slurred.

Annais recalled Amalric saying that Sabin had been limping. She turned her attention to his legs, but there was no sign of blood here either. When she raised his gambeson and tunic to inspect above his knees, he gave a cracked laugh.

'Jesu, the best offer I have ever had from you and I'm in no case to take advantage.'

Annais glared at him. 'If you were not delirious with fever, I would slap you,' she said. 'Where are you wounded?'

'I took a spear in the foot.' He raised himself up to look down his body. He was more awake now, but it was not an improvement.

'And you haven't had it seen to?'

'No time at first, and when there was, I didn't care.' He slumped back on the bolster.

Clucking her tongue, Annais went to the end of the bed and looked at his boots, which he hadn't removed. The right one was intact. The left one bore a sliced incision. Dust and dirt had caked over the blood that had soaked through the tough leather. Her stomach turned and she felt the first roll of queasiness for a month. The boot would have to be eased off to discover what lay beneath, but she did not want to see a disabling injury.

'You are looking at me as if I'm your favourite horse with a broken leg,' Sabin said huskily. 'I give you permission to dispatch me if it's unmendable . . . although I might still be good for stud duties.'

'If you were not babbling and out of your wits, I would gag you with your own leg bindings,' Annais snapped.

'Hah, I'm sure you can think of better ways to get your revenge.'

Annais opened her mouth, looked at him, and changed her mind. She could see him clearly as a small boy, as an adolescent, as a fledgling adult, holding brazen against fear and pain. It was a shield, she thought, and he would rather die than let anyone pierce through to his vulnerable core. What he needed the most – and the least – was mothering.

'Indeed I can,' she said and, kneeling, unfastened the horn toggle at the side of his boot, cupped his heel and gently tugged. She felt him stiffen and heard his breath hiss through clenched teeth, but he did not cry out. There was a slicing wound to the ball of his foot and the fleshy cushion of his largest toe. It was ingrained with dirt and in need of cleaning and stitching but, as far as Annais could tell and providing his fever did not worsen, it did not threaten his life.

'Bring water,' she said to a maid, 'as hot as your hands can bear. And a crock of honey from the kitchen stores.'

'Honey?' Letice looked at her.

'Mother Prioress at Coldingham always swore by honey

as a healing ointment for wounds, and it worked. Even those with badly inflamed cuts used to mend swiftly.' She told another maid to have two men haul a wooden bathtub up to the room and set about divesting Sabin of his other boot. 'You should have had yourself tended last night,' she reproached him. 'Surely you have seen how swiftly injuries can fester in this climate?'

'Do you nag Gerbert too?'

Compressing her lips, Annais rose from her knees and bade the two remaining maids undress him. 'Gerbert has more sense in his little finger than you have in your entire body,' she muttered as she rummaged in the nostrum satchel for the feverfew and willowbark that would cool his body and eventually dull the edge of his pain. There was tincture of white poppy too, if necessary, and leaves of the hemp plant – a substance favoured by the Saracens.

'Likely you are right.' He surrendered to the ministrations of the women who stripped him of all save his braies. The bathtub arrived, was filled with water at a little below blood-heat and the two male attendants removed Sabin's braies and helped him into it. The maids set to with olive-oil soap, while Sabin leaned his head against the edge of the tub and endured with taut jaw and closed eyes.

'Drink this.' Annais pushed a steaming cup into his hands.

Sabin gave her a look through heavy lids. 'Does your child know what a formidable mother it is going to have?'

She turned her back on him, ostensibly to kneel at the other end of the long, oval tub and examine his injury now that it had been cleaned by the water, but also so that she would not be tempted to enter into a sparring contest with him. It was his defence, she reminded herself; and he would have to be dying before he let her through.

She heard him drinking the brew, and the mutter beneath his breath at the bitter taste. She supposed she should have sweetened it with some of the honey reserved for his wound, but then decided he didn't deserve it. With grim thoroughness, she cleaned the cut. His body went rigid, but he did not complain or make a sound; however, it was telling, she thought, that he also omitted to make any flippant remarks. She suspected that for the moment they were beyond him.

Once he had been helped from the bath and dried in a succession of linen towels, the maids dressed him in a heavy cotton robe and helped him back to the freshened bed. Annais set about stitching his injuries, smeared the area liberally in honey, and then bandaged his foot with strips of washed and softened linen.

'Now you can rest,' she said as she rinsed her hands in the bath water. 'Do you wish for someone to sit by you?'

From being flushed with fever, his colour had receded as she stitched and bound. Dark shadows circled his eyes. 'I need no one to keep vigil,' he said. 'I am sure you and your women have more pressing matters to attend than to watch me sleep . . . unless any of them wish to share my bed?'

Annais straightened her spine and lifted her chin. 'I doubt that very much,' she said curtly. 'Amalric will keep watch amid his other duties and be your messenger should you have need.' She nodded to end the exchange and began ushering the other women from the room. Her foot was over the threshold, her body turned towards the stairs when his voice caught the soft space beneath her ribs.

'Thank you,' he said. It was spoken humbly and stripped of all sarcasm. A moment's lowering of the shield.

She hesitated, but did not look over her shoulder, for her own defences were raised. 'I would have done it for anyone,' she replied. 'It is my duty.'

There was silence from the bed. Head lowered, Annais hurried after the other women.

Chapter 16

Four days after Joscelin of Edessa took his leave, his cousin King Baldwin appeared at Montabard's gates with the army of Jerusalem. Heralds had arrived in advance, so the gates were open and preparations in hand to welcome the royal guest. Space was cleared in the lower enclosure to house the tents of the knights and soldiers and pavilions were hastily erected in the middle ward to absorb the overflow that was bound to come from the hall.

For the duration of the visit, Sabin had to yield his own chamber to a man of higher rank. Fortunately, four days of sodden sleep, punctuated by nourishing broths, tisanes and copious applications of wild honey, had engendered a rapid recovery and it was with equanimity that he moved from his bed to a camp tent in the lower ward. The bandaging around his foot meant that he had to wear a monk's sandal, and his limp was pronounced, but he borrowed a toy spear from one of the castle children and, using it as a walking stick, managed to get around spryly enough.

'The King has responded swiftly to the tidings of the siege at Zerdana,' he said to the herald who had brought the details of King Baldwin's imminent arrival and was now quenching his thirst in the hall with a cup of wine. Around them servants were assembling trestles and spreading them with freshly laundered napery. 'We did not think to see him for several weeks.' The herald drained his cup. 'The King had business with Count Pons of Tripoli, so we were already halfway here when the news came. The King will rest here tonight, gather more soldiers and ride out at dawn.'

Leaving the messenger, Sabin limped from the hall and into the courtyard. A glance aloft revealed the fit members of the garrison standing to attention on the wall walks to greet Baldwin's arrival with a flash of upright spears. He wondered how many of them Baldwin would take on the morrow. Probably as many as there were serviceable mounts in the stables.

Gerbert came striding from his personal apartment, dressed in his mail and wearing his ceremonial surcoat of crimson and yellow silk, three falcons embroidered across the breast. His face wore its usual anxious expression. Sabin had learned that Gerbert was not always as worried as he looked, and that the deep frown lines between his brows were as much set by habit as current emotion.

Annais arrived on her husband's heels with the castle ladies, all of them gowned in finch-bright silks and many of them twittering with excitement. Annais was flushed and breathing swiftly, but then as lady of Montabard it was her duty to make sure that everything was in order and an hour's notice was precious little warning. At least it was only soldiers rather than the entire court, Sabin thought. Providing there was enough food and shelter to go round, no one would notice the lack of attention to small details. In his experience, men were always easier to please than women. He limped across the ward and joining the ladies, murmured that consolation to Annais.

Her hands had been tightly clasped before her waist in a gesture reminiscent of agitated prayer. Now she looked at him and her posture relaxed. 'You are right, of course,' she said with the semblance of a smile. 'And this is not a formal visit with formal patterns to be followed. They are here to restock their supplies, gather troops and ride on.'

'Anything you do can only be an improvement on Lord

Gerbert's first wife's efforts,' Letice said from behind. 'She would have bolted herself in her chamber and refused to come out.'

Annais laughed. 'That sounds like wisdom from where I stand,' she said, but the conversation had calmed her.

The army of the kingdom of Jerusalem entered through Montabard's main gate. Recent rain had dampened the dust so there were no choking clouds, but the noise of hooves and the rattle of spears and harness were deafening. First came the scouts and the vanguard, then the hand-picked soldiers chosen to protect King Baldwin, and then Baldwin himself, upright in the saddle, fair beard bristling, his cloak fastened with an elaborate jewelled clasp. Waiting attendants directed the flow of the army into the middle ward where the stables were housed. Baldwin himself dismounted in the main courtyard and handed his reins to a squire while Gerbert and his household knelt in obeisance.

With a swift flick of his right hand, Baldwin gestured everyone to rise. 'I am pleased to see you in readiness, my lord,' he said to Gerbert with a wintry smile. 'I note from the decorations on your gatehouse wall that you have already entertained other company.'

Gerbert nodded. 'One of my returning patrols caught some raiders close to the keep and there was a skirmish, sire.' He extended his hand to the household. 'Sabin can tell you more since he was leading the patrol.'

Baldwin's gaze lit on Sabin and the smile deepened. 'Ah,' he said, 'the young man who is found by trouble even when he shuns it.'

Sabin gave a wry shrug. 'Certainly I have been earning my daily bread of late, sire.'

'And likely to earn more if the rumours from Zerdana are true.' Baldwin stripped his mail gauntlets and tossed them to another squire. 'I see you are wounded.'

'I took a Saracen arrow in the foot, sire. A few more days and I will be back on active duty.'

'Before that,' Gerbert said grimly. 'If I am to ride with my constable and my marshal, you must take the responsibility for Montabard.'

Neither Gerbert nor Baldwin could understand why Sabin almost choked on what looked like painful laughter.

Among the knights who followed Baldwin towards the hall was one as tall and fair as the King, but more robust of build. He hung back from the press, waiting for Sabin, who had also stayed back so that his slow progress would not hamper the others.

'So,' said Strongfist, clapping a brawny hand to Sabin's shoulder, 'has Montabard been the making of you when all else has failed?'

Sabin shook his head. 'If I was not hampered by my foot, I would run away,' he said tersely and changed the subject. 'Where's Fergus?'

'Back in Tripoli with a dose of marsh fever. I've got command of his men.' He looked at Sabin. 'I have things to say to you, but not here and now. The King is waiting and I have my daughter and son-in-law to greet.'

'I thought that everything had been said . . . or locked away as too dangerous for words.'

Strongfist plucked at his beard. 'I did too, but things have happened that make all that went before seem like comparing a pin-prick to a deep wound. I am glad to be here with the King. It keeps my mind busy, and using my sword is always what I have done best.' His gaze went beyond Sabin to the hall door and, with a shout of joy, he opened his arms.

'Papa!' Annais flung herself into Strongfist's embrace and squeezed him around the neck. He hugged her tightly against his mailed breast and lifted her off her feet.

'Sweetheart, sweetheart!' he said. When he let her go, his eyes were moist. 'Ah God, pay no heed, I am an old fool.' Laughing, he held her away and looked her up and down. 'Old enough to be a grandfather! You cannot know how delighted I was to receive your news . . . you are well?'

Annais laid her hand to the gentle swell of her belly. 'Very well,' she confirmed. 'The child has quickened and grows stronger daily.' She tugged his arm. 'Come within and take bread and wine. I have no time to talk now, I have to attend on the King, but we can talk later.'

'Yes, later.' His smile faltered and the pleasure in his eyes dimmed.

The hall was so packed with armoured bodies that it reminded Sabin of a bulging fishing net. Sword hilts jutted at every hip and easing past without getting caught up or bruised was impossible. Men clinked as they walked. Spurs tripped the unwary. The smell of hard-travelled unwashed bodies was so pungent that it almost obliterated the more wholesome aroma of freshly baked bread. The King was afforded a place at the high table together with the senior ranks, but other knights and barons had to find dining space among the closely packed trestles lining the body of the hall. On the third time that someone inadvertently trod on Sabin's injured foot, he abandoned any notion of talking to Strongfist and made his way back to his campaign tent in the lower ward.

Amalric was already there and had kindled the oil lamp suspended from the long support beam of the frame. Sabin's bed had been assembled and the floor was covered with pale gold gazelle skins, striped black along the spine.

Amalric poured wine from a ewer of green Tyrian glass into a matching goblet and gave it to Sabin who took it gratefully and sat down on a campstool. He took a swallow and arched his brows at the youth in amused question.

Amalric widened innocent eyes. 'There were several flagons set out in the butlery,' he said. 'This was the smallest one and I did not think that they would miss it.'

Sabin raised the goblet and toasted his squire. 'Oh, they'll miss it for certain,' he said with relish. 'This is the best of the best and probably intended for the King. I have no doubt that

Lady Annais will be giving the butler grief, and that the butler will be tweaking some poor serving lad's ear.'

'Shall I take it back?'

'Yes!' Sabin said with a gleam in his eye. The boy looked askance until he grinned broadly and added, 'But not until it's empty.' He pointed to the drinking horn on the boy's belt. 'You might as well enjoy the fruits of your thievery. No point taking the risk and then abjuring the pleasure. You can go to confession on the morrow.'

The youth plucked the horn from his belt with alacrity. Sabin watched him and chuckled. 'Just don't make a habit of such light-handedness,' he said. 'This is worth a whipping at the least and they would expect me either to share your pain or deal it out.'

He took another sip of the wine. Smooth and rich, dark as the kiss of an experienced woman at night. Smoky and potent as lust.

The tent flaps were open to the gathering dusk and Sabin looked out upon serried ranks of canvas, on braziers and fires with soldiers gathered around them, cooking, dicing, attending to their harness and armour. He thought about joining them, although not with a glass goblet from the high table in his hand. That was actively seeking trouble rather than waiting for it to find him.

The side of the canvas shook and there was a curse as someone tripped over a tent peg. Amalric froze, the horn halfway to his lips, his expression that of a hare cornered by a dog.

'Christ, you'd think I'd have learned to pick up my feet by now,' said Strongfist as he ducked inside Sabin's tent. His eyes widened at the sight of the glass flagon. 'Isn't that . . . ?'

'Yes, it is. My squire's teaching me bad habits.' Sabin snapped his fingers at Amalric and unfolded another stool for Strongfist to sit upon. The youth found another cup, of plain Jaffa-ware this time, filled it with the blood-coloured wine and handed it to Strongfist. The knight took a round, appreciative mouthful, washed it round his teeth and swallowed with a sigh of pleasure.

'You always land on your feet,' he said to Sabin with grudging admiration.

'Except when a Saracen manages to put an arrow through one of them,' Sabin answered wryly.

'Bad?'

'It was in danger of going sour but Annais dealt with it in her usual efficient way.' Sabin drank the wine and held out his cup for Amalric to refill. 'She is wise beyond her years,' he added. 'It must be the upbringing with nuns.'

'Hah,' Strongfist snorted. 'She was born like that. My wife always said that it was like having a little adult at her skirts, not a small child.' His tone softened. 'Annais is a fine woman and I'm proud of her.'

'You should be.' Sabin raised his goblet in salute and drank again, enjoying the warmth it conveyed to the empty space in his belly. 'Gerbert's besotted . . . even more so since she has quickened with child.' Sabin contemplated the darkness of the wine shining through the glass. 'You should have brought bread too, lad. I'm going to be as pickled as a Danish herring before I'm done.'

'I'll fetch some, sir.' The boy ducked out of the tent.

Sabin smiled at Strongfist. 'Do not ask where from, but hope it smells of heaven and is as light as his fingers.'

Strongfist returned the smile in a preoccupied way, drank, lowered his cup and, holding it between his knees, looked at Sabin. 'I have not spoken to Annais yet,' he said. 'I have come to you first, and perhaps that is not the right order of doing, but so be it.'

Sabin made a questioning sound in his throat. The wine had begun to tangle in his veins and he knew that his reactions were not as sharp as they should be.

Strongfist took a deep breath. 'Mariamne has left me,' he said.

Sabin loudly swallowed his wine and somehow managed

not to choke. He stared at the older man. 'I am truly sorry,' he said.

'Are you? I'm not . . . nor even surprised.'

Sabin's flesh prickled beneath Strongfist's weighty stare. The thorns were back.

Strongfist drank down the wine and Sabin tipped a fresh measure into his cup, refilling his own at the same time. 'She ran off with a silk merchant soon after the Christmas feast. I sent a hunting party out after them, but they were long gone. In truth, the only reason I wanted to find her was to lift her unfaithful hide with my whip.' He drank swiftly, forgetting to savour the bouquet. 'I do not expect she will be faithful to him,' he added with a curling lip. 'Another man will catch her eye and she will transfer her affections as easily as a whore going between customers. She had a reputation already . . . but with the land that was offered, I chose to ignore it.'

Sabin looked down. He would have walked away from the offer, but then his priorities were different and it was not fair to make a comparison.

'If the truth were known, I was infatuated with her at the beginning,' Strongfist said with a grimace. 'I could not believe my good fortune. Doubtless she was cursing her luck.' He tilted his gaze to Sabin. 'I think she was hoping that you might be given the custody of Tel Namir.'

'I would have run a league at the notion!' Sabin gave a humourless laugh. 'Although perhaps I did not run quite fast enough when it mattered.'

Strongfist shrugged. 'It is in the past,' he said gruffly and rubbed the back of his neck. 'I still have the land.' He lowered his arm. 'I am glad of this campaign. Being a soldier is always what I have done best.'

'So you will not pursue Mariamne and her lover further?'

'Where would be the point? They will eventually punish each other more than I could ever punish either of them. Let them lie in the bed they have made together.'

'And if she comes back to you?'

'Even on her knees, I would not have her,' Strongfist growled. 'The space she left has not been lonely; there are others keen to fill it even without a marriage contract. If I have no immediate heir for my lands, I have a daughter who is quick with a babe. When I die, my grandchild may have Tel Namir with my blessing.'

The squire returned with a loaf of fragrant bread, its top polished with honey and generously scattered with sesame seeds. There was also a wheel of goat's cheese, sticky dried dates, and another dish of cracked wheat flavoured with spices and bursting with raisins and small slivers of roasted lamb.

'I won't ask,' Sabin said with a smile as the boy laid down his haul on the small trestle beside Sabin's bed.

Amalric lifted his shoulders. 'I didn't steal it this time,' he said. 'The lady Annais caught me hanging around the kitchens, so I told her that you had sent me to fetch food for you and Lord Strongfist. She piled the bowls herself and wished you both good appetite . . .'

Grinning, Sabin drew his eating knife to cut the end off the loaf.

'And then she said that when you have finished and if you are not too drunk on her best wine, you had better come back to the hall because Lord Gerbert wants to speak to you about your command on the morrow.'

Strongfist chuckled at Sabin's arrested expression. 'I don't know how many women you've deceived in your career,' he said, 'but you'll never pull the wool over my daughter's eyes.'

Chapter 17

Baldwin led his army across the Orontes to Zerdana and discovered that while the main fortification remained intact, the Saracens had succeeded in taking some of the outer defences. However, no battles were fought over the ground, for the Saracens prudently retreated from their small gains rather than face Baldwin in head-on battle. Not that their leader, Ilghazi, gave up immediately. There were several skirmishes. The Saracens tried to lure the Franks into folly by pretended flight, but Baldwin was accustomed to the tactics and paid no heed, merely matching their movements and standing off. It was a war of patience and nerves and finally it was Ilghazi who broke, standing down his warriors and sending them back to their homes, for it was obvious that with the Frankish army in the vicinity and at full strength, shadowing his every move, there was little to be accomplished. Satisfied that for the moment the trouble was over, Baldwin sent his army's standard back to Jerusalem and retired to Antioch to refresh himself and his men.

At Montabard, Sabin settled into the routine of lord and commander. He made sure that the guards on the walls were alert to their duty, he sent out patrols to scout the immediate vicinity. To keep the men from growing stale, he organised competitions – jousting, wrestling, weapon skills, archery. He set up mock raids where men had to scale ropes in the darkness and 'rescue' a pouch of silver in a guarded room without being caught. He had the more supple of them start to learn Saracen horse-riding skills, and joined in with joyous enthusiasm until he could shoot a bow from the back of a galloping horse and hit the target. He trained them hard, and rewarded them well, and, like hounds, they answered with enthusiasm.

'For a man who claims not to want responsibility, you handle it well,' Annais remarked to him one evening when he found the time to dine in the hall rather than the guardroom.

'Needs must,' he said with a shrug. 'Even if I do not want it, I know what is required.' Stepping over the bench behind the high table, he sat down, diplomatically leaving the lord's great chair empty. Not once had he used it since Gerbert's absence.

'But you could have refused it and ridden out.'

'Could I?' His glance flickered to the loose robe swathing her belly, which was almost nine months' round.

'Not now, but you have had the summer to make your escape.'

'I promised your husband a year and a day of service.' He handed her a vellum packet. 'Messages from the field,' he said more brusquely than he had intended. 'The courier arrived as I was on my way to the hall.'

Annais flushed as she took her eating knife and broke her husband's seal. Within her, their child gave a wallowing kick. She had been experiencing a niggling pain in the small of her back for several days now. The Syrian midwife said that the child's head was lying well down, ready to be born and had seemed pleased, informing Annais by gestures that her hips were wide enough to permit the birth and that it would be soon.

'Do you want to read your letter alone?' Sabin gathered himself to rise.

'No,' she gestured him to stay. 'If I wanted solitude, I would seek my chamber. Besides,' she said ruefully, 'Gerbert does not write the kind of letters to make me blush in public. He's far too practical, God save him.'

The mingling of affection and exasperation in her tone sent a pang through Sabin that was almost envy. An attendant set down a bowl of pottage before him. Taking his silver spoon from his pouch he polished it on his sleeve and began to eat.

Annais swiftly scanned the lines of prose. They had been written by Father Jerome, her husband's chaplain, and were thus in Latin, but since she had been educated by nuns, she had no difficulty reading it. 'He writes to say that they are on their way home,' she said. 'Ilghazi has retreated from Zerdana and the True Cross is on its way back to Jerusalem.' There was a sheet of folded vellum beneath her own letter, which she opened and passed to Sabin. 'This one's for you . . .' She gave a wry laugh. 'It's identical to mine.'

'Fortunate then that it's not a love letter,' he said, forcing a smile. 'If the courier came swiftly, that means he will be home in two days.'

'Then your purgatory is almost at an end.' She eyed him shrewdly over the sheet of vellum. Despite the defensive noises he made about not wanting so much responsibility, she rather thought that he had enjoyed these past few months. Even if he refused to take Gerbert's chair, he had risen to the challenges of being lord of Montabard, and there was little strain in him to suggest that he had been performing an onerous task. However, she said nothing and demurely took up her own spoon. She was ravenous and the spiced pottage was a speciality of Montabard's Syrian cook.

That evening, she began to think that eating two bowls of the soup, no matter how delicious, had not been wise. She was taken with cramps in the stomach and severe voiding of the bowels. And then the pains began in earnest. Letice went to find the midwife, only to discover that she had gone to visit her sister in the village.

Doing the rounds, talking to the guards on the wall walk and at the gate, Sabin saw Letice emerge from the hall, looking worried. Leaving the men, he strode to meet her and, with a look of relief on her face, she told him of her difficulty.

'I'll fetch the lady at once,' Sabin said, already turning to the stables. It couldn't be the pottage, for he had eaten two bowls himself without adverse reaction. He knew little of women in childbirth. The women of King Henry's court retired to their husband's estates long before their confinement was due. When his father's wife had been carrying, she had retreated to the inner sanctum of her chamber as the birth drew close.

He did know that women died in childbirth. There had been occasional mourning at court for such a happening, and one of Countess Matilda's serving women had died following three days of protracted labour. Nor had she been in poor health, but a robust lass, confident of birthing the babe that had killed her. Increasing his pace, he reached the stables. He should have sent one of the garrison, but he had to do something to uncoil the tension that was winding within him.

By the light of an oil lamp in the stables, he harnessed Lucifer and led him out. The night was clear and star-powdered, giving him sufficient illumination to guide the horse down to the village. Lucifer's hooves were loud on the stony path. His snorting breath cut the night and alerted any listeners that someone was out after curfew.

He found the midwife at the house of her sister as she had said. Most folk would cower at banging on their door after nightfall, but not she, for by her trade she was long accustomed to being summoned at all hours. Murmuring to the other members of the household, drawing her dark-coloured shawl around her head, she followed Sabin out into the night, and untethered her ancient donkey from the ramshackle stable at the side of the dwelling.

Sabin found it difficult to keep his impatience in check, but the woman was not to be chivvied. 'There is no rush, young lord,' she said. 'It's a first babe and they always take their time.' Her eyes gleamed in the darkness like night-lit water. 'From your worry, anyone would think you were the father, not just the messenger.'

Sabin tightened his fingers on the bridle and the horse jibbed as his tension was conveyed to the bit. 'I hope that your hands are cleaner than your tongue,' he answered coldly. 'It is my lady's first child. Every one of us is concerned.'

The woman clucked to herself and, with surprising dexterity for one of her years, heaved herself across the ass's back. 'But it is not usually the men who worry about women's business unless they have a vested interest.'

'The command of Montabard is my responsibility and I must do my best for all within its walls,' Sabin said tersely. He could not believe that he was justifying himself to a wizened old woman. Nor could he quite believe the words that he had actually spoken. *His responsibility.* Declared with authority and perhaps even a touch of hubris. Thoroughly discomforted, he tugged on the bridle and jabbed Lucifer sharply in the flanks.

The return was slower than the descent, for the midwife's donkey was even less disposed to rush than she was, and when he tried to chivvy them along, he received the peaceable reiteration that first babies were notoriously slow to make an appearance. It was almost midnight by the time they were admitted into Montabard's bailey. The midwife slipped from her mount and eased the small of her back. 'I'm getting too old,' she said with a little groan that did nothing to increase Sabin's confidence.

She refused to be hastened, but he brought her as swiftly as he could to the room above the hall. Letice was waiting to take charge, and she ushered the woman inside the chamber with words of relieved welcome. The latter closed the door in Sabin's face and he heard the latch clatter down with finality.

He went below and poured himself a measure of wine. It was ordinary household stuff and he had to remember to clench his teeth as he reached the dregs and hit the must. A second measure swiftly followed the first into his cup, but he stopped after one long swallow. The command of the keep was in his care. If he got drunk, he was abusing the trust Gerbert had put in him. The voice of rebellion said that he did not care, but it was the voice of a petulant child and Sabin thrust it aside with the same irritation that he deposited the goblet on the board.

He took himself to the armoury to make a mental inventory of the sheaves of arrows and stacks of spears, but he already knew their number by heart. A diversion to the kitchens secured him a hunk of bread he did not really want and the sight of one of the castle's feral cats slinking into the shadows, an enormous rat dangling between its jaws. Small mewing sounds from a dark hollow beneath a storage shed revealed where her kittens were waiting.

Sabin finished the bread, which lay like a leaden weight in his stomach, and returned to the hall. Men slept along the perimeter on pallets of linen stuffed with straw. One or two were still awake around the fire, their faces uplit by the red glow at the heart of the banked coals. Some nights he would have joined them, but not now. An enquiry to the chambers above drew no reply except the terse repetition that it was a first child and therefore going to be long in coming.

Sabin retired, and for the rest of the night paced the wall walk, keeping vigil. The darkest hours of the watch slowly yielded to the paling of dawn and the sky became as still as a veil of stretched silk, shaded oyster to grey and tinged with the pink sheen of mother of pearl. In Damascus and Aleppo, in Shaizar and Masayef, the muezzins would be calling the people to prayer. Here, a single bell tolled a summons to the mass of a new day, and still there was no news from the women's chamber.

A shout from the guard on the lookout tower above the main gate brought Sabin striding along the walk boards to gaze out. In the gilded light of early morning, men and horses were toiling up the track like a chain of ants. Silks fluttered on spears, harness flashed as the sun spangled on buckles and studs. Gerbert was timely home. Watching the cavalcade,

Sabin knew that he should be relieved to relinquish his burden, but relief was not the feeling that flowed through him. Tersely he gave the order to open the gate and when the guard looked up in surprise at his tone, Sabin glowered at him and stamped down to the bailey.

The news that Gerbert had arrived home in time for the birth of their child came to Annais in one of the lulls between pains. At first she thought that the whispered conversation at the chamber door was the result of Sabin sending yet again to ask how she was faring, but Letice returned to her side with a smile and told her that Gerbert and the men were back, safe apart from a few minor scratches. 'And your father is here too,' she said.

Annais swallowed against tears. She wished she could be waiting the news in the hall rather than labouring to produce it. The purging of her bowels had only been the start – thoroughly natural, so the midwife had said when she arrived in a whiff compounded of donkey, woodsmoke and garlic. Her body was only preparing itself to bear the child, but there would be a long wait yet. The woman had briskly taken charge and set Annais' women to rubbing her back with warm oil, and had prepared a tisane made with various secret herbs and honey. The pains came and went at regular intervals and, as the night progressed, had grown stronger. Now and again, the midwife would make a gentle examination and nod with satisfaction. 'I've known a first babe take a week,' she said, 'but your husband should be able to greet his heir by dusk.'

'Dusk!' Annais's voice was hoarse with dismay as Soraya, the Syrian woman who was married to the knight Durand, translated what the woman had said.

The midwife waved her hand and gabbled.

Soraya flushed and looked embarrassed. 'She says that you are one of the fortunate ones, that you have wide hips and the child is lying well.'

Annais had a moment to feel ashamed before the next contraction seized her in its pincers and drove everything away but the tightening pain. Fortunate or not, she was not enjoying the experience.

'Men,' she gasped as the squeezing grip finally eased, 'have by far the better part of the bargain!'

The midwife chuckled when Soraya told her what had been said.

'Oh aye,' she laughed. 'There has to be some recompense for being born with your wits down there instead of in your skull.'

Unable to pace, stifled by Gerbert's return, Sabin took out a troop with the dual purpose of conducting a patrol and hunting. The exercise, the stretching of the horse beneath him, helped to a degree, but even at full gallop across the grassy meadows opening beneath the foothills, the wind parting his hair and stinging his half-closed eyes, he could not outride himself.

Finally, as the sun was lowering over the seaward plain, he turned the men for home with their catch of three gazelle and a brace of hares. Crossing a stream, they came across the spoor of a lion in the shingly mud at the water's edge. The wildness in Sabin demanded pursuit, but he suppressed it. If not to himself, then he had a duty to the men and to the castle. Night was falling, and even if he yielded to that wildness, he was beginning to realise that it would not be satisfied. The hunger was too great, too destructively ravenous. Better to endure the pangs of starvation than to rouse an insatiable feeding frenzy. He marked where they had seen the spoor for a further occasion, and clicked his tongue to the horse.

As they left the plain and began the long climb to the castle, they encountered the exhausted royal messenger on his spent horse and thus were the first to hear his news and receive the call to arms.

'Come now, girl, one more push,' the midwife encouraged, her hand on Annais's belly. 'Your work is almost done.'

Panting, Annais closed her eyes and gathered her strength. An hour ago, the women had helped her from the bed to the birthing stool. The pains had reached a level that taxed her endurance but could not possibly go beyond it, or else she would die. Surge upon agonising surge.

'Good, good, almost there,' the midwife encouraged through Soraya, then suddenly squeezed her hand. 'Hold, my lady,' she commanded urgently. 'Wait a moment, the head is here and we do not want your flesh to tear.'

Annais struggled, her breath coming in great sobs as she strove not to push. The midwife busied herself beneath the birthing stool. Annais felt the pressure of the child's head against the opening to her womb and thought that she would split asunder. The woman gave a short exclamation of triumph and ordered her to push again, but gently. Seconds later, Annais felt the pressure relieve in a warm slither of sensation, and the midwife rose from her knees clutching a wizened, bluish-red creature. It gave two experimental squeaks, the second louder than the first, then expanded its repertoire to a series of indignant bawls.

'A son,' the midwife cackled as exultantly as if she had borne him herself. 'My lady, you have a fine boy.' She laid the baby, wet and smeared from his birthing, in Annais's arms where he continued to bellow like a young bull. Annais was astonished, and not knowing whether to laugh or weep, did both. Helping hands swaddled the baby in warmed linen towels and his squawls diminished to grumbles and then silence. He stared around in myopic wonder. Even as the midwife cut the cord between them with a sharp pair of shears, Annais was tied by a bond that would last a lifetime.

The messenger had delivered his news and retired to the guardroom to eat and rest. In the hall, there was silence as the senior officers of Montabard digested the tidings.

Joscelin of Edessa had been out patrolling the territory around Saruj when he had encountered the army of the Emir

Balak. There had been a skirmish in a heavy downpour. The Frankish horses had slithered in the ensuing mud and Balak's lighter troops had been able to surround and capture the lord of Edessa. Demands that he hand over his principal city in return for his release had been met with derision and Joscelin and his surviving men had been removed to Balak's fortress at Kharpurt to think about their response.

'It could happen to any of us,' Gerbert said, chewing on his thumbnail. The frown lines between his grey eyes were pronounced. Not only was he anxious for his labouring wife, but this news had set a cat among the pigeons . . . a Saracen cat with vicious claws. He looked at Strongfist. 'I do not suppose that King Baldwin will move his army south now.'

Strongfist kneaded his beard. 'Not immediately,' he said. 'He will have to take on the burden of Edessa until Joscelin can be freed.'

Gerbert grunted. 'At least he was lord of Edessa before he was King of Jerusalem,' he said. 'He knows these people well, and his wife is of those parts.' He sighed. 'I will put Montabard on alert. If the King needs more men to swell his ranks then I am at his disposal. I cannot see Balak sitting on his gain like a broody hen on a nest. He will want to wreak as much havoc as possible while he thinks we are in disarray.'

Again silence fell and the men gazed sombrely at each other. It was as much a blow to Frankish pride as it was to the fabric of their rule. Joscelin of Edessa was one of their greatest knights, and for him to fall into the hands of the Emir Balak was as much a source of chagrin as dismay.

'Balak won't hold Joscelin for long,' Gerbert said fiercely. 'He will find a way to escape . . . and when he does . . .'

Sabin felt the restlessness tug at him. Although no one spoke, he knew that they all wanted to leap to horse and charge off to rescue Joscelin. It was as if the Frankish battle standard had fallen into enemy hands. But they had to plan ahead; they had to be pragmatic and ignore the heat that sprang from the belly.

Gerbert hissed softly through his teeth. Looking up, Sabin followed his gaze and saw that Letice had emerged from the opening to the turret stair, a bundle cradled in her arms. The smile on her face stretched from one side of her wimple to the other.

'A son and a grandson is born,' she announced, advancing to Gerbert and presenting the infant to him.

Gerbert held the baby along his bent forearm and parted the soft outer shawl to look upon the minute features. The child was not fully swaddled yet and Gerbert was able to lift one of the tiny, perfect hands and watch it curl around his forefinger. Suddenly his eyes were wet and he had to knuckle his tears.

'My wife . . . is she . . . ?'

Letice gently touched his shoulder. 'Annais is well,' she said, 'tired and a little sore to say the least, but safe and joyful.'

Swallowing, Gerbert passed his newborn heir to Strongfist, who, as his grandfather, had second claim. 'I have to thank you for coming to Outremer,' he said in a voice that trembled with emotion, 'for without your decision, I would have neither my wife, nor this wonderful gift of a child.'

Strongfist cleared his throat and blinked hard. 'God's will,' he said gruffly into his beard and after a moment's awkward holding, passed the baby to Sabin. 'How is he to be named?'

'Guillaume, for my sire, the first lord of Montabard.' Gerbert's voice rang with emotion and pride. His complexion was so bright that it was almost incandescent.

Sabin cradled the infant. It opened its mouth and yawned at him. Even though it was newborn, he could already see the mingling of Gerbert's features and Annais's. Guillaume had Gerbert's eyes and brows, his mother's nose and a jaw that was going to be like Strongfist's. Sabin found his own throat tightening, which was ridiculous. He knew why he had been given the infant to hold, when Strongfist could have passed him straight back to Gerbert. He was being shown that this was what he had to fight for. It was one thing to say 'for the future', it was another to hold that future in his arms, solid of flesh, light as air, warm as love.

It was with opposing feelings of loss and relief that he returned the baby to its father. Gerbert broke away from the masculine circle they had formed and, telling Sabin and Strongfist he would be back in a while, headed for the stairs and his wife.

CHAPTER 18

Little Guillaume de Montabard gurgled in his cradle, his attention fixed upon the lozenges of sunlight shining through the fretwork shutters into the women's chamber. At seven months old, his eyes were changing from the clouded grey-blue of the newborn to a lighter, lucent grey and the dark, natal hair was growing out to be replaced with curls of warm brownish-gold.

Gerbert bent over him and, as he had done on the day of his birth, gave the baby his finger. Guillaume grabbed it, conveyed it to his mouth and gnawed it experimentally with his two new teeth. Then he crowed at his father. Gerbert laughed and swept the baby out of the cradle and into his arms. He was wearing his gambeson over his tunic, but had yet to don his hauberk. That would come last, on the threshold of leaving.

Annais watched father and son with a smile on her lips and a leaden heart. Gerbert took such pride and pleasure in his son that it brought a lump to her throat when she saw them together. It made the pain of his birthing a negligible thing. Her body was still tingling from Gerbert's farewell lovemaking. She ached with a need she had small experience to name; she only knew that she had been brought to a brink and then left behind as he was consumed by his release.

'I wish you did not have to go,' she said. She bit her tongue as soon as the words were spoken. She had promised herself that she would be a proper soldier's wife, that she would let him do his duty without complaint and clinging.

'I wish it too, sweetheart,' he said and his glance flickered to the bed where they had so recently lain. 'But the King has commanded and I promised that I would go to him.' He made a face, then buried his expression against the soft flesh of his son's neck. 'It is only for a short while. Thierry is an experienced constable and the garrison is well drilled.'

'I know that.'

'And it has an excellent mistress to keep everyone in order,' he added with a smile. He came over to where she sat, her black hair loose to her waist and her chemise unlaced at the throat, exposing the top of her cleavage. The baby between them, he kissed her on lips that were still swollen from earlier kisses and cupped her breast. Her body throbbed. She wanted to pull him down, guide him inside her and cling to him, but there was no time; she could hear the servants prowling in the antechamber, and the shouts of men and horses from the ground outside the hall. Besides, she understood Gerbert well enough to know that active demanding would suggest to him that she was dissatisfied. She did not want to send him away with that kind of doubt in his mind . . . not after the behaviour of her father's wife.

'Keep whole,' she murmured fervently as their mouths parted. 'Come back soon.'

'Even the very maw of hell would not prevent me.' His grey eyes were both fierce and tender. He stroked his forefinger over the soft down on the baby's skull. 'Besides, I have a conroi of sons waiting to be begotten.'

When he had gone, the maids bustled into the room from the antechamber to help their mistress dress so that she could go down and bid Gerbert farewell in the public arena of the ward. Ignoring the women, Annais bore Guillaume to the window and gazed through the half-opened shutters on the men arming up to leave. Tied in line and tended by their keeper, the baggage asses and mules brayed and stamped. Gerbert was leaving the footsoldiers behind and taking only the swift, mounted troops King Baldwin had requested. She saw Sabin's page, Amalric, holding Lucifer's rein. The grey shone in the spring sunlight like the blade of a damascened sword. Sabin came striding from the direction of the kitchens, a large flat bread in one hand, the other resting lightly on the hilt of his sword. His great kite shield was strapped to his back, upside down, so that the pointed end stuck up behind him like the peak of a mountain.

Tousling Amalric's head, he took the reins and swung nimbly into the saddle. Gerbert emerged from the hall and answered the bread-filled hand that Sabin lifted in salute with a comment that made both men laugh. Her husband mounted his enormous bay and glanced upwards at her window. Sabin glanced too, and Annais swiftly drew back. Although she was almost certain that the men could not see her, Gerbert would not be overjoyed to think that the sights he enjoyed were on display to other men. Handing Guillaume to Letice, Annais allowed the women to dress her in a gown of soft red linen, belted with gold braid, and a veil fashioned of two layers of gilt-edged silk.

She hastened below, took the chalcedony stirrup-cup from a waiting steward and went out to bid Gerbert a formal farewell. By the time she arrived, Sabin was at the head of the ranked serjeants and knights waiting to lead them out, Gerbert's banner fluttering from the haft of his lance.

Taking the cup from her, Gerbert drained the wine and spices and handed it back down in exchange for his shield, which was also her duty to present to him. The weight strained at her arms as she lifted it up the wall of the bay's massive side. 'Perhaps I should get a smaller horse,' he said.

She shook her head and found a smile. 'It would not suit you, my lord. Stay as you are.'

'I'll try . . .' Leaning down, he touched her face and looked at her intently as if memorising every feature. Then he reined sharply about and trotted to join his men. Sabin glanced back and tipped her a laconic salute from a now breadless hand.

One of her women handed Guillaume to her and she held him high in her arms to watch his father leave. As the last horse clattered beneath the portcullis and under the gatehouse arch, she hastened to the wall walk with the baby and watched until the conroi of men became smaller than ants toiling down the path, and were finally lost to sight round a deep curve in the escarpment. When she descended to the ward, it was full of the usual sounds of people going about their daily business, but, to her ears, the noise seemed muted.

'Annais?' Letice touched her arm.

Annais shook her head. 'I am all right,' she said. There was a painful lump in her throat, but what she said was true. In a castle the size of Montabard the cisterns would run dry before the tasks did. Her nature was essentially practical. She would keep herself busy and, although not a feast, it would be enough to live on.

The red glow of sunset burned the sides of the two rowing boats like embers and dripped beads of fire from the oars as the craft were sculled across the width of the River Euphrates. The rowers, plying their way in stealth, wore dark-coloured garments and hoods. Sword hilts were slung at their left sides and daggers at their right. Occasionally mail rivets sparked in the dying sun. As the craft threaded the reeds edging the far bank, nesting waterfowl took flight and the men in the boats cursed softly. A moorhen gave its piercing, startled call once, then again in rapid succession.

'The signal,' muttered one of the men and, cupping his hands at his mouth, returned the cry. Wine-red light edged the shapes of other men running stealthily down to the water's edge. A rope plashed among the sedges, was caught by willing hands and the first boat was drawn into cover, close followed by the second.

King Baldwin jumped from the craft and splashed onto the bank. The greeting party knelt and he gestured the men to their feet. The soldiers who had accompanied Baldwin made certain that the boats were fast and, hands to sword hilts, joined him. On the far shore the rest of Baldwin's force had pitched camp – not his main army, but a splinter force of fast horsemen and seasoned warriors. From that force he had hand-picked a dozen men, Sabin among them, to accompany him across the river and deep into enemy territory around the stronghold of Kharpurt, residence of Emir Balak, and prison of Joscelin, lord of Edessa.

The leader of the group that had come to guide Baldwin was a leather-faced Armenian named Gabriel who looked anything but the angel of his namesake. He had narrow black eyes, one of them half closed by a scar that slashed from eye corner to chin. A full black moustache occupied the space beneath his hooked nose and overhung his lip so that he resembled a whiskered terrier. He spoke heavily accented but understandable French. Baldwin, whose wife came from Melitene, but a few miles distant, had a smattering of the native tongue.

'The Emir Balak guards the fortress closely,' Gabriel said, 'but it is possible to get men inside. We have villagers who take in supplies and we have been able to glean that Lord Joscelin has not been harmed, but that he is kept shamefully in chains and under close guard.'

'Will the castle withstand a siege?'

'You mean can it be taken swiftly?' Gabriel made a forward and back motion with the flat of his hand. 'Who is to say? I think perhaps not, but even for us it is difficult to come close to the walls. There is no tree cover and Balak has doubled the guards.' The Armenian flashed the King a broken-toothed smile. 'But we will bring you as close as we can.'

Baldwin chewed on his forefinger. 'Where is Balak himself?'

'That we do not know, sire, only that he is not at Kharpurt, nor within the range of our spies.' He smoothed his moustache. 'But he keeps his harem here, safe and away from the fighting.'

'So he thinks,' Baldwin growled.

As the dusk gathered and fell into night, Gabriel led them by goat tracks and narrow footpaths towards the fortress of Kharpurt in the foothills rising from the valley floor. The moon rose in a bright silver disc and washed the landscape in shades of grey, blue and dull green. The Franks and their guides spoke only by hand gestures as they toiled up the track. Any arms or armour that might clink and give them away to a sharp-eared sentry were wound in cloth. Hoods remained raised.

Sabin's every sense was attuned to the night. His eyes were at full stretch and his ears felt as if they had grown points like a cat's, so hard was he listening. A ball of apprehension floated in his stomach, but he was exhilarated too. This was as much his environment as the battlefield. He found it easy to copy the stealthy footsteps of the Armenians, to think himself into the shape of a shadow or a tree. He could understand why Gerbert and Strongfist had not been selected for this foray. They were both big men who, although skilled in battle, relied more on their strength than on fluid speed and grace.

King Baldwin was of their ilk. It was his foot that slipped on a stone and sent a shower of small pebbles rattling down the track. It was he who stumbled, or who stood out from the blending of light and shadows. But since he was Edessa's former count and it was his desire to reconnoitre Kharpurt, men held their tongues and prayed.

Finally, they came within range of the massive walls of Kharpurt. Sentries bristled on the wall walks and the iron studs on the great gate gleamed in the moonlight. The voices of the watch calling to each other in Arabic carried on the still evening air. Outside sentries patrolled the perimeter with leashed hounds, their way lit by hand-borne pitch brands.

Two guards stood on the main trackway, warming their hands at a brazier and leaning on their lances.

Baldwin stared intently at the fortress as if memorising each stone. Crouched in the bushes, Sabin kept close watch and prepared to draw his sword.

'The guards are discussing the harem,' Gabriel whispered. 'They were expecting some women to arrive today, but they are not here yet.'

Baldwin shrugged. 'We could do without the number of guards, but at least the light is useful,' he muttered, shifting position, determined to see the castle from another angle.

Sabin held his breath as more stones showered and a guard shouted to his companions below. Sabin drew a foot of steel from the scabbard.

The torches on the fortress slope swung towards them and the dogs gave tongue as they were unleashed. Sabin cursed and heard Gabriel do the same. Now they had to decide whether to remain where they were and hope they were not flushed out or make a run for the river.

Above them something skittered on the path, dislodging a greater cascade of stones. There was a flurry, a series of unearthly growls rising to a scream and then the frantic yelps of a dog in pain. Higher up the dog-handler could be heard whistling and clapping to retrieve his animals. Moments later a lean shape bounded past the gully where the men were hiding. Sabin saw compact silver muscle, eyes of gleaming jet and a muzzle pleated above a cavern of fangs. Then the moonlit image of the lion vanished into the darkness beyond.

'We are saved,' Gabriel hissed. 'They will not come lower and investigate in the dark.'

Baldwin laughed softly and seemed pleased with the notion that a lion had saved a king. It was entirely fitting. Sabin was less sanguine, especially now that the lion was somewhere between them and the river. The dog was still yelping, but must have struggled back to its master, for the sound had faded into the distance. As the men settled from their encounter, other noises alerted them. Horses were clopping up the path to the fortress. Raising his head above the lip of their hiding place, Sabin saw a bobbing procession of torches and lamps. Saracen soldiers, turbans tucked around their heads, short mail byrnies swimming with light, were escorting a group of shrouded figures mounted on mules and asses. These must be the women for Balak's harem, although it was difficult to tell even whether they were human, let alone what sex they were, so heavily were they concealed.

The patrol guards drew back and the attention of those on the walls shifted to the new arrivals. Gabriel took the opportunity to move the group out of harm's way. Warned by the earlier incident, they completed their reconnaissance swiftly and by moonset were back at the boats – fortunately without encountering the lion.

In the morning, the commander of Kharpurt sent his men to search the slopes beneath the fortress. If there was a lion in the area, it needed flushing out and frightening off. Spoor was found, and the dogs pursued the scent, dragging their handlers over rock and through scrub. But it was not news of the lion that the searchers brought back to Kharpurt, but of human footprints in the soft ground above the river, and of a woollen hood discovered by the dogs in one of the ravines. The commander pondered the signs and deciding to err on the side of caution, sent a messenger to the lord Balak on the swiftest horse in the stables. Then he ordered the guard on Joscelin to be doubled.

King Baldwin had a yen to hunt. As always, even on campaign, he had brought his hawks and they formed their own camp of bow perches to one side of the royal pavilion. In the early cool of the April morning, Sabin and Gerbert moved among the sleepy birds. Mottled sakers, the favoured falcons of the Syrian nobility, famed for their fierceness and speed and the King's great Scandinavian gyrfalcon, its jesses stitched with silver bells. And the shahins, fastest of the long-wings, some of them part of the tribute that Montabard paid to King Baldwin.

Gerbert paused by a pair of perches on the outer edge of the camp and, drawing on his hawking gauntlet, unfastened his own young shahin from its tether and brought the bird to his arm. Sabin too had a hawking glove, for Gerbert was lending him the white saker on the next perch.

'When we return to Montabard, you ought to have one of your own,' Gerbert said.

'I had a merlin when I was a child,' Sabin murmured, taking the saker onto his wrist. 'My father gave her to me in my twelfth summer, and taught me to fly her.'

'Your first falcon?'

Sabin stroked the saker's soft breast feathers. 'There were always birds in the mews . . . but yes, she was the first of my own.' A distant look filled his eyes. 'It was a long, hot summer that year and it is a thread of gold in my memory. There have not been many such threads since.'

Gerbert eyed him thoughtfully. 'So what changed after that summer?'

Sabin shrugged. The gesture looked casual, but it was a habitual one, akin to the motion of a man swinging forward the shield he always kept in readiness. 'My father died, and I lost my merlin on a hunt,' he said impassively.

'I am sorry.'

'My stepmother bought me a new one, but I had no interest. The falconers cared for it in the mews.'

'But you know hawks, you can handle them.' Gerbert nodded at the saker perching alert but quiet on Sabin's arm. 'You must have continued your education.'

'I did – at the court of King Henry.' Sabin gave Gerbert a sardonic look. 'That is why I am here now.' He moved away towards the horse lines. Gerbert's inquisitive nature was intrusive and at times irritated him to the point of gritting his teeth. His perception was sharp, but did not have that final thrust to break through the shield. It might be better if he did, rather than doing half a job. In his mind's eye – as if from the view of a hovering hawk – he could see himself, a dark-haired child, swinging the lure, and his father looking on with a smile of pride as the merlin flew to it. Warm sun on his back. His father's tunic of forest-green wool; the heavy scent of pine from the woods beyond the clearing; the sturdy dappled cob and the matching pony grazing side by side in the endless afternoon, their harness jingling. Was that why he had a preference for grey horses now? He squared his shoulders and quickened his pace, but the memory followed in his shadow.

'King Baldwin seems pleased with himself,' Strongfist commented as he prepared to mount his copper stallion.

'He is always pleased when there is a hunt in the offing,' Sabin said. He glanced to one side. Baldwin had emerged from his pavilion and was inspecting the hawks on their perches. 'Besides, he knows the lie of the land around Kharpurt now, and that Joscelin is still alive and within possibility of rescue. Today is by way of a reward to himself.'

Strongfist grunted and Sabin concealed a wry smile. Unusually for a nobleman, Strongfist had no great interest in the hunt. He used the event to exercise his horse and hone his equestrian skills, but he had little desire to perch a hawk on his wrist and his eyes would glaze over when other men began to discuss falcons and dogs with zeal.

'He should save the reward until after the rescue.' Strongfist's tone was jaundiced.

'You must admit that he has worked like a Trojan to secure the administration and ensure that the state of Edessa will not crumble for want of a guiding hand. You have seen the way the lamplight shines through his tent until near dawn. Surely he deserves a day's leisure.'

'Aye, you're right,' Strongfist conceded with a wave of his hand. 'I suppose I should not carp.'

'And would do so less if you did not have to hunt this morn.'

That brought a reluctant chuckle from the older man. He reined his horse about and went to take his place amongst Baldwin's assembling bodyguard.

The King hunted joyously and hard, flushing out cranes from the riverbank and partridge and francolin. Sabin flung his borrowed saker into the sky, watched it hover and then stoop upon a fleeing rock dove far below. In a puff and flurry of grey feathers, the saker struck and bore its prey groundwards. Bright-faced with excitement, Amalric galloped his pony to retrieve the first kill and Sabin followed at a trot. The sun was warm on the elbow-length quilted tunic he wore and he began to think about taking it off. Dismounting, he took the saker back onto his wrist.

Eyes shining, Amalric attached the limp dove to his belt. Sabin gestured and smiled. 'You can eat it for supper,' he said and, remounting, swung around to rejoin the hunt. The King had just launched his gyrfalcon at another crane. His arm was still extended, the smile still parting his lips, when an unearthly ululation split the air and hoofbeats thrummed the ground. Faster than a spring storm, Saracen cavalry galloped out of the brush, lances brandished, arrows nocked.

'Christ on the Cross!' Sabin hurled his newly retrieved saker aloft in a bate of wings and drew his sword. 'Into those bushes!' he snapped at Amalric. 'Lie down and don't move . . . on peril of your life!'

Without waiting to see if the boy did his bidding, he spurred Lucifer towards the knot of hunters with the King at the centre. No one was wearing armour, and even if they all carried swords, they were outnumbered and disadvantaged. It was death, sudden and fierce as the strike of a hawk.

He was intercepted by a Saracen warrior who jabbed his lance at Sabin's side. The blade pierced through the layers of the gambeson and slid along Sabin's ribs without doing damage, but the force and angle of the blow twisted him from the saddle. He landed hard, all the air slammed from his lungs and a glancing kick from Lucifer's off hind sent black stars rippling across his vision. He heard the plunge of hooves close to his head and tried to protect himself with his hands, but they refused to obey his will. Through an encroaching blur, he saw a yelling Saracen hurl himself across Lucifer's back. The grey reared and came down stiff-legged, and as Sabin's vision darkened beyond sight, he heard the swish of a leather whip and a stallion neigh of terror and fury.

CHAPTER 19

Someone was shaking his shoulder. Sabin groaned and opened his eyes. His vision blurred and cleared, blurred and cleared. Pain hammered through his skull and each blow went straight down to his belly.

'Christ, are you alive? Get up!'

The voice was Gerbert's, and it was raw with pain and anxiety. Sabin crawled to his knees, hung his head and vomited. The hand shook him again, harder, rattling the few wits remaining in his skull. Sabin decided that he didn't want to be alive.

'They've taken the King!'

Slowly Sabin raised his head. Although his stomach was churning like a brewer's vat, he staggered to his feet. Gerbert was hunched over him. A rag was bound tightly about his upper arm, stanching a wound that had obviously bled copiously. His face was as grey as his eyes and he was dripping wet.

'Who has?' Sabin asked. Beyond Gerbert he was slowly becoming aware of a scene of bloody carnage. Bodies of men and horses were strewed in the dust and the sweet tang of blood filled his nostrils. Birds circled in the sky – not the hawks they had flung aloft at the first onslaught, but red kites and vultures.

'Balak, who do you think?'

'But . . . but his army wasn't anywhere near this place . . .'

Sabin rubbed his temple and felt a tender egg-sized lump beneath his fingertips. He was going to vomit again.

'Not yesterday it wasn't, but plainly he moved up at speed,' Gerbert said grimly.

Sabin lurched to the water's edge and heaved. When he had recovered, he looked round to find Amalric watching him. Tear-streaks stained the boy's ashen face, but his jaw was set and he was holding Lucifer firmly by the cheekstrap of his bridle. 'He bolted, sir, but came back.' He swallowed and kept his head turned from the scene of the battle. 'I did as you said . . . I hid in the bushes and no one saw me . . .'

'Good lad,' Sabin said vaguely. Gerbert had stumbled over to the bodies and was inspecting them. Even from here it was obvious that no one had survived and Sabin wondered what Gerbert was doing. Then he realised.

'Stay back,' he said to Amalric, then tottered over to join the baron.

Expression contorted with pain, Gerbert closed the eyes of the yellow-haired knight over whom he had been stooping. 'Strongfist's not among the dead,' he said. 'They have taken him too.'

'Did you not see?'

Gerbert shook his head. 'I was forced into the river . . . By the time I'd stopped myself and the horse from drowning, it was over. They didn't stay to gloat over their victory.' He bared his teeth. 'First Joscelin of Edessa, now King Baldwin Balak has the means to bring us to our knees.'

Sabin had to wobble aside to be sick again. He wanted to lie down with the rest of the men: brutally slaughtered, but mercifully dead. Knowing that Gerbert would only badger him and shake him until his brains poured from his ears, he turned drunkenly back towards Amalric and Lucifer. 'Naught we can do save carry the news,' he said, struggling to enunciate the words through the waves of pain and nausea. How far was the nearest Christian village? Too far . . . His legs were made of wet rope. Gathering every ounce of will, he staggered to Amalric. Grasping the reins, he somehow found the strength to set his foot in the stirrup and was dimly aware of the lad boosting him up and across. Then Amalric swung up behind him, pillion fashion. Gerbert had mounted his bay, although the horse was much the worse for wear, weak in the legs and bearing several grazes and superficial sword cuts. Had their circumstances not been so dire, Sabin would have laughed. The cream of the Frankish army reduced to two wounded, unarmoured knights and a squire. How were the mighty fallen.

Another supply cart rolled into the compound at Montabard and soldiers ran to unload its cargo of olive oil and honey. Annais studied the industry from her chamber window, Guillaume cradled in her arms. For two days now the bailey had been as busy as a dockside.

'Do you think that we will be threatened, my lady?'

She looked over her shoulder at Soraya. With her liquid brown eyes and shy manner, she reminded Annais of a gazelle. 'I do not know. That is the honest truth,' she said. 'All I have to guide me is that one message from my husband. I hope not.' Four days ago, a rider had come from Gerbert who was in Antioch. The message had been brief, but then her husband was not a man of words. He wrote that the Emir Balak had captured King Baldwin, that he himself was on his way back to Montabard. She should stock the castle to the roof spaces with supplies and be on her guard. A duplicate of the letter had gone to Thierry, the constable.

Soraya looked down at the linen bandages she was preparing. 'I thought that my son and I were going to die when the Franks raided our caravan,' she said quietly. 'I had heard terrible tales of what the Franks did to their captives.'

'Probably the same tales that we hear about what the Saracens do to Frankish prisoners,' Annais said. 'And I do not doubt that some of it is true, even as much is false.'

Soraya busied herself with the linens. 'I was terrified of Durand at first,' she said. 'Even though he protected me from the others, I knew that it was because he wanted me for himself. Then I realised that if I did his bidding, I would be helping my child and myself. I did not love him then . . .'

Annais nodded, for she had an inkling of how the other woman felt. She had wed Gerbert out of duty. However, like a seed planted in good soil, affection had grown, and there had always been respect. Was there love now? She thought perhaps there was. Imagining him in danger made her stomach churn and she had missed the comfort of his body beside her at night. 'Durand is a good man,' she murmured.

Soraya found a tenuous smile. 'I know that now, and I am happy here. I do not want it to change.'

'It won't,' Annais said more firmly than she felt.

She had fed Guillaume and was rocking him to afternoon sleep in his cradle when a panting garrison soldier came to the chamber door and gasped out that Lord Gerbert had been sighted with a small escort of men, including Sabin and the boy, Amalric. Instructing a maid to watch the baby, Annais hurried to the wall walk and shaded her eyes against the late April sun. The riders were too distant for her to see clearly, although she recognised Gerbert's banner and his tall bay stallion, and pacing beside it Sabin's slighter grey. His escort contained far fewer men than had ridden out and she felt cold, knowing that some of the garrison wives would be mourning the loss of their husbands, and children would suddenly be fatherless. Muttering a prayer to the Holy Virgin, she crossed herself and sped from the wall walk to issue instructions to the cook and the kitchen servants, to the grooms and squires. Water was set to heating for bathtubs and fresh clothing shaken from storage in the coffers.

When the men rode beneath the gatehouse tower, its grisly decorations now no more than incomplete skeletons dangling by shreds of dried, leathery flesh, Annais was waiting to greet them with the women of her chamber. Two knights rode into the bailey, then came Gerbert on his bay with Sabin pressed up hard to the bay's flank one side and a serjeant on the other. Annais frowned, first in puzzlement, then in worry as she realised that they were making sure Gerbert did not fall from the saddle.

Amalric dismounted from his pony and hastened to grasp the bay's bridle. Sabin flung from the grey and, issuing terse commands to the closest of the garrison troops, prepared to catch Gerbert. Annais ran forward and was in time to see Gerbert raise himself from the saddle and swing to the ground. His skin was sheened with sweat and pallid, except for a burning spot of colour on either cheekbone. Fever had stripped his flesh. The creases that showed when he smiled were gaunt hollows and his grey eyes were as opaque as chips of polished flint. He swayed where he stood, but he refused the support of his knights.

'There is nothing wrong with me that the sight of my wife and son and a good night's sleep in my own bed will not cure.' His gaze drank Annais as if she were a pool of cold water in the desert. He extended his right arm like a wing and Annais moved into his embrace. His lips were cracked, his breath sour as he kissed her, and the heat emanating from his body was hot enough for a smith to forge horseshoes.

She broke from him in consternation. 'Jesu, you are burning up!' Sabin removed his helm and told a hovering attendant to fetch a litter.

'I have felt better, but there is no cause for all this fuss,' Gerbert growled with a glare for Sabin. 'I took on a wild young man and he has turned into an old woman overnight. Come, lead me to the hall and my son. I want to see my son.'

The querulous way he spoke the last words filled Annais with fear, for she could hear that same fear in Gerbert's own voice. He took three steps and staggered, a fourth and his legs buckled. As his weight sagged against her, Sabin nudged her aside, looping himself under Gerbert's arm to bear his weight.

'He should not have ridden,' he said, 'but pride makes fools of everyone.' Staggering slightly himself, he helped Gerbert towards the hall.

'What is wrong with him?' Feeling sick and cold, Annais hurried at his side. 'Why are there so few of you?'

'That is two questions at once,' Sabin gasped through clenched teeth. 'Only let me set him down, and I will tell you.'

He made his way to the hall and laboriously climbed the outer stairs to the solar and bedchamber. A maid had seen them coming and opened the door. Sabin bore Gerbert to the vast bed and carefully eased him down upon it.

'I'm all right,' Gerbert muttered. 'I could have walked without help.'

'As far as a goat can fly,' Sabin retorted, breathing hard. He turned to Annais. 'When King Baldwin was taken, there was savage fighting. Gerbert took a sword cut to his left arm and it has gone bad.'

Her eyes widened. She knew how dangerous a festering wound was in this climate. Sabin's gaze was knowing and compassionate, but there was also a sardonic glint that told her he was remembering the way she had treated his infected foot.

'A chirurgeon looked at it in Antioch and cleaned and stitched the wound,' he added. 'But he needs rest and intensive tending. I am afraid I make a good battle companion but a poor nursemaid.'

'At least you have brought him home.' Leaning over the bed, Annais unpinned Gerbert's cloak and pulled it wide. His left arm, which thus far she had not seen, was bound in a sling and heavily bandaged. She did not touch it – that would be for Montabard's new chirurgeon to do – but she removed his boots and bathed his face tenderly with a damp cloth.

Gerbert found a smile. 'I am in heaven and you are an angel,' he said.

'Not yet. I intend to keep you on this earth until you are

as old as Methuselah.' Annais wagged an admonitory finger and managed to keep the tears out of her voice.

'Where's my son?'

She went to fetch Guillaume from the cradle. He made a peevish complaint and fisted his eyes, but thankfully did not resort to outright wails as she bore him to Gerbert. Sitting on the edge of the bed, she held him at her husband's good side. 'God in heaven, he has grown!' There was pride and astonishment in Gerbert's voice.

'Of course he has. If he is to be as tall as his father, he has to begin now.'

'When we were under attack, I thought of you and him . . . indeed it was all that was in my mind. I mustn't give up, I mustn't die.' His voice cracked and tears oozed through his lashes and down his fever-glazed face.

'Hush, it's all right.' She spoke to him in the soothing tones of a mother to a child. 'You are home, you're not going to die.' She glanced at Sabin. He had moved away and turned his back out of decency, but he was not deaf. The fact that he was lingering meant that he had more to tell her, and she was not sure she was going to be strong enough to hear it.

Montabard's physician arrived with his satchel of nostrums. He was a young Italian named Luigi who had rested at the keep on his way home from Jerusalem two months ago and ended up remaining longer than a night. Annais returned Guillaume to his cradle. Awake but crotchety with tiredness, he began to wail, but Soraya rocked the cradle with her foot and spoke softly until the wails subsided to small, sleepy grumbles. Thanking her with a look, Annais went back to her husband.

Examining the wound was a difficult chore, for Gerbert was obviously in agony and even to touch the bandages made him catch his breath and groan. However, Luigi gently persisted. When laid bare, the injury had an unpleasant smell that rose in waves of heat. Pus oozed between the stitches and poisonous red streaks stretched into the healthy flesh north and south. Luigi's expression did not change. His only sign of concern was a single click of his tongue.

'Can you do something for him?' Annais rubbed her hands together then clasped them at her mouth as if she were praying.

'I can try, madonna. The poison in the wound is spreading into his body and must be stopped. I have to open up the stitches, clean his flesh and rebind it. The rest is in the hands of God who has been merciful enough to spare him thus far.' She nodded and compressed her lips.

He gave her a compassionate look from large dark eyes. 'You do not have to stay if it disturbs you too much, madonna.'

Annais shook her head. 'No, I am accustomed to caring for the sick. I was raised in a convent, and although elderly nuns are different from a full-grown man, I am not squeamish.' Her expression grew fierce. 'Besides, he is my husband.' Luigi nodded approvingly.

By the time he had finished, Annais wished that she had never agreed with such pride to stay. She and Sabin pinned Gerbert to the bed and Luigi did his work. Probing the wound, which made Gerbert arch like a bow and scream, revealed a shard of steel from the blade of the sword. Red-fingered, Luigi held it aloft in triumph. 'This is what was causing the trouble,' he said. 'With good fortune and rest he will heal now.' He proceeded to wash the deep slash in salt water and stitched the macerated flesh back together. A honey poultice was packed over it and soft linen bandages wrapped around the arm. Gerbert had been given white poppy in wine and, as it took effect, he subsided into a restless doze. Luigi sat at the bedside to watch his patient and from his satchel removed a dog-eared vellum book, a medical treatise, he said, written by a Greek physician called Paul of Aegina. Within moments, his nose was buried.

Feeling sick and faint, Annais moved to the embrasure to draw in lungfuls of clean air. Sabin brought her a cup of wine and gently pushed her down on the stone seat beneath the window. 'He will be all right,' he said gently.

Annais found a wan and meaningless smile and turned the cup in her hands. The wine rippled and shook, but Sabin had been wise enough not to fill it to the brim and it did not spill. She wanted to weep, but could not afford to . . . not until she knew everything. Standing at her side, Sabin was quiet, but it was not an easy or comfortable silence. He was waiting to speak, allowing her to gather her second wind. She took a trembling sip of the wine and looked at him. There was a bruise the colour of spilled woad at his temple, and weary smudges beneath his eyes. She realised that he was still wearing his mail.

'You should unarm.'

'Presently,' he said. 'Truth to tell I have worn it for days on end and an hour more will make no difference.'

Annais drew a deep breath. 'There is more, isn't there? You have not told me the whole.'

He gazed out of the embrasure for the space of several heartbeats, then turned to look at her. 'Your father was captured with King Baldwin,' he said. 'Or at least we believe he was.'

Heat prickled at the back of her neck. She pressed her fingers against the cup, anchoring herself to consciousness by the hard pressure of her fingertips on the cold, glazed sides. 'Tell me,' she heard herself say, and, as if from a distance, listened to Sabin relay the story of their ambush and the fight that had followed. When he was finished, the silence fell again. If Annais had been filled with suppressed emotion before, now she was so swollen with it that she had grown numb, and it was a blessing.

'As soon as the meltwater has gone from the Euphrates, I am returning to Kharpurt and joining the Armenians. There is a plan to spring Joscelin of Edessa from captivity, and that plan must now involve King Baldwin and your father. It will be of more use than remaining here when there are men like

Thierry and Malik and Durand to hold the keep. Besides, Gerbert will be on his feet soon enough.'

She set the cup to one side knowing that if she drank the wine she would be sick. 'You are certain that my father was taken captive?'

Sabin bit his thumbnail. 'We searched all the bodies,' he said. 'His was not one of them, and he was close to the King when the fighting began.' His expression was bleak but resolute. 'I will bring him home alive, I promise you . . . and I promise myself . . . or I will not come back at all.'

'Do not say that! It is tempting fate.'

He smiled. 'No more than usual. Don't worry, you won't be rid of me that easily.'

He left to remove his mail and wash the sweat of travel from his body. She went to the bedside to look at Gerbert, deep-sunk in drugged sleep. Her stomach was a hollow cavern. She was terrified and she could show that terror to no one. Perhaps that was how Odile had felt; perhaps that was why she had preferred to remain closed in her chamber, cocooned from the blows of the world outside.

Chapter 20

His heart slamming against his chest wall, his breath whistling in his throat, Strongfist obeyed King Baldwin's bellowed order to cast aside his shield and throw down his sword, thus baring them both to the lances and scimitars of the surrounding Saracens.

Through a blur of stinging sweat, Strongfist could see the bodies of his companions strewn along the riverside like flotsam; and each hard-drawn breath sucked the stench of the slaughterhouse into his lungs. Himself and five others surrounded the King like the points of a star. Everyone else was dead, or too badly wounded to fight on. He stared at the bristle of steel points and past them into the fierce dark eyes of turbaned warriors. A slim thread of command was all that stood between life and death for King Baldwin and the remnants of his bodyguard. Strongfist prayed with silent vehemence. It was one thing to die in the heat of battle, another to be executed as the blood cooled and a man had time to understand what was coming.

The Saracen ranks flurried and parted, the warriors bowing down to a man riding an exquisite black mare. His mail coat shone like polished sea-coal and was mirrored by his eyes. He wore an immaculate white turban set with a ruby the size of a pigeon's egg. Rubies adorned his fingers too, winking like clots of blood set in gold. The hilt of his scimitar was similarly blistered. A grey-bearded attendant on a pied mule accompanied him, and it was he who spoke out in accented French.

'In the name of Allah the All Merciful, know that you are in the presence of the lord Balak, Prince of Saruj, lord of Khanzit. Yield yourselves to his great mercy and you shall be spared.'

Baldwin bowed his head. 'I yield myself and my men to the superior force of Lord Balak.' Although flushed and breathing hard, Baldwin had control of himself. Having been a lord of these wild north lands before he was king, he knew the rules and how to play by them.

The spears withdrew a fraction and Strongfist's tension came down a peg, although his heart continued to hammer in his chest. The lord Balak spoke, his voice harsh and dusty.

'The lord Balak says that he is pleased to offer you hospitality at his fortress of Kharpurt,' the translator declared. 'There is no need to visit in the secret of night when he can show you everything by the clean light of day. He is certain that you will be eager to see your kinsman and he promises that you and your knights will be kept in the same luxury as Joscelin of Edessa . . . until a suitable ransom can be agreed.'

The words were as smooth as honey, but there was no mistaking the underlying threat. Strongfist wondered grimly what form a 'suitable' ransom would take. For Joscelin, Balak had demanded the fortress of Edessa, and had it flung back in his face. What would he seek for the King of Jerusalem?

Balak's warriors surged amongst them, searching and removing all weapons and anything of value. Strongfist had already discarded sword and shield, but now he was stripped of his meat dagger and the fine English hunting knife that had belonged to his grandfather. His hands were lashed behind his back with rawhide cords and a Turcoman warrior took his stallion on a lead rein. Strongfist craned his neck and tried to gaze past him to the strewn dead, seeking the bodies of Gerbert and Sabin, but the Saracen took it as a sign that Strongfist was planning to escape and clubbed him with the blunt end of a lance. The blow struck Strongfist's temple hard enough to form stars before his eyes, and ran a long graze down his cheek. He reeled but instinctively gripped the saddle with his thighs, knowing that if he fell they were likely to kill him rather than let him become a hindrance. He prayed that either Gerbert or Sabin had escaped, for then at least Annais would know what had happened to him. If not . . . He had a vision of her confronting the loss of her husband, her father and her friend. His little grandson would lose three of his strongest protectors. A babe among wolves. He clamped his jaw to resist despair. His grandfather had endured the great battle of Hastings field and the loss of most of his kin. His progeny, by the very fact of their existence, had inherited his tenacity and will to survive . . . but although the thought was a crutch, it gave Strongfist little comfort.

Leaning against a merlon, Gerbert pressed his hand to his ribs and struggled to catch his breath. Sweat glistened on his brow and his heart was beating so hard that it made his body tremble. Sabin knew better than to tell him he should not have climbed to the wall walk in the first place. The wound fever had left Gerbert as querulous as a woman in the week before her monthly bleed, and anyone who spoke a word out of line was dicing with his temper.

That Gerbert had made any kind of recovery from the wound was little short of a miracle. Sabin had been convinced he was going to die, but Luigi's skills as a physician and Annais's tender, diligent nursing had pulled him back from the brink. The wound still oozed and was not healing well; he was beset by an almost permanent low fever, but he had declared himself well enough to rise from his bed and inspect the castle's defences.

Gerbert steadied and drew himself upright. His chest still heaved and his lips were tinged with blue. 'You think I am being foolish,' he growled.

Sabin shrugged. 'What I think does not matter. I have been

called a fool and worse on many occasions, but it always made me more determined to go my own way.'

Gerbert gave a snort of reluctant amusement and turned to look out through the crenel gap on a land lush with the meltwater and greenery of spring. For a long time, he was silent and Sabin did not seek to intrude on his thoughts. Besides, given Gerbert's condition, there was no guessing what they might be. Sometimes they were lucid and clear, but on other occasions, depending on the level of his fever and how much white poppy he had consumed, he would ramble and lose his way.

'I have a boon to ask of you,' he said eventually, fixing Sabin with glittering eyes and red-branded cheeks. 'I bound you to me for but a year and a day. That time has long passed. I know I cannot keep you, but I ask you for the sake of my wife and son to dwell on at Montabard.'

Sabin paced along the wall walk and paused by the next crenel. The shahins were riding the air high above the walls on curved wings. He watched them and knew that Gerbert was watching him in his turn. 'You know that their lives are mine, saving that I go to join the rescue at Kharpurt,' he said quietly. 'You would swear a holy oath on that?'

Sabin turned his gaze from the falcons. 'If my word is not good enough for you, then neither is a holy oath. Why do you want me to stand protector when you will not trust me?'

Gerbert grimaced. 'I am in pain,' he said. 'Forgive my clumsy words. I do not doubt your honour. It is my concern for Annais and Guillaume that makes me zealous.'

'You could ask Aymer, Thierry, Durand . . . or Malik. Their steadfastness is proven,' Sabin said curtly.

'So is yours.' Shuffling forward, Gerbert clamped a heavy hand down on Sabin's nearest shoulder. 'I did not intend to insult you. What I meant to say was that Thierry and Durand have sworn their oaths to me. I know that you are bound to no one save by your own choice, but I ask you, in friendship, to swear fealty to my wife and my son.' The hand squeezed, forestalling Sabin as he drew breath to reply. 'Think upon it,' Gerbert said. 'Say no more now. I do not have the stamina to listen, and your own thoughts may need consideration.' The grip slackened, but the weight increased, becoming a need for support. Sabin gestured to the two attendants who had been standing in the background, prudently out of earshot, and they hastened to assist their lord.

'My will outstrips my flesh.' Gerbert's voice was constricted with pain and frustration as the men almost carried him towards the stairs leading down to the ward. 'No, do not follow me. Complete your inspection and consider what I have said.'

Sabin sighed and continued along the wall walk. He spoke to a pair of guards, checked their weapons, asked after their concerns, and went on his way. He did not have to think about what Gerbert had said. He would give his loyalty to Annais and Guillaume without question. If Gerbert wanted to bind him with a ceremony, then so be it. A year ago he would have packed his saddlebags and fled at speed from such a commitment, but the past months had changed him, forging a weapon of a different temper from the light blade that had arrived in Outremer. While unease still haunted him at the notion of binding himself, it was no more than a fading whisper from the code by which he had once lived.

Strongfist had never been shackled in his life although he had frequently seen felons thus encumbered. To have iron bracelets secured at his wrists and ankles and linked by chains so that he could only shuffle like a bear was humiliating and grossly uncomfortable. The irons chafed and he had been forced to tear strips from his tunic to bind around their edges. King Baldwin had done the same, and filaments of gold embroidery twinkled on the frayed silk wrapped at wrist and foot.

He and his men shared a cell somewhere in the bowels of the fortress. Since there was no window in the room, there was no telling day from night save by the changing of the guards outside the door and the routines of food provision and slop emptying. What light they had was provided by three inadequate oil lamps that did little but chase the shadows from the corners into the centre of the room. Strongfist tried to keep a tally of the passage of time by marking the wall with a chip of stone he had found among the floor rushes, but it was a crude indicator and he had no confidence in its accuracy.

Baldwin had been half hoping that they would be thrown into a cell with Joscelin of Edessa, but Balak was cannier than that, and they had no news of how the other captive was faring, or if he was even aware of their presence in Kharpurt. Most wearing of all was the lack of outside news. They did not know what havoc Balak was wreaking while he held the King of Jerusalem and the Count of Edessa captive. They did not know whether a ransom was being collected, or an army gathered to march upon Kharpurt, and they did not know if they would ever see fresh daylight again.

Strongfist was enduring the captivity with more resilience than some of the more restless men. Family and employers had often called him a 'great ox' in jest, and his almost bovine indifference was standing him in good stead now. No nervous rash had erupted on his skin. He had not taken to biting his nails, plucking out his beard, or become involved in the petty squabbles and occasional spurts of violence as tensions boiled over.

He sat now near the door in a puddle of weak light cast by one of the oil lamps and with his chip of stone painstakingly etched a tafel board into the floor beneath the rushes. He had been saving date stones from their food ration to use as counters. It kept his hands occupied and gave him a focus.

The key grated in the lock and the heavy bolts shot back. Time for the second meal of the day, he thought. In the morning they were given flat bread, fruit and cheese. At night, there were usually stewed grains with spices and vegetables, occasionally with slivers of goat meat meagrely stirred through. Their rations were short, but not so much as to bring about starvation, and the food was at least edible.

The door opened to reveal a torchlit corridor lined with armed guards. Two men entered, each bearing steaming bowls of the vegetable grain mixture. Depositing these in the middle of the floor, they went back out, returning moments later with a dish of dried dates and figs and a fresh water jar. Finally, the slop bucket was changed. As the second man left, he passed very close to Strongfist and surreptitiously dropped something into the straw by his hand. Then he stooped out of the room and the door swung shut behind him.

Baldwin and the others advanced to the food. Without spoons they had to eat in the eastern fashion, taking the mixture from the edge where it was cooler and rolling it into mouthful sized balls with their fingers. Strongfist grubbed in the straw and found a small needle case such as women wore on their belts. It was made from the wingbone of a goose and delicately carved with a polished, tightly fitting stopper. The hair rose on Strongfist's forearm. Rising to his feet, he brought the object to Baldwin and told him what had happened.

With a brightening glance, the King wiped his hands on his chausses, took the needle case and, with difficulty, because of the size and greasiness of his fingers, pried out the stopper. Inside was a furled strip of parchment covered with spider lines of brown scrawl. Baldwin rose to his feet and clanked over to the nearest lamp. Squinting, he strove to read the words.

'It is from Joscelin,' he said at length to a response of cheers. 'He says that the servant who brought the food is one of his spies and that he is in contact with allies outside the walls. They can do nothing for the moment, until the meltwaters subside from the river, but as soon as that happens, they will attempt a rescue.' His breathing had quickened as he read the note. 'It is too dangerous to engage in speech with his man, or even to pass messages with any degree of frequency, but he will do what he can.' Baldwin twisted the parchment, pushed the end in the lamp flame until it caught fire, and then held it until it had burned down almost to his fingertips. He dropped the flaming ember on the ground and crushed it beneath his heel until it was naught but black powder and a few white flakes that he stirred among the rushes. 'At least now we have a means of communication,' he said, 'and hope, no matter how slim.' The men returned to their meal with renewed gusto, their conversation charged with a cheerfulness that had not existed before. Strongfist tried not to feel too optimistic; it was but a small glimpse of light, but it made it easier to believe he would see the outside world and his loved ones again.

Annais took her harp from its protective leather case and tuned the strings. Gerbert enjoyed hearing her play as much as she loved playing and the moments were a pleasure to them both. Tonight she thought that the music might soothe him. Heavily dosed with feverfew to cool the heat of his blood and white poppy for his pain, he lay on their bed with Guillaume. The baby was free of his swaddling and was doing his best to grab his foot and suck his own toes.

'I could watch you both for ever,' Gerbert said as she brought the harp to a stool by the bedside and sat down to pluck the strings. 'There can be no sweeter sight on this earth.' His voice was a mumble, induced by the effects of the potions he had drunk.

'Flatterer!' She plucked out the sweet tones of 'Stella Maris', a tune she knew so well that she did not have to think about the movement of her fingers. In the privacy of their chamber, she had removed her veil and her dark braids fell to her waist, gleaming in the lamplight like polished dark oak.

'I'm but a simple man. I report what I see.' He reached out to touch the baby's plump, firm flesh. 'Others might revel in a different sight, but this is all to me.'

Annais cast him a silent smile over the top of the harp. She did not want to break the mood by ceasing to play and embracing him, nor, she thought, had that been his intention.

The notes sprang from the harp in droplets both sweet and sharp, bright as gold, soft with melancholy. Tears welled in Gerbert's eyes and he pinched them away with thumb and forefinger. Annais raised her head and gazed at him in alarm.

'I am weeping for myself.' His throat rippled as he struggled for control. 'No, don't stop. If you love me, play on.'

Annais bit her lip but did as he bade. Gerbert's mood was often difficult to gauge, especially in the evening when he was tired and in pain and the syrup of poppy had yet to do all its work. She knew that he was unwell. She and Luigi had nursed him back from the brink of death, but its shadow still breathed down his neck, and although he fought it at every turn, the outcome was at best a stalemate.

His lids closed and he slept. Annais set the harp aside. Lifting Guillaume from the coverlet, she kissed him and buried her face in his soft, warm skin, stifling tears of her own.

During the night, Gerbert's fever rose, and by morning, he was raving. Annais and Luigi bathed him with tepid water, changed the wringing sheets, wafted cool air over him with fans made from palm fronds, but the heat came from within and finally all they could do was sit by his bedside and pray.

At nightfall, all their attentions harvested a weak result as the fever dropped sufficiently to leave Gerbert lucid. Wrung out, limp, as exhausted as a shipwrecked sailor heaved onto the shore but lacking strength to crawl above the tideline, Gerbert raised his hand and plucked at Annais's sleeve.

'Fetch Father Jerome and Sabin,' he whispered. 'There are things to be said and done before . . . before morning.' As he spoke, he cast his gaze towards the shutters, open to a tranquil starlit dusk. Annais followed his stare and the hollow feeling in the pit of her stomach expanded until she felt as if she might disappear into it.

Sabin was in the bailey, talking to the senior serjeants after a training session for the garrison, but he came swiftly at the summons from the bedchamber.

'My lord?' He advanced to the bedside and saw from the looks on the faces of those gathered in the room that he was attending at a deathbed. Annais was as pale as a shadow with huge, haunted eyes. The senior officers had been brought from their posts and stood grim-faced and anxious. Father Jerome knelt at the bedside, telling his prayer beads from one hand to the other.

Gerbert was propped up against several bolsters. His flesh had sunk against his bones and was the grey of a dove's breast. He beckoned Sabin closer, and his chest trembled with the effort of drawing breath to speak. 'You know the matter we discussed on the walls?'

'Yes, my lord . . . you wish to see it done?' Sabin looked briefly at Annais.

'I do . . . and more than that.' Gerbert licked his lips. 'Before these witnesses, I charge you with the protection and well-being of my wife and son. It is my wish that if I die, you shall undertake the care of Montabard and the care of my son until he is of an age to hold this place by his own sword, and that you shall do this by right of marriage.'

There were several indrawn breaths followed by a stunned silence. Sabin blinked, and blinked again, but the scene did not dissolve and the words continued to ring in his ears. It was not a dream.

'Do not refuse me . . .' Gerbert's voice had sunk to a dry whisper. He started to cough and Luigi, who had been standing at the head of the bed, swiftly set a cup to his lips. Gerbert took a couple of swallows, but most of the liquid dribbled down his chin and stained his cotton shirt.

Sabin looked at Annais who was ashen, her brown eyes huge with shock, and was angry. Not even a dying man had the right to do this. 'You know I will care for them,' he said. 'There is no need to ask this.'

Gerbert bared his teeth. 'There is every need,' he gasped. 'We are at war with Balak.'

'That makes no difference, I will do my best whatever.'

'Until someone else is appointed by right of marriage.' Gerbert closed his eyes. His breathing was harsh and the blue tinge around his lips had increased. 'You know the rules in Outremer. If I do not do something about my successor, then Antioch will.'

Sabin wanted to object, to say that he had always been a breaker of rules, but the words lodged in his throat.

'Promise me,' Gerbert wheezed. He seized Sabin's arm in a grip as strong as death itself and beckoned to Annais. Looking as if she too would rather run from the room, she inched to the bedside. With a supreme effort of will, Gerbert leaned forward, took her hand and placed it in Sabin's. 'I charge you to honour my wishes,' he said. 'Swear to me . . . both of you.'

Sabin felt Annais's fingers flinch against his, but she controlled the movement before it could become outright recoil. Her breathing was as swift and shallow as Gerbert's. 'I swear,' she said. Her voice held a higher pitch than normal, but it was clear and firm. She fixed Sabin with a look that dared him to baulk. Over his own hand and hers, he felt Gerbert's talon grip.

'I swear,' he responded, and cold sweat sprang on his palm where hers touched. He didn't want any of it . . . not like this.

Gerbert held on a moment longer, then let out his breath on a deep sigh and slumped against the bolsters. His grasp relinquished and Annais took back her hand. Sabin did not miss the way that she smoothed it against her gown, as if obliterating the feel of his skin against hers.

'Do it for Montabard and for Guillaume,' Gerbert said huskily as Luigi set the potion cup to his lips and made him drink. 'I hold you to it.'

Sabin inclined his head and stepped back so that the other senior officers of the castle could have their time with Gerbert and receive instruction, but since that instruction involved him too, he could not retreat too far. When it was finished,

Gerbert was so exhausted that he could scarcely breathe. Only Annais and the priest stayed with him; everyone else went about their business.

'Courage, man.' Thierry clapped Sabin on the shoulder as they descended to the hall. 'It may not be what you intended for yourself, but there are worse fates.'

'You think so?' Sabin said grimly. 'Would you rather change places with Joscelin of Edessa or the King?'

There was a band of tension at Sabin's brow, as if he had forgotten to remove his helm after battle practice. 'I still do not understand why he chose me,' he said. Grabbing a flagon off a trestle, he poured wine into a cup.

'Then you are either wilfully blind or fishing for compliments,' Thierry growled.

Sabin took a rapid gulp and pushed his free hand through his hair. 'Neither,' he said. 'I know I am good with a sword, I know I can handle men and administrate, but always if forced to it, or challenged, never of my own seeking. Surely he would have done better to appoint you, or Durand.'

Thierry helped himself to wine. 'All men have their own niche,' he said. 'I work best when I know the plan, but I need someone to give me that plan. Durand is a fine soldier but he has the imagination of an ox. As you say, you can fight, you can handle men. You are the young stallion champing at the stable door.' Thierry smiled. 'Men like myself and Durand are here to serve as your steadier stable mates – like that mule you have for your grey.'

Sabin laughed harshly at the comparison and drank again.

Thierry studied him. 'Can you truly say that you do not desire this task – even if it is being thrust upon you?'

Sabin sighed. 'No,' he admitted. 'I do desire it. But it comes with a deal of baggage and I am not sure that my back is broad enough to carry it all.'

'Lord Gerbert is certain . . . and he has ever been a good judge of men. No one has protested. We know you. There is no telling who might be given Montabard if it is left in the hands of the administrators in Antioch. Besides, they have enough on their trencher with the King in captivity.'

Sabin raised his cup in a rueful toast. 'To faith,' he said, and wondered what Annais was thinking. He had felt the flinching of her fingers beneath his. If she had not been fond of Gerbert when she wed him, then she was now. To watch him die and then be forced to marry another man before Gerbert was even cold in his shroud was more than grinding salt into an open wound. He knew that he should have ridden away long ago . . . but he hadn't, and now he was trapped, and so was she.

Chapter 21

Annais looked down at her husband. The fight was over and Gerbert's expression wore peace instead of the ravages of pain and fever. His brow was smooth; his lids were closed over sightless eyes. She and her women had spent the day bathing and dressing him for the night vigil in church. He wore his court robe of blue silk and soft indoor boots of tender kidskin stamped with the image of falcons in gold leaf. The rings that he had owned but seldom worn in life bejewelled his broad fingers and a cross of gold set with peridots adorned his breast. The hilt of his sword was clasped between his hands, the blade pointing down his body, and his feet rested upon his shield. He would go to his grave without these accoutrements, which would be stored until his son was old enough to bear them, but for the vigil Gerbert was arrayed in full glory. He looked as if he were asleep. If she had not seen him die, she might have been fooled.

'Do you want to rest awhile, my lady?' Soraya's soft, accented voice invaded her thoughts as the young woman touched her arm. 'It will be a long watch in church tonight.'

Annais shook her head. 'No,' she said. 'If Gerbert is at rest until the trumpets of Judgement Day, then I can manage for a day and a night. There will be time enough for sleep when it is over.'

There was a knock on the door. She turned, expecting to

see the senior officers of the keep arriving to bear Gerbert to chapel, but it was Sabin alone. He had changed his soldier's garb for a court gown of red silk damask patterned with golden lions. The deep embroidered neck opening was pinned not with his usual thistle brooch, but with one of Saracen gold set with rubies as small as beads of blood. He was wearing his sword and had donned his ceremonial belt of gilded leather instead of the one he wore when on active campaign.

Annais was suddenly aware that he and Gerbert were dressed for the occasion, but that she was still wearing the garments in which she had nursed her husband, held his dying body . . . washed and tended him when it was over.

'We are not ready yet,' she said, and bade Soraya have more water brought, and a pot of scented soap.

'No, I have not come for that.' Approaching the bed, Sabin looked down at Gerbert and crossed himself.

'Then for what?'

Sabin drew a deep breath. 'The oath he made us swear. If you want to reject it, I will understand. Taken under duress, it would not be binding.'

Annais lifted her chin. 'He is not yet cold and you stand over him and talk of revoking his dying wish?'

Sabin gave her a hard stare. His eyes were as bright as the peridots in the cross on Gerbert's breast. 'Would it be better to wait until he is cold and beneath the ground to discuss such matters?

Annais shuddered. She wanted to shriek at him to get out, but that would resolve nothing. Besides, she had more respect than he did for the sanctity of the dead.

'It is the living that concern me,' he said, as if reading her mind. His tone had gentled somewhat. 'I will hold you to nothing that is not of your will.'

Annais shook her head. The rawness of grief had left her numb. She did not know what her will was. 'Do you desire absolution of the vow?' she asked. 'Is that why you are here? If I revoke it first, then you cannot be blamed?'

He clenched his fists. 'I have no intention of revoking the vow,' he said. 'It is true that I argued against it at the beginning, but if you and Guillaume are to be kept safe, then I understand why Gerbert wanted the match. It need be a marriage in name only, if that is your preference.'

Annais swallowed and shook her head. 'I will not revoke the vow,' she croaked. 'It was my husband's dying wish, and I know he had the best intentions. He did not trust you when you came to us – indeed, he did not want you, but he took you out of obligation to his new family. If he changed his mind, it was based on merit, therefore I must have as much belief in you as he did.' Her voice wobbled. She had not thought herself capable of any more tears, but they welled over her hot, sore lids and trickled down her face. 'Is that the answer you wanted?'

'I am sorry . . . I had to know.'

She turned away from him and wiped her face on a linen kerchief that was already sodden with tears. 'Now you do.' She blew her nose. 'What would you have done if I had revoked the oath? Ridden away?'

He tensed. 'No,' he said. 'I could have done it once, but not any more.'

Two attendants arrived with the soap and water she had requested. Also two storage jars, one of hot, one of cold. 'I will return in a while, when you are ready to bear Gerbert to the chapel.' Sabin gave her a stiff, formal bow and strode from the room.

Annais let out a quivering breath, sat down at the bedside, and wept.

In Outremer, a week represented a year's mourning. Seven days after Gerbert's body was laid to rest, Annais and Sabin were married in the chapel that had so recently hosted a funeral. There were no rich clothes, no celebrations, no feast. The ceremony took less than a thousand swift heartbeats to perform, witnessed by the priest and his altar attendants, by

Durand, Malik and Thierry for Sabin, by Letice and Soraya for Annais.

Sabin presented her with a gold bezant as a symbol of his intention to provide for her, and a wedding ring of African gold. He slid it onto her finger atop the one she had from Gerbert. Father Jerome pronounced them man and wife in the eyes of the Church and the pact was sealed with a kiss of peace. The meeting of lips was brief and impersonal, the clasp of hand upon hand no more than part of the ritual.

Following the ceremony, Annais went with Sabin to the Great Hall. Her arm rested lightly along his in the fashion of the court and she carried herself spine-straight like a queen. They matched pace for pace in slow dignity, turned and took their places in the great carved chairs on the raised dais. One by one, the knights and vassals of Montabard came to kneel and swear their oaths to the new lord and his lady. If there was any jealousy and dissent among the men, it was no more than a twinge. Few envied Sabin his position with the King and Joscelin of Edessa in captivity and the Emir Balak wreaking havoc in Frankish-held territory.

When the oath-taking was over, Sabin and Annais parted company, he to his duties, she to the women's chamber.

Annais gulped down the cup of wine that Letice poured for her, but shook her head at the offer of a stronger potion to give her ease. 'No,' she said. 'It helped me to sleep on the first two nights, but I need a clear head.' She massaged her aching temples and wondered if Sabin had been as eager as she to have the terrible ceremony ended. Certainly he had not lingered in the church and his lips had been as dry and passionless as her own. Letice had moved from her side and was eyeing the bed. 'Will you both sleep here tonight?' she asked neutrally.

Annais turned the new gold wedding ring on her finger. 'I have been trying not to think about that,' she said. The bed where she had spent her first night as lady of Montabard. The bed where she had learned what it was to be a lover as well as a dutiful wife. The bed where Guillaume had been born and Gerbert had died. Now it waited to receive the cycle all over again.

'You must,' Letice said gently. 'It cannot be ignored, and it is best to be prepared.'

Annais poured herself another measure of wine. 'Sabin promised me that if I wished, it would be a marriage in name only.' Her gaze returned to the bed as if pulled by an invisible leash. She tried to imagine lying in it with Sabin and abruptly turned from the vision with churning stomach.

'Even if you keep to separate chambers, for the sake of appearances you must spend at least one night together,' Letice said, her tone compassionate but insistent. 'No one need know what you do together, but they must see that you are one.'

She was right, Annais acknowledged. Given that she was no virgin, bloody proof of consummation would not be required . . . but she would still be expected to couple with Sabin. An unconsummated marriage, after all, was one that could be annulled. She wondered if Sabin was prepared to take that risk. Was she, for that matter? 'Have the bed made up with fresh sheets,' she said. 'But do not garland it with flowers or make it look like a bower for a bride and groom.'

Letice nodded with compassion in her eyes. 'It shall be done,' she said.

Annais spent an hour feeding Guillaume, changing his swaddling, playing with him. His eyes were so like Gerbert's, his brown curls too, that it was like gaining comfort from twisting a knife in her heart. She cuddled him and wept a little. When he became sleepy she laid him in his cradle and, leaving him to her women, went below to the hall. After all, she was lady of Montabard and this was her wedding day. The thought left her unsure whether to laugh or to cry.

Although she had not ordered a feast to be prepared, they still needed to feed the guests and witnesses who had come to Montabard to pay their respects. There was plenty of bread, both leavened and flat, goat's cheese, olive oil, lamb served with boiled wheat and almonds, and the thick honey and sesame sweetmeats so favoured in this part of Outremer. Not in the least hungry, she nibbled at the food. Since Gerbert's decline and death, she had felt little inclination to eat and the green silk gown, which had once suited her so well, hung on her like a sack.

Sabin did not try to coax her to eat, as her women would have done. He merely placed a dish between them to share and ate his own portion. But then she could see that he was occupied with the news brought by a Templar knight on his way south, who had paused to refresh himself at their board.

'Fortunately for us, Emir Balak has not seen fit to exploit King Baldwin's captivity thus far,' the knight said around mouthfuls of lamb and wheat. 'There have been skirmishes, but little more than usual.'

'I have kept up the patrols,' Sabin said, 'but there has been no trouble.' He toyed with a silver salt dish. 'It is all to the good that no one has panicked and that the rule of the kingdom has not fallen into disarray. Patriarch Bernard has the control of Antioch and Eustace Garnier of Caesarea has been elected bailiff of Jerusalem. They are both more than competent.'

The Templar grunted agreement and washed down his food with a swallow of wine. 'It is like anywhere,' he said, gazing pointedly around the crowded hall. 'Fill the gap with an able deputy and the ordinary folk scarcely notice.'

Sabin looked wry, but said nothing. He took a moderate swallow from his own cup, which was still more than half full. He was staying sober, and Annais did not know whether to be grateful or worried by the detail.

'I would offer my congratulations,' the knight said, 'but since they come on the heels of tragic circumstances, I do not suppose they would be in order.'

'My wife and I thank you none the less,' Sabin said politely and sent Annais a glance intended to reassure. She replied to the Templar with an inanity she was not later to remember.

'I heard Gerbert de Montabard died of a wound taken when the King was captured.'

'That is so,' Sabin replied woodenly, but the Templar did not take the hint and continued to probe.

'Were you there when King Baldwin was taken?'

Sabin nodded. 'But out of the fighting. I was thrown from my horse and left for dead – the reason I am here now. My lady's father is a captive in Kharpurt with the King.'

'Is he?' The Templar raised his brow. 'I suppose that is slightly better than being dead, but not much.'

Sabin winced for Annais's sake. 'Have you heard any news of Balak from your own territory?' he asked to change the subject.

'Enough to know that he is not about to set out for Jerusalem.' The knight reached for a handful of raisins and almonds. 'He may have acquired a glorious reputation in capturing the Count of Edessa and the King, but he would rather make himself lord of Aleppo on its back than destroy the Frankish kingdom. Of course, if he conquers there, he will likely turn his attention on us . . . but we have a few months' grace at least.'

Sabin digested the news thoughtfully. By the time Balak was ready to assault the Franks with any purpose, Baldwin would be free. That was if everything went to plan.

'There is talk of raising a ransom,' the Templar said. 'That is one of the reasons I go to Jerusalem. Queen Morphia has been very busy.'

'From what I have heard and seen of the lady, she is not one to sit at home and wring her hands,' Sabin replied, recalling the flashing dark eyes beneath the pearl-fringed headdress when he had seen her in Jerusalem. Being Armenian herself, she probably knew of the rescue plan, but it was always wise to divide eggs between baskets.

Having eaten his fill the Templar excused himself, pinned his cloak and went out.

Sabin turned to Annais. Her portion of food on the trencher

was still untouched and she was as pale as whey. 'I know this is difficult for you,' he said quietly.

'Is it not for you?' she asked.

He pushed the congealing food away. 'Of course it is.'

'You do not show it.'

'Well, that is because I have grown accustomed to either running away from problems or brazening them out if it is too late to run. Believe me, I am neither smiling nor calm behind the face I wear.'

'Then what are you?'

'Terrified,' he said. 'And that is something you are more than privileged to hear.' Now he did drain his cup, but when offered a refill by an attendant, accepted less than a half-measure. 'But then there should be no secrets between husband and wife.'

Abruptly he excused himself from the high table and went to talk with the serjeants and soldiers. Annais watched him pausing here and there to listen. Once he laughed at a jest and seemed genuinely amused. Was that part of the façade, she wondered? Gerbert had always talked to the men too, but in a paternal or avuncular way. Sabin's manner was more brother to brother – it was bound to be so when he was a younger man; however, there was still no doubt as to who held the command.

He did the rounds of the hall and returned to her. Sighing, pushing his free hand through his hair, he said, 'Do you want to make an end of this and retire?'

An end or a beginning? She inclined her head and summoned her women. Her stomach was clamped to her spine.

'I have told the men that, under the circumstances, there will be no bedding ceremony,' he added as he summoned Amalric. 'Although Father Jerome will bless the bed.'

'I do not know if I can sleep in it,' Annais said.

'With me?'

She made a small gesture. 'So much joy and grief has been

heaped upon it that it is like a mountain. It is already so high that I fear I will never reach the top and see what lies beyond.'

He said nothing.

'You think I am being fanciful,' she said.

'Not at all. I was wondering how I would sleep tonight in a bed that is only mine by default. Not well, I suspect.'

Father Jerome arrived with an attendant bearing a casket of holy water and oils. Sabin held out his arm and Annais took it. Soraya picked up the hem of Annais's gown so that it would not trail on the floor and they moved in procession to the foot of the stairs.

Once above, Sabin waited patiently for Father Jerome to perform the blessing rites on the bed and themselves, although Annais could tell from the very stillness of his face that the patience was part of the mask he wore. However, that stillness was a source of strength and she drew on it, attuning her breathing to the slowness of his, even while her heart continued to pound and cold sweat made her palms clammy.

Father Jerome concluded his task, wished them well, and departed the room with his attendant. Sabin followed them to the door, ushering out the women and Amalric. Then he shut out the world and secured the bolt. Once it was done, he wandered the chamber, restless as a dog in new territory. He unlatched his swordbelt and cast it across a chest . . . a chest that was filled with Gerbert's tunics and hose. It was too soon, too painful for Annais to distribute them among the poor or make them into new garments.

'Will you transfer your things to this chamber?' she asked him as she moved to the embrasure. His own coffer was still in the small room he kept above the guardhouse.

'Do you want me to?'

Dusk was falling and a scattering of stars shone in the sky outlined by the open shutters. She inhaled the scents of spicy cooking and dusty heat beginning to cool. A bowl of lemons stood on a side table; picking one up she rubbed her thumb over the porous yellow skin, then pressed her nail beneath the surface. An almost invisible spray shot from the wound and a sharp tang filled the air. 'There is room for them,' she said without looking round.

'That is not what I asked.'

'I would have refused if I objected,' she said. Her nail dug past the pith into the flesh of the fruit, and she felt it yield and burst. The scent grew stronger. How could she want him to when Gerbert had not been dead a week? Sabin's question engendered feelings of guilt and self-loathing. Standing beside him in the chapel, she had longed for nothing more than to lean on him, to put her arms around him and feel his healthy, living flesh. To make the world go away. 'By all means move your things,' she said wearily. 'People will expect to see them. Gerbert always conducted his business from here and it is the seat of the lord's authority.'

He was silent and she did not have to turn around to know that he was grimacing.

'There is not sufficient space in your chamber,' she said.

'I know that. You do not need to convince me, but neither do I have to like this one.' He drew off his tunic, then sat down on the bed to remove his boots. The disrobing went no further than that. Shirt, hose and braies remained.

'Since there are no witnesses and we are not expected to display a bloody bridal sheet on the morrow, there is no need for all the rituals of a wedding night. Besides,' he added wryly, 'I am not sure that I would be capable of performing the deed, even if required.'

'With your reputation?' The words were out before she could bite them back. Turning from the window, she faced him, her face bleached of colour. 'I am sorry. That was unfair of me.'

He gave her a steady look. 'Sometimes a little reputation goes a long way,' he said.

She swallowed. 'But you are still scarcely a washed lamb.'

He conceded the point with a gesture. 'I admit that I was

one of the wilder youths at court, especially after my father died. It was easier to futter and brawl than to think . . . and at court, if you had silver in your hand and on your tongue, and you were the foster son of a prince, then the court whores were accommodating . . . some of the barons' wives too.' His expression became sombre. 'If I used them for my escape and to assuage the rampant lusts of adolescence, then they used me because of my youth and stamina. I developed a reputation when I started reaching for the higher apples on the tree, the ones that were harder to pick and better guarded . . . not out of carnal desire, but for the challenge.'

'Until you were caught.'

'Until Lora died for it, yes,' he said.

'And what of my stepmother? Was she a challenge too?' She waited for him to deny it. It was another blow below the belt, but she wanted to see how he handled it.

He shifted uncomfortably. 'I was a youth of sixteen again,' he said, 'and she was the baron's wife. Old habits die hard when you are pushed up against a wall and threatened with everything that you desire and loathe.' He gave an involuntary shudder. 'Yes, she was a challenge, but it was a lesson in refusal, not seduction.' He looked at her. 'I am not a monk. There have been women since Tel Namir – you would be blind not to know that – but if not abstinence, I have learned restraint.'

Annais absorbed the information without a flicker of emotion. 'What arrangements will you make if our marriage is to be in name only?' she asked. 'What happens when need goes beyond restraint? Do you make a fool of me in my own household, or do you go on discreet "hunting trips" and find yourself a gentle doe or a plump partridge to assuage your hunger?'

'I would hope that before it came to such a pass, our marriage would be one to suit all needs,' he said. 'But if not, then I would do my best not to bring scandal into the household.'

'Let us hope you have more success than of yore.'

He looked bleakly amused. 'Your trust commends you.' He rose from the bed. 'I can sleep on the floor if you wish. It will be no burden.'

'No, I would feel guilty, and if you are telling the truth about your condition, I have nothing to fear, do I?'

He made an open-handed gesture of acknowledgement. 'No,' he said. 'Not at the moment.' Drawing back the sheets, he got into bed, pulled the covers back over and arranged the bolsters at his back.

Annais swallowed. She felt queasy and tired; she could not remember what it was like to have a night of unbroken sleep and not awaken to feelings of dread and grief.

'Come.' Sabin beckoned her with his forefinger. 'I give you my promise I will not touch you. You cannot stand there all night.'

What he said was true, but Annais could not dispel the notion that she was committing some sort of betrayal by joining him. Even though Gerbert had made them swear an oath, he had been doing it for the good of Montabard. She doubted that he would have taken joy in the sight of his wife and Sabin FitzSimon sharing the Montabard family bed. Reluctantly she came and sat on her side of the mattress. She was intensely aware of Sabin's brooding scrutiny and a shiver of apprehension danced down her spine.

He got out of bed, came around to her and, sitting at her side, removed her shoes. She tensed as his fingers explored the lacings of her gown, but having loosened them, he made no attempt to divest her of the garment. Finally, he turned his attention to her veil. His touch was butterfly light as he removed the securing pins and then lifted the gossamer silk from her hair. 'You should loosen your braids,' he said. 'It will lessen the tightness across your brow.'

When she neither spoke, nor sought to push him away, he performed the task himself. Unfastening the gold fillets that secured the ends of the braids, he combed his hands through the heavy deep-brown plaits, unwinding the strands. Annais was wary at first, but he offered no more than the performing of a service. She supposed that he was accustomed to acting the part of lady's maid. Secret assignations without the help of an attendant would call for such skills . . . if of course the woman ever had the time to let down her tresses.

When he had finished, he lifted the bedclothes and tucked her in, then returned to his own side of the bed and lay down. 'Do you want me to leave the lamps burning?' he asked.

Annais shook her head. 'I do not fear the dark,' she said. 'There are far worse things in this world of which to be afraid.' Raising her hand, she wound a tendril of her freed hair around her forefinger. It was sticky to the touch, a little greasy. She could not remember when last she had washed it – such things did not matter when the heart faltered and almost stopped beating. In the space of two short years, she had gone from virgin, to wife, to mother, to widow and back to wife again. It was no use saying that she did not want to dance any more, because the dance went on regardless.

Sabin shrugged his shoulders against the bolsters. 'You have my permission to kick me if I snore,' he said.

From somewhere, Annais found a smile. 'Thank you.' She touched his sleeve. It was safer than touching his hand but still managed to convey her gratitude for the way he had handled matters.

He said nothing else, but leaned over and snuffed out the lamp. She felt him settle against the bolster and heard his breathing become slow and measured. However, she sensed that he was not sleeping; instead, rather like a hound at rest across a door, he was keeping watch. The notion comforted her. She had thought that she too would lie awake all night, but at some point she slept and when she woke to the sound of Guillaume's cry from the antechamber, and one of her women shushing him, the bailey cockerels were crowing and the light through the shutters was grey.

She could tell from the slow rise and fall of his chest that Sabin was asleep, although his limbs were neatly positioned and his slumber appeared controlled rather than relaxed. She suspected that any sudden noise would galvanise him off the bed and put a sword in his hand in less time than it took her to blink. In the glimmer of dawn, she could see the dark edge of stubble surrounding his mouth and edging his jawline. Studying him, Annais felt an ache of tenderness and grief. They had survived their first night together, now all that remained was to cope with all those that followed.

Chapter 22

Harsh light burning down on the inner courtyard caused Strongfist to squint in pain. The prisoners had been brought out for what was supposed to be the mercy of fresh air while the straw of their prison was forked out and changed. After the barely lit dark of their malodorous cell, the beat of the sun was so fierce, so blinding that it was almost like a weapon. Some men were brought to their knees, their shackles clanking and painful tears squeezing between their lids.

The yard was used to exercise horses and a turbaned groom was shovelling up collops of dung. He glanced curiously at the Franks but stayed well away from them as if their presence might contaminate him. The guards, however, patrolled close and fingered their swords, making it clear what would happen if there were trouble.

'Do they truly think we have the strength to overpower them and escape?' said Ernoul of Rethel with a wondering shake of his head. He was Baldwin's young nephew, fair-haired and red-cheeked.

Strongfist shrugged. 'I suppose they cannot afford to take the chance, no matter how remote it might be. If our news is correct and Lord Balak has ridden away to Aleppo, they are bound to be wary. Give them a few more days and they won't be quite so zealous.'

Ernoul nodded agreement and shuffled off to speak with

his uncle. Strongfist began to walk around the perimeter of the yard within the band of shade cast by the walls. The steps he took were bitesize, determined by the length of his chains, but at least he was treading solid ground instead of shuffling through rank straw. As he crossed the gateway, a guard barred his path. Without looking at the man, Strongfist shambled past and began another circuit of the ward.

The sun hammered down and the louse bites in his scalp, his beard and armpits began to itch fearsomely. Strongfist thought of the once despised baths in Jerusalem with longing. Cool water; clean, scrubbed skin; fresh linen underclothing smelling of citrus and sunlight. He plodded the courtyard like an ox yoked to a sesame mill. Round and round. If they were to escape then he must keep his body strong. From the messages that passed, he knew they had perhaps another month to wait, but plans were progressing. It helped that Balak was busy subduing Aleppo and seldom at Kharpurt – although much of his domestic household was lodged within its walls.

Strongfist sat down in a patch of shade to take a rest and leaned his back against the cool, hard stone. From his position, he could see the larger courtyard beyond the scowling guards. A group of heavily swathed women clustered around a well, drawing water and decanting it into clay jars. They too were attended by a guard, although he was slouched on his lance and his posture was bored.

Ernoul joined Strongfist and slumped down, forehead pressed to his upraised knees. After a moment he glanced through the archway at the women. 'They'll be the lowlier members of Balak's harem,' he said. 'You shouldn't stare. If the soldiers see you, they'll pop your bollocks with the blunt end of a spear.'

Strongfist winced and lowered his gaze. 'My lust is for the water,' he said. 'My mouth feels like a cave in the Sinai.' From the corner of his eye, he was aware of some of the women lifting their water jars and, balancing them gracefully on their heads, moving off towards another part of the fortress. The senior women of the harem would inhabit an inner sanctum, away from the prying eyes of all but the most privileged men. Those who came to fill the jars were, as Ernoul said, the secondary wives and the slaves.

It was with enormous relief that he saw two soldiers bringing one of the filled jars towards them. From their treatment thus far, it was plain that Balak intended them to suffer but not enough to sicken and die. It would be foolish of him to lose his treasure or treat it in such a way that he incurred the wrath of all Christendom.

The prisoners were given a dipper of water each – enough to dull the edge of their thirst without quenching it – and then they were lined up to be returned to their cell. This time they were taken by a different route that traversed the main courtyard. A couple of women were still drawing water from the well and they kept their backs turned and their faces hidden. As Strongfist shambled past a tower opening, the Saracen commander of the garrison emerged, a shrouded woman at his side. He stopped to wait for the prisoners to pass, his expression fastidious and filled with contempt. Strongfist glanced at him in passing and at the woman yet more fleetingly, but what he saw stopped him in his tracks. The woman's dark blue eyes widened, then lowered and she drew back into her companion's shadow. The Saracen's hand hovered over his scabbard.

Ernoul gave Strongfist a shove from behind that pitched him against the man in front. Recovering the power of motion, if not his wits, Strongfist stumbled forwards, propelled by another hard push from Ernoul.

The Saracen did not follow, except with his eyes, which remained narrowed until the chain of prisoners had vanished through a small doorway further along the tower.

'Why did you stop?' Ernoul demanded as they were thrust back into their cell. His voice was pitched high with agitation. 'You've called attention to yourself now.'

Strongfist collapsed in the thick, fresh straw. 'The woman . . .' he said in a parched voice. 'The woman he had is my wife.'

'What?' Ernoul stared in disbelief. 'Are you sun-touched? How could you tell that it was even a woman under all those layers?'

'I did not need to see every part of her. I would recognise her eyes anywhere.' Strongfist flushed beneath the younger man's scorn. The raised voice had brought the others gathering around.

'That's foolish!' Ernoul scoffed. 'What would your wife be doing in the harem of a man like Balak?' He looked round for approbation and received it.

'I am telling you, it was her!' Strongfist snarled. 'As to what she is doing here—' He broke off and glared at the ring of grinning faces. 'She absconded with a silk merchant and I thought it no one's business but mine.'

That wiped away most of the smiles. Those who thought it cause for jest were nudged by their neighbours, or hid their mirth behind their hands. It wasn't comfortable to think about what one's own wife might be doing in one's absence.

'So you truly think she is here?' Baldwin looked dubious.

'I know it, sire. And she knows that I know.'

The King narrowed his eyes and rubbed his beard.

'It is the truth,' Strongfist said. 'What has happened to bring her here, I know not, but I am neither mistaken nor out of my wits. I would be glad never to see the bitch again.' Wounds had torn open that he thought healed and he could almost feel the sting of salt in them.

'Do you think she would help us?'

Strongfist shrugged. 'She will help herself,' he said bitterly. 'If she desires to be free of Kharpurt then she will give us her aid. If she is content with her lot and whatever lover is currently spreading her legs, then she will not hesitate to betray us. Use her,' he said, 'but do not trust her.'

The men shuffled and muttered, no one knowing what to

say. One by one, they drifted away until only Baldwin and Ernoul remained.

The King gripped Strongfist's shoulder. 'I am sorry,' he said. 'If indeed it is true, and the woman is your wife, then it is a difficult burden you bear.'

'My back is broad,' Strongfist said with an unconvincing smile. 'And heavier loads are carried by others. A fickle wife is nothing, save to my pride.' He set his jaw, determined to show as little emotion as possible now that he was over the first shock. But inside both heart and pride were bleeding.

Annais knelt before the open coffer in the bedchamber and lifted out the shirts and braies that had belonged to Gerbert. It was almost six weeks since he had died, and she had made herself attend to the task of clearing the belongings that could be put to better use than gathering dust and entangling her in painful memories. Durand and Gerbert had been of a similar breadth across the shoulders. Annais would not notice him wearing Gerbert's shirts and braies, for they were underclothes. Decisively, she pressed them on Soraya, and when the young woman both thanked her and protested at the generosity, Annais waved her hand in negation.

'No, take them, with my blessing. They would drown Sabin . . . and in truth I would rather start afresh than clothe him in garments that Gerbert has worn. He deserves better—' She broke off and buried her head in the coffer again. She could imagine Sabin's expression should she offer him Gerbert's castoffs. The line they trod was already as sharp as a knife-blade.

Two pairs of chausses followed. The shoes went into the alms pile. The rich, fur-lined cloak was set aside for Guillaume's future, as were the gilded belts and the court dalmatic of embroidered silk. Annais decided to make some tunics for the child out of the best of his father's gowns. She returned what she was going to keep to the chest and had it removed to the women's chamber, leaving an empty place where it had stood. Next to that place was the coffer containing Gerbert's mail hauberk, oiled and stored in waxed leather, his helm, his sword, his spurs. That had to stay, for the contents were of high value and part of Guillaume's inheritance. As yet Sabin's equipment remained in his own room and he spent as little time as possible in this chamber. If he had to hold an audience, he would do it in the hall, or the guardroom, depending on the circumstances. He left the domain of the solar and bedchamber to her and her women. When they shared the great bed at night, he kept to his own side and was distantly courteous. Often he would wait until she was asleep before he came to bed. Frequently he did not sleep there at all, using the excuse of his duties to keep him up late, and bedding down in his former room so as not to disturb her. Or else he would take the men on patrol and stay away for a couple of nights.

Her task finished, Annais rose from her heels and dusted her hands. He was giving her time to grieve for Gerbert and, in a way, he was right, but the 'marriage in name only' was putting considerable strain on both of them. He was treating her not as his wife, but with the respect and distance owed to her as Gerbert's widow. Her gaze fell on the bed. It would have to end, she thought, for both their sakes, and sooner rather than later. The thought made her shiver. What would it be like to take Sabin's weight in the act of procreation? To taste and touch him? Would it be different to her experience with Gerbert? Flustered at her own thoughts, she pressed her hands to her face and turned away from the bed. Perhaps she would have to stop thinking as Gerbert's widow too.

Soraya was gazing at her with concern and knowing in her great dark eyes. Her arms were piled with Gerbert's clothes. 'Is there something wrong, my lady?'

Annais gave a shaken laugh. 'No,' she said, and then, 'Yes.' She went to the window and looked out on the courtyard. 'I don't know what to do.'

'You only think that, my lady,' Soraya said in her gentle voice. 'It will come to you.'

Annais screwed up her face. 'You are optimistic.'

The young woman looked at her earnestly. 'I was once in your position – worse, in fact, for the man who took me under his wing was my enemy and my husband was killed by his companions. I told myself that I had to take each day – each moment – as it came . . . not look forward and not look back.'

'It worked?'

'Not always, but enough . . .' Soraya jutted her chin in the direction of the wall. 'That bed is a prison for both of you. You need to spring the lock before you can be free.'

'And how am I to find the key?'

Soraya moved her shoulders. 'That I cannot tell you, my lady . . . but surely you will find your own way.'

Annais gazed out across the courtyard. Letice had taken Guillaume for a carry around the castle in order to give Annais a moment's peace. At almost eight months old, he had the frightening combination of being curious about everything coupled with the ability to crawl faster than an ant up the side of a honeypot.

Now she watched Letice cross the space in front of the hall and, lifting the baby high on her arm, point. Guillaume bounced up and down and pointed too. An instant later Sabin strode into Annais's line of vision and she realised that the patrol must have returned. He was still clad in his mail but had stripped off his helm and coif and given them to Amalric. Hoisting Guillaume out of Letice's arms by a fistful of linen smock, Sabin swung the infant aloft and perched him on his shoulders. Guillaume squealed in delight and tangled his fists in Sabin's hair for purchase. Sabin gave a mock wince and said something to Letice that made her nod and laugh.

Annais felt a melting tenderness at her core, tinged with a degree of sadness. It should be Gerbert holding his son like that, not the slender, wiry man who stood surrogate in

Gerbert's place. She would weave memories and stories of his father for the child, but those memories would hold Sabin's features.

'Have a tub prepared,' she told Soraya. 'Lord Sabin will want to bathe.'

The maid took the pile of clothes to her coffer, then set about her task. Two younger women slid aside a thick curtain and drew out a large wooden bathtub, banded with oiled iron hoops, and brought towels made of heavy, sun-bleached cotton from a deep chest. Annais removed the chatelaine's keys from her belt and unlocked the chest containing the oil and candles. Here too was stored soap made from olive oil and scented with essence of lemon. Back in England, the only soap available was made from mutton fat, and while it certainly performed the task for which it was intended, the smell was less than delightful.

She filled a smaller flagon from the large wine pitcher in the antechamber before sending a maid to bring bread, cheese and figs, and another to fetch clean garments.

From the top of the stairs, she heard the girls giggle and Sabin's voice speaking with breathless good humour. Then, stooping under the door arch, he entered the room, Guillaume still perched triumphantly on his shoulders. The baby was leaning over now and sucking experimentally on a fistful of Sabin's hair. Sabin reached up and swung his burden round, tossed and caught him, and presented him, squealing with delight, to his mother.

'He is going to be a skilled horseman one day,' he said, 'providing he learns not to pull too hard on the reins.' Grimacing, he rubbed the top of his head, then wiped his slimy hand on his surcoat.

Annais laughed and shifted Guillaume to her hip. 'I suppose it depends on the quality of his mount too,' she said.

'Oh, there's no doubt in the least about that.' Sabin responded to her tone in a similar vein. In the light from the window, his eyes were vivid amber, ringed at the pupil with green. 'This one's a bargain . . . depending on what you are seeking, of course.'

There was a moment's hesitation. Annais's loins were heavy, as if the force of his stare had pierced to her vitals. 'I have heard that you should never look a gift horse in the mouth,' she said.

His lips twitched and he inclined his head at her riposte. 'Or anywhere else,' he said. 'For the Good Lord knows what you might find.' He unlatched and discarded his swordbelt and scabbard, following them with his surcoat.

A procession of attendants arrived bearing pails of hot and cold water from the kitchen cauldrons and set about filling the tub. Annais handed Guillaume to Soraya and, with her heart in her mouth, came to help Sabin unarm. The air was so laden with steam and tension that she found it difficult to breathe.

'The patrol went well?' she asked as he bent over and she tugged the hauberk over his head. The greased rings slipped against her fingers and the weight of it dragged her arms down.

'Yes . . . that is, there were no signs of raids or encroachments.' Sabin took the hauberk from her and draped it across the top of Gerbert's coffer. She saw him pause as he noticed the bare wall where the clothing chest had stood. When he turned from the task, his brows were raised.

'I have begun sorting in your absence,' she said, and knew that her face was burning.

Again he measured her with a glance, but said nothing before breaking the eye contact to remove his gambeson. The rest of his clothes followed. Annais busied herself sorting them out, casting the shirt and braies into a rush-work laundry basket, setting the tunic and hose aside to be aired and brushed. By the time she had finished, Sabin was safely in the tub and swilling himself with the herb-scented water.

She handed him the dish of soap and the cloth. She dipped

a pitcher in one of the spare pails of mixed hot and cold water and tipped it smartly over his head. The sound of his splutter made her smile and succeeded in dissipating some of the tension building within her.

'I hope you don't bathe guests in such a wise,' he gasped.

'At Coldingham I was taught perfectly well how to bathe guests,' she said pertly. 'Since it was an ancient and honoured custom, the Prioress made sure that all the secular girls in her care knew what to do.'

'Surely she didn't encourage you to drown them and get soap in their eyes!'

'You are exaggerating. It's your own fault. Sit still . . . and don't look gift horses in the mouth.' She lathered his hair and sluiced him again. Guillaume had been set on the floor by the maid, and he crawled over to the tub and pulled himself up on its wooden side where he proceeded to giggle at his stepfather and point. Sabin threatened him with a soapy fist, which only made Guillaume squeal the louder.

'I yield,' Sabin declared. 'How am I ever to discipline either of you when you give me your tongue and he laughs in my face?'

Treacherous pleasure, akin to happiness, washed over Annais. This was the first occasion since their marriage that there had been any form of lightness or banter. That it was a fragile mood, she knew well, but the fact that it was present at all could only be a good omen. Even the environs of the room were no threat: the oppressive presence of the bed was negated by the company of the servants and the child. It was a public arena, not a tortured private one.

'I'm sure you will think of a way.' Annais handed him a dry wash cloth to press against his face. A white scar snaked along the tanned line of his forearm. She followed it down to his splayed fingers, thin and hard, then hastily averted her gaze and fetched one of the large cotton towels. Sabin took it from her and stepped from the tub. She busied herself finding him fresh raiment and by the time she returned to him, Sabin had tucked the towel around his hips and padded away from the tub. He poured himself a cup of wine and tore a chunk off the bread. Guillaume was industriously crawling towards him. Sabin scooped him up and broke off a piece of crust for the infant to gnaw.

Annais watched with wonder. 'Most men would run a mile from a baby, let alone do as you are doing,' she said.

Sabin's lips curved sheepishly. 'I was seven years old when my youngest half-brother was born – twice that age when my stepmother birthed the children of her second husband. Before I left for King Henry's court, I had plenty of time to grow accustomed to small brats.'

'Do you ever think of them?' She lifted Guillaume out of his arms in exchange for the shirt and braies.

'Of course I do. I may have left my old life behind but the memories still cross the divide. I wrote to Simon only last month when—' He broke off and changed what he had been going to say. '—and told him that I was making a life here and not to look for me on returning pilgrim ships. Oh, and I sent Helisende that bolt of gold silk I promised her.' Between mouthfuls of bread and swallows of wine, he donned the garments.

'You should move your baggage here,' she said. 'There is room now and it would be more convenient for all.'

He looked at her thoughtfully and she wondered if her cheeks were as red as they felt. It was stupid to feel as if she were importuning him, for the suggestion was eminently practical.

'I know you still need somewhere for your own solitude—'

'My monk's cell,' he interrupted with a pained smile.

Now her face was indeed burning but she was determined to finish. '—but surely you can keep your clothes here.'

Behind them came the noise and slosh of the bathtub being emptied. Sabin donned the hose that the maid had brought, an indoor tunic of soft indigo-dyed linen and a narrow leather belt. 'Why not?' he said, and turned his attention to Amalric who had arrived with the message that the constable and the steward were waiting in the hall to make their report. 'We'll talk later.' He kissed Annais's cheek, surrounding her with the fragrance of citrus and olive, and left the room.

She pressed her hand to her face, and frowned, for she had not missed the way he glanced at the bed. That she thought, was the obstacle. Remove it, and matters would ease considerably. But it was also a symbol of the continuity and power of the lords of Montabard and for that reason alone it had to remain. One day it would be Guillaume's and the castle with it. For now it was held in trust . . . and because of that obligation, it was a shackle.

Sabin dealt swiftly with the outstanding business presented by his steward and constable. He read such letters as had arrived in his absence and replied to the messengers when the words required were verbal. One such courier had ridden in earlier that day, a slim, yellow-haired Armenian with a pox-scarred face. His news was swift and simple. The river was low, Balak was absent, struggling with his recalcitrant subjects in Aleppo, and an attempt was to be made to rescue the King.

'I will come,' Sabin said without hesitation, although inwardly he grimaced. Montabard was safe enough to be left, he judged, but the news came when he needed a little personal leeway.

Business finished, he did not return to the solar and Annais, but, refusing company, turned a circuit of the wall walk. His first impulse when he had ridden out on patrol had been to go to a certain house in one of the villages and ease his need with one of the women there, but he had curbed the urge. Even if the tale did not get back to Annais, it would have shown a lack of respect for his wife among the soldiers. Onan's sin was somewhat less pleasurable, and carried a penalty when confessed, but a lesser one than adultery, and could be accomplished almost as swiftly as voiding the bladder.

Still, that temporary release might as well not have existed when he had walked into the bedchamber and set eyes upon Annais with her wide, doe-brown gaze, slightly parted lips and swift breathing. Once he would have acted decisively upon such signs, but now he was more circumspect. He had noticed how she had turned away rather than see him naked, and her reaction could be as much about uncertainty and fear as it was about desire. He scooped his hands through his hair and laughed at himself. Doubtless her responses were akin to his and the only thing to do to find out for sure was to grasp the rose by the thorns and find out if the deed was worth the boldness. There was little opportunity to procrastinate. The messenger from Kharpurt had made sure of that.

Reaching the end of the wall walk, he paused to watch the sun setting on the seaward side of the hills, a great orange orb melting into a copper and violet sky. In the dusk, he descended the stairs and made his way to the hall. The trestles were being set out for the evening meal and attendants were bringing piles of flat bread from the kitchens and flagons of wine. He climbed the outer staircase to the solar and found the women about their usual duties of spinning and weaving. Guillaume was napping in his cradle and there was no sign of Annais.

Soraya came to him and gave him an eloquent look from her kohl-lined eyes. 'My lady said that she had gone to seek you out . . . perchance you have missed each other in passing.'

Sabin smiled at the irony of the remark. 'Perchance, yes,' he said.

'Will you stay and wait for her?'

'No.' His reply was swift. 'I want a word alone . . . and I am too restless this night to sit – attractive though the surroundings might be.'

Sabin went back out and, as he dropped the curtain behind him, the women exchanged glances. One or two sighed rather nostalgically. There was a debate as to whether the women should leave the chamber in order to give the couple privacy later. Letice thought it an excellent idea, but it was the gentler Soraya who spoke out.

'No, let it be,' she said. 'I doubt they will need these rooms this side of dawn.'

Sabin crossed the compound and, at the gatehouse, paused to speak with the guards who were preparing to change the watch. Then, kindling a brand from the stack in the corner, he climbed the stairs to his quarters, intent on preparing his belongings to be brought to the rooms above the hall.

His chamber door was shut. He hesitated before it, drew a breath, and set his hand to the latch.

Annais was sitting on his bed, her hands folded in her lap and her posture composed, although he could tell straight away from her expression that it was artifice.

'You are not surprised to see me?' she said.

'When I did not find you in the women's chambers and I knew you were not in the hall, I suspected this is where you were.' He set the torch in a bracket beside the door and came further into the room. 'I was going to give the order to move my belongings across the ward.'

She watched him with wide, dark eyes and moistened her lips. 'But not yet,' she said. 'Not at this moment.'

He smiled at her. 'It can wait a while,' he said. 'Certainly longer than a moment.'

She rose from the bed leaving a small indentation on the tightly drawn coverlet. 'Your monk's cell,' she said with an uncertain gesture as she went to the flagon and cups standing on the coffer beneath the arrow-slit. He followed her and took her elbow before she could pour the wine.

'Do you really want a drink, or is it a matter of form?' he asked.

Annais faced him. A rapid pulse beat in her throat. 'You said earlier that you wanted to talk,' she said hoarsely.

'That was earlier.' Sabin's voice was equally constricted. 'What I want now—' He broke off to run his finger from her temple to her throat. 'Well, you must know, or you would not be here now, for I do not think that you have come with the intention of talking either.'

They stared at each other, holding back for a final instant. Then she stepped against him and coiled her arms around his neck and his mouth sought hers. The first kiss was a wild plunder and Sabin knew that the fierceness could not be sustained at this level for more than a few minutes. A part of him did not care. A part of him desired the pounding, immolating heat of a hard, fast coupling, but he held back, leashing himself.

Taking his mouth from hers, he buried his face in the soft warm flesh of her neck. Her rapid breathing sawed against his ear and she clung to him tightly. He drew her with him to the bed. 'This certainly isn't a monk's cell now,' he said hoarsely, 'and nor is the kind of worship about to be offered.'

She gazed up at him, her eyes as dark as a doe's. 'Should you not extinguish the light?' she asked.

He glanced at the oil lamp on the coffer and then at the torch, flaring smokily in its socket. 'Do you want me to?'

'I . . . Gerbert didn't like—' she broke off. 'I am sorry. I do not want to invite his ghost in here too.'

'You won't,' Sabin said, although he grimaced inwardly. 'Let the light remain.' He could imagine Gerbert's staid character preferring that the lamps be extinguished. Coupling was a duty as well as a pleasure, and it was easier to believe in the duty if the act was conducted without too much sensuality.

As he had once done before on their wedding night, Sabin unpinned Annais's wimple and unbound her hair, but this time he ran his fingers through the strands with slow beguilement and this time it was soft beneath his touch and silky with recent washing. This as much as anything revealed to him that the degree of her mourning had changed since their first night together. He unfastened the side lacings of her gown and slipped his hands inside, to the warmer layer of her chemise. Through the fine cotton, he felt the arch of her rib cage and the sleek curve of her breasts. She made soft, needful sounds in her throat as Sabin rubbed fabric against flesh and her nipples hardened beneath his coaxing.

It was like playing a tune, he thought; she was his harp, and he the caller of the notes. Slowly, tenderly, ruthlessly, he built the melody and watched the pleasure-pain flash across her face, felt the clutching of his fingers as he composed another strand, heard the catch of her breath. Then he too was caught in the spell he had woven; he could not detach himself from the song, but found mind and body blending with the rising notes of the paean.

Between kissing and fondling, sucking and stroking, they removed each layer until skin encountered skin. Hot, damp, salty with need and need controlled. She was sobbing now, and would have bitten her lip at the exquisite sensations being drawn from her body, save that Sabin was biting them instead: small, capturing nibbles that stole her breath and spoke of a ravening hunger barely held in check. The notion of being overtaken by that full feeding frenzy filled her with lust and joy and just a hint of fear. She bit him in return, and arched against him, watching his hands smooth their alchemy on her wet body, the tips of his dark hair trembling with sweat in tune to his heartbeat. She parted her thighs and felt his rigid flesh like a brand against her thigh, then higher, twice seeking, and on a final adjustment, sheathing with a slow burn that made her cry aloud.

He raised above her, braced on his forearms. 'Did I hurt you?' he panted. His eyes were the golden green of a lion's, the pupils wide and dark. Against her abdomen, she could feel him breathing in and out.

'No,' she swallowed, shaking her head, raising her hand to his hair then letting it fall to his throat, to the grooves of muscle in his shoulders. Her voice dropped to a whispered, almost tearful laugh. 'No, but in God's name I am swept away. I do not know how I will survive.'

He smiled, and the slow, triumphant sleepiness melted her

loins so that her flesh rippled around his. 'You might not,' he said softly, 'and neither may I, but we should strike out for shore all the same.' He dipped his head and sealed his lips upon hers, at the same time thrusting forward. Annais closed her eyes and clasped her arms around him. At first, she held back, clinging to the rock of what had been familiar with Gerbert, but although the movements were similar, they were not the same and her hold began to slacken. She dug her nails into his skin as the surge dragged her into the tumult. He kissed her, sharing breath as they shared bodies, and his tongue moved in counterpoint with his hips. Annais moaned in her throat. She thought that she had known and understood lust, but now realised that she knew nothing.

'Wait!' she gasped. 'I cannot . . . I . . . Oh Jesu!' The river had brought her to the sea and, as she was hurled into the surf, the seventh wave struck. Rigid, she shuddered in the grip of white-hot pulses of sensation, and in the midst of the wildness, felt him join her and, with his release, return to her some semblance of familiarity.

There was a long moment of silence while the shipwrecked survivors accumulated their scattered senses. He kissed her throat, her mouth, her breasts. She ran her hands down his narrow flanks, over his taut buttocks to the small of his back and smiled to feel him involuntarily twitch and thrust forward again. Within her she felt a sleepy throb like the slow blink of an eye.

'Now I understand why you are considered dangerous,' she murmured.

'No more so than any man with half the wit God gave.' He nibbled her earlobe. 'Besides, you have small room to talk. One look and the marrow melts from my bones. You do not know how difficult it was . . .'

'What was?' Raising her hand, she pushed the hair from his eyes and traced the line of his eyebrows with her forefinger.

'To hold back, to wait until you were ready . . . when all I wanted to do was plunge headlong to my own release.'

Her finger continued a tactile study of his features. Yes, she thought, that was indeed the danger. From what she had heard other women tell of their marital duty, and from her own experience with Gerbert, waiting was not something that most men thought about. Their pleasure was their wife's duty.

'And I have waited a long time,' he said softly.

'Since Scotland? Do not tell me.' She gave him a disbelieving stare.

She felt his quiver of amusement inside her own body. 'In Scotland you were a prim little nun and even if I was wayward, I had recently been taught some hard lessons. Yes, I thought about you then, but only when I was bored or out of sorts. You were like an irritation that couldn't be scratched – as doubtless I was an irritation to you.'

Annais sniffed. 'Hah! Indeed you were. Even if you did keep your distance, you gave me small cause to trust you . . . especially after what happened at Tel Namir.'

'You can flay me no more than I have already flayed myself,' he said, sobering.

She shook her head. 'I would be foolish to belabour you with that now. It is in the past . . .' Her fingers descended to his chest hair and she tugged gently on the wiry strands. 'So tell me, my lord, how long have you waited? When did irritation become desire?'

He narrowed his eyes and pondered. 'When I saw you with a knife in your hand on board our ship . . . when you played your harp in Fergus's garden in Jerusalem . . . when you hung that icon on your wall at Tel Namir . . . but they were only flashes. It didn't become a constant ache until you married Gerbert.' He gave a wry smile. 'I thought about riding away, but I was pledged to him for a year and a day . . . and when that time had passed, I found I could manage the ache of being in your presence better than the desolation of being out of it.'

Annais blinked on silly tears. Dangerous indeed, she thought. Few women were vouchsafed such declarations of devotion – if they were true, of course, and not just blandishments. After the life he had led at Henry's court, she supposed that he was accustomed to telling women what they wanted to hear. But then he had no reason to lie to her, and she had witnessed his heroic forbearance these last few weeks. Bringing her face down to his, she kissed him, making the salute serve where words would not. He returned the embrace, and for a while they preened and intertwined like courting swans. The soft stroking fanned the embers of what had gone before and they made love again, slowly this time, with pauses for detailed exploration of fingers, and palms, wrists, elbows, all the small places that had been overlooked in the drowning need of that first time. She laughed and squirmed when he touched a particularly ticklish place, and then gasped when he used the same feather touch elsewhere. The excitement built by gradual but inexorable degrees. Sabin chuckled at her frustration as she parted her legs and rubbed her thigh along his flanks. He held back, teasing, then rolled her over so that she was on top of him, sought and thrust. The look of astonishment, almost worry on her face told him that she and Gerbert had never adopted this particular position . . . but then Sabin was almost certain that Gerbert had never had a court whore or a Jerusalem courtesan teach him the enticing variations that lent spice to bedsport.

'So,' he said with a grin. 'Do as you will.' He slipped his hands to the warm, smooth flesh of her buttocks. 'Treat me gently, and I promise to be brave in my suffering.'

She gave a breathless laugh. 'Do I have to confess this to Father Jerome?'

He encouraged her to rise and ease down. 'Only if you are accustomed to confessing what you do abed. Besides, with the souls of a garrison of soldiers in his care, he'll have heard it all and more.'

She pursed her lips and contemplated. Suddenly a gleam entered her eyes. 'So if I do this it is not a sin?'

'No,' Sabin said with a grin.

'And this . . . and this?'

He caught his breath. 'Only if you stop,' he managed in a congested voice.

'I have to leave soon,' Sabin said regretfully. The sky had darkened from dusk to the colour of blue-black damask silk, salted with stars and a sickle moon. He watched it through the open shutters and ran his hands through Annais's loose hair. The oil lamp had gone out, leaving them only the light from the window, translucent as fine stained glass.

'Do you mean from this bed, or from Montabard?' she murmured sleepily.

'Oh, not from the bed until dawn, and then only to put in an appearance for propriety's sake.'

'I thought you did not care for propriety.'

'That was before I became a sober married man.' He smiled and twined a tendril of her hair around his forefinger.

'So you mean from Montabard.' Her tone sharpened as she emerged from the haze of wellbeing.

'A messenger came from the Armenians tonight. They are preparing the assault on Kharpurt—'

'Was there any news of my father?' She rose on her elbow.

He took her hand and kissed her fingers. 'I wish I could tell you yes, but the messenger did not know the names of those with the King, save for his nephew Ernoul. I would say it is very possible – you know we searched the dead after the battle and he was not among them – but I do not want to raise your hopes.' He meshed his fingers through hers. 'I will get him out if at all possible.'

'But be careful what you risk.' Suddenly her face was stricken. 'I would not lose you too.'

He had been going to make a jest about his nature and taking risks, but one look at her face stilled his tongue. 'I will do my best to stay alive,' he said, stroking her hair.

She moved closer to him, pressing her thigh against his, her heart filled with dread. 'I understand that you must go . . .

that if you have a prize falcon, you do not clip its wings, but fling it from your wrist into the sky. I am trusting you to return to me. Do not destroy that trust.'

He did not swear that he would return, for only God had that power. Nor was he so sure that she should trust him. He closed his eyes against the spectre of a raw November night and a girl called Lora. She had trusted him to destruction too. This was different. He would make it so. Gathering her in his arms, pressing his lips against the pulse in her throat, he murmured soft love words and willed the night to last for ever.

Chapter 23

The walls of Kharpurt rose out of the heat-haze like a castle in a troubadour's lay. Sabin swallowed against the tension cording his throat, for what they were about to attempt also belonged in the realms of troubadour fantasy. He wore a voluminous robe of coarse brown fabric that amply concealed his sword. A fortnight's growth of beard darkened his chin and a colourful felt hood covered his head. Accustomed to riding a spirited Nicaean stallion, he was now trying to adjust to a small grey donkey. Ahead of him, Gabriel straddled a bay mule, playing the master to Sabin's servant. They were going to enter Kharpurt on the pretext of seeking an audience with the captain of the garrison regarding permission to trade. Behind them on the track lumbered an ox cart filled with carded fleeces and goatskins. The driver was a small, tough man in middle age with a youth at his side and two heavily swathed womenfolk in the back of the cart. Behind again were two priests. All the usual traffic of daily life at Kharpurt, which was an administrative centre as well as a fortress.

Sabin's hands perspired on the donkey's rope bridle as the guards inspected the two farmers in front of him and Gabriel before allowing them through the shadow of the gateway and into the fortress. Gabriel drew rein before the soldiers and Sabin halted a little behind him, eyes downcast, shoulders hunched in a servile manner.

'Permission to trade in what?' one of the guards queried as Gabriel made his request.

'My brother makes jewellery in gold and silver and while he toils in the souks and bazaars, I bring his custom to places further afield.' Gabriel flapped back the skin covering a pannier on the mule's side and produced an ornate silver belt buckle.

The guard took and examined it. He rubbed a covetous thumb over the intricate surface.

'Keep it,' Gabriel said with an ingratiating smile. The soldier closed his fist over the silverwork and gestured them to enter. Passing into shadow beneath the iron teeth of the portcullis, Sabin suppressed a shiver.

The main courtyard was bustling. As well as Gabriel's silvertrader and servant, several petitioners had gathered, hoping to see the garrison commander, and there were sundry itinerant craftsmen passing through the fortress on their way elsewhere.

Sabin tethered the mule and donkey to the brass wall ring and sat down beside them to wait while Gabriel hefted the pannier of silverware by a thick leather strap and entered the fortress.

As Strongfist had done a few weeks since, Sabin watched the women come to the well and fill their stone jars. His gaze rested on them briefly then perused the rest of the compound, noting where the fighting men were. He reached into his tunic as if to scratch a louse bite, and felt for the reassurance of his sword. His heart was thundering, his mouth dry.

Another man entered the compound with two young falcons in a wicker cage. An imperceptible forefinger signalled to Sabin, who rubbed his eyes. The falcon-seller entered the fortress, followed by a well-dressed Armenian. The latter's servant strolled over to gossip with Sabin and drew a short knife to pare his nails.

'Five,' said Sabin to the man who was named Pieter and was as skilled with a knife as a fishwife. 'But only two who look as if they'll put up a fight. And none with bows.'

'Reasonable odds,' Pieter said, adding, with a swift glance from under his brows, 'Gregor's here.' Another servant joined them, his gaze swiftly assessing the opposition as Sabin's had done.

From the corner of his eye, Sabin saw two guards move towards them. He tensed and the hilt of his sword bumped against his pounding ribs. With a burst of relief, he realised that the soldiers had no interest in the three 'servants', but were moving to flank an old man and a youth who had emerged from another courtyard bearing bowls of bread and fruit. The group fell into step and disappeared into a small, dark archway at the end of the wall.

'Ah,' said Gregor, a wealth of eloquence in the word.

Sabin rose to his feet and stretched. He took a few paces as if easing cramp and walked closer to one of the remaining guards. Gregor sidled to the mule's other pannier and rested his hand along its top. The tension was palpable, as the seconds seemed to last for minutes and the minutes for hours. Then they heard what they had been waiting for: a cry from within the fortress and a triumphant roar of command. Gregor's hand emerged from the pannier with a loaded crossbow. He sighted and shot and the guards were down to two. Sabin launched himself at his chosen man, dodged beneath the tardily raised lance, wrenched it into his own hands and used it. Pieter wrestled the third guard to the ground and used his short knife to slit the man's throat.

Someone was blowing frantically on a horn to summon help. Gregor, Pieter and Sabin sprinted to the archway at the end of the wall and plunged from broad sunlight to the dimly lit head of a twisting staircase. Sabin cast off the enveloping robe and drew his sword. Gregor descended the stairs first, knife in one hand, sword in the other.

Around the first turn, there was nothing but more steps descending, gritty and narrow. Sabin glanced over his shoulder towards the light of the courtyard, but as yet there was no pursuit. Around the second turn and Gregor suddenly raised his voice and yelled a warning. A guard came running up the stairs from the darkness beneath them and Gregor's sword swiped. The tip of the steel rang against the wall, but the blade connected and the man screamed and fell. Another guard following hard on his heels tried to back and run, lost his footing and tumbled down the stairs, becoming wedged at the next turn. Gregor pounced upon him, seized his head, jerked with the knife and stepped over his shuddering body. Sounds of raised voices and a scuffle caused the three men to quicken their pace. The stairs turned again and opened into a dimly lit anteroom with two barred doors at its end. One chamber was open and the old man who had been carrying the food lay dying across the threshold, his blood soaking into the flat loaves of bread.

Within the room someone was retching and choking. Sabin rushed forward and saw Joscelin, lord of Edessa, throttling his guard with the chain of his manacles. A second guard was slumped against the cell wall, run through by his own lance. There was a sound like the snap of a thick, dry branch and the Saracen dropped, a dark patch flooding the front of his breeches as his bladder relaxed.

'Never underestimate the wolf, even when he is chained!' Joscelin snarled at the corpse and kicked it. He glared at the men standing in the doorway. The other knights who shared his cell crowded at his shoulders, ready to fight.

'My lord.' Gregor went down on one knee, swiftly followed by Sabin and Pieter. 'My lord, we have come to free you.' 'Hah, and about time!' Joscelin's voice was a roused snarl. 'Get me out of these things.' He thrust out his manacled wrists. Pieter produced a short axe from his belt, and Gregor a spare sword. Within moments, the lord of Edessa was free, armed and ready for a fight.

Sabin stooped to the strangled guard and prised the ring of keys from the man's fingers. Striding to the other door, he sought to unlock it. Behind him Saracen reinforcements pounded down the stairs, intent on foiling the escape. Joscelin was waiting for them with a bared sword and a store of bitterness. One of his knights had the fallen guard's scimitar, the other a lance.

Trying to blot out the clash and swipe of weapons, knowing that at any moment he might feel a blade at his back, Sabin thrust the next key in the line into the lock and grated it round. 'My liege, your rescue has come!' he bellowed at the top of his lungs, lest Baldwin take it into his head to use his chains as Joscelin had done. Setting his shoulder to the door Sabin barged it open and stumbled into a fetid-smelling cell. His eyes widened upon the hollow-eyed, gaunt-faced men staring back at him. For a moment he recognised none of them for, when last seen, they had been well-fleshed warriors, richly clad for a day's hunting. The same garments clothed them now, the brave hues now as filthy and discoloured as beggars' rags. After an instant of shock, Sabin rallied. 'My liege.' He did not go down on one knee and bow his head. There wasn't time with a full-blown battle raging at his back.

One of Joscelin's knights arrived with the axe and, seizing it, Baldwin set about springing himself and his men. Sparing a rapid glance around, Sabin sought and found Strongfist among the gathering, thin as a cadaver, but his eyes burning with life beneath the craggy brows. Heartened, Sabin plunged out of the cell and joined the fight, followed moments later by the freed prisoners. It was bloody and grim, but brief . . . and this time, to balance the battle on the banks of the Euphrates, the Franks were victorious.

Gaining the courtyard, Sabin discovered it strewn with the bodies of the garrison. The two 'priests' of earlier were laughing and slapping each other, their swords reddened to the hilts. A grinning Gabriel strode up to Sabin and punched his shoulder. 'Kharpurt is ours, let no man doubt it!' He shook an exultant fist. 'Not a Saracen left alive in the place. This is a spear up the arse for Balak!'

Sabin blotted his perspiring brow on the back of his wrist, and having wiped his sword, sheathed it. 'What of their commander?' He had known that there would be little mercy shown, but it was unusual to massacre every last soldier, especially if rich ransoms were to be gained.

'Ah, that was none of our doing.' Gabriel's smile broadened, but behind it lay unease. 'He was murdered in his bed by one of the Frankish slave women from the harem . . .'

Strongfist looked at the heap of chains that had so recently dragged him down and now lay at his feet like a shed snakeskin. He rubbed his chafed red wrists. 'I had begun to think that I was doomed to die in this place,' he said. 'Keeping hope alive on promises is not always easy.'

'We had to wait for the meltwaters to subside and the river to reach its lowest ebb,' Sabin said. 'And for Balak's attention to be elsewhere.' He gazed around the cell and could not suppress a shudder. 'I would have run mad within a week.'

'Some of us almost did,' Strongfist said wryly. 'But those with less imagination acted like that donkey to your stallion. We anchored them to sanity, and they gave us a purpose.' He managed a smile. 'I will never scorn a bathhouse again. Jesu, I am as lousy as a gutter orphan.'

'And as starved.' Sabin started towards the door. 'I suppose we should have waited until after you had finished breaking your fast.'

Strongfist grunted with pained amusement. At the cell door he paused and kicked aside the straw to reveal the small tafel board he had carved in the dirt of the floor. He stood for a moment in contemplation. 'I do not want ever to play that game again,' he said, revulsion curling in his voice.

'I do not blame you.' Sabin waited patiently, his hands at his sides, while Strongfist took a final inventory and farewell of his prison. 'I am only relieved to have found you alive,' he said. 'After the battle on the riverbank, I did not know what happened to you . . .' He wondered how to broach the news of all that had occurred during the three months of Strongfist's captivity – starkly, without gentleness, or in stages, like forging the links of a chain. It was an unfortunate image and he gave an involuntary grimace.

'Nor I you . . .' Strongfist raised his head and now made determinedly for the light. 'I thought you and Gerbert must be dead. The onslaught was too terrible to hold out hope of anything else.'

'I—' Sabin began and stopped. The words that had always come so easily to him as a courtier were elusive now when it truly mattered.

Strongfist climbed the stairs, all his breath given to the toil. Reaching the top, he emerged into the burning brilliance of the sunlight and clutched the wall for support while his eyes adjusted and his lungs recovered from their labour. Sabin followed him out, his own chest heaving, if for different reasons.

'Gerbert survived the battle,' he said, 'but he suffered an arm wound that would not heal. I took a blow to the head that knocked me senseless and the Saracens left me for dead.'

Strongfist slowly straightened and looked at him in dismay. 'You say Gerbert's wound would not heal?'

Sabin nodded. The words were bitter in his mouth. 'It took two months for the infection to kill him. If not for Annais's nursing and the skill of our physician Luigi, it would have been much sooner, I think, but they fought tooth and nail to keep him alive. There is little comfort in such news, I know, but at least he had the time to make his farewells and set his affairs in order.'

'And small mercies are to be appreciated,' Strongfist said, his mouth twisting.

'If I could have given my life for his, I would,' Sabin said quietly.

'Don't talk like a fool.' Strongfist's tone was harsh with the anger of grief. 'God has spared your life; you should give praise and use it to the hilt. I certainly intend to use mine.'

Sabin stiffened beneath the reprimand. It was justified, but he thought that Strongfist probably harboured such feelings of guilt himself, for he too had survived while others were dead. 'There is more that you need to know,' he said, approaching the eye of the storm.

Strongfist looked at him from beneath tangled brows and the blue eyes, although hollow and bloodshot with exhaustion, were knowing. 'You sound like a bridegroom about to give his bride unwelcome news on her wedding night,' he said.

'In a way it is news of that kind . . .'

'Go on,' Strongfist said curtly.

'Before Gerbert died, he made provision for Montabard, and Annais and Guillaume . . .'

'As I would expect. You are telling me that my daughter is already remarried.'

'Yes,' Sabin said. 'To me.'

Strongfist stared. A sound started somewhere in his chest and rumbled upwards. It was laughter . . . of a sort. 'Dear Christ in His heaven!' Strongfist choked. Tears filled his eyes and streamed down his face. He had to clutch the wall again for support. 'When I warned you to stay away from her, I was pissing in the wind, wasn't I? I might as well have thrown you together on your first day out of Scotland.'

Sabin compressed his lips. 'We are legally wed in the eyes of the Church. I honour your daughter and I will do my best for her son . . . my stepson now. If it displeases you, I am sorry, but it was Gerbert's dying wish. We were wed a week after his death, but it was not until I left to come to Kharpurt that we shared a bed as man and wife. There has been no scandal or shame – nor will there ever be.'

Strongfist shook his head and wiped his brimming eyes. 'I believe you,' he said hoarsely. 'Against all odds, I do believe you. If I didn't, weak as I am, I would heave that sword out of your belt and smite you dead. And if you break your word, the same.'

'I won't break my word,' Sabin said with quiet intensity. 'If such a thing as love exists, then I love Annais. Whatever her pleasure and pain, they are mine too.'

Strongfist looked sceptical. 'And yet you had the strength to hold back when she was Gerbert's?'

'It didn't take strength,' he said. 'If I had made so much as one improper move, Annais would have taken that scramaseax of hers and thrust it hilt-deep into my heart. Besides, there is love at first sight – so the troubadours say – and there is the love that you take on piece by piece – like armouring yourself . . .' A thoughtful look crossed his face. 'Or perhaps like removing your armour. How many people would you allow within the space between your heart and your shield?'

Strongfist subjected him to a scrutiny that pierced like a lance and then drove inwards. 'I am a simple man and I live by simple ways,' he said flatly. 'Not for me the courtier's polished words. So often they are shells without a kernel, and how can you know whether such a shell is a guardian of the truth or a concealment?'

'You trust your intuition, not the man,' Sabin said. 'I would not blame you for holding my past against me.' He drew himself up. 'I know that I am hardly the son-in-law you would have chosen, but I will prove your fears ungrounded.'

Strongfist's mouth curved within the bushy straggle of his beard. 'See that you do,' he said, extending his hand to clasp Sabin's forearm in a powerful grip – although not quite as powerful as it had been three months ago. 'If you were amongst a line of prospective husbands for my daughter, I may not have chosen you – too unpredictable and dangerous. I would have looked for someone like myself – like Gerbert. But since I have seen both sides of you, lad, and Gerbert saw fit to name you his successor while his son grows to manhood, it's a coin I can learn to live with.'

Sabin returned the smile, although it was a struggle. Strongfist's response was as near to good grace as he was going to get . . . and just now there were greater concerns about which to worry.

CHAPTER 24

Baldwin and Joscelin had called an assembly in the main hall. Seated on a trestle table, grease and saffron in his beard from the chicken leg he was devouring, the King addressed the company. 'There are sixty-two of us all told,' he said. 'We command a fortress of medium stature in the heart of enemy territory. We can count on some support from the Christian villages in the vicinity, but not to the extent of rendering us secure. As soon as Balak receives the news of what has happened, he will bring his army up in force.' He broke the chicken leg in two; having demolished the thigh, he tossed the bone to a saluki hound hovering on the periphery of the gathering. The drumstick he pointed at his audience.

'Joscelin and two guides who know the lie of the land will go for aid. The rest of us will defend Kharpurt. In my estimation we can hold out against a siege until our own army arrives.'

'What about supplies?' Waleran of Birejek queried. He had been captured with Joscelin and was cousin to both him and Baldwin. He had the family traits of fair hair and sharp cheekbones. 'Is there enough food and water so that we are not driven to surrender by hunger or thirst?'

'There is enough and there will be no surrender.' Baldwin's voice was so quiet and steady that he might have been passing the time of day, but the narrow look in his eyes was chilling. 'Either we hold this place, or we die. Balak will not suffer the defilers of his harem to live, and the surrounding territory is too hostile for us to slip away unseen. Our strongest hope of success lies in holding these walls.'

A brief silence ensued as men digested his words. There were some frowns, but no dissent, for what Baldwin said was the brutal truth. Kharpurt was indeed their best means of protection until reinforcements could be brought up. If they could hold Kharpurt, it also meant that Baldwin would have a foothold in Balak's territory.

Sabin was aware of the sharp glance that Strongfist had cast him and knew that the older man was thinking of his daughter and the duty owed to her. But done was done. No man could turn his back now unless he left as one of Joscelin's companions, and the chosen ones would be expert guides.

As they left the gathering, Sabin felt Strongfist's elbow in his ribs. 'You do not have to stay,' he muttered, head bent towards Sabin's ear. 'My daughter needs you more than Baldwin and Joscelin do.'

Sabin's eyes narrowed. 'I promised Annais that I would bring you home, and I will not break my word.'

Strongfist made an irritated sound. 'I am past my prime,' he said as they crossed the courtyard. 'It will not matter if I do not return.'

'You are not exactly in your dotage,' Sabin retorted. 'And it will matter to me, and to Annais. Baldwin thinks we can hold this place . . . do you say him nay?'

Strongfist rubbed an agitated hand over his dirty beard. 'No, of course not . . . but it is not wise to put all your eggs in the same basket.'

Sabin smiled grimly. 'Annais and I knew the risks when I climbed into this particular basket,' he said. 'And I'm going to do my best to see that Baldwin doesn't drop it. I . . .' The words dried in his throat and he stared.

The woman emerging from another building across the courtyard was tall and slender. Her citrus-green gown flowed like an illuminator's paints melting in the rain and a diaphanous veil floated in a cascade of gold filaments atop her raven braids.

Strongfist muttered an oath and the prison-pallor of his skin turned corpse-grey.

Unperturbed, the woman advanced on them, her walk graceful, the slight sway of her hips, pronouncing her femininity without exaggerating it. Numerous gold bangles slithered and jingled on her wrists and her dark-blue eyes were rimmed in kohl of the same deep tint.

'Mariamne!' Strongfist's voice emerged as a wheeze.

'My lord.' With a curl to her reddened lips, she dipped him a mocking curtsey and inclined her head to Sabin.

The hair at Sabin's nape prickled. It was like standing in the middle of a dry thunderstorm. He flicked his gaze to Strongfist's hand, which was hovering rather too close to the hilt of the scimitar he had taken from the bloodied grasp of one of the dead garrison. Mariamne noticed too, but seemed unperturbed.

'I thought you would have sought me out before now,' she said.

'Why should I do that?' Strongfist's voice was still husky. From white, his complexion was now flushed and his eyes watering. 'Why should you think I have any desire to know about the welfare of an unfaithful whore?'

She tensed. 'A whore sells herself for money,' she said. 'Never in my life have I done that, but I have often enough been sold by men. Does that make them pimps?'

Strongfist spluttered. Sabin's first instinct was to step between him and Mariamne, but after one involuntary movement, he paused and held back. Mariamne flashed him a scornfilled glance.

'So, if not a whore, what are you . . . apart from an adulterous wife?' Strongfist growled.

'Does it matter any more?' She made an impatient gesture and the gold bangles clinked together. Rings adorned her fingers too, one of them set with a blood-red stone the size of a robin's egg. Her nails were perfectly manicured talons. 'Strike me with your fists, if you want, beat me with the buckle end of your belt to ease your wounded manhood, but it will change nothing.' She raised a thin, black brow at him. 'But before you do, be very glad that I preferred not to thrust a knife in your ribs when you bedded me.'

Strongfist drew a loud breath over his larynx, but she forestalled the words he was preparing to speak.

'Why do you think that the captain of Balak's garrison was not there to direct his men?'

He stared at her with the whites of his eyes. 'You killed him?'

She gave a little shrug. 'He deserved it, the swine, and I was willing to take the risk that you would prevail over the garrison. If you hadn't, I would have cut my own wrists.' She jutted her chin at them in proud defiance.

Sabin thought that he understood. It was a fine performance, as good as any he had given in his troubled past. Whatever undesirable traits Mariamne possessed, cowardice was not one of them.

Strongfist opened his hands. 'I thought never to see you again.' His tone contained weariness and distaste, and, incongruously, a trace of longing.

'Nor I you.'

With an effort, he tore his gaze from hers. 'I do not want you back. Do as you will with your life as long as it does not tangle with mine.'

'What of Tel Namir?'

'What of it? You abandoned it when you abandoned me for your silk merchant – much good it has done you. What happened? Did he desert you when he became jaded by your whore's tricks?'

A flush mantled her cheek. 'We were set upon by robbers,' she said. 'He was killed and I was sold into the harem at Kharpurt. Call it just retribution if it salves your pride.'

'I doubt that anything will ever salve my pride,' he growled.

'For the sake of chivalry alone, I will extend you my protection while we are still in Kharpurt, but when we leave this place, I never want to see you again.'

She nodded stiffly. 'That will suit me well,' she said and turned back the way she had come, her walk graceful and unhurried.

'Bitch,' Strongfist muttered under his breath, his stare fixed on the supple sway of her spine and hips. 'Heartbreaking bitch.'

Sabin glanced at him. 'Despite what you say, would you take her back?'

Strongfist shook his head. 'No,' he said vehemently. 'Never.' But his gaze lingered and the way he spoke made Sabin wonder.

Annais watched her son pull himself to his feet using the stout foot of his father's chair, then, clinging to the seat for support, walk his way to the bench beside it, where his toy wooden horse was standing. He squealed with delight at his own prowess, and Annais joined him, clapping her hands. She was certain that he was the cleverest child that had ever lived, but the other women, many of them mothers themselves, prevented her pride from swelling out of proportion. Having observed the way that Soraya doted on her son and small daughter, Annais understood that it was a common condition and to be kept within bounds. It was difficult though.

Her flux had come at its appointed time, a week after Sabin's departure, so she knew that she was not pregnant. In part she was disappointed, for it would have been something of Sabin to keep should the worst happen . . . but the practical side of her nature was relieved not to be with child. It meant that her energy was not diluted by a developing baby, but she could concentrate on the one she had and the duties of being the lady of a fortress under threat of war.

Going to Guillaume, Annais swept him into her arms and cuddled him fiercely. She often brought him to the battlements. It reminded the guards to whom they owed their duty, and it gave them a sense of continuity. It also awoke the protective paternal instinct in many and Annais let them hoist Guillaume aloft in their hard, mailed arms and show him the lands beyond Montabard's walls. She allowed them to carry him across the ward to the soldier's fire in the bailey and to become part of the ring of men standing around it. At the moment, Guillaume lived in the feminine world of the women's chambers, but the time would come when he would leave it for the masculine world beyond. It was never too soon to begin his training, and the training of the men who were to serve him.

Letice entered the bedchamber. 'A messenger has just ridden in from Antioch,' she announced, eyes bright.

Annais rose to her feet and lifted Guillaume to her hip. Her heart began to thump. It could be anything. News about supplies, a letter from the Patriarch concerning administration, a request for an escort for a merchant train . . . or it could be news about Sabin and her father. Eyes full of hope and fear, she faced Letice.

'That is all I know,' Letice said. 'He would say nothing more.'

Then it had to be news from Kharpurt. Annais handed Guillaume to Soraya, sent a summons to the senior knights, and hastened down to the hall.

The messenger had been furnished with a cup of wine and a platter of bread and fruit. He had discarded his mail and helm, but still wore his padded undertunic. Although it was reasonably cool in the hall, his face shone with the sweat of his ride.

'My lady.' Hastily swallowing his mouthful of food, he rose to his feet and bowed. The steward, who had been attending him, moved politely out of earshot.

She inclined her head in reply and came straight to the point. 'Who sends you? What is your news?'

If he was taken aback by her abruptness, he was too well

trained to show it. 'My lady, I have come from Joscelin of Edessa to bring you tidings and a request for soldiers.'

'Your lord is free?' Her breathing quickened. 'The rescue at Kharpurt has been successful?'

'Yes, my lady.'

'That is good news! What of the others? Are they with him?' A prickle of unease walked beside her pleasure. If Kharput was no longer in Saracen hands, why was a messenger here and not Sabin in person? And why asking for soldiers?

'No, my lady . . . not yet . . . although Lord Joscelin bids you be of good heart for your husband and your father are both alive and well.' He hesitated and his gaze flickered down the hall. Turning her head, Annais saw Durand, Thierry and Malik advancing, and beckoned them to join her.

'Tell us,' she said to the messenger. 'Tell us everything.' The man took a fortifying drink of wine and told his story. He spoke of the taking of Kharpurt, which was in itself nothing short of a minstrel's tale. 'Since the fortress is within enemy territory and since it is worth keeping, King Baldwin decided to hold on to it and use his rescuers as a garrison. There are sufficient supplies in the castle to withstand a siege should Balak bring up his army.'

Annais began to feel cold. At her side, she could sense Durand's increasing tension. 'So most of the men are still at Kharpurt?'

'Yes, my lady. It was decided that Lord Joscelin would fetch aid, since he knew the area the best of anyone there and the tribesmen are loyal to him – not all of them would be as loyal to King Baldwin. He left Kharpurt and made his way to the banks of the Euphrates. One man went back to reassure the King and those men remaining that all was well. Since Lord Joscelin could not swim, he and his guides made floats from goatskins and paddled their way across like dogs.' He spoke the words boldly, looking for and receiving exclamations at Joscelin's resourcefulness and bravery. 'When they came to a village they knew to be friendly, they took horses and rode for Turbessel where my lord's wife and court were waiting to greet him.' The messenger paused to drink again while his audience hung on his words. 'He tarried there not more than a night but set out to Antioch to raise troops to rescue the King.' His mouth turned downwards. 'Unfortunately Patriarch Bernard felt that the army of Antioch was not of sufficient size to face Balak's army alone and bade Lord Joscelin make all haste to Jerusalem and gather an army there . . . And so my lord is doing.'

There was a brief, intense silence, broken by Annais, her voice tight with strain. 'How long will it take?'

'That, my lady, I do not know.' The messenger spread his hands. 'It depends on the state of the roads and the speed of my lord's horse. He will not tarry, I swear to you.'

'Patriarch Bernard should have given Lord Joscelin the men of Antioch,' Durand growled.

The messenger said nothing. It was not his place to argue policy, just deliver it. 'Lord Joscelin will field a rescue force as soon as he can,' he said. 'He asks that you spare as many soldiers from Montabard as possible and bring them with all haste to the muster at Turbessel.'

'He shall have everyone we can spare,' Annais said fervently, and the men at her back nodded vigorous agreement. Her relief that her father and Sabin were safe was swallowed by anxiety. If Balak's army should take Kharpurt before succour arrived, then what price the lives of the men within?

Chapter 25

Sabin donned the quilted undertunic and with Strongfist's aid struggled into the Saracen hauberk.

'Not a bad fit,' Strongfist said. He walked around Sabin, considering him from all angles. 'Could do with some links adding here, but that won't be difficult.' He gave an admiring click of his tongue. 'It's good quality.'

'So it should be,' Sabin said. The hauberk had been the property of Kharpurt's Saracen commander whose corpse now rotted outside the walls with the rest of the garrison. Having belonged to a man of wealth, the quality was superb. Strongfist was wearing his own hauberk, which, along with the rest of the Frankish prisoners' gear, had been stowed in the armoury. However, the flesh that he had lost during five months of privation meant that he no longer filled the garment and found its weight a burden.

Sabin rotated his arms to test for ease of movement. He latched his swordbelt at his hip and attached the scabbard, then fitted the Saracen helm on his head. It bore a spiked crest that shone like silver.

Strongfist snorted. 'All you need is a scimitar, and you could be one of them.'

'You think so?' Sabin looked down. 'My hose are not baggy enough and my boots should have pointed toes.' He rubbed his smooth chin. 'I need a beard too.'

'Fool,' Strongfist said, but fondly. 'At least I suppose you are now fit to go on guard duty.'

Sabin lifted the bow and quiver of arrows from the bench where he had laid them while he dressed. 'There was no sign of Balak's army yesterday,' he said. 'Let us pray our luck holds from another dawn to dusk.'

Strongfist agreed and set his hand to the hilt of his sword. 'It is more than a week since we heard that Lord Joscelin was safely across the river,' he said. 'Our own relief army cannot be long in coming. Patriarch Bernard is certain to send out troops from Antioch.'

'Is he?' Sabin moved from the guardroom to the stairs that led up to the wall platform. 'From Montabard's dealings with Antioch, I would say that Bernard is a cautious old bird.'

Strongfist cocked his brow. 'Your point being?'

'My point being that Joscelin may leap up and down and demand that men be sent immediately, but I suspect Bernard will think matters through before he commits himself.'

'Not with a kingdom at stake.'

'Precisely because there is a kingdom at stake. The army of Antioch is not large when compared to the force that Balak already has in the field.'

Strongfist tugged on his regrowing beard. He had shaved it off to be rid of the lice that had infested it during his imprisonment. 'You do not believe a relief army is coming?'

Sabin half turned. 'Of course one is coming. Joscelin of Edessa is loyal to the bone and tenacious, but whether it is the army of Antioch or that of Jerusalem is debatable. If it is the second, then pray hard that we don't see the glitter of Saracen spears at our gates for a while yet.'

'Balak will not find us easy meat.'

'Indeed,' Sabin panted as he reached the top of the wall walk, 'but we dare take nothing for granted.'

Strongfist clenched his hands in his belt. 'When did you become such a prophet of doom?' he demanded with exasperation. 'I think I preferred you when you were a wild young man.'

Sabin gave him a sour grin. 'I'm not being a prophet of doom,' he said, pressing one hand to the stitch in his side. 'But a commander needs to look at both sides of the coin. If you had preferred me as I was, you shouldn't have taught me anything.'

'I didn't teach you command, lad.' Walking to a merlons, Strongfist rested his arm on the gritty stone and looked out over the scrubby, mountainous landscape. 'You had that already and, if the truth be known, in better measure than me. I'm just a soldier who follows orders better than he leads.'

'You make no pig's ear of ruling Tel Namir,' Sabin said.

'Hah, anyone with half a brain and one hand tied behind his back could do that,' Strongfist snorted. 'Tel Namir lies in peaceful territory. It's like a milch cow. As long as I care for it, then it will feed me. It is no more than common sense.'

'Well, perhaps you showed me steadiness,' Sabin said quietly. 'I had never dwelt for any length of time in its presence before.'

Strongfist grunted, but he did not look displeased. 'Surely you had that with your father, even if he died untimely.'

Sabin grimaced. 'I stood on quicksand where he was concerned. I loved him hard, but his nature was not yours or Gerbert's. I have learned a great deal this past couple of years.'

'No, lad, you've grown up.' Strongfist set a large hand to Sabin's shoulder. 'If we get out of here alive, I'll be proud to call you son to the world.'

Sabin reddened at the compliment. 'You are generous.'

A smile curved the straight set of Strongfist's lips. 'Mayhap I am, but that's in my nature too.'

It was so rare for the older man to jest or tease that it took Sabin a moment to understand and respond with the appropriate grin.

Strongfist left after that, for he had promised to help in the armoury. One of their number was a smith and was occupied in making spears and arrows from the fortress's store of supplies. Strongfist was content to pump the bellows in the forge while the smith heated, hammered and quenched the metal into much needed weapons.

Towards noon, the men stopped to rest. The sun beat down like a brazen shield boss, and the heat from the forge struck up to meet it in searing blows of air. Melting in sweat, gasping with open mouth, Strongfist staggered outside and collapsed in the shade of the wall. Off came his tunic, off came his shirt, but it gave him little relief for the air was as hot as the inside of a frying pan.

Carrying a large stone jar, Mariamne came around the corner from the well. Unlike the native women, who had learned to balance such burdens on their heads from a young age, Mariamne bore the water in her hands and walked with a lurch that was out of keeping with her usual grace. Strongfist watched her, pretending indifference, but then gallantry got the better of him and he rose to help her.

'Sit,' she panted, gesturing him down. 'It is for you anyway.'

He took the jar and set it on the ground. Water slopped over the lip and clotted in the dust.

'That is kind of you.' His tone was impassive. Dipping his hands, he scooped a palmful of water and sluiced it over his hair and face. It was cold and fresh from the well and the contrast against the burning heat of his skin made him gasp with shock and pleasure.

'Not that kind,' she said. 'We have been carrying water to all the men. My duty fell your way, that is all.'

'And after me, will it fall Sabin's way?' He cupped his palms and sluiced again.

Eyeing him through narrowed lids, she handed him the drinking horn that had been thrust through her belt. 'You did not complain at the time . . . I even wondered if you knew.'

Strongfist took the horn from her, dipped it and drank deeply. Water ran down his beard and trickled in sparkling rivulets down his chest. 'Oh, I knew,' he said softly, 'but it was easier to ignore. What man willingly admits that a woman has put the horns on him? Besides, you didn't have your way with Sabin . . .'

'He told you that?' Her tone was scornful.

'I didn't need to be told. For all your wiles and my ignorance, I know the lad better than that. You were what he left behind in England. He had already had his fill of your sort.' He dipped the horn and drank again, more slowly this time.

'My sort?' She raised a plucked black eyebrow. Fine, dry lines like delicate embroidery seamed her forehead.

'Dissatisfied married women with the bitterness and boldness to do something about their state. I know I wasn't your choice, even if you played the role.'

'No, you weren't,' she said. The scorn departed her expression, which became thoughtful. 'Not having a choice. Perhaps that is the crux of the matter.'

'Well then, you have several now.' He wiped his mouth on his wrist.

She met his gaze. 'Yes,' she said. 'I have several now, for what use they will be to me.'

He returned the horn and she pushed it into her belt. Her once sharply manicured nails were clipped short and her hands were rough. A pang seared him and, as always, his emotion showed on his face.

Her lips curved. 'For what it is worth, you are a good man,' she said. Hefting the water jar, she moved on to the smith, who was emerging from the forge, wiping his hands on a rag.

Strongfist watched her and thought that it was worth dross. From behind and above, there came a bellow from the wall walk: Sabin's voice pitched deep for loudness and strength. The cry was caught and repeated along the watchtower until the stones rang with the sound and the echoes filled the spaces between. The water in Strongfist's stomach lay like a cold stone. Grabbing his shirt, he ran to the nearest tower and scrambled up the stairs. The thundering of his heart and the weakness of heat-punished limbs made him slow, but finally he was at the top and pushing open the heavy wooden door that led onto the battlements.

Sabin's tanned complexion bore a greenish undertone and his mouth was set in a tight line. Gasping from his climb, Strongfist lurched to the wall, leaned against a merlon and peered through the narrow crenel. Summer dust choked the horizon and the rising cloud was punctuated by the dazzle of sun on spears and harness. Outriders had fanned out from the main troop; their single dust trails led the eye to swift, small horses and warriors with round shields and tasselled lances.

'It is Balak,' Sabin said, his breathing as swift as Strongfist's. 'Our own relief army had better not be far behind.'

There was a flurry on their section of wall walk as King Baldwin arrived at the run. He looked for a moment and then bared his strong, square teeth in a snarl. 'Let them come,' he said. 'We are ready to send them to hell. They will batter themselves bloody, but they'll not take this keep while I am its commander.'

An hour passed and still the dust cloud grew. At the front it had resolved itself into the vanguard of Balak's army and the first soldiers were making camp just out of arrow-shot of Kharpurt's walls. It was obvious that they feared no attack from within.

'There's not much that we can do in daylight with a garrison of sixty men,' said Waleran of Birejek. 'Of course, it might be different at night.'

Sabin nodded. 'But we should wait until they have built their siege machines. That way we cause the most damage. If we make our sortie too soon, then we put them on their guard to no gain.'

Horns blared below their walls. The two men looked through the crenel and saw a herald approaching from the Saracen lines. A white banner streamed from his lance and he rode a white gelding with black mane and tail.

'Ever been under siege before?' Waleran asked.

Sabin shook his head.

Waleran smiled, but there was little humour in his expression. 'This is the part where Balak offers us easy terms of surrender – and death if we refuse. We'll send a man out to parley, of course, but the outcome is not in doubt.'

Sabin raised his brows. 'And are the easy terms or the punishment for refusal to be believed?'

Waleran folded his arms. 'I wouldn't trust Balak as far as I could throw a Turkish lance,' he said. 'Smooth as a snake, he is, and warm when the sun is on his skin, but his blood is cold and he is as venomous as the deadliest viper.'

That answered the second part of the question. Although the siege had scarcely begun, Sabin was finding it difficult to adjust to the notion of being surrounded and attacked. It was the feeling of being backed into a corner and held at bay rather than having open ground on which to fight or flee that disturbed him. Strongfist, with his bovine, stoic nature, was far better equipped to cope with such a situation than he was.

Baldwin arrived from another section of wall walk and slapped his hand down on Sabin's shoulder. 'I need a man to go out and meet Balak's herald,' he said. 'And since you served your apprenticeship as a squire in a royal court, you will do admirably.'

'I will be honoured, sire.' Although Sabin's stomach gave a momentary lurch, he was relieved. Having something to do was better than the waiting – even if the task was facing snakes. He was under no illusions. Baldwin might have selected him for his courtly training, but he was also expendable.

'More than that, you'll be observant,' Baldwin said. 'You have sharp eyes; I expect you to use them.'

They found him a horse in the stables; not the one that had belonged to the dead commander, which would have been a calculated insult to Balak, but a fine black mare with a white star marking.

'Whatever terms Balak offers, you are to listen politely and refuse,' Baldwin instructed. 'Although I yield him the courtesy of an answer, it is immutable. We fight to the last drop of blood.'

'Sire.' Sabin met the King's gaze briefly. The blue eyes were as cold and clear as glass. Baldwin meant every word. Sabin hoped that the Saracens had sufficient honour and restraint not to take Baldwin's reply out on Baldwin's messenger. He mounted the mare, took the lance with the requisite white banner tied to the socket, and rode out.

The terms offered by Balak, and delivered by his herald in accented but fluent French, were too good to be worth a moment's consideration. A safe conduct for Baldwin to wherever he wished to go and leniency towards the garrison in exchange for yielding up Kharpurt before sunset. Looking into his opposite's flat dark eyes, Sabin knew that the only place Baldwin would be going if he yielded was another prison – one impregnable to all assault. And as for leniency towards the garrison . . . the sword instead of the rope was the only probable mercy. The manner in which Kharpurt had been taken had left Balak smarting with humiliation, and the fact that his harem was within Kharpurt and had been subjected to the pollution of Frankish men was another shame to be expunged in blood.

'Emir Balak is generous to offer such terms,' Sabin said, bowing and smiling. 'However, I am advised by my lord, King Baldwin, to refuse them since they do not accord with his own wishes. Emir Balak should know that a mighty Frankish army is on its way to Kharpurt and, if he is a wise man, he will withdraw his troops before sunset reddens the sky.'

The herald smiled back, his teeth a dazzling white between his red lips. 'Emir Balak, may Allah's blessings fall upon him, is indeed a wise man – wise enough to know the difference between the hot air of bluster and the true breath of fire. If your King does not come to terms by the setting of the sun, then you will all die.'

'Tell Emir Balak that he has his answer,' Sabin replied and

reined the black around. All the way back into Kharpurt, his shoulder blades itched. He was aware of the garrison on the battlements, their arrows nocked to give him cover and dissuade any sudden charge for the gates on Balak's behalf. However, the Saracens withdrew to their camp without incident.

Sabin gave Baldwin the ultimatum and Baldwin laughed. 'He must think I was born yesterday! A safe conduct indeed! What would be the point of keeping me prisoner all these months if he is prepared to yield so much for so little?' He looked keenly at Sabin. 'Tell me what else you saw.'

'Not a great deal, sire,' Sabin said and gratefully took the wine that Strongfist handed him. It was dark and strong and he needed it.

Baldwin frowned. 'I hope you have more to say than that.'

Sabin swallowed. 'Balak's army is as large as you see from the battlements. Indeed, you have a better view from here than I did on the ground. Of course, that means nothing. If our walls are impregnable, then feeding such an army while conducting a futile siege will put a considerable strain on Balak's resources and leadership.'

'And?' Baldwin continued to frown. His fingers twitched impatiently.

'The point is that they appear not to have brought any siege equipment with them, and there are no vast forests around here to cut down trees and construct such. We are not about to be assaulted by trebuchets, rams and perriers.' Sabin took another deep drink of the wine. 'But Balak must believe that he can take the keep.'

'You think so? Then why offer such generous terms at the start? It would usually take days of negotiation to reach that point.'

'Perhaps because he doesn't expect you to yield,' Sabin said. 'Perhaps he doesn't want you to yield because his satisfaction will lie in humiliating you and wreaking vengeance on the garrison.'

'But no one is going to open the gates to him or let his followers inside,' said Waleran of Birejek, 'so how does he intend to take this place without siege machinery? He cannot afford to tarry. Our own army will be here any day.'

Sabin swirled the remaining wine in his cup and looked at Waleran. 'I think that he intends to undermine one of the tower walls and make a breach that way,' he said. 'I did notice carts heaped with faggots and brushwood and panniers of spades. I would say that come sunset, he will begin undermining our walls and if that is the case, we perhaps have less grace than we imagine.'

Baldwin's mouth tightened. 'You speak my own concerns aloud,' he said. 'But I consider the walls strong enough to hold out until our army arrives. I have faith in Joscelin.' He stared around the gathering of men. 'I stand by my word. Who stands with me?'

Whatever doubts some of them, including Sabin, may have harboured, they all shouted their support for Baldwin. It was a matter of pride and principle. Besides, no one believed for a moment Balak's sugared terms of surrender. They had no choice.

Chapter 26

'They will kill us, won't they?' Mariamne's voice was calm, her hand steady as she poured the wine.

Strongfist cupped his hand around the bowl of the goblet. 'They have to break through first,' he said gruffly. 'Do not let it worry you.'

She gave him a withering look. 'I hear the sound of them mining the walls day and night and there is no sign of succour on the horizon. I am not a child to have my fears comforted by a soothing pat on the head.'

'Then why ask in the first place?' Sabin had heard the beginning of the conversation. Now he straddled the bench beside Strongfist and thrust out his own drinking cup. 'Is that not what you were seeking – comfort?' There was no shortage of wine to assuage their increasing extremity, although no one was getting drunk on it. The fact that there was wine at all in a former Muslim stronghold owed much to the raiding abilities of Balak's forces and the garrison commander's penchant for the brew of the grape.

Mariamne glared at Sabin. 'No,' she said so curtly that he knew he had caught her on the raw. She served him without a tremor.

'Of course they will kill us if they break through,' Sabin said. 'Or most of us anyway. Nor will you be spared for your sex. Is that what you wanted to hear?'

She gave an arid smile. 'It is not what I wanted to hear,

but you confirm what I have been thinking.' Her glance flickered to another trestle where Baldwin was taking a brief respite from his command to play chess with Waleran of Birejek. 'The King will not surrender . . . but then it is not he who will die.'

'And you think that we should abscond over the walls at night before we do?'

'Yes I do,' she said. 'But I know that I am crying in the wilderness for all the heed any of you will pay.'

'Anyone escaping over the walls has still to win past Balak's army,' Sabin said. 'And then cross the river.'

'Joscelin of Edessa did it.'

'With two experienced Armenian guides. And there is only one Joscelin of Edessa. Besides, Joscelin walked out of the gates and all he had to do was get past Balak's outriders, not his entire army.'

Strongfist cleared his throat and gave Sabin a look that warned him not to press the point. 'We will do what we can,' he said, the heartiness of his tone ringing false.

Mariamne shook her head and moved away to serve others. Strongfist grimaced and rubbed the back of his neck. 'Why do I feel as if that woman has my bollocks in her hands?' he said.

'Probably because she does.' Sabin set his wine aside.

'Is there a way out – if it comes to the crux?'

Sabin pursed his lips. 'Over the walls by rope,' he said. 'But that's hardly something you can do by stealth unless you are swift and the guards outside not vigilant. You could bribe Balak's guards, but it is difficult to know what with. We are not men of high importance and privilege like the King. Disguise might work, but not for long. I speak some Arabic, but not of the local dialect . . . and if we had a woman with us, that would immediately arouse suspicion.'

'She could disguise herself as a man.'

Sabin looked pained and bit down on his thumbnail. 'You are entering the realm of troubadour's tales now,' he said.

Outside the sound of mining ceased. The men in the hall held their breath and looked at each other. Faintly, through the open shutters, the cry of a muezzin calling the faithful to prayer pierced the taut silence.

Sabin slumped on the trestle and Strongfist washed his hands over his face. They both knew that once the miners had dug far enough beneath the foundations of the tower, they would fill the tunnel with brushwood and set it alight. The fire would burn through the props and bring the tower tumbling down, giving Balak's men an opening into Kharpurt. This time, however, the miners had only stopped in order to pray.

'We should pray too,' Baldwin raised his voice. 'All of you, on your knees, and make obeisance to God.' Crossing himself, he knelt and bowed his head. Everyone followed suit and for a moment the room was filled with the sound of scraping benches, clinking armour fittings and the rustle of clothing as men followed Baldwin's example. Then there was silence. They had no priest to lead them in prayers; each man was alone with God. Sabin wondered how many were bargaining for their lives. I will never sin again if you let me live. I will give half of all I own to the Church. I will offer my son to Christ . . . Behind the walls, beyond the reach of their Frankish arrows, doubtless slender brown-skinned men were striking similar bargains with Allah.

'Thy will be done,' Sabin murmured.

'God helps those who help themselves,' responded Mariamne from close by. Despite himself, Sabin was amused and almost choked on suppressing a laugh.

A hundred miles away, the same saying was on Annais's lips, much to the consternation of the other women of the household.

'My lady, it is too dangerous!' Soraya's gaze was wide with anxiety.

Annais stiffened her spine. 'Queen Morphia has ridden

north to aid her husband's cause, and it is only fitting that I should join her – to pay my respects and offer support. I can find out more about my father and my husband if I join the court. There is nothing I can do at Montabard save bite my nails to the quick and worry myself into a stupor.'

Soraya wrung her hands. 'But at least you are safe here.'

The young woman's tone roused Annais from the morass of her own concerns. Paying proper attention to Soraya, she saw her fear. 'I will be safe at court too,' she said. 'Queen Morphia is hardly going to ride into the heart of Balak's territory. She has her daughters with her and the youngest is little older than my son. Guillaume will have plenty of attention.'

'You are taking the baby?' Soraya looked horrified.

'Of course. I do not know how long I will be gone. There will be nurses and maids attached to the queen's household. I am not asking you to accompany me.'

'But Guillaume is used to me.'

'So he is, but he's young enough to adapt.'

Soraya bit her lip. Annais fought her impatience. Soraya had come to Montabard as a spoil of war, had converted to Christianity and married Durand. She was pragmatic, and strong in her own quiet way, but she had never once left the security of these walls since that time. 'It is your decision,' Annais said. 'I will not force you. Of course, your husband will be leading my escort. Think on it.'

Leaving the women, she entered the inner chamber and went to her travelling coffer. She would need her court gown – the one of cream silk in which she had been wed. And she would need sensible travelling garments. Cotton and linen for the heat of the day, wool and fur to keep her warm at night and protect her from the mountain winds. Morphia was currently lodging in Antioch with the Patriarch, but would soon leave for Edessa's main city of Turbessel. The army of Jerusalem was already on its way there.

Letice followed her. 'You are certain about doing this?' she said with a troubled frown.

Annais busied herself fetching items to place in the coffer. 'I have been certain ever since I heard that the Queen was bringing her court to the north. She could have sent representatives, but she chose to come herself and bring her children.'

Letice considered her gravely without speaking.

'You think me foolish?' Annais's tone sharpened.

'No,' Letice said slowly. 'In your place I would probably do the same, but since my heart is not engaged, I can stand back and worry for you.'

Annais's chin trembled. She wanted to say that there was no need, but it wasn't true. Sometimes she felt like a thread unravelling from what had been solidly woven cloth, and with no notion of how to restore the pattern. 'I would know if they were dead,' she said and blinked as her eyes stung. 'Wouldn't I? I would know.' She gave Letice a beseeching look.

Compassion softened the other woman's gaze. Coming to Annais, she put her arms around her shoulders and kissed her temple like a mother. 'Yes,' she said. 'You would know.' Even if it wasn't the truth, at least it was a sustaining lie.

Strongfist was coming from his duty on watch to snatch a few hours' sleep when Mariamne called to him. Pausing in midstride, he turned and went to her. She was standing at the foot of the tower where Balak's troops were undermining the foundations. A basket of bread was looped over one arm and the ever-present water jar rested at her feet.

'Well?' she said. 'No shine of armour on the horizon to report?'

He shook his head. 'No.'

She tilted her head. 'It will be moonless tonight. Perhaps now is the time to consider putting a rope over the wall.'

Strongfist pushed his hand against his sword hilt. 'If you wish to go, I will hold and lower the rope,' he said, 'but do not expect me to leave the King.'

'No, you are too honourable for that.' Her tone was mocking. 'You would rather die at his feet like a faithful dog.'

Strongfist swallowed the retort about faithless bitches that came first to his lips. 'It will be better if you wear men's clothing,' he said.

She laughed and her eyes gleamed. 'Would it now?' She pushed her tongue into her cheek and looked at him through her lashes. 'I dare say I could lay my hands on some.'

Strongfist opened and closed his fists. He knew where he wanted to lay *his* hands. Mariamne stepped closer until they were almost touching. 'Would you like to see me in hose and braies?'

His throat closed. He raised his clenched fist but when he stroked her cheek with his knuckles, it was a tender caress. When he had faced her for the first time in Kharpurt, he had sworn an oath that he would have naught to do with her, but in the days of their besieging, it had been impossible to keep. She had been everywhere: fetching, carrying, cooking and tending. He had half expected her to try to attach herself to Waleran or Baldwin because of their status, but she behaved towards them no differently than to any of the men. Sabin she actively avoided, and he treated her with the frozen courtesy that Strongfist had come to realise was out of his own reach. He still ached unbearably when she was near.

'You know how I would like to see you,' he muttered. His other hand spread at her waist and drew her against him.

She laughed and reached up to stroke his short beard. 'Tell me . . .'

Strongfist opened his mouth, but his words were stolen by the violent shuddering of the ground beneath his feet. It was like the time he had stood on the battlefield at Dorylaeum as a young footsoldier and felt the vibration of hooves as the Saracens pounded towards their lines on their swift Turcoman horses.

'What in God's name—'

Mariamne screamed as the walls above them shimmered as if in a heat haze. The shimmer became a ripple and the ripple a wave. A huge crack ripped up through the tower walls, sundering rock from mortar. Stones bounced and the air filled with the roar of tumbling masonry.

Strongfist seized Mariamne's arm and ran. Boulders and dust rained down, pounding, bouncing, splintering to send out lethal shards, and the rumbling sound increased until it blotted out all else. Dust filled Strongfist's lungs. A sudden blow to his back punched the wind from his lungs, tore his grip from Mariamne's sleeve and sent him sprawling. Mariamne screamed again, the sound cut off in mid-shrill and overpowered by the thunder of falling rubble.

Retching, choking for breath, Strongfist struggled to his feet. Mariamne lay two paces behind him, her body pinned beneath a slab of rock. Dust boiled around them and the tower was a jumbled pile of rubble, still quivering and settling. Blood ran from Strongfist's temple into his eye, but he felt neither the pain nor the heat of the trickle. All he knew was that in a moment Balak's army would be swarming over those stones and he was standing directly in their path. Desperation lent him the strength of Samson, and he heaved the boulder from the middle of Mariamne's back as if it were made of no more than a balled-up piece of parchment. Her eyes were closed. Blood trickled from her nose and the corner of her mouth, but she was still breathing. Strongfist swept her up across the back of his shoulders like a shepherd with a stray lamb, and staggered towards the undamaged buildings. He was vaguely aware of Sabin sprinting out to help him, of lurching up tower stairs that seemed to spiral for ever, and at last, with bursting lungs and darkening vision, of yielding his burden and falling to his knees. He hunched over, wheezing, gagging, barely aware of the others in the room: the King, Waleran, Ernoul, several knights.

Sabin gripped his shoulder with compassion and urgency. 'I am sorry,' he said.

Strongfist absorbed the words blankly. He stared at Mariamne. She stared back, her blue eyes fixed and wide, the pupils huge and unresponding to the shadows of the men stooping over her. Her mouth was filled with blood and her breast was still. When had she died? She had still been breathing when he picked her up, he was certain of it. He had not felt her soul fly her body, but it was gone as surely as their hope. 'No.' He shook his head in denial. 'No!' His breath rasped in his throat like tearing silk.

Sabin's grip increased, the thin fingers steady and tight, anchoring him down against the desire to leap to his feet and rip the room and everyone in it to pieces. 'In moments Balak's army will be upon us,' Sabin said. 'Here.' Stooping, he drew Strongfist's sword from the scabbard and thrust it into his grip. 'This is the only language that matters now, and you have always said it is what you do best.'

Strongfist tightened his fingers around the leather-bound hilt, clenching until his joints cramped. He reached his left hand to stroke Mariamne's cheek as he had done moments before, and this time used the pad of his thumb to close her eyes. Making the sign of the cross on his breast, he rose unsteadily to his feet.

He wanted to run back down the tower stairs, to throw himself at the first men to clamber through the gap created by the fallen tower, but obligation held him back. His life was not his own to lose. It belonged to Baldwin and it was his duty to guard the King unto his dying breath. Tears streaking channels down the white dust on his face, he clenched his jaw, straightened his shoulders, and readied himself.

Balak's army swept into Kharpurt, alight with the spirit and rage of a nest of displaced hornets. The Armenian soldiers and knights were either slaughtered on the spot, or dragged up one of the towers and thrown off the walls to their broken deaths. Only when it came to the final stand did the Saracen leader stay his hand and spare the men standing back to back, protecting Baldwin at their centre.

Strongfist shuddered. It was as it had been on the banks of the Euphrates. Slaughter all around and himself still standing as if his life was either charmed or cursed. The moment brought him to breaking point and regardless of the reprieve he would have leaped upon the threatening wall of scimitars, but Sabin thrust out his foot and brought him down, then seized his sword from his hand. Strongfist struck out, but Sabin was too quick and his fist swiped air.

'It's over. You'll be no use dead,' Sabin hissed. 'Not even to yourself!'

Strongfist lunged and Sabin kicked him in the gut. He collapsed, wheezing, the pain in his mind a match for the pain in his belly, and as suddenly as the light going from a snuffed candle, he did not care any more.

The prisoners were roughly manhandled back to their original cell and once again the shackles were brought out. Strongfist accepted them with broken docility and it was Sabin who now had to prevent himself from struggling. Even without the memories of that night in November when the *Blanche Nef* had gone to her grave, the notion of being bound and helpless made his skin crawl as if there were tiny insects scuttling between it and his bones.

'Tonight Lord Balak will decide how to deal with you,' the interpreter said, pausing on the threshold, his figure blocking the light from the oil lamp in the passage. 'In the morning you will know.'

He strode from the room and the guards swung the great door shut and barred it. Now there was no light at all, for the prisoners had been left without so much as a single lamp. Sabin stared wide-eyed into the darkness and felt like a living corpse, walled up in a crypt.

'If Balak was going to kill us, he would have done it back in the tower,' said Waleran of Birejek's disembodied voice from somewhere on his right.

'You mean he's not going to save us for a public spectacle on the morrow and hurl us over the wall like everyone else?' said Ernoul, his voice rough with bravado.

'I doubt it,' Baldwin said. 'His decision will be whether to keep us here or move us. He knows that our army is on its way and since he has compromised the defences by undermining one of the towers, I think he will move us deeper into his territory.' Sabin prayed grimly that Baldwin was right about Balak's intentions. He clung to the thought of Annais and Guillaume. He had to emerge from this not only alive, but with his wits intact, for their sake.

Beside him, Strongfist was murmuring quietly to himself and, although he could not see him, Sabin could sense from the movement of the air that he was rocking gently back and forth. For good measure, Sabin added a prayer for his father-in-law's sanity.

Annais travelled from Antioch to Turbessel in Queen Morphia's entourage. From the moment the Queen had learned that Annais's father and husband were among the men garrisoning Kharpurt, she had received the warmest of welcomes. She was furnished a place among the Queen's ladies and Guillaume joined the children of the royal nursery. Morphia and Baldwin had four daughters, ranging in age from three to twelve, but there were younger infants too, belonging to the other women. Although Baldwin and Morphia had been married to cement alliances, theirs was a match where respect, affection and love had overtaken duty. For the sake of the kingdom of Jerusalem, the Queen was doing all in her power to resolve the crisis, but it was as a wife, mother and lover that she was moving heaven and earth to have her husband restored to her. Since Annais felt the same and had had the strength of will to venture forth from behind her own walls, Morphia had taken her to her heart.

A week after their arrival at Turbessel, Annais was in the royal apartments, playing her harp for the Queen's easement. Morphia had been occupied all morning in affairs of state. Although the kingdom possessed a strong administrative system, she involved herself rather than performing a purely decorative role.

'One day my daughter will be Queen of Jerusalem,' Morphia said. 'And while the rule will devolve upon the husband we choose for her, she will not be without power of her own. A woman should know the business of governance so that she can be effective in her lord's absence.' Her mouth was firm and decisive and her fingers clenched as if physically grasping the power of which she spoke. 'Melisande will learn by example.'

However, even a queen was subject to the curse of the monthly flux and Morphia had conceded an hour's rest in her chamber with a cold cloth at her forehead, goatskins of hot water at her aching back, and Annais's harp lulling the air. The afternoon was somnolent. A large black fly buzzed drunkenly at the half-open shutters until finally blundering its way out into the bright sunshine. One of the Queen's women fanned her mistress with a date frond whilst two more prepared a tray of wine and sweet cakes. In a smaller antechamber the younger children were napping in the afternoon heat, Guillaume among them, his thumb tucked in the corner of his mouth and his golden-brown hair tumbled at his brow. By bending slightly forward, Annais could just glimpse the end of his blanket, and Soraya, seated nearby on watch. The latter had overcome her fear to travel in Annais's entourage, and was coping well, although Annais suspected that she would be happy when the time came to go home to Montabard.

Princess Melisande considered herself too old to take a nap. She was a thin, gangling child, her father's fair hair darkened on her to the shade of old bronze and her eyes a deep grey-blue lit with amber flecks. An encouraged and competent reader, she had abandoned her leather- and ivory-bound book and was kneeling upright on the silk cushion in the embrasure, peering out of the window. Nearby, her sister Alicia, was toiling diligently over the piece of braid she was weaving to make herself a belt. Her tongue protruded between her teeth and there was a look of rapt concentration on her elfin features.

Watching the girls and the picture they made, Annais thought that it would be pleasant to bear a daughter, even if sons were the required coinage of power. Women shared so much that a man would never understand, even one as perceptive as Sabin. She thought that Sabin might enjoy a daughter too, and smiled a little at the image that filled her vision, albeit that the smile was wistful and her throat tight.

Melisande suddenly gasped, leaned forward a little, then turned back into the room, her eyes as bright as new candles. 'My lady mother, a messenger's just arrived from my cousin Joscelin.' The words were formal but their manner of announcement was like a thunderclap.

Morphia sat up on the couch, already peeling the damp cloth from her brow. 'Messengers come and go, child,' she said, but was already hastening to the window herself, her hands plucking her starred silk tabard to hold it above her dainty slippers. 'How do you know he belongs to Joscelin?'

Melisande blushed furiously. 'It is Stephen de Burzey,' she said. 'I know his face.'

Her mother gave her a sharp look. 'I hope that is all you know,' she said, kneeling beside Melisande to look out. After a glance, she said briskly to one of her women, 'Fetch him to me at once, and tell Countess Maria that a messenger has come from her husband.' A clap of her hands dismissed her other ladies. Annais started to put her harp away in its case but Morphia wagged her finger. 'No, stay and play,' she said. 'I do not want silence.'

Annais sat down again and rippled her fingers down the strings, feeling the successive strands of horsehair press against her fingertips. Moments later Joscelin's wife hastened into the room accompanied by two maids. Countess Maria was slender and small, her sallow skin given life by a gown of jewel-red silk. Her hands fluttered, never still, as if they were borrowed from small birds. Her dark eyes were liquid and tragic.

'Oh, my dear.' She hastened to embrace Morphia. The

taller woman stood as rigid as a statue and looked over Maria's shoulder to the messenger standing in the doorway.

Annais followed Morphia's frozen gaze and felt the chill pierce to her own marrow.

He was of about Sabin's age and possessed the same wiry build. His face was flushed with the exertion of his ride and his eyes held a storm of troubles. With obvious weariness, he knelt to Morphia and bent his head.

The harp slipped in Annais hand and her fingers slashed across the strings in discord as she grabbed it to prevent it falling from her lap.

Morphia jumped at the sound, but did not turn. 'What has happened?' she demanded in a clear, steady voice. 'Tell me.' She gestured the young man to rise with an imperious flick of her long fingers.

'Madam, Lord Joscelin sends you his greeting and his news.' He moistened his lips. 'Our army came to the walls of Kharpurt too late. The Emir Balak had succeeded in undermining one of the towers to make a breach . . .'

'And my husband?' Morphia stood like an effigy. Imperious, regal. Even the pleats of her purple silk dalmatic looked stiff. 'Am I then to mourn him?'

The messenger swallowed. Perspiration made an oily gleam on his travel-grimed face. 'No, madam. There had been some hard fighting . . . very hard indeed, but King Baldwin was not among the slain.' He raised his eyes to her for an instant and they were filled with the horror of what he had seen. 'The Saracens threw all the defenders over the walls, the dead and the living, to be broken and mingled in the ravine below. Lord Joscelin had word from one of his spies that Balak is bringing the King to his fortress at Harran, which is beyond our abilities to assault.'

Annais whimpered behind her lips. Morphia's head gave the slightest turn and the messenger's blue glance flickered briefly.

'Was anyone with my husband?' Morphia asked. 'What

of Waleran of Birejek and Ernoul of Rethel? Surely the Saracens would not slaughter them?'

'I know not, madam.' The young man gave an uncomfortable shrug. 'Lord Joscelin's spy said there were five Frankish prisoners, but he could not tell their identity from where he was hiding – save that one was the King.'

Morphia absorbed this without expression. 'And Lord Joscelin?'

'He has sent envoys to Emir Balak petitioning for the King's release, and the army is returning to Turbessel.'

Morphia thanked and dismissed him. When her daughter Melisande followed him from the room, she sent a woman in pursuit as chaperone, but it was an absent gesture: her mind was clearly focusing on the news.

The messenger's words had sliced through Annais like a sword blade, severing all reaction. She stared numbly at Morphia. No words came, no movement of hand or eye. Behind the blankness of her stare, she was seeing Sabin and her father lying shattered at the foot of a castle wall. She had watched the kites and vultures picking at the brigands who had dangled from Montabard's battlements. She did not have to imagine what would happen to the bodies . . . she knew.

Then Morphia was at her side, her grip hard on Annais's sleeve and her voice clear and firm. 'Nothing is carved in stone,' she said. 'Your husband and your father may be among the prisoners and they may be among the dead – but now is not the time to mourn them or fall into a faint over what might have happened. You must endure and you must be strong. I need your support.' She gave Annais's arm a small shake to emphasise her point.

Feeling sick and cold, Annais nevertheless responded to the tone of voice. 'Yes, madam,' she said woodenly.

'Good. I know I can rely on you.'

Annais was not so sure, but the Queen's command and a goblet of heavily sugared wine bolstered her resolve. Morphia was right. They had the bare facts without the clothing of detail. That would come later, and there was no gain in moping in a corner and thinking the worst.

The Queen set about cementing diplomatic relations and opening talks, not only with Balak's representatives to discuss a ransom price, but also with Balak's allies and enemies. No road was to be left untravelled lest it lead to a way out of the crisis.

Annais was occupied from dawn until dusk: fetching, carrying, attending the Queen at formal meetings, and taking her turn with the children. She played her harp to soothe the spirits and entertain the nobles who came and went at the royal summons. Time to worry was in short supply and mostly found at night on the edges of slumber or in chapel when prayers were led for the souls of those who had died and those who they hoped still lived. Annais was always surprised to see her prayer beads still round and full when she emerged from these sessions, for she was certain that her busy fingers ought to have worn them away.

Joscelin returned to Turbessel with the army, intent on a brief respite and garnering of more troops before moving on to harass Balak's territory around Aleppo. He could tell the women no more than they knew already. Baldwin and the remnants of his bodyguard had been removed to Harran. The identity of the survivors was unknown.

'Unless we press Balak hard, there will be no ransom,' he said grimly on a visit to Morphia's chambers shortly after his arrival. 'He is not to be reasoned with.'

Morphia narrowed her eyes. 'Not at all?'

Joscelin let out a harsh breath and dug his hands through his receding hair. 'Not that I would call reason. He wanted Edessa from me. I doubt he'll settle for less from Baldwin. The only ransom he will accept is one that will beggar the kingdom – especially after what happened at Kharpurt. What we do is harry him and strike at his interests – make his underbelly so sore that he changes his mind about what is reasonable.'

'Will that not bring fresh danger upon my husband?' Morphia remained quite still, only betrayed by the gentle quiver of one of her ear jewels, glimmering silky grey in the window light. 'Supposing he changes his mind to Baldwin's detriment – tosses him over Harran's wall?'

'He can no more afford to do that than he can currently afford to let Baldwin go. Trust me.' Joscelin touched Morphia's rigid shoulder. 'I laid my own chains of captivity on the altar of the Holy Sepulchre in Jerusalem. So will Baldwin lay his.'

Morphia smiled, but her eyes were shadowed. 'I pray you are right,' she said.

Sitting in silent attendance, pretending to sew, Annais saw the weariness in Morphia's expression. The Queen drew a deep breath and braced her spine. Beneath the gossamer silk of her veil, her throat gave a single ripple. Unlike prayer beads, the human spirit was worn down by the constant pressure of their predicament. To see the moment of doubt was oddly comforting to Annais. It was a glimpse beneath Morphia's iron control to the vulnerable woman beneath.

It was the waiting that took its toll, Annais thought. The long, interminable waiting, and the war in the soul between hope and despair.

Chapter 27

Half a day's ride from Harran, Balak's army halted in an abandoned village and made camp for the night. The Turkish commander in charge of the Frankish prisoners bade them dismount and set six of his men to guard the King, Waleran and Ernoul with poised spears. Sabin and Strongfist, being of lesser rank, were taken under close scrutiny to fetch furze and kindling from the backs of two laden donkeys standing among the pack beasts. The Saracens saw no reason why they should toil in the service of the Franks when the Franks could do it themselves.

Sabin loosened a bundle of kindling and hefted it to his shoulder. It was a task he had performed several times now on their march. From what he had been able to glean, they would arrive at Harran on the morrow. The notion of being shut up in darkness again filled him with dread. One night had been sufficient to set a tremor in his fingers. Any longer than that and his captors would have been treated to the sight of a crawling, gibbering wreck.

'Do you think Joscelin has reached Kharpurt yet?' Strongfist asked as he shouldered his own bundle of kindling. He had survived the first shock of his wife's death and the slaughter at Kharpurt, but the grape-coloured shadows beneath his eyes and the lines between nose and mouth revealed the toll taken upon him.

Sabin shrugged. 'Whether he has or not is of no consequence.

'The bird is now in a different cage – or will be soon.'

'No talk,' said their guard in heavily accented French, wagging his finger back and forth.

Sabin tightened his mouth and began to walk, his shoulders hunched to bear the burden of the firewood. Suddenly the ground beneath his feet shook as it had done on the day that the tower collapsed.

'What . . . ?' Strongfist's gaze widened in alarm. The donkey brayed in terror, kicked up its heels and bolted, catching Strongfist a blow with its rump that sent him sprawling. Sabin dropped the firewood. Behind them, the deserted building shook as if the mud bricks of which it was fashioned were turning to liquid. The guard's horse reared and plunged, eyes rolling with terror. A chunk of baked mud from one of the buildings flew through the air and struck the guard a crushing blow to the back of his skull. He fell without a sound, twitched and was still. The ground continued to rumble, shivering buildings to rubble, tumbling the scrubby thorn trees, panicking the horses and mules. Terror and confusion boiled with the dust.

Coughing, Sabin stooped to the dead Saracen, appropriated his spear and scimitar, grabbed his mount's bridle and vaulted into the saddle. As another loose horse plunged past him, Sabin seized the reins, brought the beast around and yelled to Strongfist who was staggering dazedly to his feet.

'Quickly!' Sabin cried, thrusting the reins into Strongfist's hand.

'The King—' Strongfist looked over his shoulder.

'—is out of reach. Hurry, man!'

Strongfist grabbed the bridle and hauled himself across the horse's withers. Beneath them, the growl of the earth was shuddering to a halt and the billows of dust were beginning to settle. The entire movement of the earth had lasted for less than sixty heartbeats.

'Hah!' Sabin yelled to his mount and lashed the reins down on its neck. Already frightened, the horse leaped forward. A turbaned figure barred his way and Sabin used the scimitar.

The figure screamed and fell away. Sabin pounded the horse's flanks and the beast took the bit between its teeth and bolted, with Strongfist's mount racing at its tail.

Through clouds of grit and debris the horses galloped into the dusk. A whine of arrows chased them and the thunder of pursuit, but both were soon halted. Sabin supposed that he and Strongfist were the least important of the Frankish hostages. It mattered less that they escaped than that Baldwin should be prevented from following their example.

By the time Sabin and Strongfist had managed to control their blowing horses, the sky was livid violet in the west, streaked with a deep line of vermilion-red. The road was strewn with boulders shaken down from the hillsides by the force of the earth tremors, and Sabin marvelled that neither animal had slipped and broken a leg in the headlong flight.

A chill wind was blowing down the pass, leaching the remnants of heat from the end of the day. Sabin's teeth began to chatter as reaction set in. Gingerly he slackened the reins and allowed his foam-flecked mount to pick its way down the path in such light as remained to them. But soon he had to dismount and lead the horse, his own legs trembling like those of a newborn foal.

'You know they will kill us if they catch up with us,' Strongfist said as he too dismounted and paused for a moment, leaning his weight against his horse's flank.

'Better to take our chance than be locked up again,' Sabin said. 'Besides, since we are the most expendable, there would be nothing to stop them killing us in Harran. Balak only needs Baldwin.' He handed Strongfist the lance he had taken from their Saracen guard. 'Here, it's only half a weapon, but better than nothing.'

Strongfist closed his fingers around the haft. A pale silver moon was rising, escorted by a handmaiden's scattering of stars.

'We couldn't have brought Baldwin with us,' Sabin said. 'Even in the chaos he was too well guarded.'

Strongfist's face contorted. 'You are right, of course,' he said. 'And you see straight to the heart of my discomfort.' He hefted the spear, testing its balance. 'What now?'

'Keep moving,' Sabin said. 'Follow the sky and the stars westwards until we reach friends.'

'You think Balak will come for us?'

Sabin shrugged. 'They may send out hunting parties from Harran, but we are only small fry. It will be humiliating to lose us, but I am sure Balak can live with it while he still has the king.'

Strongfist looked unhappy at the reminder.

'You remember what Mariamne said in church?' Sabin touched his arm.

'What?'

'God helps those who help themselves . . . and we can best serve Baldwin by doing just that.' Turning to his horse, he groped in the compact roll behind the saddle. 'Flat bread and goat's cheese,' he said. 'At least we have food. Look in yours.'

Strongfist did so, emerging with some strips of dried meat, and a chunk of boiled sugar, studded with almond slivers and sesame seeds. It was enough to nourish them overnight, and there was a three-quarters-full waterskin on Sabin's saddle.

They exchanged half shares and, leading the horses, began to pick their way westwards.

In Turbessel, the earth tremors had brought down several buildings and given the town the sort of rattling meted out by a housewife shaking a pan over the fire. Morphia's exquisite set of Tyrian glass goblets had crashed from the sideboard shattering all but two, and a groom had suffered a crushed hand when a door had swung shut across his knuckles. Annais had been wide-eyed with fear at first, thinking that the wrath of God was being visited upon them, but Morphia and Countess Maria had taken the event in their stride. 'Not a year goes by without some shuddering of the earth,' Morphia told her. 'Perhaps not so much in Jerusalem, but here it is a part of life . . . like riding a half-broken horse. You grow accustomed.'

Annais was not sure whether to be comforted or not.

The city walls had withstood the thunder. Accompanied by their women, Morphia and Countess Maria rode out to inspect the damage. Joscelin had left Turbessel in order to harry Aleppo and its environs and, for the moment, the women were nominally in command of the city. They distributed alms in the form of silver coins, food and wine, but although the quake had been sharp, the damage caused was not as great as it might have been. A few houses had been destroyed and part of the wall near the main gate had tumbled.

On the third morning after the quake, Morphia again summoned her grooms and her women and went to see how the rebuilding work was progressing. The sky was hot and blue. Sweat prickled Annais's brow and stung her eyes. The smell of ripe dung wafted on the air, and the sound of loud braying as a train of asses laden with kindling were drawn to the side to let the royal party pass.

As they approached the gates, Morphia's chaplain bestowed alms on the beggars crowding there, but the charity-giving was disturbed by a flurry at the gates themselves. Morphia's guards closed protectively around the Queen and gestured her ladies to draw together, but it swiftly became obvious that the commotion was one of excitement and joy rather than an incipient riot.

Moments later two Saracen horses pranced through the entranceway, a chestnut mare and a bay gelding with tasselled bridles and saddlecloths.

'Jesu . . . Holy Mary, Mother of God!' Annais's hands flew to her mouth, but in shock rather than a belated attempt to smother her oath. Her lips formed her husband's name against the pressure of her fingers and her eyes widened to drink in the sight of the two men astride the horses, surrounded by an escort of grinning, exclaiming soldiers.

'Sabin!' Before the word had been whispered. Now she shrieked it at the top of her lungs, not caring who heard.

His head came up and his eyes sought hers among the crowd. He looked as wild and unkempt as a desert wolf, his hair tangled and dusty, a grizzle of beard outlining his jaw. A sheathless scimitar was thrust through his belt and his tunic bore dark stains of blood and sweat. His lips parted and she saw him say her name in reply. Suddenly she was thrusting past the guards, shouldering and pushing her way through the crowd, using her elbows like a fishwife, her only thought to reach him.

Sabin swung from the horse, fought his way to her and, without a care for the onlookers, pulled her fiercely into his arms and crushed his mouth down on hers. It was a rough embrace, devoid of courtliness and consideration . . . and it fulfilled all of Annais's dreams. She kissed him just as fiercely back, her fingers clenching in his long hair, her body arching to his.

'Ah God, ah Christ, I dreamed of this when I was on the verge of madness and it kept me whole,' Sabin gasped as they broke the embrace, only to kiss again and again until their lips were bruised and aching.

'I thought . . . I did not know if you were dead. I told myself not, I would have known . . . but . . .' Weeping, laughing, she clung to him. Then Sabin disengaged one arm and turned her on the other to face her father who was watching the two of them with a poignant expression and wet eyes. 'Papa!' she cried and, feeling a strand of guilt at having ignored him, ran from Sabin's embrace into his. New tears poured down her face and she felt her father shaking as he too wept.

'Child, child, I thought I would never see you again . . .'

He swallowed deep in his throat, striving for control. 'How is my grandson?'

'Walking!' Annais laughed through her tears. 'And learning words so swiftly that already he chatters like a magpie!'

Strongfist swiped his hand across his eyes. 'It will heal me to see him,' he said. 'Already I feel closer to being whole than I have in an age.' He held her away and pushed her gently back towards Sabin. 'Your place is first at your husband's side,' he said. A look passed between him and Sabin, of acknowledgement and acceptance, which was intercepted by Queen Morphia, a flush mantling her high cheekbones, and a certain tautness to her jaw.

Belatedly Sabin and Strongfist knelt and bowed their heads.

'Get up,' Morphia said. 'A lapse is understandable in the circumstances.' Her tone forgave them, while reminding them that she was Queen and expected respect. 'Now tell us what you are doing here. Are you alone as it seems? Do you have news of the King?'

It was very late. In the guest chamber, the scented oil lamps had burned down and been replenished, the wine flagons emptied and refilled. Queen Morphia had been given a full accounting of what had happened between Joscelin's flight from Kharpurt and Sabin and Strongfist's escape from the detail sent to Harran, and had retired to her own apartment to digest the news and decide how next to proceed.

Strongfist drained his cup, wiped his beard and eased to his feet. 'I'm for my bed,' he said, 'before the dawn catches me out of it. Do not expect to see me early on the morrow.' Standing up, he stretched, and smiled at Sabin as the young man rose to acknowledge the farewell. 'Not that I expect you and my daughter will be rising early yourselves.'

'Queens and small children will not wait,' Annais said, rising too and kissing her father's cheek. Her complexion was flushed, partly with wine, partly from the path the conversation was taking.

'Well then, make the most of the time you have remaining.'

A smile set tired creases in Sabin's cheeks and lit in his eyes. 'I remember the days when you warned me against such occupation.'

'I remember the days when your reputation was different to that you hold today. Besides, the advice was for my daughter, not you.' He saluted them both and passed quietly beyond the archway curtain, his tread heavy with weariness.

Sabin sat down on the bench, adjusted the cushions and poured the last of the wine into their goblets. He was heavy-eyed and very tired, but reluctant to yield the sweetness of these moments for slumber. Annais sat down beside him and cuddled into the embrace of his arm.

'He took Mariamne's death hard,' Sabin murmured. 'I think that he was prepared to hate her for what she had done, but when it came to the crux he could not. Then he began to think that there might be a chance for them if they could survive Kharpurt.'

'Do you think there was?' There was doubt in Annais's voice, perhaps even a hint of antipathy.

Sabin sighed. 'If the truth be known, no,' he said, 'but I would never say as much to your father. At least since she is truly dead, he can mourn her in a proper fashion now. Before, his mourning was tainted.'

Annais digested his words and nodded agreement. Then she twisted to look up at him.

'What?' he asked.

'I cannot believe that you are here,' she said. 'I have to pinch myself to make sure you are real.'

Sabin grinned. 'I can pinch you if you want . . . although I am sure there are better ways of convincing you how real I am . . .'

Her gaze narrowed, but her eyes were melting. 'I'm sure there are . . . if only I could remember them. It has been so long.'

'Is that an invitation to be reminded?'

She made a slumberous sound and twined her arms around his neck. 'What do you think?'

'I think it is well that I have a better memory than you,' he said and, taking her hand, led her to the bed with its feather mattress and scented linen sheets.

Chapter 28

'Snow.' Fergus rubbed his hands and held them out to the heat of the charcoal brazier. 'It puts me in mind o' the Eildon hills where I used tae ride when I was a lad. I mind many folk didna like it, but it does me fine.'

Sabin and Strongfist exchanged grins. Fergus's Scots accent was always more pronounced when he was reminiscing. A bellyful of spiced wine had made him loquacious. Indeed, the strong brew seemed to have gone straight to the tips of his hair, for it bushed out from his scalp like a dandelion seedhead.

'Always used to give me chilblains,' Strongfist said. 'I never felt the ground I was walking in the harshest winters because my boots were so stuffed with fleece. Some years I lived in my gambeson too.'

'I remember some good snow brawls at court . . . and at my father's keep at Fotheringay.' Rising to his feet, Sabin took his cup of spiced wine and moved to the window embrasure. Outside the dusk was filled with a mass of whirling white flakes. The sky was darkening into nightfall, but it had been dull all day, with a burden of snow, and the accompanying wind was bitter enough to freeze the features off a man's face. Yet he welcomed the weather. It was an excuse for coddling oneself over a hearth, mending weapons, taking stock, and talking companionably with friends and lovers. After the parched, burning summer, it was pleasant, too, to see the ground clothed in white.

He hadn't thought of his father in a while, or if he had, only in the course of ordinary remembering. The sharpness of the pain had dulled to the ache of an old scar. In his mind's eye he saw himself, a child forming the powdery snow into balls in sheepskin-mittened hands and hurling them at the slender, laughing man with bright brown hair and fox-gold eyes.

'Good thing you arrived when you did,' Strongfist said to Fergus, 'otherwise you'd be a corpse in a drift by now.'

'I'd ha' stopped in the monastery down the pass if I'd thought the snow was going tae outrun me,' Fergus retorted. 'Credit me wi' some sense.'

'If you had sense you would still be in Jerusalem,' Strongfist said. 'Not that it isn't a pleasure to see you.'

'Ach, Jerusalem's so full of officials and diplomats that the streets almost run with slime,' Fergus said.

'I thought it was full of Venetians . . . or so we heard.' Sabin turned from the embrasure, caught Annais's eye and winked. She was kneeling on a gazelle skin rug that had been placed atop the floor rushes, a sleepy Guillaume cuddled in her lap.

'Aye, them too, the blood-sucking weasels.' Fergus made to spit on the floor, belatedly recalled his manners and swallowed instead. 'Do you know what they demanded as the price for helping us besiege Tyre?'

Sabin shook his head. 'No, but doubtless you are going to tell us.' Although Montabard was a frontier fortress, they received the news often enough from Jerusalem via Antioch. Venice and the kingdom of Jerusalem had been locked in negotiations for some considerable time. The maritime power of the Venetians was second to none, and their demands in return for the borrowing of that power were also second to none. There was a plan to snatch the lucrative port of Tyre from its Muslim rulers, but it couldn't be done without help from the sea.

'Aye, I'll tell ye,' Fergus growled. 'They're to get a street with a church, and a bakery and a bathhouse, free of all obligation . . .'

'That's not so bad,' Strongfist settled himself more comfortably in his chair. He contemplated his cup. Sabin signalled and a servant moved to refill it from the flagon mulling near the hearth.

' . . . in every town of the kingdom,' Fergus added with a ferocious frown. 'If that's no' greedy, I don't know what is. And they're to be allowed to use their own weights and measures for all transactions – amongst us all, not just themselves.' He spread his free hand and counted off his fingers. 'They're to be given houses in Acre, and if they help capture Tyre and Ascalon, they're to receive a third of the cities, and they're to be paid a yearly sum of three hundred Saracen bezants from revenues at Acre . . . tcha!' He gulped down the rest of his wine and the servant crossed over to him.

Sabin smiled. 'I think I want to be a Venetian,' he said.

'If you were, laddie, I'd nae be supping wine sae freely at your board. The bastards also want a say in what the kingdom charges other nations in customs dues. The Patriarch has agreed for now, but King Baldwin won't wear it. It'll make his crown worthless.'

'Merchants are always avaricious because they know their value,' Sabin said, 'but you are right. The King will not be happy with that last clause.'

'If he ever wins free of captivity,' Strongfist said morosely. 'Balak shows no signs of being open to negotiation.'

'Why should he when just by holding on to Baldwin he keeps the upper hand?' Sabin answered. He pressed the knuckle of his index finger to his forehead. They had discussed this point repeatedly like a serpent swallowing its own tail. They were due back in the field in a fortnight's time. Joscelin and the northern army were planning a series of raids on the area around Aleppo where Balak's rule was weak and disputed. The intention was to harry the spider, force him out onto the strands of his web and persuade him to yield his parcelled treasure.

Fergus turned to Strongfist. 'So where are ye going?' he asked Strongfist. 'North with the laddie, or to Tyre with me?'

'I thought you did not like Venetians,' Sabin said mischievously.

Fergus glowered. 'I don't, but needs must when the devil drives and if the bastards are at sea, I dinna have to share their campfires, do I?'

Sabin smothered a grin. 'I suppose not.'

Strongfist shook his head. 'I've sat on my arse at enough sieges to know that I'd be bored out of my skull by the first nightfall. No, give me a warrior's work, not an engineer's. Besides, I have a score to settle with Balak.' His expression grew bleak. 'I will never forget what happened at Kharpurt, but if I take the field against Balak, I can perhaps put it behind me.'

'Suit yoursel'.' Fergus stooped to look at Guillaume who was now asleep in Annais's lap. 'He's a fine wee lad and the spit o' his father. I mind that I mun say a prayer for Gerbert before I leave.'

'I say one for him every day,' Annais said quietly. 'I honour his memory, as Guillaume will do as he grows.'

'I know that, lass.' Fergus's voice was gruff.

The door opened and Letice entered. She had been across to the kitchens to have a word with the cook and the cloak she had donned for the short walk was starred with snowflakes. They sparkled and melted on her veil, and her cheeks were flushed with the brightness of the cold. Her braids shone below her veil, bright as new copper and barely stranded with silver. Strongfist's gaze dwelt on her briefly before sliding away to the middle distance. She glanced at him, and then walked past to hang her cloak on one of the pegs hammered into the wall.

Sabin eyed the interchange thoughtfully and raised his brow at Annais who returned him a conspiratorial look.

Later that evening, when they were in bed, she turned on her side to face him. 'Letice and my father,' she said.

'I noticed.'

'What do you think?'

'You can bring a horse to water, but you cannot force it to drink. It has to be thirsty of its own accord.' By the light of the night candle her hair shone like black water. He reached out to take a tendril between his fingers. 'But it might be good for both of them.'

'Yes,' she murmured. 'And I have an idea.'

Sabin gave a theatrical groan and received a kick. He yelped and complained of Annais's cold feet.

'I shall not tell you,' she sniffed.

'I promise I am all ears now.' He pulled her closer and drew the fur coverlet up around their heads. 'You know I was but teasing.'

'Then perhaps I should tease you too and say nothing.'

He kissed her in the tender spot behind her earlobe and cupped her breast. 'Tell me,' he said. 'I promise to listen.'

'I'm not sure . . .' She stretched her throat to give him better access. 'Perhaps I prefer the persuasion to the telling.'

'Do you? So do I.' He moved over her and for a while was so persuasive that by the time she was convinced, she was exhausted and glowing and there was not an inch of her that was cold.

Lying against him, regaining her pleasure-scattered wits, she smiled. 'All I was going to say is that when we leave for the court at Turbessel, I will bring Letice with me as my senior lady and leave Soraya here. Soraya is uncomfortable with the outside world, but she is capable of performing the duties of a chatelaine. It is not as if I will need her to play nurse to Guillaume. Usually I am nearby, and when I am not, the Queen and Countess Maria keep nurses for the children. Princess Joveta is only just four years old, and Maria's daughter Stephanie but a babe in arms. Letice will enjoy the change and if anything is to develop between her and my father, it can do so in its own good time rather than being forced.'

'It seems a fair suggestion,' Sabin said huskily. He was

still recovering his breath. 'I did wonder if your father might go with Fergus to besiege Tyre, but the wounds inflicted at Kharpurt run deep. I think he is right when he says that they will not begin to heal until he can bandage them with battle.' He felt her stiffen. She rubbed her cheek against his shoulder.

'I do not like to think of either of you in battle,' she said.

Sabin said nothing. There was no comfort to offer her except to say that he and her father had been trained to the sword from birth and that their equipment was of the best. She knew those things already. She also knew that they had not been enough to save Gerbert from a drawn-out and painful death.

'I hold Guillaume in my arms,' she said, her voice muffled against his flesh. 'I have fed him at my breast and watched him fall asleep. I have tended his hurts when he has fallen over, and protected him as fiercely as a lioness protecting her cub. But how will I protect him when he is a young man stepping out in the world with a sword at his hip?'

'You can't,' Sabin said. 'And that is your burden to bear. All you can do is fit him for what the world will throw at him. That will be his protection.' He grimaced. 'My life might have been easier if that had been done for me.'

'Did not the Countess Matilda care for you?'

'She did her best to be fair,' he said neutrally.

Annais rubbed her forefinger against his bicep. 'But fairness is not love.'

'No.'

'What of your mother?'

He shrugged. 'She chose to serve God. My father never held anything back from me. I know that I was conceived in the town of Durazzo on his way home from the great crusade. My mother was travelling under his protection and she had nursed him back from the brink of death when an old injury festered. They were not habitual lovers and they lay together but once. By the time she realised she was with child, their ways had parted. Since a nun cannot keep a baby, and since the only other recourse open to her was to give me to the Church or renounce her vows, she sent for my father and he took me into his household.'

Annais paused her stroking. 'I could not have given up Guillaume for a life in Holy Orders. Indeed, I would kill anyone who tried to take him from me.'

'But then you have no vocation and no difficult choices to make,' he said softly. 'If my mother had left the cloister, she would have had to live as my father's mistress. If anything happened to him – which it did – she would have been left to fend for herself.'

Annais made a sound that said she understood, but was not happy with the verdict. 'Does she still live?'

He shook his head. 'She died when I was a small child. The Abbess at her convent wrote to my father to tell him. I visited her grave when I was in Normandy with the court, but it looked like all the others and there was nothing it could tell me that I did not already know.'

She made a small, comforting sound in her throat.

Sabin looked at her and smiled, albeit wryly. 'It is all right,' he said. 'I can view it from a distance these days and without too much pain. My father told me that my mother was the daughter of King William the Conqueror's chief falconer. I was thinking how fitting it is that I should have come to Montabard with its shahins. Here, for the first time, I feel as if I belong.'

Chapter 29

Spring 1124

Princess Joveta had a fever. Rubbing her eyes, grizzling to herself, she lay on a settle in the women's room, covered by a light woollen blanket. She had spent the night shivering and vomiting and, at first light, her mother had sent for the royal physician. He had dosed the child with a tisane of feverfew and given instructions that she was to sip water lightly sweetened with honey.

Annais sat with the child while the Queen was absent in conference with her ministers. Joveta preferred Annais above all Morphia's women and was so frequently at Annais's side that newcomers to the court sometimes mistook them for mother and daughter, although their only resemblance was the colour of their eyes.

'Hush, sweetheart, hush,' Annais soothed, stroking the little girl's flushed brow. She hoped that the fever was caused by something Joveta had eaten and was not going to sweep through the rest of the royal nursery. Infants were so vulnerable, and bouts such as this were responsible for many a child's death. Guillaume was only eighteen months old, Joscelin's daughter Stephanie even younger. Nor was it wise to be complacent about the older children, Joscelin's heir and namesake, aged eleven, or Joveta's three sisters.

'My head hurts.'

'That's because you didn't sleep last night. Master Gregorio has given you a potion to make you better. It will begin to work very soon.' At least, she thought, Joveta had not vomited it back up. That had to be a good sign. 'Here, take a sip for me, sweetheart, and I'll play you a magic tune on my harp.'

Joveta allowed herself to be propped up and obediently took a couple of swallows from the goblet of honey and water. The goblet itself was made from green chalcedony, purported to ward off poison. 'Why is it magic?' Joveta's little voice was rough and cracked.

'Because it comes all the way from Scotland,' Annais said in a soft voice. 'From the Eildon hills where the Fairy Queen dwells with her court. Sometimes, if you are in that country and you listen hard, you can hear the sound of her silver bridle bells as she rides by with her knights and squires.'

Joveta's gaze widened. 'Have you heard them?'

Annais smiled and shook her head. 'I grew up in a nunnery and walls will stop such sounds. But sometimes, when I had been riding in the cold, windy air, perhaps what I mistook for the call of the bird was the chime of a fairy bell.'

She fetched her harp and drew it carefully from its leather carrying case, noting that Joveta, although heavy-eyed, had forgotten her tears. Having spent a few moments tuning the strings, Annais began to stir them with her fingers, creating a gentle breeze of notes. 'Imagine you are standing on a hill-side,' she murmured. 'Cool green grass beneath your feet and white daisies scattered about. A breeze strokes the heat from your body and you feel as light as air . . . There is a stream running down the hillside and you can hear it bubbling over the stones . . .' She made the harp suit the words.

'Can I hear the fairy bells?'

'You have to go higher up the hill for that . . . to the very top where no one goes except sometimes a shepherd and his sheep. Close your eyes the better to hear . . . no, not tightly, just let your lids lie like petals over your eyes . . . .'

Annais continued to pluck the harp, picking out sweet,

individual notes. Joveta's breathing slowed and the flush left her cheeks. When Annais ceased playing and held her hand above the child's body, the furnace-like heat was much reduced. The feverfew was doing its work. Feeling less anxious, Annais continued to play until she was certain that the little girl was asleep.

Finally she set her harp aside and rose from the couch. A little distance from Joveta's sickbed, some of the other women were sewing and talking quietly. The nurses had taken the rest of the children out to play and, for the moment, the room was peaceful. She sat down beside Letice and picked up the edge of the embroidery on which the older woman was competently working.

Letice cast a glance towards the couch. 'How is she?'

'Improving. I hope the worst is over.' Annais drew an ivory needle case from the pouch at her belt, selected a fine silver needle and searched among the skeins of thread for the right colour.

'Aye, it is always a cause for anxiety when they are so young.'

Annais threaded the needle and set it into the bleached cotton. 'It is the common lot of women to worry their nails down to the quick.'

'Indeed so,' Letice said. Her stitches were swift and neat. Annais watched her hands for a moment. They were large for a woman's, but surprisingly deft at the delicate work.

'I hope there is news soon,' Annais said.

Letice gave her a keen look and squeezed her hand. 'Bless you, of course there will be. Lord Joscelin's courier service to the Queen is second to none. He's a competent commander, and those are skilled men he has with him.'

Annais tilted her head in acknowledgement and did not add the obvious detail that Balak was a competent commander too, with seasoned troops at his back. There had been a rebellion against his authority in the city of Membij and the rebels had appealed to Joscelin for help. Joscelin had leaped at the opportunity to poke Balak in the eye and ridden out in haste to Membij's aid. Now came the waiting: the dragging minutes, hours and days of silence while her father and Sabin gambled their lives.

'Are you not concerned?' she asked Letice.

'Of course I am . . . although my anxiety is bound to be less than yours.'

Annais sewed in silence.

Letice said, 'I know that you and Sabin have been quietly building a marriage bed for your father and me.' She raised her hand as Annais drew breath. 'No, do not deny it. Age has the advantage of conferring experience, if naught else.'

Annais flushed with chagrin, but Letice's eyes were bright with humour.

'Oh, I do not blame you. Indeed I am flattered that you would choose to consider calling me mother, but I am not sure it is the right thing – and neither is your father.'

Annais's gaze widened. 'You have discussed it with him?'

Letice shook her head. 'No, but I have seen his awkwardness. He is still in mourning for the wife he lost at Kharpurt – or so it seems to me.'

Annais stabbed the needle into the fabric and took several hard, angry stitches, which she had then to undo. 'Then perhaps he needs a new interest – beyond war – to help him forget. She is not worth the depth of his grief.'

'And I need a husband, poor dried-up stick that I am.'

'No! I never thought like that, I swear I did not!' Annais was mortified and Letice swiftly patted her again.

'I know that, child,' she said. 'And indeed I do like your father. He is a good man . . . but you can only help matters so far. The dish has to cook by itself.'

Their conversation ceased then, because the Queen returned from conferring with her ministers and hearing the day's news. There was little to report, except that the siege of Tyre was progressing slowly but steadily in Frankish favour. There had been alarm when the Egyptian army had come marauding in the south, but the danger had faded away like mountain mist under the burn of a summer sun. A threat to Tyre from the Egyptian fleet had been dealt with by the Venetian galleys, which had positioned themselves to intercept any invasion from that quarter.

The Queen briefly relayed her tale to her women and went to check on her youngest daughter who was now sound asleep, her thumb in her mouth.

'You see,' Letice said with a smile and a mischievous eyebrow. 'All is well with the world . . . unless you happen to be a citizen of Tyre.'

'Shall I sit behind your saddle and support you?' Sabin asked.

Strongfist raised his head, which had been bowed over his horse's mane. He was hunched over his saddle, his fingers gripping the reins by instinct rather than conscious effort. They had been clenched around the leather for so long that they were set and cramped with a corpse-like stiffness that was not far from being the truth. 'I am not a puling infant to need a nursemaid to hold me in the saddle,' he snarled. 'When I need your aid, be assured that I will ask for it.'

Sabin frowned at his father-by-marriage. Strongfist had taken a spear in the side during a disastrous skirmish outside Membij. The tip had broken bone, but damaged no vital organs. However, the wound was in danger of going sour, and the hard ride of their retreat had done more damage and caused Strongfist considerable pain. Strongfist was not the kind to cry out, yet Sabin had heard the sounds suppressed in his throat and seen the clenched jaw. He had been alarmed to see blood at the corner of Strongfist's mouth, but it turned out to be the result of a bitten cheek, not a punctured lung. But should a splinter of bone work its way inwards or riding put too much strain on the damaged area, then the danger became mortal. He tried not to think about that. Last year he had returned Gerbert to Montabard, injured but alive, only to watch him die of a protracted bout of wound fever.

Annais had watched him die too, her husband, the father of her son. Time was a healer, but he knew that she would always remember the manner of Gerbert's homecoming. Now Sabin was bringing her another wounded man, beloved to her heart, and the image in her mind would be strengthened. He felt like a messenger of doom.

'Turbessel is not far,' he said. 'We'll be there before dusk and you'll receive all the succour you need . . . a soft bed and syrup of poppy for your injuries.'

Strongfist glared at Sabin. 'I know how far we've to ride.' He caught his breath as his horse jolted him. Sabin winced in sympathy, and turned his head for a moment, giving Strongfist time to adjust. The battle for Membij had been a sound defeat, but not a disaster. Once they had licked their wounds, they still had the wherewithal to go back and try again, but he wondered if they had the heart. Joscelin's deputy, Geoffrey the Monk, who had been his regent at Edessa, had taken an arrow in the throat. Several fine and experienced knights had either been killed or badly injured. Balak was a formidable commander, but his abilities were no greater than Joscelin's. What he had at the moment were luck and confidence.

By the time they approached the walls of Turbessel, the spring sun had passed its zenith and a chill breeze had begun to pry its way through openings in cloaks and tunics. Two wounded knights had died on the last part of the journey and men and horses were stumbling with weariness. Joscelin called a halt to muster the straggling army and gave instructions that they were to march into the city in good order. No dispirited slumping, no bowed heads, no dusty, blood-spattered armour. Even if his army had been defeated, Joscelin had no intention of riding into his capital city like a whipped cur.

Wineskins were passed around and men drank deeply while they summoned their courage and beat the miles and the defeat from their garments and armour.

Strongfist was unable to sit straight, but fiercely declined the suggestion that he might join the wounded in one of the baggage carts. 'I'll ride through those gates with a horse beneath me, and if I die in the doing, then so be it,' he wheezed at Sabin. 'All you need do is help me put on my helm. I cannot raise my hands high enough.'

Sabin plucked Strongfist's arming cap and helm from the strap behind the saddle cantle and, drawing Lucifer close, reached up to place them on Strongfist's head. The nasal bar came down, covering the broad, strong nose. Strongfist's eyes glittered like chips of sapphire glass and his cheekbones glowed as if he had spent half a day drinking in a tavern. A fever was setting in. Sabin wondered grimly how much longer Strongfist's resolve would hold him in the saddle. His thoughts must have shown on his face, for Strongfist scowled at him.

'My grandsire fought the Norsemen at Stamford Bridge, then marched south to Hastings with a spear wound in his leg. He stood on that ridge where the abbey now stands, and he fought your bloody Norman ancestors with his axe, his spear and his bare hands from dawn until nightfall. He stood packed shoulder to shoulder with dead men who could not be moved from the shield wall, so great was the press. And when the Norman King finally gained the battlefield, my grandfather retreated in forced march back to York with a piece of a Norwegian spear still in his leg.'

Sabin's lips twitched. 'So you are not thinking of dying just yet,' he said.

Strongfist's look was baleful. 'You waste so much of your breath on clever words that it's a wonder you have any left on which to live.'

Satisfied that his father-by-marriage was still lively enough to be truculent, Sabin allowed himself a full smile. Nevertheless, when they set out again, he rode unobtrusively close, ready to grasp Strongfist's bridle should he fail.

Joscelin's desire to enter Turbessel in full military array was partially successful. The cavalry drew in their reins so that the horses paced with heads tight in to their chests and stepped high. The armour shone more than it had done before their stop, and the burn of the wine in their blood made men stride out those final paces.

The citizens waited on the walls and lined the roadway from the main gate. At first, the cheering was ragged, but Joscelin knew his people. During the pause on the road, he had changed to a fresh horse and donned a parade surcoat embroidered with gold. Preceded only by his standard-bearers, he rode at the head of the line and raised one arm on high, his fist clenched and the gilded arm brace catching the late rays of the sun. The cheering increased in volume. Fists in the crowd punched the air in reply to Joscelin's signal and the walls echoed with cries of defiance that were almost exultation.

Buoyed by their reception, Joscelin's army did its best to respond. Men sat straighter in the saddle if they could. The footsoldiers did their utmost not to limp. Those who bore banners held them aloft to stream in the evening wind.

'How to make a homecoming victory out of a difficult defeat,' Sabin murmured to Strongfist, who was rigid in the saddle. He had forced himself upright, but the cost showed in his taut expression. Sabin reached to his bridle.

'Do not you dare,' Strongfist said through his teeth.

Sabin took his hand away, but not his scrutiny.

It seemed to take an aeon, but at last they arrived at the palace. Grooms and attendants came running to take the mounts of the senior men. Amalric was there for Sabin, but a thumb jerk sent the youth to Strongfist's tawny stallion.

'Attend him first,' Sabin commanded. Swinging from Lucifer's back, he gestured another knight to help him and together they brought Strongfist down from his horse.

'I tell you I am all right!' Strongfist cried and, on the last utterance, dropped like a stone.

Because Sabin was prepared, he caught him, but the weight strained his arm muscles and almost brought him down too. Carefully, he and the other knight laid Strongfist on the ground and removed his helm. Sabin folded his saddle blanket and used it to cushion the unconscious man's head.

'Leave the horses,' he commanded Amalric. 'Fetch a litter to bear him within.'

The youth sped on his errand, almost colliding with the two women who were rushing out into the ward. Turning at the squire's breathless acknowledgement, Sabin's eyes lit on Annais and Letice.

Annais met his gaze, flew into his arms for a brief embrace, then, reassured that he was whole, fell to her knees beside her father. Letice had already stooped and laid her hand to Strongfist's brow.

'He took a spear in the ribs,' Sabin said, feeling raw with guilt. It was not as if he could have prevented it happening, but being the one to bear the news raised echoes of that terrible homecoming with Gerbert. The sharp gaze that Annais cast him compounded those echoes. He rubbed his neck, turned his back and walked several paces away. Suddenly it was hard to breathe and there was a stinging pressure behind his lids.

Murmuring to Letice, Annais rose to her feet and hastened to Sabin's side.

'He's strong,' Sabin said, only managing to speak after he had swallowed. 'If you had heard him swearing on the ride . . .'

'I know . . .' She wrapped her arm around his. 'Do not blame yourself. I would rather you brought him to me than a stranger—'

'As I brought you Gerbert?' he said harshly.

'Hush.' She laid her fingertips swiftly to his lips. He grasped her wrist in his, trapping her to him and kissed her hand. 'I cannot help but see it,' he said, his voice muffled by her flesh. 'And do not tell me that you do not see the same thing.'

'Seeing with the mind is not the same as seeing with the eyes of now,' she said. 'Just because you have brought my father home wounded does not mean the same outcome as before.'

Sabin shuddered and turned to face the litter. The men-at arms had picked it up and were bearing it within, Letice pacing at the side and holding Strongfist's hand.

'God sometimes works in very mysterious ways,' Annais said, and although her expression was pensive, it was not despairing.

'Very mysterious indeed,' Sabin said bitterly.

Recognising that he was as much in need of care as her father, and that, for the moment, the latter had all the attendance he required, Annais tugged gently on her husband's sleeve. 'Come,' she said. 'Let me unarm you, and you can tell me all that has befallen.'

Chapter 30

As the spring advanced in Turbessel and the snow on the mountains gave way to the green of grass and the mottled dots of grazing sheep, Strongfist's wounds gradually healed. It was a protracted battle and not without setbacks. On several occasions, he developed a high fever and the injury threatened to turn from sour to putrid. Letice took responsibility for most of the nursing. It was she who sat with him, who bathed, bandaged and tended him. Annais was only an auxiliary who took occasional watches when Letice had to sleep; the arrangement was at Letice's insistence.

'You have a husband and son to care for, and the demands of a queen,' Letice said one morning as they stood by the sickbed, where Annais had been taking a turn at watching.

'But still, it is not fair that you should do all the work,' Annais replied.

Letice waved the comment aside. 'I came to Turbessel as your companion, but when you requested my attendance, there was more than one motive . . . and fortunately so. It is no burden to me. I have the time and the patience.' She gestured to the bed and its occupant. 'How is he?'

'I—'

'Trying valiantly to sleep amid a chorus of female chatter,' Strongfist interrupted. Before either woman could move to help him, he drew himself to a sitting position. If he was somewhat stiff about the task, nevertheless, he managed it without wincing. 'I'm sure he will tell you himself,' Annais said and, having kissed her father's cheek in greeting and farewell, went to find Sabin.

Strongfist smiled as he watched his daughter leave. 'I did not mean what I said about the female chatter,' he said.

Letice returned the smile and fetched his tunic, hose and boots. 'I know.'

'But I heard everything that was said.'

She lifted her shoulders. 'I do not suppose that you learned anything of which you were not already aware.'

His eye corners crinkled. 'There has been much talk of leading horses to water and then standing back in the hopes that they might drink.'

Letice laughed but beyond that did not respond. She helped him to dress, her manner efficient but not overbearing, and let him do the parts he could manage himself, patient when he lacked speed.

'I am like an old man I used to know at my brother's castle of Branton,' he said, shaking his head at his weakness. 'But he claimed four-score years and I am scarcely half that age.'

'Then you must have crammed twice as much into your life,' she said.

Strongfist grunted with amusement. 'I know not,' he said, 'because I never asked him his story. Perhaps I should have done.'

'But you have your own to live.' Letice wound his leg bindings neatly from ankle to knee and tucked the ends in at the top. She had noticed that he preferred this older, distinctly English style of dressing. 'Besides, you are not suffering the difficulties of age but of wounding. Given time you will improve.'

'How much time?' Strongfist gazed towards the open window where spring sunshine was dappling through the fretwork. 'High summer? Summer's end? Balak might be at the gates of Turbessel by then.'

'If that happens, then one man will make no difference.'

She stood back, her hands at her hips, and studied him. 'I would say that you will be hale and well long before the sun reaches its zenith.'

He eyed her keenly. 'You believe that? You are not just cozening me like my daughter?'

Letice folded her arms. 'I never cozen,' she said. 'Ever.' Reaching to the side of the bed, she produced his walking stick. It was fashioned of mountain oak, something of a rare wood these days as forests were cut for fuel and building. At first, he had been reluctant to admit that he needed a stick, but since the alternative was languishing in bed, he had grudgingly agreed to try it out. Now he accepted it as a prop to his returning strength and balance, and used it to move gingerly from the bed to the window embrasure.

'So,' he said nonchalantly to Letice, 'do you think that we should oblige them and perhaps drink just a little?'

She faced him. Her braids were the hue of new-hulled chestnuts, just here and there a glitter of silver like spider-strands on a bright autumn morning. Her eyes were a dark green-hazel, rayed at the pupil with flecks of reddish-brown, and seamed with fine lines that showed humour and experience. Suddenly his breath was short, although not in the same manner as when he first set eyes on Mariamne. This was a slower, far subtler burn that had caught him by surprise as it suddenly licked into flame.

She raised her brows. 'Oblige them, or oblige ourselves?' she said.

He cleared his throat. 'Both, I suppose.'

Letice studied him thoughtfully. '"A little" and "suppose" are not urgent encouragement to a baulky mare,' she said, but there was a smile tucked into the severity of her lips.

Strongfist tugged his beard. 'I have no skill with words,' he muttered. 'I do not want to frighten you or see loathing in your eyes.'

'Why should I loathe you for consideration?' she said. 'If we are going to drink, it ought to be full measure.' She came to his side and gave him a candid stare. 'You do not frighten me . . . but I wonder if I frighten you.'

Strongfist looked indignant, but she held his gaze and raised her hand to lay it over his. 'You will soon be clean-shaven,' she said with a smile.

The gesture of her hand over his was intimate. After a brief struggle, he found the courage to close his fingers over hers. 'Yes,' he said, 'you do frighten me . . . but then I am not accustomed to women. I have dwelt with them all my life and still they are more a mystery than my sword or my horse. I don't have the courtly ways or the patience to conquer in that area.'

She considered him, the smile remaining in her eyes. 'Perhaps not,' she said, 'but you have steadfastness and a charm that is your own. Some very pretty scabbards hold fine-looking swords that shatter when put to the test. I do not believe you would do so.' She leaned towards him.

He inhaled the scent of her, felt her warmth, and thought, Why not? She was a widow; he was free to remarry where he wished. If the ghost of Mariamne had trodden hard on his shadow, her haunted step had lightened with each day that his wounds improved, courtesy of the care of this woman at his side. Before caution could reassert itself, he took her in his arms, but gingerly because of his damaged ribs, and he kissed her. And Letice held his face between her hands and kissed him back.

They were married on a fine morning in May when Strongfist was able to bear the weight of his sword on his hip without discomfort and stand without tiring for the duration of the wedding mass afterwards. Taking a brief respite from duty, Fergus arrived from Tyre to bear witness to the marriage and join the celebrations.

'It's a braw lassie you've got yourself,' he said as he gave the bride a smacking kiss on the mouth and a hearty slap on the rump. 'A buxom, bonnie armful. She puts me in mind o' my Margaret.'

Letice decided to take his words and actions as a compliment, only murmuring to her new husband that there were men who were far more challenged than himself in the matter of courtly ways and that he was never to consider himself inadequate again.

In high good humour, Strongfist threw back his head and laughed, squeezing her to his side. The throng of guests repaired to an inn where the wedding feast had been prepared. Fergus descended upon Sabin and Annais like a wild, redhaired dervish.

'And how's my other bonnie lass?' he demanded, engulfing Annais in a hug that drove the breath from her body.

'Squashed,' Sabin said helpfully, since his wife could not speak. Guillaume gripped her skirts and stared up at the fuzzy red-haired giant in astonishment. The child's eyes were huge and his lower lip quivered as he deliberated whether to cry. Sabin swiftly lifted Guillaume in his arms and set him on his shoulders so that the little boy was higher than Fergus. He couldn't see Guillaume's expression, but since no squalls deafened his ears and the small hands clung to his hair like a rider grasping the reins, he judged that disaster had been averted. The move had also cunningly prevented Fergus from clasping Sabin in a similar bone-cracking embrace.

'Och, it's good to see you all.' Fergus snatched up a passing flagon and hugged it to his silk-clad chest. Coarse red hair poked above the throat-lacing of his shirt. 'I'm right glad that Edmund's found himself another woman. I felt bad about Mariamne. If I had known what a slut she truly was, I'd not have pushed the match.'

'That part is over,' Sabin said quietly. 'And whatever the things she did, calling her a slut is a harsh judgement.'

Fergus shrugged and swigged from the flagon. 'That's a matter of opinion, lad, but I'll no' tarnish his wedding feast by airing mine more than once, and never in his hearing.' He winked up at Guillaume, who leaned over and buried his face in Sabin's hair. 'A stout wee lad,' he said. 'You'll be wanting brothers and sisters for him foreby, I warrant.' He looked at Annais, his eyes shrewdly assessing her slender figure. She swiftly clasped her hands before her waist as if closing a door inadvertently left open.

'As God wills,' Sabin answered. He could almost see the old rogue calculating how long they had been wed and measuring it against their progress or lack of it in that area. He changed the subject. 'How is the siege progressing?' He thought that it must be going slowly for Fergus to spare the time to come to Turbessel, and with such a fiery surplus of energy that once the drink got inside him, he was going to be the devil himself to control.

'Och, Tyre will fall, it's only a matter of time.' Fergus rested his free hand on the sword at his left hip. 'It's taken a while because they had plenteous rain in the winter and early spring and it filled all the cisterns. They're starting to run short o' water now though, and the Venetian blockade means there are no supplies coming to them from the sea.' He nudged Sabin. 'I know it's been hard for the northern army and ye've taken some blows, but while you're keeping Balak occupied, it means that he's not able to send help down to Tyre. Every soldier o' theirs you wound means one less to man their walls and their siege machines.'

Sabin looked wry. Every sortie against Balak meant less of their own troops too, and they were no further forward than they had ever been.

'Is there any sign of a ransom being agreed?'

Sabin shook his head and sighed. 'Balak sends his representatives and the Queen sends hers. They take sherbet, they talk, but that is all it is. Smooth words and no substance. Balak has no reason to release the King unless it be in exchange for his kingdom.'

'Aye, well, once Tyre is in our hands, we'll give him a reason.' Fergus clenched his fist to emphasise his words. Then, seeing a friend among the wedding guests, he took himself off to bend the man's ear. Sabin exhaled with relief and gave Annais a rueful grin.

'Subtle as a wild bull in a street of pottery-sellers,' he said, 'but he means well.'

Annais removed the hand she had laid across her belly and smiled, although the expression did not quite light her eyes. 'I know that . . . and he is kin, so we make allowances. Who knows, when the time does come to give Guillaume a brother or sister, he or she may inherit that red hair. Both his sons have it and I am told that it comes from my great-grandfather.'

Sabin screwed up his face. 'That would be easier to bear than certain other traits,' he said, and tumbled Guillaume down from his shoulders into his arms. He had not missed the wistful note in his wife's voice. They had been very careful thus far, very careful indeed.

'If you want—' he began, and saw that she had been thinking along the same lines as him, for she shook her head.

'I do want,' she said, 'but not here, not in Turbessel when so much is at stake and the Queen needs me and you are so often away on skirmishes and patrols. Let it wait until we return to Montabard . . . unless you . . .'

'What man does not want to see himself live on in his children and to boast to other men of his virility?' He smiled at her. 'I would not regret the news that you carry a child, but for the moment I think it remains best to be careful.'

She nodded and the moment passed, with agreement and wistfulness on both sides.

The wedding feast was a noisy, joyful affair. Men and women were eager to release their tension in drink and dancing, to forget the protracted war with Balak and the fact that their King was held captive deep in the enemy's territory. Some bought pleasure with wine; others used it to seek oblivion, or to release their emotions in weeping.

Strongfist and Letice danced a measure, circling and

turning to the cheers and whistles of the guests. Sabin and Annais joined them, and Guillaume came too, performing his own version of the steps to the great amusement and pride of the adults.

The open inn door spilled light and music into the courtyard beyond. An entertainer from the town had brought his dancing bear to the celebration and it shambled to the music of an oud, its brown fur gleaming with the reflection of the torches burning in sockets either side of the door. Sabin was outside with Guillaume, watching the beast, when a horseman came thundering into the tavern courtyard, slid to a halt and even as he drew on the reins was already dismounting.

'News!' he bellowed. 'I have great news from the palace!'

The oud fell silent and the bear dropped from its hind legs to all four paws. Laughter and conversation raggedly ceased and the crowd turned its attention to the stranger.

'Balak is dead!' the man bellowed, his voice cracking with excitement. 'Of an arrow wound at Membij!' Tossing his reins to one of the onlookers, he strode inside the tavern to deliver his tidings to the other revellers. An instant later a massive cheer shook the hostel to its foundations. Sabin lifted Guillaume in his arms and pushed his way within. Annais was squeezing towards the entrance to find him. Meeting near the door, they hugged each other joyfully. Fergus appeared and pummelled Sabin's arm.

'Did ye hear?' he demanded with savage exultation. 'Did ye hear? Now we have the bastards by their short hair. There'll be no relief force for Tyre. Hah!' Seizing Annais, he gave her a bruising kiss on the lips, and then, full of drink-fuelled energy, hurtled in search of fresh victims to embrace.

The messenger came hurrying towards them. Having delivered his news to the wedding feast where many of the guests were knights of the northern army, he had other destinations in the city to visit. As he made to pass, Sabin caught his sleeve. 'How did it happen?'

'A stray arrow from the citadel with Balak's name upon it,'

the man said and his smile was still bright with relish although he must have told the tale a hundred times. 'The Queen has summoned a meeting for the morrow.'

'Who inherits King Baldwin's captivity?'

'The Emir Timurtash, so I'm told.' The messenger nodded to terminate the conversation and left.

'That is good news too,' Sabin said. 'Timurtash is not forged of the same bitter steel as Balak. It is likely that we will be able to negotiate a ransom price with him for Baldwin.' He smiled suggestively at her through half-closed lids. 'And then we can return to Montabard.'

The rejoicing continued long into the night, for now there was not only a wedding to celebrate, but the death of the kingdom of Jerusalem's most formidable opponent. There might be threats from other neighbouring sultans and emirs along the Frankish borders, but none as potent as Balak had posed.

The newlyweds were escorted to a fine private bedchamber on the floor above the main room. The bed was garlanded with spring flowers and made up with fresh sheets of woven cotton and a coverlet of fine-spun wool, embroidered in the Armenian fashion. The priest blessed husband and wife with holy water and did his best to ignore the bawdy jests that flew thicker than arrows in a battle. Strongfist took it in good part and Letice endured with steady fortitude.

Fergus's comments were by far the coarsest, with many references to siege engines and battering rams. Sabin managed to grab him and propel him out of the room before his comments cut too close to the bone. Fergus swung a wild punch, fell over, and then began to snore. Sabin dragged Fergus by the armpits into the side of a timber-covered walkway, covered him with his cloak, and left him to sleep it off.

'Reminds me of my days at King Henry's court,' he said to Annais as they went to find their own sleeping space in one of the outbuildings that the innkeeper had refurbished for the wedding guests. 'I was always either in the same state as Fergus or helping out one of the other squires . . . or,' he added softly, 'in some woman's bed.' His hand rested lightly on her waist as he spoke, and suddenly the atmosphere burned with tension.

'I thought King Henry didn't approve of drunkenness and debauchery?' She gave him a look of mock severity. Her eyes were as dark as the darkness, but gleaming like jewels.

'Well, he was always strict about the drunkenness, so what went on usually took place away from his scrutiny. As to the debauchery . . . well, you don't beget a score of bastards by living the life of a saint.' He pushed open the door of the outbuilding. It had been swept out, washed with lime and draped with woollen hangings. There was a mattress on the floor stuffed with fragrant bracken and herbs and the floor was strewn with thick, fresh straw. It was inevitable that the conversation and the surroundings should remind Sabin of another tavern and a November evening when he had stood on a similar, if more opulent threshold with Lora. For a moment he hesitated in the doorway, but when Annais gave him a questioning look, he shook his head and stepped inside.

Guillaume was so tired that he flopped like one of Joveta's cloth dolls and within moments of being laid down on the mattress and covered up, was soundly asleep. Watching Annais tend the child, Sabin's heart filled with a pain of love and lust so strong that it stung his eyes.

She smoothed Guillaume's brow, then rose from her stoop. For a moment, they looked at each other, and then she went into Sabin's arms and raised her head to meet the downward slant of his.

Mindful of the sleeping child, they kissed and caressed in silence, but the constraint of making no sound heightened the intensity of sensation, driving it inwards, turning the core of the act to molten white heat. Annais forgot all about the precaution of fleece and vinegar and clasped herself fiercely around Sabin, refusing to let him go. And Sabin followed her willingly, letting the healing fire of now immolate the memories of the past and overlay them with the promise of the future.

Chapter 31

'You handle a falcon well . . . for a Frank,' said Usamah ibn Munqidh, with an approving nod at the young shahin perched upon Sabin's gauntleted wrist. The Saracen lord was of a similar age to Sabin and, like Sabin, was raven haired, with eyes of changeable lion-hazel and a thin, quick smile. The likeness had been remarked upon more than once, much to the amusement of the two men who jestingly called each other 'brother' and had taken to sharing each other's company. Usamah was the nephew of the Emir of Shaizar, who had travelled to Turbessel to broker a ransom arrangement between Timurtash, inheritor of Balak's lands, and Queen Morphia for the release of her husband and his relatives.

'It is in my blood,' Sabin replied in Arabic. 'My grandfather was chief falconer to a king.' He took no offence at Usamah's patronising tone. The Saracen's charm and good humour offset his superior air. Besides, he deserved to be cocksure. Shaizar was an impregnable fortress, and the Munqidh lords of his family were respected, formidable warriors as well as being accomplished diplomats and men of high education. Since the rulers of Shaizar were keen huntsmen, Sabin and the court at Turbessel had been out with hawk and hound, with trained cheetah and bow and spear for the best part of a week, entertaining their Saracen guests.

Sabin stroked the bird's breast feathers with a gentle forefinger. 'When I was a squire, the King of England let me handle his white gyrfalcon.'

Usamah's eyes gleamed. 'Ah, one of those I would like to have, but I do not think they would do well in our country.'

'They might among the mountains where it is high and cold.'

Usamah shook his head. 'No,' he said. 'Look at the way you Franks do not prosper away from your own lands. Each creature has its own natural territory.'

Sabin smiled politely and did not argue the point.

The grooms brought the horses around. Usamah had a fine black mare with hard blue hooves and a sweeping elegance of carriage that made many a Christian lord watch her with envy. But then, as Usamah was fond of saying, the lords of Shaizar excelled in all things.

Usamah gained the saddle and drew the reins through his fingers. Gold tassels fringed the mare's browband and saddlecloth. Usamah's turban was pinned with an emerald the size of a walnut shell.

Sabin mounted his own horse. The women were emerging from the palace to bid the men good hunting – although everyone knew that more than hunting was on the day's agenda. There was the business of King Baldwin's ransom to negotiate. Discussions had taken place long into the night between Joscelin, Morphia and the Emir of Shaizar. Now the Emir and Joscelin would speak further while they rode, and there was to be another immediate council on their return, involving the Queen. Morphia was tenacious of her power.

Sabin eyed his Saracen companion. 'Do you know how much it is going to cost us for King Baldwin's return?'

Usamah smiled, revealing a dazzle of white teeth. 'That is easy,' he said. 'A king's ransom.'

Sabin made a face. He had asked for that.

'Not so much that it is refused,' Usamah temporised. 'Emir Timurtash does not want the responsibility of holding your

King. To him, the money – whatever the sum – will be more useful.'

He waved his hand and his groom rode up on a dappled gelding. Perched behind him on the crupper was a cheetah, a gilded collar around its neck, a chain of silver links running between it and the groom's hand. At first Sabin had been somewhat unnerved at the sight of the huge cat, but he had gradually grown accustomed to its presence among Usamah's hunting menagerie of hawks and hounds. He had been surprised to find that it had paws like a dog's, with claws that remained set and did not retract – the reason, Usamah said, for its great speed.

The women came among the men, handing up farewell cups of wine to the Franks, sherbet to the Muslims, and wished all good hunting. Annais smiled at Sabin's stirrup and gave him first the wine, and then Guillaume, who was clamouring to sit in the saddle. The warm wind ruffled his light brown curls and shone in his eyes, making them a pale, almost translucent grey. 'A fine boy,' Usamah said. 'Although he looks not like you.'

Sabin gave the Saracen an amused look. 'There would be hell to pay if he did resemble me, since he is the son of Gerbert de Montabard, God rest his soul. Gerbert died of a battle wound when my stepson was still in swaddling.'

'Ah.' Usamah nodded. 'I remember him. Occasionally he visited Shaizar on business for your King.' He looked speculatively at Guillaume, and the narrow quality of his gaze caused the hair to rise at the back of Sabin's neck, although he could not have said why. Feeling thoroughly disturbed, he returned the infant to Annais, then his empty cup.

'Good hunting,' she said. 'Be careful.'

Setting his qualm aside, Sabin forced a smile. 'That's a contradiction,' he teased, 'but I promise to do my best to keep my hide whole.'

Usamah was curious about Sabin's life at King Henry's court and asked detailed questions about Frankish ways, which

Sabin answered with good humour. They talked of the different domestic habits, of bathing and diet, of weapons and military training. Usamah wanted to know what had brought Sabin to Outremer.

'Were you following your God, or was it the notion of land to plunder and infidels to kill?' he asked.

Sabin shook his head. 'I was fleeing trouble at home.' He told Usamah about the circumstances of his arrival in Outremer. 'It was supposed to be a pilgrimage of atonement,' he said. 'And somewhere to dwell for a while until the dust settled.'

'So you will go back to your people and your homeland one day?' Usamah's hazel eyes were shrewd.

'There is nothing there for me. In truth, if I returned, I suspect all that settled dust would blow up again within days of me stepping over my family's threshold.'

'But you would be returning as a man, not a fickle youth.'

'Precisely,' Sabin said wryly.

During their conversation, they had fallen behind from the main hunting party, although Usamah's groom still attended them with the cheetah on his saddle and Amalric rode behind, armed with several spears and a bow. As they pushed their mounts through a cane-brake of licorice trees to catch up with the hunt, Usamah's fawn saluki bitch nosed into a thicker part of the undergrowth and began to growl. There was a burst of vigorous rustling, a squeal and then the dog yelped and shot backwards, its chest and flank ripped open to the bone. A boar charged out of the undergrowth, its yellow tushes stained with the saluki's blood. Usamah exchanged his falcon for a spear from his groom and hurled it at the boar. The point penetrated its shoulder, but did not pierce deeply enough to create a mortal wound or lodge in the flesh. Shaking off the lance, the pig darted back into the thicket.

With pounding heart, Sabin gave his own hawk to a white-faced Amalric and armed himself with a spear. Sabin had often hunted boar in England and Normandy, but only as part of a general crowd and he had never been of sufficient importance at court to be granted the privilege of making a kill. The boar was a formidable enemy. Unlike a deer, it would turn and fight while still fresh, and its tusks were powerful enough to disembowel dog, horse or man.

'If we wait, it will come out again.' Usamah's eyes were agleam. 'And when it does, I will strike and kill it.'

Sabin adjusted his grip on the boar spear and nodded at Amalric to stay back. He remembered Annais's words about 'good hunting' and 'being careful' and gave a humourless grin. He reached for his hunting horn, intent on sounding the alarm and summoning the others, but the boar crashed out of the undergrowth and dashed for the denser woods on the other side of the path. Amalric yelled as the boar sprang past him. Usamah's groom tried to strike the beast with his own spear and succeeded in piercing the hump of its shoulder blade. But the weapon had a weak shaft that snapped off, leaving a protruding stump. Squealing, bleeding, the pig pivoted on its haunches and charged straight at Usamah's mare, hitting her side-on. She staggered and went down with Usamah under her, and the pig galloped off into the bushes. Sabin swung down from his horse, grabbed the mare's bridle and hauled while Usamah scrambled out from beneath her. She struggled to her feet, but held her offside hind leg gingerly. Although not broken, it was clearly sprained.

Cursing harshly, blood trickling from a graze on his cheek, Usamah ordered his groom to hand over his own horse, seized the man's spare spear, and thundered off in pursuit of the boar. Cursing similarly, but in Christian terms, Sabin galloped after him.

The boar had fled into a brake thick with more licorice trees and asphodel. Although the scrub was dense, the boar had been slowed by its injuries and was leaving a thin trail of blood. Usamah followed it with determination, his spear poised to strike. His hand was swollen and it was obvious from the way he held the weapon that his little finger was either broken or dislocated.

Sabin hefted his own lance and looked along its length to the bright, sharp point. He could see no imperfections in the wood, so, as long as his thrust was true, he stood in no danger.

Usamah bared his teeth at Sabin in what was supposed to pass for a grin. 'You do not like the boar as an opponent, I can see it in your face,' he panted.

'I have not hunted them often,' Sabin said. 'I know that a wounded boar is perhaps the most dangerous of all beasts.'

Even as he spoke, the pig came crashing out of the trees. Usamah yelled and spurred to meet it, but his hand was injured and the thrust that was supposed to pass between its ribs and open its heart was not strong enough and turned on the bone, and the pig's weight slammed into the horse's forelegs. Again, Usamah's mount went down, and although the Saracen threw himself clear of the horse, he was still in the path of the boar's stained, razored tushes.

Sabin spurred forward and, without time for thought, thrust down hard with his lance. The pig let out a gurgling squeal that ended abruptly as it staggered and keeled over, narrowly missing the stunned Saracen. His horse threshed to its feet and stood trembling. Sabin yanked out his spear on a river of blood and the sweet smell of it filled his nostrils and made him feel desperately sick. The boar twitched, but it was no more than a spasm in a creature already dead. Dismounting, Sabin hastened to help Usamah rise. By now the fingers of the Saracen's right hand were swollen a deep purplish-red and an angry graze blazed on his brow.

Sabin stooped, his hands braced on his knees, and breathed slowly and deeply. The nausea lessened, although it did not go away. He did not think that he was ever going to develop a passion for hunting boar.

'You saved my life,' Usamah said gravely.

Sabin straightened. 'And my own.' He forced a smile. 'I would have done the same for any man who was my companion.'

'You are generous.'

'No, it is the truth. I acted upon the spur of the moment without time to think about either spending generously or holding back.'

'Even so, I will mark down what you have done for me, and I will not forget it.' Usamah held out his good hand and Sabin clasped it across the corpse of the boar.

'There is one thing,' Sabin said.

'Name it, and, if it is within my power, it is yours.'

'Then tell me why you gave my stepson such a strange look before we set out to hunt?'

Usamah turned to his shaken mount and smoothed his hand upon its sweat-damp neck. 'I was not aware of having looked at the child with anything more than idle curiosity,' he said.

'Then you have a strange way of expressing idle curiosity.'

Usamah said nothing for several heartbeats. Then he sighed and turned his fierce gaze back to Sabin. 'Once the ransom sum is agreed, your King is to be set free, but there will have to be guarantors for his payment. Emir Timurtash has requested that certain Frankish hostages be housed at Shaizar until the sum and the conditions are met in full.'

'"Certain Frankish hostages?"' Sabin went cold.

'Since, next to the fighting men, your children are the rarest and most precious commodity that you have, Timurtash demands that at least ten of them be held against the payment. He demands the Princess Joveta and Joscelin of Edessa's son. It is likely that he will also ask for the child of Gerbert de Montabard.'

'No!' Sabin snarled. It was an instinctive reaction and one so strong that he even reached for his sword. The sight of Usamah's damaged hand flashing to his scimitar in a gesture of self-defence caused him to release his grip from the hilt and instead clench his fist around his belt. 'No,' he said in a more controlled voice. 'I will not let him go.'

'Not even for your King?'

'Not for all the gold in Christendom,' Sabin said furiously. He collected his mount and swung into the saddle. 'If you have influence, then use it. Let that be the price of your life.'

Tension crackled between the men and was not dissipated by the arrival of the groom and cheetah on foot and Amalric still astride.

'I will see what I can do,' Usamah said, nodding stiffly. 'But do not expect miracles.'

Having calmed from her initial shock on hearing about Sabin's encounter with the boar, Annais salved a graze on his arm and made doubly sure that he was unharmed beyond such minor damage. They had the momentary privacy of a small side chamber off the royal rooms. It was little more than a large wardrobe used to store spare napery and bed linen. Constrained by lack of space, they stood in each other's breath.

'Even a scratch can turn bad,' she said when he displayed impatience at her fussing.

'I did it on a licorice tree. It wasn't as if I was tushed by the beast.'

She gave an involuntary shudder and bound a strip of linen over the injury. 'And now I hear that the Emir of Shaizar's nephew is in your debt for his life.'

Sabin shrugged. 'So he says, although I have already called it in.'

She drew back her head and stared at him. 'What do you mean?'

He glanced to the door curtain, but there were no sounds nearby to suggest that they were about to be interrupted. 'The ransom price has been fixed at eighty thousand dinars and the ceding of some land around Aleppo. Usamah told me that Timurtash desires hostages for surety against the payment. He wants one of the Queen's daughters, Joscelin of Edessa's son and other children belonging to the royal court . . . and that may mean Guillaume.' He expected shock and exclamations of horror, but her expression did not change.

'I know,' she said calmly.

His gaze widened. 'You know?'

'The Queen told me while we were at our stitching and you were off hunting.'

'Why did you not say something sooner?'

'I was waiting the right moment to tell you, indeed I would have done so now, but you have arrived at the destination before me.'

Sabin stared at her, unable to believe how calm she was. 'We must take Guillaume back to Montabard immediately,' he said. 'Usamah says that he will put in a word with Timurtash against Guillaume being selected.'

Annais shook her head. 'I have already promised the Queen that I will stay. She asked me to accompany Princess Joveta as one of her nurses, and I said that I would.'

'God's blood, you did what?' They were standing breast to breast like lovers, but tender emotions were not uppermost in Sabin's mind.

'I said that I would,' she repeated calmly. 'Joveta knows me well and prefers my company to that of the other women. She is scarcely more than a babe in arms. She needs attendants with whom she feels safe.'

'And for that reason you will put yourself and Guillaume in jeopardy? What happens if Baldwin reneges on the ransom?' His own voice, although held low, was harsh with fear. 'What do you think will happen to the hostages then? Do you know what Balak did at Kharpurt when he overran us? He didn't stop to worry whether the women in that place were Christian, Muslim, with child, innocent or guilty. He ordered them all pitched over the wall to their deaths . . . every single one.'

She went as pale as a lump of Caen stone, but did not flinch. 'Timurtash is not Balak,' she said. 'You saved the life of the nephew of the Emir of Shaizar who is Timurtash's friend and ally. Surely that is a powerful counter-balance to any threat that might be made on our lives.'

'A counter-balance about which you did not know when you offered your services,' he snapped. 'What were you thinking?'

'I was thinking of Joveta. I spoke with my heart . . . and I am not ashamed that it has ruled my head.'

'I would be within my rights to throw you over my saddle and drag you back to Montabard. No man would blame me.'

'Indeed not,' she said with quiet vehemence. 'But the Queen would.'

'At least you would be safe!'

The composure broke and indignation flickered across her face. 'How can you say that when you gallop off to hunt boar and return covered in blood? You expected me to bring you a stirrup cup and a smile when you rode off to skirmish at Aleppo and Membij. I was supposed to sing carefree songs at my spindle when you left our marriage bed for Kharpurt, where only by the grace of God were you yourself not hurled over the walls to die. I see most clearly . . . my lord . . . that sauce for the gander is not sauce for the goose!'

'Of course it is not the same!' He looked at her in pure exasperation. 'You are a woman.'

She drew herself up. 'And I have a queen to follow who will do what she must for the sake of the kingdom. She has asked it of me and I have agreed.'

'Without consulting me!'

'You were away pig-sticking,' she spat. 'I do not recall being given a choice in whether you went to Kharpurt or not.'

'But that was—'

'Different?' she finished for him on a curled lip. 'For once the shoe is on the other foot.'

He wanted to grab her, shake her, tell her that he would not allow her to go, but he swallowed the fury and felt it burn like a hot coal in his belly. More than half of it, he knew, was fear. She was right. It was different when he put himself in danger. It had never mattered to him, and he had never given much thought to whether it mattered to her. Now that the tables were turned, he disliked the sensation intensely.

Seizing her by the shoulders he drew her up to him and kissed her hard, parting her lips, flattening them against his own. Born of frustration and meant to dominate, his purpose failed because she matched him. She clasped her hands at the back of his neck and her nails dug into his flesh. He felt the wildness in her. Before it had always been covert, even in extremity a little held back by her convent training, but now it was undammed and had he not been so pent up himself, he would have been hard pressed to stay with her.

Her rib cage heaved as she strove to breathe without breaking the kiss. Her hand went down between them and, as Sabin closed his eyes and groaned in his throat, he heard her whimper. It was foolhardiness bordering on stupidity, but for the moment, neither of them cared. The wall chamber was cramped, there was no room to lie down, and the difference in their heights would make coupling against a wall something of a trial, but there was a bench cut into the stone and in seconds Sabin had made use of it, sitting down, drawing her after him.

She poised above him, her brown eyes narrow with concentration and hot with desire. 'I suppose you learned this as King Henry's squire too?'

'God no, I'd use a bed unless I was desperate.'

'And are you desperate now?'

'Bursting at the seams,' he said, his hands on her thighs beneath her gown, and then her buttocks, cupping them, pulling her up and forward, and then, blissfully, down. He squeezed his eyes tightly shut, his body quivering with tension, that single moment almost bringing him to the loose.

Her breath locked in her throat and then emerged on a strangled cry. She bit her lip and leaned forward, muffling her voice against the thick, soft linen of his tunic and shirt.

Her nails scored him again and she took her pleasure without urging or encouragement, but as her right. And as she moved upon him and he gritted his teeth against the intense pleasure-pain, Sabin thought dimly that this was the part where he did not so much lose the battle, as lower his weapons and yield.

'I am going to the Queen,' he said a short while later. His breathing had recovered, but his heart was still racing and his fingers were somewhat heavy as he adjusted his braies.

Annais gave him a sharp look, the pleasure-haze clearing rapidly from her eyes. She smoothed her hands down her creased skirts and raised her arms to adjust her skewed veil. 'You tell her that you will not permit me to go, and I will not forgive you.'

Sabin gave a twisted smile. 'It had crossed my mind,' he said, 'but I would be cutting off my nose to spite my face. If I am going to Morphia, it is to offer my services. The hostages will require a Frankish entourage as well as a Saracen one. If it is your intention to be mad, then it is mine to protect you . . . and I will not take no for an answer – from a queen, or from a wife.'

She drew a breath and parted her lips, but her words went unspoken as the curtain across the chamber entrance was ruffled aside by Amalric. The youth's grey eyes were alight and his complexion blazing. So consumed was he with his own emotions that his lord and lady's state of disarray completely passed him by.

'Tyre has surrendered!' he cried, his adolescent voice cracking with excitement. 'The messenger's just arrived! The Queen's going to announce it in the hall. I've to summon as many as I can find!' With that, he was gone at the run.

'That has to be a good omen,' Annais said, her eyes luminous. 'Surely things are beginning to turn in our direction.'

Smiling, Sabin rose to his feet and took her hand to lead her from their brief sanctuary into the public domain.

'Including Fergus,' he said. 'I think I would rather be a hostage!'

A week later, arrangements finalised, the hostages set out for Shaizar where they were to be held in honourable captivity until the full eighty thousand dinars was paid. A deposit of the first twenty thousand had been sent to Timurtash together with a promise to cede five towns in the vicinity of Aleppo and an assurance that the Frankish army would aid the Emir to be rid of his Bedouin enemy, Dubais ibn Sadaqa.

Sabin watched the last baggage mules being led into line and donned his spurs. There were seven children all told, and eight adults. Joscelin of Edessa's son was the eldest child at eleven years old, and sat his own small Arabian horse with the confidence of an accomplished rider. His tawny hair gleamed in the sun and anticipation of adventure shone in his dark blue eyes. Sabin strolled over to the back of a covered wain. The younger children were travelling in this, since riding any distance was not practical for them and their guardians. Leaning his arm on one of the curved willow struts, he peered under the canvas at its occupants.

Princess Joveta grinned cheekily at him from her place between Annais and Letice. The latter's presence had been requested by the Queen because Letice was steady in all circumstances and Morphia felt that all the children would benefit from her influence.

Guillaume scrambled across two six-year-old boys and their nurse with the eager clumsiness of a puppy and held out his arms to Sabin. 'Papa!' he cried.

Sabin swung him up in his arms. 'I'll take him awhile on Lucifer,' he said and turned to find Strongfist standing behind him.

'God keep you all,' Strongfist said, his throat working. He lifted Guillaume out of Sabin's arms and gave the child a fierce hug. 'I'll spend not just every coin I have, but every drop of blood in my body to see you all home safely.' He kissed Guillaume who wriggled and squealed in protest.

'Horse,' he demanded, clenching and unclenching his fists. 'Want horse.'

Strongfist handed him back to Sabin and swiped his forefinger beneath his eyes. 'Oh for the innocence of the young.' He clasped Sabin's hand in a fierce grip. 'Bring them back whole . . . and yourself too.'

Sabin forced a smile. 'Do you doubt it?'

'I try not to . . . but like you I wear the scars of other battles.' He did not mention Kharpurt by name, but it was there in his eyes. As Sabin had done, he went to the cart and leaned within. 'I'll be praying for all of you,' he said.

Annais came to the end of the cart and embraced him tenderly. 'God willing, we'll be free before summer's end, and we have been promised great hospitality at Shaizar. I do not say that you fear needlessly, but neither should you build mountains from a grain of sand.'

'I am your father, give me leave to fear,' he replied in a constricted voice and squeezed her hard for a moment. Then he released her and she drew back so that Letice could take her place.

Strongfist's words were a hard knot in his throat. He swallowed, for they were choking him, yet he could not unravel them to speak.

Letice cupped the side of his face. 'I will miss you,' she said, her own voice lacking its usual steadiness. 'Do not let Fergus lead you into misdemeanour, and take care of yourself. I do not want to greet a worried shadow on my return, but a whole man . . .'

He gave her a haunted look and took her hand, moving it so that it was across his lips. The ache in his throat was unbearable by now. He kissed her fingers.

'Find a scribe,' she said. 'Write to me. Even if your letters do not arrive, it will be a comfort to know that you have done so.'

He nodded. 'And you,' he croaked. In his mind's eye he saw himself dragging her out of the cart, throwing her across his horse and galloping home to Tel Namir, then shutting the gates and sending the rest of the world to perdition. But that was only the dream. In reality he pulled her towards him for one last kiss, and then let her go. Somehow, he found the strength to leave her, to walk across the courtyard and join the other onlookers. He had not wept since Kharpurt, and that was over a dead woman, but he knew he was going to weep over a living one with considerably more anguish.

The party of hostages set out from Turbessel, their departure waved off by the entire court, and it seemed almost like a feast day parade, for everyone was clad in their finest robes for the occasion and the Saracen deputation in their turbans and silks, with their hunting dogs and cheetahs, gave the entourage an exotic air. A closer glimpse showed the sharpened steel in scabbards, the watchful eyes, and the tension like a taut wire strung with bright glass beads. Surrounded by the trappings of wealth, afforded every courtesy, the Frankish delegation were still hostages and heading for an uncertain captivity.

Chapter 32

The fortress of Shaizar crowned a steep ridge that bound the eastern side of the Orontes valley. The river guarded its north and east approaches and the castle itself was cut off from the plateau continuing the ridge by a deep moat. The only passage across the river was over a bridge manned by guards and defended by a small citadel.

The fortress had three entrances: two serving the town and one leading over the bridge that went directly into the castle itself. As the Emirs of Shaizar had boasted, so the Franks now saw for themselves: the place was indeed impregnable, except perhaps to treachery. When Sabin mentioned this to Usamah, the Saracen smiled.

'No one in Shaizar would yield up its secrets to a Frank, whatever the temptation,' he said. 'Try my people if you will, I do not mind.'

'That depends upon how restless I become,' Sabin replied as he handed over his sword and hunting knife to a courteous but watchful steward, retaining only the short blade he used for eating.

Usamah shrugged. 'I see no reason why we cannot spend some time hunting,' he said. 'You are scarce likely to abscond while your dependants are within the castle, and you volunteered yourself to be a hostage after all.'

Sabin flicked a wry look at Annais who was descending

from the baggage cart, a child clinging to each hand. 'I had no choice,' he said.

They were given their own apartments separate from the Saracen household, the chambers well appointed with skilfully woven rugs on the walls and even on the tiled floors. The beds had coverlets of silk; the bolsters and sheets were of the finest woven cotton perfumed with oils of rose and lavender. Fine robes of linen and silk had been laid out for the guests and indoor shoes of gilded kidskin. There were ornate brass ewers of scented water in which to wash hands and face.

Sabin ran his fingers over the exquisite embroidery on one of the silk robes. 'At least we are to be held hostage in luxury.'

'I have seen few enough guards,' Annais said, stifling a yawn. The time of her flux was due and she felt heavy, achy and out of sorts.

'When there is only one way in and out and sheer drops around, you don't need to stand over your captives with a sword.' He gave her an assessing look. 'You should sleep. Your eyes are darker than caverns.'

'I am all right.' She rallied and raised her chin. Moments later though, another yawn almost cracked her jaw.

Sabin gave her a look of exasperated amusement and drew her down onto the bed. 'Sleep,' he said. 'Let someone else be responsible for a short while. I will wake you if there is need.'

Usually she would have protested, but she really was beginning to feel unwell and all she needed to convince her was the pressure of his arm refusing to yield. After a moment she relaxed against him and allowed him to swing her legs onto the bed and slip off her shoes. 'You promise to wake me?'

'On my honour.'

She felt his thumb at her ankle gently smoothing over the point of the bone, then his lips at her brow. Then nothing as she sank down into a sleep so deep that it was fathomless.

Sabin stood over her for a while, looking at her, unconsciously biting his thumbnail. She had seemed more tired than usual these last few days. He had not been unduly concerned. Even if she had done no more than sit in a baggage wain, the bumping and jarring of the journey was a discomfort and the company of small children could be exhausting. But surely not exhausting enough to set such dark rings beneath her eyes, or cause her to fall asleep the moment she lay down. 'How is she?' He turned to face Letice.

'Sleeping,' he said with a brief gesture and a frown. 'You sat at her side in the cart. Did you notice a change in her?'

Letice gave him a thoughtful look from her dark hazel eyes. 'Only the changes that are a woman's lot to bear.'

His frown deepened and then realisation struck. It must be the time of her flux, although usually the visitation was a minor inconvenience and when they had made the journey between England and Jerusalem, she had been robust at every phase of the moon. 'Ah,' he said and rubbed the back of his neck.

Letice hesitated as if she might say more, but the moment passed and she too kept her own counsel.

Annais woke from her sleep with such heaviness in her breasts and loins that she thoroughly expected her flux to begin. She still felt tired, but was able to find sufficient energy to face the remainder of the day and to eat a gargantuan meal of spicy stew and boiled grains. She was aware of Sabin watching her with concern, but that seemed to lessen as he viewed the amount of food she consumed.

'I was worried for you,' he said, 'but no one could be deeply ill and eat as much as that.'

A dish of sweetmeats was set before them: pine nuts and sesame seeds in a confection of boiled sugar, honey and spices. Annais reached eagerly, craving the sweetness on her tongue.

'I was tired, nothing more,' she said.

'And very hungry.'

She made a face at him and he smiled, heartened at her response.

The next morning, the feeling of heaviness was worse. Annais slept late and when she woke, felt sick. She lay in bed, gazed at the painted ceiling, counted the days, and knew that she could fool herself no longer. Her flux should have come with the waning moon, but that had been twelve days ago. The symptoms were beginning to suggest a gathering of life rather than a bleeding away. She laid her hand to her belly. It was as flat as ever, but her breasts were sore and full.

Slowly she sat up. She would not tell Sabin yet, she thought. It was far too early. Even if she was fairly certain herself, it was still a precarious time and she might yet bleed. She knew of several women who had miscarried in the early months before the quickening. She would wait until then before telling him, and hopefully by that time they would be free.

King Baldwin arrived from Harran two days later accompanied by a detachment of Saracen warriors. He came clad in fine silks and wearing his own mail coat, newly burnished until it shone like a basket of silver coins. His sword rested at his hip, and he was afforded every grace and honour. With him rode his nephew Ernoul and Waleran of Birejek. They too had been restored their mail and weapons.

The Emir of Shaizar greeted Baldwin with kisses on both cheeks and treated him as an honoured and welcome guest. Food, drink and entertainment were provided in lavish quantities. Baldwin was gifted with a fine saker falcon with golden bells attached to the jesses, a robe of embroidered damask and a ring set with a lustrous black pearl.

'You see,' Usamah told Sabin. 'We are terrible in war, but we can be the most generous of hosts when it is in our interests. My uncle remembers the good service that King Baldwin did to him in granting him remission of a payment we were supposed to make to Antioch several years ago. Now the debt is repaid and the ground is level again.'

Sabin sipped from his cup of sherbet and watched some women from the harem dance for the pleasure of the company.

Unlike the 'dancing' girls he had witnessed in the brothels of Jerusalem, these women were modestly clad and their movements were graceful rather than suggestive. The entertainment was intended to be aesthetic and appeal to the mind as much as the body.

'As soon as your King repays the rest of his ransom, then you will all be free to go,' Usamah added, lifting his cup of frosted pomegranate juice to his lips.

'What of Waleran and Ernoul?' Sabin asked. 'Do they depart with King Baldwin to Antioch?'

Usamah stroked his luxuriant black beard and his gaze slipped past Sabin's. 'The agreement was that the King alone should be freed,' he said. 'Emir Timurtash gave no such undertaking for those with him. Like you, they will be treated with honour and respect, but they are to be held at Shaizar for the moment.'

Sabin had been expecting such a response, but still his gut tightened. Although the Saracen courtesy was impeccable, it was plain that there was to be no leeway of any kind.

Later that night, Baldwin privately visited with the men, women and children who, for his sake, were to remain at Shaizar until the terms of his ransom had been fully met. He sat on a woven rug on the floor, four-year-old Joveta cradled in his lap, and looked over her sleepy fair head at the gathering.

'I will do everything within my power to have you free of this place within a few short months,' he said. 'Even if I have to tax the country dry to raise the coin, I will do so.'

'And what of the other promises, sire?' Sabin asked.

Baldwin shot him a bright look. 'What promises?'

'To cede the towns that Aleppo demands, and to lend your aid to Timurtash in suppressing Dubais ibn Sadaqa.'

'You think I would put my own daughter's life in danger? Or that of these other small children?' A note of distaste entered Baldwin's voice and his blue gaze was frigid.

'No, sire,' Sabin said. 'But matters often change when a different light shines upon them.' It was the nearest he would come to suggesting that Baldwin might alter his mind once he was free.

'I will do all in my power, I have told you that. If you were so uncertain of my word, then you should not have volunteered for the task of standing hostage.'

'I sought reassurance, sire, not to offend.'

'Then be reassured, and I will take no offence this time, although you sail very close to the wind.' He gave his sleepy daughter a last squeeze, kissed her brow, and raised her from his lap. 'Time for your bed, sweetheart,' he said. 'I swear that even if you were as light as a feather at the start, you have grown as heavy as a war shield on my arm.'

Annais hastened forward to take the little girl and lead her away to the waiting mattress in an alcove beyond the main room. Sabin excused himself from the gathering and followed her.

'Why did you speak to him like that?' Annais demanded in hushed tones as she removed the child's dress, leaving her in her cotton chemise, and tucked her beneath the covers.

'I was reminding him of his responsibilities,' he said. 'So that his conscience remains a shield and not a feather.'

'You think he would go back on his word with so much at stake?' She smoothed Joveta's hair and murmured soft words to the child. Joveta clutched a corner of her blanket and raised it to tickle her nose. Her eyelids drooped, revealing lashes that were as thick as the fringes edging the floor rugs. Sabin moved silently past the child's mattress and went to gaze down at Guillaume who was sprawled on his back like a puppy.

'That depends how much we weigh in the balance,' he said softly. 'And how much of his payment he thinks that he can remove from the scales before he ruins the transaction.'

Her brow furrowed. 'You do truly believe he would do that, don't you?'

Sabin crouched by his stepson and gently pulled the cover over his sleeping form. 'Let us say that I hope he would not, but that kings often have to make decisions of the head, not the heart. In two months' time when we are home in our own bed at Montabard, you can call me all the names that you wish and I will accept them meekly.'

'You will indeed,' she said, but the words were spoken as a token gesture and Sabin felt a pang at the sight of the trouble he had put into her eyes. Yet he could not have kept silent. Baldwin had had to hear the words spoken by one held hostage for his sake. It drove home the necessity to remember, made it harder to barricade the door of conscience.

'I am sorry,' he said. 'I was never much good at being held at the behest of others. I feel like a beast in a cage. Put my doubts down to my own failings.'

She came swiftly to his side. 'You could never fail me.'

He laughed bitterly. 'Oh, I could. You do not know how easily.'

'Never,' she repeated, and, taking his hand, linked her fingers through his.

Sabin was not particularly comforted. Given their present circumstances, the weight of her trust felt like a shackle. 'Play your harp for me,' he requested. 'Something to ease and lift the spirit.'

Annais took her harp from its case and sat down with it among the company and played the tunes that she had brought with her from Coldingham, a lifetime ago. 'Love me broughte and Edi be thou hevene quene.' The notes dropped from the strings like clear, cold rain on parched skin and for a brief span, reality was relegated to insignificance by imagination.

CHAPTER 33

Bright daylight pierced Strongfist's eyeballs like a fistful of needles. 'Christ,' he groaned. 'Close those shutters.'

Fergus's wife, Margaret, gave him an exasperated look, but did as he asked. Even so, the sunlight still dazzled through the latticework. 'You know that you are to stand guard duty before noon?' she said.

'What hour is it now?' His head felt as if there was a giant inside it, kicking to get out.

'High morning. I left you as long as I could. You and Fergus drank enough last night to fill a cistern.' She clucked her tongue in disapproval and moved away. Strongfist heard the sound of liquid trickling into a cup. She returned with a goblet of pomegranate juice and water. He took it and, with no great enthusiasm, drank. His gut was rolling like a ship in a storm. Last night the court had arrived in Antioch complete with Morphia and Baldwin. Strongfist had not been on duty; Fergus had been newly come from Tyre with Margaret and their sons, and, naturally, they had been caught up in the celebrations.

'Where is Fergus?' he asked.

'Asleep on the floor where he dropped, but at least he is not on duty today.' Margaret jerked her head in the direction of the smaller antechamber. They were renting a house not far from the palace, and, although it afforded them the privacy that it was impossible to obtain in the royal quarters, space was cramped. Margaret moved around the room, finding Strongfist's equipment and laying it together, her manner briskly efficient. He watched her with aching eyes and was filled with longing for Letice.

She pushed a platter of bread and a hard-boiled egg at him. 'Here, you will need to eat. It will be a long day.'

The sight of the food almost made him gag, but to please her and to pretend he was not as ill as he felt, he forced it down before summoning Amalric, whom Sabin had left in his charge.

'Perhaps the King will have something to say in council about the hostages,' Margaret said as Strongfist pushed his arms into his quilted tunic and the youth tugged it down over his body.

'I hope so.' He looked at her. 'Fergus says he will give up his share of the gains he took in Tyre to go towards the ransom.'

She raised a sardonic brow. 'Was that before or after you got drunk?'

'Before. I'm sure he will tell you when he wakes up.' His tone was hesitant. Fergus's share from Tyre was around five hundred dinars, and he knew that Margaret might not see her husband's generosity in quite the same light as he did.

'Oh, I am sure he will,' Margaret said with a determined nod and pursed lips. For a moment she kept Strongfist dangling, then gave him a hefty push. 'Oh, away with you,' she said. 'If five hundred dinars help to buy back your family, do you think I will put my silk gowns and rare perfumes first?'

'But it is a great deal of money for one man.'

'So it is . . . and perhaps even more for one woman, but nothing if it helps friends and family. I will hear not another word on the matter from you.' She smiled. 'Even if Fergus might hear many from me . . . and, yes, I am jesting.'

Amalric assisted Strongfist into his mail shirt and then the surcoat of scarlet silk. Margaret handed him his swordbelt.

'Thank you,' he said, making it clear that it was not the

belt he was talking about. 'You and Fergus give me reason to count my blessings.'

'Fool!' she said, but with affection, and presented him with a round red cheek to kiss. Mindful of his sour breath, he gave her a quick peck, and turned away to seek out his spear and shield.

Strongfist spent the rest of the day guarding King Baldwin. It demanded vigilance, for the King was a prime target for assassination and a royal bodyguard needed eyes not just in the back of his head, but all over his body. By the time evening arrived, Strongfist's headache was like a huge black thundercloud. He swore that never again would he try to match Fergus drink for drink. He had not succeeded when he was eighteen years old; why should it be any different a score of years later?

Baldwin was dwelling at the residence of the Patriarch of Antioch, Bernard de Valence, and the two men had retired to the Patriarch's private solar. A squire served them with wine and sweet cakes, bowed and departed. Strongfist remained in the room, guarding the door he had just closed. Outside two more knights stood on duty.

Strongfist knew how to be deaf. It was a lesson perfected long ago in the service of Prince David. He looked straight ahead and stood as still as an effigy, essentially becoming part of the background. Baldwin and the Patriarch were so accustomed to the presence of armed guards that they paid him as much heed as they would a lizard on the wall.

At first, their discussion was easy and quiet. They talked together as old friends and there was the occasional burst of soft laughter. Strongfist's attention wandered. He gazed at the embroidered wall hangings and thought longingly of his bed and a cold lavender-scented cloth for his brow. His eyelids started to droop and he forced them open.

'You cannot do that!' Patriarch Bernard's raised voice jerked Strongfist out of his threatened doze. He turned his head and saw that the prelate had risen from his chair and was standing over Baldwin. 'Those towns are not yours to cede, and well you know it. Yes, you are overlord to Antioch, yes, you are the regent, but you have no right to give away a boy's patrimony.'

'It is one of the terms of the treaty,' Baldwin retorted, also springing to his feet. He stood taller than the Patriarch and whatever advantage Bernard had gained by his initial stance was now lost. 'Do you realise what is at stake?'

'Indeed I do . . . but I would ask the same question of yourself. Will you risk knives in your back for the sake of helping your enemies in Frankish territory? Do you think you will gain the support of your own camp if you deprive Bohemond's heir of his rightful inheritance?'

Strongfist frowned as he tried to follow the gist of the conversation. The principality of Antioch was held in trust for young Bohemond of Taranto, a youth of sixteen, whose father had been the first Prince of Antioch but had died when Bohemond was an infant. The lands had been many years in the hands of the King of Jerusalem and overseen by the Patriarch.

'I gave my word.'

'And that counts above your word to one of your own?'

Baldwin bit down viciously on his thumbnail. Patriarch Bernard turned to pour from flagon to cup and looked across the room. Strongfist hastily averted his eyes and stared at the lozenge pattern on the wall.

'What then should I do?' Baldwin asked. 'Whatever my choice, I break my oath.'

The Patriarch turned round with the goblets and handed one to the King. 'My advice would be to deny Timurtash. He wants, nay, he *needs* the money. He has difficulties of his own to contend with. He must have known when he made his demand that he would not receive everything for which he asked. It is like negotiating for a piece of carpet in the souk.'

'My daughter is not a piece of carpet,' Baldwin said

savagely. Strongfist echoed the sentiment strongly. He compressed his lips and fingered the hilt of his sword.

'No, sire, indeed not, but your other daughter is betrothed to young Lord Bohemond and you would be diminishing the patrimony of your grandchildren if you cede the land to the Saracens. I think you must take the risk.'

'A risk that you would not take when you sent Joscelin of Edessa all the way to Jerusalem to collect troops, rather than letting him bring the army of Antioch to the relief of Kharpurt.'

'That would have been a disaster, sire. Our troops could not have stood against the force that Emir Balak had mustered.'

Baldwin exhaled hard. 'I suppose you are right,' he said. 'On both counts, but it does not mean that I like either of them.'

'Nor I, sire, but the decisions have to be taken.'

They sat down to drink their wine and their conversation sank again to a level where Strongfist could hear no more than the occasional word. There was no more laughter. The mention of 'Timurtash' and Shaizar were no comfort. His palms were slick with cold sweat. He envisaged leaping at Baldwin and the Patriarch with drawn sword and forcing them to swear that they would do nothing to jeopardise the lives of the hostages. But then what was a royal oath worth? He wondered if he could get word to Sabin, but Shaizar was an impregnable fortress and it would be nigh on impossible for Sabin to escape, let alone two women and a small child. Besides, with the wellbeing of Princess Joveta in their care, he knew that wild horses would not persuade Annais and Letice to leave, lest it be with their charge.

The Patriarch rose to depart the royal chambers, brushing past Strongfist as if he were another of the marble pillars supporting the roof. Strongfist bowed and straightened, and, with narrowed eyes, watched the prelate leave.

Baldwin poured himself another cup of wine and sat down, feet outstretched towards the warmth of the brazier. He drank, sighed, pushed his hand through his thinning hair and rose to prowl the room like a caged cat. For the first time, he seemed to notice Strongfist standing by the door.

'You can go,' he said. 'The Queen will be here soon and I am not expecting other guests this night.'

'Sire,' said Strongfist stiffly.

Something must have glimmered in his tone, for Baldwin frowned and bade him come forward. 'Ah,' said Baldwin as recognition dawned, and with it understanding. 'I am sorry that guarding me fell to your duty tonight.' He grimaced and looked down at the goblet in his hand. 'Patriarch Bernard is right,' he said. 'I cannot cede lands that are not mine.'

'And what of the hostages, sire?' Strongfist asked huskily.

'I think that Patriarch Bernard is right in that too,' Baldwin said. 'Emir Timurtash wants his eighty thousand dinars too badly to worry about the gilding on the gingerbread. My own child is involved in this. I feel as you do.'

'Then I hope, sire, that you and the Patriarch are not proven wrong,' Strongfist said, bowed again, and made his escape before he did something rash. The King had lied. He could not even begin to feel as Strongfist did.

'Aye, Baldwin's playing a dangerous game, but he's canny, and so is the Patriarch,' Fergus said. 'Timurtash won't act.'

Strongfist rubbed his hands over his face. The thundering headache of earlier had been joined by a tight band of tension between his temples. 'And if he does?'

'There's no use worrying about what you cannot change. Even if you were to draw your sword against Baldwin it would make no difference to what happens to the hostages . . . and if you are considering that, then get a hold of yourself, man.' A lecturing note entered Fergus's voice.

Strongfist's expression filled with remembered loathing. 'When he came to me and said that he was sorry, I wanted to seize him by the throat. Do not ask how I kept myself from doing so, for I do not know.' He met Fergus's shocked blue stare. 'Oh, I have calmed now. My fingers still itch, but I find that washing my hands helps.' His lip curled. 'I would not make a good king, Fergus. I hate these power games.'

Baldwin's gamble paid off. Timurtash sent envoys to Antioch protesting his disappointment and alarm at the fact that the King of the Franks had gone back on his word, but that he would show lenience this once and let it pass. Strongfist breathed again. Perhaps all would be well. Emboldened by the lack of iron in the Saracen response, Baldwin gambled further. Since the territories surrounding Aleppo remained in his grasp, why not try for Aleppo itself? Accordingly he made an alliance with Timurtash's enemy, the Bedouin leader Dubais, and together they laid siege to the city. The terms of Baldwin's ransom had stated that he would aid Timurtash against Dubais. Made furious by the second betrayal, Timurtash sent a contingent of troops to Shaizar with explicit orders.

Usamah's cheetah was chained in the courtyard. Its leash was long, giving it room to wander, and it had a bed fashioned from an old gambeson with an underlay of straw. Lying with head on paws and half-closed eyes, it allowed a maid to groom its amber and black coat with a brush made from hog's bristles.

Sabin had grown accustomed to the cheetah's presence. Although the lords of Shaizar owned several hunting cats, this was the only one permitted in the family enclave and it was treated as an honorary dog. Still, he did not think that he would emulate his hosts and take to keeping such a pet at Montabard. There was still something edgy and dangerous about the beast. All that quiescent power. He had seen it run down a gazelle and strangle it without effort. A child would not stand a chance.

On that thought, his gaze went to the hostage children and their nurses who were playing ball across the courtyard. His gaze lit on Annais as she threw and caught and encouraged. Something was weighing on her spirit, but he was not sure what.

Several times she appeared to have been on the verge of telling him, but then had hung back. He had his suspicions and had deliberately not pressed her. Sometimes ignorance was an easier burden than knowing.

His misgivings concerning Baldwin had been proven correct when the King had reneged on the agreement to cede the lands surrounding Aleppo. For a while the hostages had been locked in their chambers and threats issued – not so much by the Emir and his family, but by some of the guards who considered that the Franks were being treated far too well. The fuss had gradually died down. Timurtash had accepted with resignation the fact that Baldwin would not hand over the territories, and the hostages had again been given the liberty to wander within the environs of the fortress.

The maid finished grooming the cheetah and turned her back. The cat rose, stretched its long, wiry limbs, and then squatted on the quilt to urinate. Turning round in time to see the deed, the woman gave an indignant shriek and clapped her hands. A string of voluble Arabic curses issued from her lips. The cheetah darted out of her way, to the end of its chain, and stared at her disdainfully.

Sabin chuckled as a laughing Usamah joined him. 'It would be interesting to see men mark their territory in a similar way,' he said.

'I am told that some do.' Usamah strolled over to the cheetah. A gesture sent the grumbling maid to unfasten its tether and the Saracen wrapped his hand around the silver chain. 'Do you wish to hunt?' he asked Sabin. 'I have a mind to go down among the cane-brakes by the river.'

'As long as you are not intending to chase boar,' Sabin said wryly.

Usamah grinned. 'That depends on what we can flush out, but I was thinking more of water fowl and perhaps gazelle.'

Sabin might not be as passionate about the hunt as Usamah, but the notion of riding out for a while, of exercising the lethargy of confinement from his body, filled him with eagerness. 'Your uncle permits this?' he asked as the cheetah padded forward to sniff his leg.

'He has given full permission for me and the men to put arrows into any Frank who tries to escape,' Usamah said pleasantly. 'I do not want to hunt down a man, but I will if necessary.' He turned towards the stables. 'You know I cannot give you weapons, but you can borrow one of my falcons.'

Within the hour the hunting party had assembled and ridden out. Sabin was not the only Frank to be enjoying the rare freedom of a day on horseback. Waleran of Birejek, Ernoul, the King's nephew, and two other Frankish knights were included in the group. All of them were filled with high spirits and eager to be away from the fortress for no matter how short a time. Just to straddle a horse and feel the air streaming past their faces was a luxury that had once been taken for granted.

Annais watched them ride out and smiled to hear the men's enthusiasm. Their voices dipped and swooped like those of excited children and there was much jesting and not a little horseplay. They were relieving tension, she knew. It was difficult for young, active men to be confined like this. Difficult too when they were at the mercy of the actions of others.

'Look at them,' said Letice with amused contempt. 'Do men ever grow up?'

Annais smiled. 'Not in the same way that women do, but perhaps I envy them a little.'

Letice looked at her askance. 'You would join that hurly burly?'

'If I were a man, yes, and doubtless I would enjoy it. As it is, I shall bite my nails and worry until they return in one piece.' She watched Sabin break away from the group and trot towards them on Lucifer. The stallion's hide shone like a silver mirror and his hooves were the hard blue of sword steel.

Leaning down, Sabin swept Guillaume onto his crupper and gave the delighted, squealing child a swift ride around the courtyard. Annais clenched her fingers in her gown as Sabin put the horse through several sharp twists and turns, but she swallowed the cry of warning that rose in her throat. He had schooled the horse until its moves were as near perfection as a mortal beast could come. There had been little else to do while they waited out their time. Finally, Sabin swung Lucifer and cantered over to the woman, drawing the horse to a dusty halt before their noses. He tumbled Guillaume into Annais's arms, saluted, and rode back to the hunt which was now on its way out of the gates.

Letice wiped grit from her eyes with her veil while Annais shook her head and smiled through her exasperation.

'Have you told him?' Letice asked.

Annais's smile faded. She shook her head and placed her hand to her belly. 'Not yet. He was like a cat on a hot griddle when Baldwin reneged on the ransom agreement. I did not want to burden him.'

Letice frowned at her. 'It is not something that you can hide for ever,' she said. 'Soon your waistline will outgrow the laces of your gown, and it will be difficult to cite eating too many sweetmeats as the reason.'

Annais glanced involuntarily at the side fastening of her gown. She had let them out once so far and there was still plenty of room; Letice was exaggerating. The sickness and lethargy had been more difficult to conceal, but she had blamed it on the change of diet from Frankish to Saracen and, fortunately, the worst seemed to have passed. 'I will tell him soon,' she said. 'When the time is right.'

Letice gave her one of her looks. 'Make sure that it is soon,' she said. 'He will not thank you to find out when you are six months along.'

Annais grimaced. 'By that time, hopefully, we will be free,' she said, and turned her attention to Guillaume who was clamouring for her to throw the ball in her hand.

The women returned to the game, but had not been about it long when a troop of Saracen horsemen thundered into the courtyard. Their mounts milled and plunged – high-spirited Arabs and barbs with the dished faces and flagged tails of the breed. The men's armour was of high quality. Some were archers and carried light horse bows and quivers filled with black-feathered arrows, others bore lances, and all wore either swords or scimitars.

Annais and Letice exchanged glances. These were not the soldiers of Shaizar, many of whom they had come to recognise during their three months as hostages.

'What has Baldwin done now?' Letice muttered.

'This may have nothing to do with Baldwin,' Annais said, but, even as she spoke, was aware of the scowling glances being cast in their direction by the dismounting soldiers. One of them in particular was fingering the hilt of his scimitar as if it would please him to draw the weapon and use it.

'And pigs might grow wings and fly,' Letice retorted darkly.

Grooms and stable lads came running to take the horses, and a detachment of Shaizar's guards arrived to join the newcomers. A rapid conversation ensued with much gesticulating. At the end of the talk, both sets of soldiers turned towards the women and children, and the man who had been fingering his scimitar now unsheathed it in a hiss of steel. Guillaume was too young to appreciate the danger and toddled to grab the ball that Joscelin of Edessa's eleven-year-old son had dropped in his fear. The boy was as pale as a winding sheet beneath his sun-bleached hair and his blue eyes had widened until there was a ring of white around the iris. Another, younger, boy began to whimper and, at the sound, Joveta ran to Annais and pressed her face into the security of her skirts.

Hakim, one of the Shaizar guards who spoke a little French, came to them and raised his voice. 'You are all to go inside now,' he said harshly. As he shouted, Guillaume too headed for his mother's skirts, but made sure that he kept tight hold of the ball.

'Why, what has happened?' Letice asked.

The Saracen with the drawn scimitar raised it so that a line of light shimmered along the blade.

'No questions,' Hakim barked, and – in the same tone of voice so that the newcomers would think he was still haranguing the women – added, 'You are considered disrespectful. If you would keep your tongues, hide them behind your teeth for my friend needs little encouragement to cut them out. For your very lives, do as you are told.'

They were herded together and jostled from the courtyard to their chamber. As the oldest male and the heir to Edessa, young Joscelin was singled out for particularly rough handling and by the time they were thrust inside their room and the door locked, he had a bloody lip and was shuddering violently with the effort of not weeping before the enemy. Thrusting comforting hands away, he huddled into a corner and stood against the wall, his face pressed into his upraised arms, blood smearing his sleeve. Guillaume had no such restraint set on his behaviour and roared his indignation and fright fit to bring down the painted ceiling. Joveta joined him and they screamed in unison. Annais set aside her own panic to deal with theirs, cuddling and rocking until the howls subsided to hiccups.

'I don't like the man with the sword,' Joveta said in a quavery little voice and, knuckling her eyes, stared apprehensively at the door.

'Nor I,' Annais admitted, 'but he's gone now.'

'Will he come back?'

'Not at the moment. Hush, you're safe. I won't let anything happen to you . . .' Empty words. How could she prevent it? But it would be over her dead body. Guillaume still had the ball clutched tightly in his hand. It was made of numerous coloured leather strips stitched together and stuffed with fleece. He had been absently gnawing on it, but now he handed it to Joveta. She took it solemnly as if it were a royal orb.

Leaving her and Guillaume with Letice, Annais went quietly over to Joscelin and touched his shoulder. It was rigid beneath her hand and he twitched as if he would shrug her off. 'I know that you have your pride,' Annais murmured, 'and I will not intrude on it. But should you wish for comfort, you have only to ask.'

He nodded without raising his buried head. At the other end of the room a key grated in the door lock and for an instant everyone recoiled. Joscelin's head now jerked up with the swiftness of a hunted gazelle's, the dried blood flaking on his smooth child's skin, his eyes wide with fear. When the door opened to reveal nothing more sinister than Aiesha, one of the Emir's senior concubines, with two of her women bearing fruit and sherbet, the boy slumped with relief. So did Annais, although not as visibly. Leaving him, she hurried back to the others.

Aiesha's gaze darted like a swallow and would not settle on any of the hostages. The other women hung back and they too kept their eyes and heads down.

'What is wrong?' Annais asked Aiesha in the halting Arabic she had learned from Sabin and Soraya. 'Who are these men?'

Aiesha shook her head. 'I can say nothing,' she whispered with a frightened look over her shoulder. 'It is more than my life is worth.'

'Please, we are all afraid.'

Again, Aiesha shook her head.

'Do they belong to Timurtash? Has King Baldwin gone back on his word?'

The dark eyes flickered and filled with panic. 'I know nothing,' Aiesha said, but that brief gaze had told a different, frightening story.

Her task completed, Aiesha backed towards the door with the other women. 'You should pray to your God,' she said, 'and hope that He is merciful.'

They were left alone for the rest of the day and their fears grew like baker's dough left to prove. Dusk approached and they lit the lamps. No one came and the sense of impending disaster increased until it was darker than the shadows in the corners of the room. Annais passed her prayer beads through her fingers, counting them off, murmuring paternosters and aves until they lost their meaning, but there was vague comfort in the rhythmic pattern of the words. She played her harp; she sang to the children. Guillaume fell asleep in her lap, Joveta against her side.

A sickle moon had risen in the arch of the unshuttered window and it was almost full dark outside when they heard the sound of the hunt returning, and, beyond and above it, a sudden clamour in the courtyard. The door burst open, armed guards strode into the room, swords drawn, and the children woke and began screaming.

Two guards placed themselves by the window and drew the shutters fast. The clamour outside diminished and ceased and, for an instant, there was absolute silence, even down to a lull in the children's sobs.

Footsteps approached, some striding hard, others stumbling. Harsh curses flowed in the Saracen tongue and she heard Sabin's voice raised and breaking in answer. There came the sound of a blow followed by a grunt of exhaled air. Six more guards shouldered into the room, manhandling between them Sabin and two of the knights who had gone hunting that morning. A vicious red graze deepening at one end as if gouged by a ring lay high along Sabin's left cheekbone and the flesh beneath his left eye was rapidly swelling shut. The guards flung him down on the floor and the other knights with him. Then, with a final flurry of kicks and blows, they left, and the key turned in the lock.

'Papa!' Before Annais could prevent him, Guillaume had abandoned her skirts and launched himself at his stepfather like a missile from a stone thrower. Sabin took the child's flying weight with a painful exhalation of breath. It took an obvious effort of will to lift his head from the ground and sit up. Blood was threading down his cheek from the wound. He curled his left arm around Guillaume and used his right cuff to soak up the trickle. The guards at the shutters said nothing, but stood with swords drawn and eyes as narrow as blades.

'Sweet Jesu, what is happening?' Giving Joveta to Letice, Annais crawled across the floor to Sabin. 'Why have they turned on us?' She had to stop herself from leaping upon him in the same way that Guillaume had done, but she could see from his hunched posture that he was hurting from more than just a cut cheek.

'What do you think?' he croaked. 'King Baldwin has gone back on his word yet again.'

'He has denied the ransom?'

'If he had done that, we would all be dead by now,' he said with the irritation of pain. 'No, instead of aiding Timurtash to defeat Dubais, he has made an alliance with Dubais and together they are besieging Aleppo. It may yet be the end of us all and not just—' He broke off with a hiss as Guillaume inadvertently kicked him in the ribs.

Annais took Guillaume back into her own lap and looked at him anxiously. 'What have they done to you?'

'Enough to make me suffer, not enough to die,' he gasped. 'One of Timurtash's goblins jabbed me with a spear haft. If Usamah had not intervened then he'd have used the pointed end – and he still might.' He looked around at the women and the children. 'They have not harmed you?'

'No, but they were rough with young Joscelin.' She glanced along her shoulder at the boy, sitting palely quiet and a little aloof from the others, his upper lip purple and swollen. Then she looked back at Sabin. 'You said "the end of us all and not just—" What else were you going to say?'

Sabin's expression was grim. 'I do not want to tell you, yet I must because it cannot be hidden. When we returned from the hunt, a detachment of Timurtash's guards was waiting for us. Usamah argued with them, but to no avail. The Emir has the last word in matters of authority at Shaizar . . .' His throat worked and she saw his anguish. He had to force the words out and they came like blood from a squeezed wound. 'Waleran and Ernoul . . . they are to be shriven by a priest and then they are to be executed . . . and word sent to Baldwin that more deaths will follow unless he complies with the treaty.'

'Jesu!' Her hand flew not to her mouth but to her belly and his gaze followed it, before slowly lifting to her face.

'I already know,' he said quietly. 'I may be ignorant, but I am quick to learn.'

She bit her lip. 'I was going to tell you . . . I just . . .'

'Perhaps you thought I would not be strong enough to shoulder the burden?' His tone was gentle but wounded.

Annais swallowed. 'I did not know how you would respond. It is my fault that we are in this coil. If I had listened, if I had refused the Queen as you wanted . . .'

'And you thought I would rail at you now, because of that?'

'No, but I wondered.'

'Christ,' he said under his breath, covering his face with his hand.

Annais swallowed, feeling utterly wretched. 'I was hoping that we would be free long before this . . . so I took the coward's way out and waited.'

He took his hand away and looked at her. She saw pain through pain, but at least he was meeting her eyes. 'You are no coward,' he said. 'If you had refused the Queen your guilt would have been a millstone around your neck and you would still have had no freedom. You would not have been denying Morphia, but a child. I would have carried that burden of guilt too, no matter that I sought to prevent you at the time.' He laid his hand at her waist. 'But I wish that you had found it in you to tell me earlier.'

'I wish it too . . . but I did not know what to do. I wanted to give you joy – not trouble.'

He pulled her to him. 'It is our joy and our trouble.' His voice had a ragged edge. 'You did not conceive this child alone, did you?'

Feeling weak with relief, she pressed against him, but, mindful of his shallow breathing, composed herself after a moment and pulled back. 'In truth,' she whispered, 'I did not know whether to feel hope or despair.' She gripped his hand where it still lay against her waist.

Although the shutters were latched, they did not deaden all sound and now they heard the muffled notes of a priest's voice raised in a Kyrie eleison and two other voices wavering with it, off-key and raw with terror. The song died away to silence. Then rose again, but only one voice. They heard scuffling and then a heavy, dull sound, of the kind swords made when they struck the straw-stuffed dummy on the practice post at Montabard. But there were no straw dummies in Shaizar's courtyard, only men.

Annais caught the scream in her throat and locked it there. Sabin bowed his head and she felt a shudder ripple through him. The priest's voice continued to sing with steady strength, but Ernoul's rose to howl Waleran's name in horror. Annais stuck her fingers in her ears. Ignoring the pain from his kicked ribs, Sabin pulled her against him and she buried her face against his breast. Over her head, he gazed towards the shutters and the grim guards standing either side. He listened while they pinned Ernoul down, heard the shrieks, the blow, a gurgle, another blow and then silence. The voice of the priest rose again, clean and bright as the edge of a blade, one side hope, the other despair.

Chapter 34

Winter arrived with heavy rain, wind and snow. The waters surrounding Shaizar became a marsh that attracted hordes of wildfowl. Although hunting parties went out most days, there were never Franks among them and the relaxed atmosphere of the early months was replaced by one of taut vigilance. Usamah still came to talk with Sabin and match wits over a chessboard, but the visits were less frequent and although they were cordial on one level, the deeper camaraderie had been strained by the deaths of Waleran and Ernoul.

'I am sorry,' Usamah had said in those first days when there were still dark stains on the courtyard floor. 'But it is a fact of war. Hostages are a surety for the word of the giver. If that word is broken, then all must suffer the consequences. Be thankful that they were not worse.'

'As yet they still might be?'

'You know the risks as much as I.'

They had not discussed the matter since, had been at pains to skirt around it like dancers encircling a fire. But the heat remained and to step too close was to risk being burned. Occasionally Usamah would bring him news of the outside world, but in general he was circumspect. Aleppo remained under siege from Baldwin and Dubais. The execution of Waleran and Ernoul had made no difference to Baldwin's resolve. After his outburst of rage, Timurtash had backed down for he had troubles beyond those posed by Franks and Bedouins. His brother was dying and Timurtash wanted to be certain of his inheritance. Therefore he remained at home in Mardin and refused to commit himself to Aleppo's defence. All this Sabin was told piecemeal over the gaming board, but he was never sure how old the news was and how complete.

They celebrated the Christmas feast in a subdued fashion, and prayed for the relief of a ransom payment. None came. The winter days lightened towards spring and the rains ceased to fall quite so hard. The feast of the Virgin arrived – Candlemas – and they were permitted tapers of beeswax to celebrate the occasion. Annais was becoming unwieldy as she began the eighth month of her pregnancy. She had resigned herself to giving birth in Shaizar, not Montabard. Even if the ransom were to arrive immediately, she was beyond the stage where she could risk travelling any distance.

Aiesha had obtained leave for Annais to bathe with the women of the harem. Her skin was massaged with fragrant oils to increase its suppleness, so that there was less chance of permanent stretch marks. A Saracen midwife was summoned to examine her and listen to the babe's movements through a trumpet fashioned of blown glass pressed upon the skin of Annais's swollen belly.

'She says it is a boy,' Aiesha declared with pleasure. Gold bracelets tinkled on her wrists. Here in the harem her face was exposed, revealing smooth honey-coloured skin and delicate features. Several missing teeth marred her wide smile.

'How does she know?'

'The way he kicks, the way he lies . . .' Aiesha reached to a heaped platter of honey-drenched dates and daintily selected one between finger and thumb. 'Fatima is never wrong. Four sons I have borne and two daughters and she predicted correctly each time.'

Annais laid her hand upon her belly and, beneath her palm, felt it ripple. The midwife smiled broadly and spoke again, holding up her spread right hand.

'What does she say?' The woman's dialect was difficult for Annais to understand.

'That he will be born five weeks from this day.' Aiesha licked her fingers and selected another date. 'At night, two hours after moonrise.'

Annais felt the small hairs prickle at the nape of her neck. She had to subdue the urge to cross herself for she did not want to offend the women, although from the way that the midwife was looking at her, she suspected that her thoughts were as clear as glass. 'And will he and I be safe?'

Aiesha spoke to the woman, who then looked at Annais. '*Inshallah,*' she said. 'If God wills it.' There followed a torrent of words too swift for Annais to be able to pick out even one.

Aiesha made a face at the woman. 'She says that too much honey is bad for the teeth and will make me fat. I tell her that many things make women fat.' She pointed to Annais's belly.

Annais laughed. 'You would rather have a honeyed date than a man?' she asked.

Aiesha chuckled. 'That depends on the man,' she said. 'Your husband could make me fat any time he chose!'

Their mirth was curtailed as a messenger came to the harem door and delivered his news through a screen to the swathed attendant. She brought the message to the reclining women, and, on hearing it, Aiesha exchanged glances with the others. The play and laughter was put aside as swiftly as sweeping gaming counters into a box.

'Is something wrong?' Annais struggled up from the couch.

'We have visitors,' Aiesha said. 'The Atabeg il Bursuqi has ridden in with his bodyguard and he will require food and entertainment. You must return to the other hostages.' Her tone was preoccupied, her mind already busy with the new task in hand.

'Who is il Bursuqi?' Annais asked Sabin. They were eating food from the hastily prepared feast, which the unexpected guests were eating in another part of the fortress. Annais avoided the honeyed dates, the figs wrapped in almond paste, the pine nuts boiled in sugar, and settled instead for the spicy lamb stew served with boiled grains. 'They have gone to a great deal of trouble, he must be important.'

He looked up from his portion of bread stuffed with minced chicken and nuts. 'From what I remember and from what Usamah has told me, he is the ruler of Mosul and a man more powerful and influential than Timurtash.' He chewed and swallowed. 'More motivation too.'

'Then what is he doing here?' Ever since the execution of Waleran and Ernoul, Annais had been on edge, waiting for the next betrayal . . . the door flying open, guards bursting into the room, weapons drawn. 'Surely such a man would not come to Shaizar without good reason.'

Sabin shrugged. 'He has good reason. Cementing friendships with the Emir of Shaizar can only be to his benefit, and I am sure that our presence here has drawn him through the hills like a siren song to a sailor.'

'Why?'

'Because he is strong and Timurtash is weak.'

She frowned at him, unsure of his meaning. Sabin was eating with apparent calm, but she could tell from the tense set of his shoulders that he was as troubled as she was. 'You think he will try and take us away from Timurtash?'

'I think he might negotiate with our hosts for a slice of the ransom. Last time Usamah spoke to me, he said that matters were not going well for King Baldwin outside Aleppo. I could glean little else, but I do not believe that Timurtash has the inclination or the strength to make too much trouble for Baldwin. I suspect that il Bursuqi does.'

There seemed little else to say. She did not want platitudes. Like the sweetmeats, they might seem pleasant, but their effect was ultimately detrimental. And speculation was like deliberately swallowing vinegar. Suddenly she was no longer hungry.

*

It was late in the evening when Usamah summoned Sabin to play a game of chess in his chamber. As Sabin rose to his feet, he touched Annais's shoulder in reassurance. 'He's not desperate to play chess at this time,' he murmured. 'I think I am going to learn what il Bursuqi is doing here.'

She nodded and compressed her lips. Sabin gently squeezed her shoulder and went with the guard.

Usamah's chamber walls were adorned with embroidered silk hangings in hues of crimson and gold. Round shields decorated with star and circle designs hung between the fabrics. A charcoal brazier burned in the centre of the room, mitigating the chill of early spring. Upon a quilt near the door, the cheetah dozed; as Sabin entered, it roused to watch him through indolent lids, its eyes like chips of amber.

Usamah sat in his favourite place near the window splay. Soft light from ceramic lamps pooled the small table before him with gold and he was toying with an ivory chess piece, walking it over, beneath and round the lean fingers of his right hand.

Two white-robed musicians sat in a cushioned corner, playing a duet of lutes. The scent of rose-oil perfumed the air as if a woman had recently left. Sabin took his place opposite Usamah. 'I thought you would be otherwise occupied tonight, my lord,' he said.

Usamah's teeth flashed. 'I was for a while.'

Sabin returned the smile. They both knew that it was not what he had meant. 'It is interesting, the difference,' he said, picking up a chess piece of his own with which to toy. 'The Franks think of the Saracens as oily-tongued and false because they prefer drawn-out diplomacy to plain speaking. The Saracens think the Franks uncivilised because they grunt out their demands on the instant and fail to observe the courtesies.'

Usamah looked amused. 'Very true indeed.' He looked from his chess piece to Sabin. 'So whose rules shall we play by tonight?'

'I will do my best not to be a boorish guest,' Sabin said, 'but I hope you will forgive any lapses.'

'Well then, I will try to accommodate some of your brusque ways. Let us play.' Usamah set his piece, a king, back on the board, and Sabin put down his pawn.

'Your wife, she is well?' Usamah gestured Sabin to take the first move.

'She is well,' Sabin confirmed, 'although somewhat uncomfortable.'

'Aiesha tells me that the birth will be soon.'

Sabin's lips curved. 'I had come to that conclusion myself without benefit of a midwife.'

Usamah responded to Sabin's move. An emerald ring gleamed on his forefinger. 'You know that you have but to ask and I can arrange for one of the women from the harem to entertain you.'

'It is generous of you, but there is no need.'

'There is always need,' Usamah said, eyeing him shrewdly.

Sabin shook his head. 'Once in another life I would have leaped at your offer, but not now.'

Usamah raised a cynical brow. 'You love the woman to distraction?'

'I would give my life for her.'

Usamah shook his head. 'You Franks are indeed strange.'

'It is more than love,' Sabin said slowly. 'It is pride and allegiance and . . . and putting myself between her and death for my own sake. For honour . . . and for what honour I once lacked.' He advanced his pawn and bent his head to the chessboard.

'And which you are not going to talk about?'

'No,' Sabin said and folded his arms. 'And since Saracens are subtle and courteous, you will not ask.'

Usamah chuckled softly as he made his move. 'You are good company for a Frank.'

'I must be if you prefer it to that of your guest, il Bursuqi,' Sabin said pointedly. 'Or am I being too brusque?'

'A little, but I can overlook it.' The Saracen waited for Sabin to make his play. 'If I am not with him just now, it is because he and my uncle wish to speak in private of their own affairs. It is a while since we played chess and talked together. I have things to tell you that will soon be common knowledge to all.'

'Good or bad?' Sabin tried to sound indifferent, but his stomach had responded to Usamah's words with a queasy lurch.

'That depends on where you stand.' Usamah stroked his beard and studied the board. 'Il Bursuqi is an important lord, and he has the strength that Timurtash lacks.'

Sabin narrowed his eyes and, waiting, did not speak. He had said as much to Annais, and he had a healthy suspicion that he knew what Usamah was going to say next, but when Usamah spoke, Sabin was false-footed and the silence of anticipation became the silence of dismay.

'The people of Aleppo appealed to him when Timurtash would not come to their aid.' Usamah lifted and placed a pawn, the ivory clicking on the inlaid board. 'He agreed to help them and brought his army to Aleppo . . . whereupon Dubais fled and your King retreated to Antioch rather than stand and give battle.' He gave Sabin a calculating look. 'We hear now that King Baldwin is returning to Jerusalem. It seems for the moment that he has relinquished his campaign in the north and left il Bursuqi in command of the field.'

Sabin took a deep breath and strove to steady himself. 'But surely it is like a game of chess,' he said. 'You calculate what you can afford to lose, and if one strategy does not work, you seek others. I would have expected King Baldwin to visit Jerusalem sooner rather than later. He has been absent from it for two years. It does not mean that he is in retreat.'

'Indeed it is like a game of chess,' Usamah said with a narrow smile. 'But your King's attack has been routed and now it is the turn of il Bursuqi to make his play.' He poured lemon sherbet for himself and Sabin and lifted the fluted cup to his lips. 'It is politic for my family to show friendship towards him.'

'Of course.' Sabin gave an ironic tilt of his head and raised his own cup. The sherbet was as sharp as a new blade but with a fortunate sheath of sugar. He managed not to suck in his cheeks.

Usamah swallowed and set his cup down. 'My uncle has offered him certain of the hostages to take into his custody. It is felt that with them in il Bursuqi's personal keeping, King Baldwin will have more incentive to comply with the terms of the ransom agreement.'

This was the news that Sabin had been expecting, but a chill still raised the flesh along his forearms. 'But your uncle is the trustee of the hostages,' he said. 'That was the agreement.'

'It was not my uncle who first broke his word, but your King. Il Bursuqi has given an undertaking that they will be treated as if they were his own family.'

Sabin was less than impressed. Men of il Bursuqi's kind were not averse to disposing of family members who stood in their way. 'You said certain hostages. It would not take a fool to realise that you mean the Princess Joveta.'

'It is your move,' Usamah said pleasantly, gesturing to the game. Sabin was tempted to dash the pieces aside and overturn the board, but he quelled the impulse, keeping the violence as an image in his mind instead of letting it rage through his body. He could not think. The pieces meant nothing. He stared at them until his eyes grew sore and blurred.

Usamah nodded. 'The Princess Joveta is indeed to enter il Bursuqi's household. Of course, in her present condition, your wife cannot accompany the Princess. You and she will remain here, and so will the boy, Joscelin.'

Sabin swallowed. The sherbet was bitter in his throat. 'When will all this take place?'

'At dawn tomorrow when il Bursuqi departs. You have leave to tell the others what is to happen.' Usamah fixed Sabin with a hard stare. 'The decision is final. There is no point in arguing.'

Sabin shook his head and blindly moved one of the pieces. His suppressed rage suddenly changed and he was assaulted by the urge to laugh. He bit his lip. His shoulders shook. He put his head down on the table and could not tell if the sounds choking from him were of despair or mirth.

Usamah waited, patient but puzzled.

At last, Sabin raised his head and wiped his eyes on the back of one hand. 'I am sorry,' he croaked. 'Is it not ridiculous? We are indeed as struggling ants beneath the eyes of God.'

'Everything is as Allah wills it,' Usamah said, a slight frown between his eyes as if he suspected Sabin of more than just the usual Frankish blasphemy.

'My wife only agreed to stand hostage because of the fondness that Princess Joveta harboured for her. Now you tell me that she and the Princess are to be separated . . .' He blinked at Usamah, his vision stinging and salty from the sweat he had rubbed into his eyes. 'It seems so futile, does it not? A good jest at our expense?'

Usamah shrugged. 'Everything happens for a purpose,' he said. 'Every deed has its consequence, *inshallah*.' He nodded at the chessboard. 'That was a rash move, but a brave one, my friend.'

'You will find it part of the Frankish nature,' Sabin said huskily, managing to rally some of his scattered wits. There was still a lump in his throat, but the tension that had been gathering within him as the weeks slowly passed had been eased back to a point where he could control it.

Usamah smiled. 'Indeed,' he said and bent to his chess pieces. The cheetah came to lie at his side and he absently set one hand to its spotted pelt. It sighed and half closed its lids, but a glint of feral amber still flashed upon Sabin.

Sabin came away from the evening with Usamah feeling as if he had been tied in the path of a storm. His skull thundering with a massive headache, his legs weak, he was escorted back to the other hostages. Suddenly his guards paused and bowed, pressing as close to him as splints to a broken limb as an entourage approached from the direction of the hostages' quarters. Usamah's uncle was pacing at the side of a slight man with obsidian-black eyes and thin, hawkish features. His belly was as round as an egg on his slender frame and he walked with a bow-legged stride as if his horse were still between his legs. A peacock plume pinned in place by a large red jewel wafted on his turban. Wedged between his guards, Sabin deemed it politic to bow also. This, he surmised, must be il Bursuqi himself, and he had obviously been inspecting his new 'merchandise'. Sabin clenched his fists but he succeeded in keeping his head down until the Atabeg had passed.

The moment that the guards had delivered him to the hostages' chamber and locked the door, Annais descended upon him. It was obvious from the look on her face that she now knew why il Bursuqi was at Shaizar.

'He says that he is going to take Joveta with him on the morrow!' Her voice was high-pitched with indignation and distress on the child's behalf. Joveta herself was fast asleep and without an inkling of what was about to happen to shatter the fragile security of her world.

'Yes, I know.' Grimacing, Sabin rubbed her arm in a comforting gesture. 'Usamah told me.'

'Is there nothing we can do?'

'I wish there was, but we are less than pawns in a deadly game of chess. We will be moved where they wish. Yielding some of the hostages will cost Shaizar nothing and earn them il Bursuqi's extravagant goodwill.'

'But Joveta is little more than a baby, and if they take her, I cannot go with her.' Annais pressed her hand to her distended belly. Her eyes were bright with tears of distress.

'I will go in your stead,' Letice had been standing a little apart, but she had been listening to the conversation and now she stepped forward and laid a hand on Annais' arm. 'Joveta knows me well enough and we are comfortable together.'

Annais chewed her underlip.

'It is the best we can do,' Letice said. 'What else is there?'

Annais nodded and drew the palm of her hand across her eyes. 'You are right,' she said. 'And thinking straight while I am snivelling like a child.'

'Nay, you have enough on your trencher. You missay your own sense and courage.' Letice gave her a maternal kiss on the cheek.

'Surely King Baldwin will move swiftly when he hears the news. He has to.' Annais felt Sabin stiffen and looked at him, alarm dilating her pupils. 'What is it? What else has Usamah told you?'

Sabin sighed. 'That King Baldwin has abandoned the siege of Aleppo and turned south to Jerusalem.'

Annais inhaled sharply. 'Does he not care about us? Do we mean nothing to him?'

'There is coin to be raised in Jerusalem and perhaps more easily than in the north,' Sabin said. 'He probably did the right thing in withdrawing from Aleppo rather than risk a battle with il Bursuqi.'

Annais swallowed and turned her head aside. 'How much longer will this drag on?' she whispered. 'Am I to see my children grow up as captives and under constant threat for their lives? If I had known . . .' She did not finish the sentence.

'You would still have done the same,' Letice said. 'Looking back means that you never see the road ahead.'

'She is right,' Sabin murmured, drawing her closer. 'And I speak as one who has lost his way more times than I care to remember.'

Annais leaned against him. 'Perhaps I do not want to see

the road ahead,' she said, 'even if I was the one who set my feet on the path.'

In sombre mood, they retired to their beds. A while later, Joveta woke from a nightmare and climbed into bed at Annais's side, wriggling and snuggling like a small puppy. Her hair had been recently washed and smelled of the almond soap that the Saracen women used; her breath was a softness that barely stirred the air. Feeling grief and guilt too deep for tears, Annais held her close and kept watch while the hours of the night burned away in the faint glow from the single lamp in the wall niche. A cockerel crowed and grey light filtered through the fretwork shutters like an enemy. Turning her head on the pillow, she saw that Sabin too was awake, and she guessed that he had not slept either, but kept his own silent vigil.

It was a hard parting. When the guards came to the hostage chamber to fetch those who were to go with il Bursuqi, Joveta shrieked and screamed. She clung to Annais and finally had to be prised off like a limpet from a rock. Letice she kicked and bit. And then she was violently sick.

'Leave her to me.' Letice raised her hand to prevent Annais from intervening. 'The sooner this is done, the better for all.' She cast a swift glance at the guards who were running out of patience. Having wiped the child down, Letice wrapped her firmly in a blanket, swaddling her as if she were an infant. Arms and legs bound, forced to be still, Joveta ceased to struggle. A blank, despairing expression entered her eyes and she became as limp as the cotton-stuffed doll among her small bundle of possessions. Burdened with the child's weight, unwilling to bring her near Annais lest another tantrum ensue, Letice kissed the air between her and the young woman and went to the door.

'It won't be long until we are all free,' she said. 'Hold that in your thoughts, and have a care to yourself and the baby.

God bless you.' The last word was spoken swiftly and ended on a gasp as the guards bundled her and Joveta out of the door and banged it shut.

Annais's eyes filled with tears. Turning, she blindly sought the comfort of Sabin's breast, but she could not blot from her mind the sight of Joveta screaming in Letice's arms, then lying limp as if dead.

Chapter 35

Damp from his first bath, snuffling as he breathed the strangeness of air, the baby furled his tiny fists and yawned. He had a fine down of dark hair that the lamplight sprang with gold, dainty eyebrows feathered with paintbrush precision, and skin so soft that Annais almost hesitated to stroke his cheek. Almost, but not quite.

He had been born exactly as the midwife said, two hours after midnight in the early morning of the fifth day of April. He was not a large baby, but he was robust, and Annais knew she had borne him. Her belly was like a mound of collapsed dough after the first proving, and the place between her legs throbbed and twinged. The midwife had dosed her with various potions to stem the bleeding and ease the discomfort, but had declared herself well satisfied with the condition of both mother and son.

The baby rooted against her stroking finger. The first time, with Guillaume, she would not have known what to do, but now she drew down her chemise and put him to suck. He mumbled at her nipple for a moment and then latched on. His small jaw set to work. The women of the harem laughed with pleasure at the sight and cooed to each other with delight. The differences that separated Saracen from Frank did not matter. They were all united as women, and childbirth was a danger and a joy common to all.

Since the birth had taken place in the harem, Sabin had

not been permitted anywhere near, although messages as to the progress of the labour had been sent out to him, the last one an hour ago when the baby was born. Even now, as a Frankish male and a Christian, he was not allowed to set foot within these chambers and would be unable to visit Annais until she left them.

Once her son had finished feeding, Annais prised him gently from her nipple and handed him, milk-filled and sleepy, to Aiesha. 'Will you take him to my husband, and tell him that I am well . . . ?'

'Of course.' Aiesha wrapped the baby in a shawl of silk edged with inscriptions from the Koran and fringed with gold.

Annais frowned as she watched the woman bear him to the door. Although she trusted Aiesha – had no choice in the matter – it was still a wrench to watch her leave the room with him. It was as if the cord between them had yet to be cut and there was a pang in her loins, squeezing deep and then stretching taut. She knew in her heart that the pains were caused by giving suck, but it was still as if being separated from her baby had caused them.

'Come, you must sleep now. It has been a day and a night since you have done so. You must gather your strength.' A Frankish-speaking concubine presented Annais with an infusion of aromatic herbs. There was honey in the brew to take away the acrid taste and as Annais sipped, she realised how tired she was.

'I want to go home,' she said and suddenly tears spilled and overflowed. She raised the palm of one hand to wipe them away and sniffed loudly like a child. She had not cried once at the birth pains, except to give vent to the effort of pushing the baby from her womb, but now she had an ocean. They wrenched from her, further hurting her tired, aching body.

'Hush, lady. Surely you will, and soon.'

The voice was as soothing as the honey spooned into the drink to negate the foul taste of the herbs. 'Will I?' Annais choked. 'How can you give me guarantees when the Emir cannot?'

The woman gave her a wounded look and her eyes grew wary. Annais managed an exhausted, bitter smile. She had failed the game; she was not supposed to answer back except with soft words of her own. 'Never mind,' she said, swallowing against the tightness in her throat and using a corner of the sheet to wipe her eyes. 'You are right, I should sleep.' For the moment, it was ten times better than being awake.

Lacking a chapel, the hostages had fashioned a small prie-dieu in a corner of their chamber, and it was here that Sabin had spent the night in prayer while Annais laboured to deliver their child. His knowledge of the process of childbirth was not great, but for the moment far larger than he desired. Pain and the risk of death. It was something that he had faced often in battle, but there had always been a choice. However, a gravid woman had none. She could not turn aside and say that she had changed her mind. She could not remain at the back of the ranks or flee if the battle raged too hard. It was her lot to stand in the front line and win or die.

Now and again, whispered messages on her progress had been brought to the door – isolated gleams of hope and flashes of fear in the darkness. The news that the child was born, a son, and that Annais was well had driven him to his knees. He was still there now, head bowed at the prie-dieu, the feeling of battle-sickness on him as it often came in the aftermath of great physical or mental exertion. Yet the battle had not been his. He was merely its cause.

The door opened and the guards stood aside to admit one of the women from the harem. She was swathed from head to foot, only her eyes showing, and she carried a small bundle similarly wrapped. It was making soft noises as she tiptoed across to the prie-dieu.

'Your son, my lord,' she said in Arabic and placed the baby in his arms.

The tiny body was securely bandaged in linen swaddling and only the baby's face remained free to air and movement. In the gathering light of dawn, father and son examined each other. 'He weighs no more than a kitten,' Sabin said and swallowed. He had held Guillaume when a few hours old, had thought himself accustomed, but this was totally different, and if he had not already been kneeling, the feel of the child's body in his arms would indeed have felled him. Flesh of his flesh, bone of his bone. Suddenly the infant's little face was a blur.

'Your lady is tired, but she has weathered the labour well,' the woman said with approval in her voice. 'She may look as graceful as a lily, but she has the strength of an ox.'

He smiled at that. 'Stronger than me,' he said. A drop of moisture splashed onto the baby's cheek and it screwed up its little face and moved its head from side to side. 'When can I see her?'

The woman clucked her tongue and folded her arms. 'She must stay in the harem until she is recovered,' she said. 'But I will arrange for her to be brought out for a while so that you may speak with her.'

Sabin inclined his head, but inwardly he grimaced at the strictures imposed by being a prisoner. Had the birth taken place at Montabard, Annais would have been confined to their bedchamber for several weeks, surrounded by her women, but he would have had the right to be there too, not excluded and forced to be grateful for the few crumbs thrown.

'The child will need to be baptised,' he said. 'I request the visit of a priest.'

'It shall be done.'

The door opened on Usamah and two sleek golden hounds. He was wearing calf-high boots and his hunting tunic. An attendant waited in the corridor, Usamah's cloak held over his arm.

'I understand that congratulations are in order, that Allah has granted you the joy of a son,' Usamah said and came to look briefly down at the baby in Sabin's arms. 'A fine seedling,' he said. 'May he grow to be as excellent a warrior as his sire.'

Sabin snorted. 'A fine warrior I make,' he said. 'I doubt I could swing a sword these days.'

Usamah eyed him thoughtfully. 'There is no reason why you should not practise as you used to. Besides, the boy is missing out on his training.' He flicked a glance towards the alcove where young Joscelin of Edessa was still asleep. 'What happened before . . .' He made a small gesture. 'It was regrettable, but that situation no longer exists. Nor, with a wife and two infants, do I think that you will do anything to endanger them.'

'They become hostages of a double nature,' Sabin said wryly, curling his arm yet more protectively around his son.

'You could see it in those terms. My uncle will not object to you taking manly exercise in the yard, providing your swords are made of wood. I am sorry I cannot take you hunting. He would not permit that, but I would have enjoyed your company.' He peered more closely at the baby, but Sabin suspected it was for form's sake rather than a genuine interest in the child. 'How is he to be named?'

'Edmund, for his living grandfather.'

Usamah made a non-committal sound and turned to leave. On the threshold, he paused. 'You may chafe at your confinement,' he said, 'but you should be thanking Allah for his infinite mercy.'

Sabin looked reluctantly up from his absorption with the child. 'Why do you say that?'

'Because il Bursuqi intends to take that which Baldwin refused to cede. He is marching on your fortress at Kafartab even now, and from there, it is only a short journey to Zerdana. You may complain that you have lost your ability to swing a sword. Be grateful. Many will not live to see the end of another summer. Il Bursuqi's army is the largest assembled for many years and he has the support of all his neighbours. The Franks will be pushed back to the coast.'

'There are always intentions,' Sabin said more evenly than he felt. The news had jolted him, but he wasn't going to show it to Usamah.

'Indeed, but some are more likely to be realised than others.'

'You do not ride to join il Bursuqi yourself?'

Usamah smiled. 'We are the guardians of Shaizar and the pass down to the sea. We have demonstrated our goodwill to il Bursuqi's cause by giving him the most important of the royal hostages. I will tell the guards you have permission to train.' With a brusque nod and a click of his fingers to the dogs, he was gone.

As if sensing Sabin's tension, the baby whimpered and started to fret. The woman held out her arms to take him back. Sabin hesitated, then reluctantly gave him to her. 'If you need me,' he said, 'I will be in the courtyard with Joscelin. Tell my wife . . .' He paused. 'Tell her . . . No, I will tell her myself as soon as I may.'

He watched her leave and then returned somewhat shakily to the prie-dieu where he offered up a prayer of thanksgiving for the lives of Annais and his son. Then he went to the laver and sluiced hands and face. Although he had not slept, his mind was racing like a mill wheel in spate and his limbs felt twitchy. His father had once said that the darkest part of the night came in the hour before dawn. The old and sick gave up their souls and babies were born. It was a time of waiting and vigil; a time when a man should think of the hope beyond the despair. Except he hadn't been a man then, but a boy, and his father had been slowly dying of the wasting disease that was eating him up from the inside out. The dawn after that had been a long time coming.

Parting the curtain that separated the sleeping quarters from the main chamber, Sabin went to rouse young Joscelin of Edessa.

Chapter 36

Strongfist swung his arm to test the fit of his hauberk, which the armourer had been repairing and refurbishing.

'How does that feel, my lord?'

'Good. A little tight when I flex my arm.' Strongfist tucked his left fist into his right armpit to emphasise the point.

The armourer moved in close, peered and set to work with pincers and T-bar. 'Now?'

Strongfist tried again. 'Better,' he said, and drawing his sword, gave a few flourishes. Beyond the armourer's workshop, Tel Namir's blacksmith was sweating at his forge, hammering out spearheads, shield fittings and horseshoe nails. The clang of hot metal on steel filled the air and so did the smell, carried on wafts of charcoal smoke and steam. The entire bailey resembled a bustling market place as the occupants of the castle prepared for war. 'I need to be able to wield my sword without impediment.' Strongfist swung again and watched the edge slice the warm wind.

The armourer nodded approval, and moved in again to adjust his work, meticulous despite the fact that he had several other customers awaiting his attention. Ever since the call to muster had gone out in response to il Bursuqi's seizing of Kafartab, his workload had increased tenfold.

'How many men can the King raise?' he asked as he tweaked and manipulated.

Strongfist shrugged. 'Not as many as il Bursuqi, but I hazard over a thousand knights and more than two thousand foot . . . when the King arrives.'

'Will it be enough?'

'If it is not, we will soon know.' Strongfist bared his teeth in a humourless smile. 'Kafartab has fallen, and the Saracens have laid siege to Zerdana. There can be no avoidance of battle this time.' He gazed around the frantic activity in the bailey. Three days ago, he had returned to Tel Namir to gather men and horses. He could have sent a messenger in his stead, but that would have meant kicking his heels in Antioch. He preferred to be active because it made him feel less helpless.

The information filtering out of Shaizar had been scant . . . apart from one terrible day six months ago when they had heard in full detail about the beheading of Waleran of Birejek and Baldwin's young nephew Ernoul. Strongfist would have run amok with fear for the wellbeing of those dear to him had Fergus not taken him in hand and got him blindly, obliviously drunk. As Fergus said, Annais, Letice, Guillaume and Sabin ought to be safe. Slaughtering the less important hostages would not achieve the desired result, and sacrificing grown men who were warriors was less reprehensible than taking the lives of little children. But, like the sword of Damocles, the threat hovered and there was nothing he could do except pray and bite his fingernails down to the quick.

He knew that Baldwin was struggling to raise the coin to rescue the hostages. Sixty thousand dinars was no piddling sum to be whipped up by a few rattles of the begging cup. Such an amount required the squeezing of the last drop from the lemon and, as always, promises of aid were easier to secure than barrels of silver and gold.

'That will do, my lord, although I will need to rivet in some rings.' The armourer gestured for him to remove the hauberk.

Strongfist beckoned to Amalric who had been waiting in attendance nearby. Stepping forward, the youth helped him with the heavy garment and only staggered a little as he took its weight. He was growing up fast, Strongfist thought. The slender boy of four years ago had sprouted like an ear of wheat and now stood at Strongfist's shoulder.

'Remind me to give you another bout of sword practice this evening,' he said, tousling Amalric's corn-coloured hair. 'You still need to work on your follow-through on the backswing.'

'Yes, my lord.' Amalric draped the hauberk across the armourer's workbench.

Amalric's early training had been at Sabin's hands and the latter had done a commendable job of teaching his pupil the basics before Shaizar had got in the way. Strongfist had taken up where Sabin left off and was enjoying educating the youngster. He was quick to learn, adept and resourceful. He would make a fine serjeant – perhaps even rise to knighthood one day . . . if he lived. The thought brought a frown to Strongfist's face. If any of them lived . . .

'My lord.' Amalric was shading his eyes and pointing towards the castle gateway. Strongfist turned and saw a troop of knights and mounted serjeants trotting into the bailey, raising a cloud of yellow dust. The silks of Jerusalem fluttered on their banners and the men were apparelled for war. Mail shirts caught the hard, pale light of the spring sun. Sword hilts glinted at right hips, side-arms on the left. Axes showed the blue curve of honed steel. Strongfist abandoned the armourer and ran towards the troop, clutching his scabbard to hold it steady at his side.

The leading knight dismounted from his sweating stallion, removed his helm and pushed down his coif to reveal a blaze of red hair that clashed dreadfully with his puce complexion.

'Fergus!' Strongfist embraced him and thumped him on the shoulder. The smell of sweat and horse was so pungent that it was almost visible. 'What are you doing here?'

'Tel Namir's only a short detour from the road to Antioch. I thought we'd claim hospitality for the night and ride on towards Antioch on the morrow.' Stepping back, Fergus thrust his helm into the hands of a squire and pushed his hands through his dripping hair. 'In truth, I didna know if ye'd be here. I thought I might be bedding down wi' the bare bones of a garrison.'

'No.' Strongfist wrapped his hands around his swordbelt. 'I came back to organise the local muster myself, but I was going to ride at dawn. I'll be glad of the company.'

Fergus licked his lips. 'And I'll be glad of a drink if you have anything decent. The wine in our flasks tastes as if something has died in it.'

Strongfist grinned. 'No usquebaugh to keep you company then?'

Fergus grunted. 'I wanted to quench my thirst, not pickle it.'

Leaving his adjutant to take his horse to the water trough with the others, Fergus followed Strongfist to the keep and collapsed on a bench in the first aisle of the hall.

'Christ, my thighs feel as if they've been rubbed with crushed glass,' he groaned, spreading his legs. 'The King's driven us harder than a houseful of whores on the eve before Lent.'

Strongfist snorted at the comparison. 'He needs to if he is to save Zerdana from the same fate as Kafartab. Where is he now?' He signalled and an attendant brought flagons of wine and water. The latter was cold from the keep's deep well and it was this that Fergus drank first, swallowing and swallowing as if there were a fire in his belly.

Finally, gasping, he surfaced for air and swiped the back of his hand across his mouth. 'On the road to Antioch. Said he'd billet at the Templar hostel. He's more stirred up than I've seen him since his return from Harran.'

Having dealt with their horses, Fergus's troop started to traipse into the hall and flop onto the benches. The thick stone walls meant that the air inside the keep was much cooler than the burning May heat outside.

'It is time that something did stir him,' Strongfist muttered.

Fergus licked water from the edges of his moustache. 'Well, there are certain rumours and tidings abroad,' he said, pouring himself a goblet of Tel Namir's dry, blood-coloured wine. 'We heard that not only is il Bursuqi marching to besiege Zerdana, but that he has negotiated with Shaizar for the custody of some of the hostages.'

Strongfist had just taken a drink from his cup. Now he choked on it and Fergus had to pound his back.

'What?' Strongfist wheezed. Coughing, he clutched his ribs.

'Patriarch Bernard sent a message down to Jerusalem after the fall of Kafartab, but it's not common knowledge – although it will be soon.'

'Then how do you know?' Strongfist glared at Fergus out of watering eyes.

'Och, get a hold of yourself, man. I was in the King's chamber when the messenger arrived. We were having a counsel about the loss of Kafartab and making plans to ride north. All of us were sworn to secrecy at the time. If I have told you, it is because you are directly involved, and it wilna be a secret once we join the final muster.'

Still coughing, Strongfist jerked to his feet and took several paces down the hall. He had to move; he could not contain the agitation and rage boiling within him. It hurt to breathe. 'Do you know which hostages?' he asked when he could trust himself to speak.

Fergus spread his hands. 'Of that I canna be sure. The Princess Joveta for certain; she's the fruit in the dumpling.' And where Joveta went, Annais did too, and Guillaume. Letice and Sabin perhaps, but there was no guarantee that the Saracens would keep the party together. He rubbed his hands, washing them so hard that his knuckles cracked. Facing the bright arch of the open hall door, he thought about riding now. It stayed a thought. No matter that the light would be good for several hours, those hours were needed to finish preparing. You did not leap into a chasm without a rope to haul you back up. 'What if il Bursuqi threatens to kill them unless we yield to him?' he said.

Cup in hand, Fergus rose stiffly from the bench and limped over to clap his arm on Strongfist's shoulder. 'That won't happen.'

'Won't it? Look at the fate of Waleran of Birejek.'

'That was different. That was over an agreement already made and those who died were grown men. Besides, if anything happened to the wee lass, il Bursuqi would have the men of Shaizar to face. They gave up the hostages for goodwill, but also in good faith.'

Strongfist grunted. He had given up trusting in 'good faith'.

Fergus studied him through narrowed lids. 'You canna live your life by what if,' he said quietly. 'That way lies discontent and madness. Take what is and make the best of it.'

'Christ, you begin to sound like a priest.'

'Then I'm in trouble.' Fergus downed his wine and poured another cupful. 'One way or another the coil will unwind. My sons will be riding with the army of Antioch this time as fledged knights. Do you think you are the only one with cares?' He lifted his hand from his friend's shoulder. 'I'm away to find a bath.'

Strongfist pushed his hands through his hair. He had always thought of himself as a self-sufficient, pragmatic soldier, able to turn the blows that life dealt him. But the price of that self-sufficiency came high. He had yielded the loneliness and the indifference in exchange for a woman's softness in his bed, for a daughter's smile and a son-in-law's company. For the arms of an infant grandson wrapped around his neck. The price of loving came higher still and threatened to beggar him.

Cursing softly, he went back outside into the scorching heat to see how the armourer was progressing. One way or another the coil would indeed unwind, and either he would unravel with it, or hold as taut as a strong rope across a chasm.

Chapter 37

Strongfist knelt to hear mass, his right hand clasped upon the cross around his neck. It was barely past dawn and the air was still cool from the passage of night; there were even pockets of cold, refreshing dew on the grass. All that would soon burn away as the sun rose from the streaked layers of cloud to the east and began to beat relentlessly on the Frankish army. Day and night they had ridden first north and then eastwards, picking up soldiers on their way, heading to a confrontation with il Bursuqi that could no longer be avoided. Their scouts had reported that he had withdrawn from Zerdana to besiege the smaller Frankish-controlled fortress of Azaz, which had been proving a thorn in his side. The garrison had sent messenger doves pleading for help, and Baldwin had returned the birds with the reply to hold out, that help was at hand.

The priest intoned the words of the mass, and Strongfist murmured his responses, comforted by the ritual and the knowledge that if he died in battle today, at least he had been confessed of his sins and cleansed. At his side, Fergus fidgeted with a leather arm brace, adjusting the buckles. Strongfist cocked a distracted eyebrow. His cousin, although devout, had ever had a problem with moments of stillness. Fergus's lips moved automatically. He latched the strap on the brace, changed his mind and slackened it off.

Strongfist cleared his throat irritably. Fergus ceased

fiddling, bent his head, signed his breast and sighed heavily.

'. . . *In Nomine Patris, et Filii, et Spiritus Sancti,* amen,' Patriarch Bernard intoned, making the sign of the cross in the air before the open altar. His jewelled, embroidered robes glistened in the new sun as if fashioned of wet gold and behind him the planted banners of Antioch, Jerusalem and Edessa streamed in the breeze. Dominating them all was the staff bearing in its pearl and gold cruciform top the sliver of the True Cross on which Christ had been crucified. The holiest relic in Christendom. As always, a lump constricted Strongfist's throat as he gazed upon the symbol. Every man present was sworn to fight to the last drop of blood to protect it . . . and it might well come to that this day.

The benediction finished, men began rising from their knees and seeking their commanders. Strongfist beat dust from his chausses and adjusted his hauberk so that it hung straight. Amalric brought his tawny stallion round from the horse lines. Sweat creamed the horse's satin coat and its eyes showed a white rim of agitation. Strongfist laid a soothing hand on its neck, fondled its dark muzzle and murmured steadying words. Beyond the boy and the destrier, he watched the men of Montabard being organised into line by Durand and Malik. They were to fight under the banner of the Patriarch, but Strongfist had their immediate leadership.

He set his foot in the stirrup and swung into the saddle. The high pommel and cantle and the long stirrup leathers gave him a firm seat that only a full-on blow or his death would dislodge. His face full of fear and eagerness, Amalric handed up Strongfist's lance and shield. Strongfist slung the latter onto his back by the long strap and looked down at the youth.

'I want a promise from you that you will stay back with the baggage detail,' he said as he gathered the reins. 'If our lines should break and we are overrun, your orders are to flee. I want no dying-breath heroics, you are too young.'

Amalric's scowl was fierce, his narrowed eyes as pale as glass in the brightening light.

'You will give me your word on this.'

'If you do not return, how will you know if I have kept it?' The boy's jaw jutted in pugnacious challenge.

'I won't, but you will. And if you cannot, then you are not worthy of future knighthood. Now, swear to me.'

Amalric continued to frown, but made the sign of the cross on his breast. 'I swear,' he said moodily.

'Good.' Strongfist gave a decisive nod. 'God willing, it will not come to that, but it is always wise to be prepared.' He touched his heels to the dun's flanks, using the sides of his heels rather than his spurs, and, keeping the reins in tight, trotted over to join Fergus. The latter was astride his black Nicaean destrier with his flame-haired sons at either side. Boys of nineteen and twenty-one years old, the latter recently knighted, the former still a squire.

Beneath the nasal bar of his helm, Fergus's moustache bristled as if every hair was standing on end. 'Well,' he said with a chequerboard display of teeth, 'we got ourselves into some hard situations when we were a similar age to these wee lads here. No one who was at the battle of Dorylaeum or the siege of Antioch will ever forget how hard-pressed we were. It seems tae me that we've reached another marker in the road. Either, by God's grace, we'll prevail, or we'll fall.'

It was stating the obvious, but such was Fergus's pragmatic tone, coupled with the wry smile on his face, that Strongfist felt oddly comforted. Beyond the hill where they had encamped, upon the flat ground before Azaz, il Bursuqi's amassed forces waited to meet them. From the information supplied by the scouts and outriders, the Saracens vastly outnumbered their Frankish counterparts. And since the Saracens too had their spies, il Bursuqi would know just how much of an advantage he had. Strongfist had weighed the odds the previous evening while sharpening his sword and putting an edge on his dagger. Not in their favour, but he had concluded that it did not matter. Whatever happened, he would either reach his wife and daughter through the Saracen lines, or die in the effort to reach them.

He touched his breast and felt beneath his surcoat and over his hauberk the outline of the simple wooden cross he wore around his neck. His own life didn't matter, just let the hostages be safe.

With King Baldwin, Patriarch Bernard and Joscelin of Edessa at its head, the Frankish army advanced through the increasing light and heat to meet the Saracens before the walls of Azaz. Banners rippled in the breeze like ribbons of dyed water and above them all sailed the stave bearing the reliquary of the True Cross. Strongfist's mouth was dry. He reached to his waterskin, thumbed off the stopper and took a swig. The liquid was fresh from the spring and cold, scented with beeswax from the lining of the skin. It was difficult to swallow, but he forced himself. Who knew when he might have the opportunity to drink again . . . if ever.

As the Frankish troops approached the Saracen army across the baked dust, it seemed to Strongfist that he was gazing upon an ocean. Serried ranks of archers and lancers were poised, their armour glittering like sunlight on wave crests, their banners billowing like sails: a tide held back by the waiting word of the captains but, when unleashed, threatening to surge over and drown by sheer weight of numbers.

Fergus whistled softly through the gaps in his teeth. 'More of them than I'd like,' he said, 'but not so many as to cause despair.' He reached to pat the battle-axe thrust through his belt. 'They're canny fighters, but they'll nae withstand the kiss o' my bonnie love.'

Strongfist found a smile despite the grim nature of the moment. Fergus was never more at home than when involved in a skirmish. It was as if the fierceness of his hair was a manifestation of his nature and every now and then it had to boil over. Out of bowshot range, the Frankish army halted and faced the Saracens across the scrubby terrain. At the back of il Bursuqi's army, the walls of Azaz were lined with defenders. Silence fell, punctuated by the jingle of bits and the whine of the wind. Strongfist felt sweat crawling down his cheeks. He had bound a band across his brow so that it would not drip into his eyes and blind him. The waiting drew out like an archer holding at the nock while his arm strained with tension. It was the usual Saracen ploy to send in skirmishers: light swift lancers and archers who would pour arrows and darts into the enemy force to soften them up. It was what had happened at Dorylaeum, except on that occasion the Frankish army had stood firm and the Saracen javelins had been unable to pierce the heavy shields and mail. However, this day, there was no sign of skirmishers breaking from the ranks.

'They're going to try to overwhelm us by force o' numbers,' Fergus said, speaking Strongfist's thoughts aloud, his voice curling around the words. 'Either their leader's a fool, or overcertain of his success.'

'Why should he not be confident?' Strongfist said. 'King Baldwin has retreated before him until now. Il Bursuqi took Kafartab without difficulty and all the Saracen lords in the north have either bowed to his authority or joined his ranks.'

'Och, I don't blame him for being arrogant, but it's nae over yet.' Fergus kissed the haft of his axe. 'Indeed, it's scarcely begun.'

His last word was drowned by a resounding series of highpitched yells from the Saracen lines. Spears flashed like a shoal of turning fish as they were raised and levelled. Joscelin of Edessa cantered down the Frankish front, his sword raised, his stallion's hooves raising puffs of dust. His voice roared out, as loud as a bull's in a market place full of cattle.

'Just like the old days, eh?' Fergus said.

Strongfist swallowed. His responding grin was a rictus as he adjusted his shield and brought his own lance to bear.

'Steady, lads,' Fergus said to his sons. The elder one was

licking his lips, the younger was striving to control his prancing, sidling horse.

A horn blared from the Saracen line and the waiting was over. The tide was on the roll, the glittering comber of spears flashing towards the Frankish lines.

Strongfist heard the responding trumpet of their own horns and lashed the reins down on the dun's sweat-spumed neck. The Frankish cavalry pounded at the Saracen line as if the shore was moving to meet the sea. Would the wave smash on the rock, or the rock shatter beneath the force of the surge? He could hear Fergus bellowing in Gaelic as he always did when he fought. The hot wind blasted his face; the dun's mane blew in ragged pennants. He could feel its shoulders straining for the next stride and the bunch and thrust of its haunches. Closer, closer. He trained his lance upon a Saracen riding a thin-legged bay. The man's round shield was small, protecting a small area, whereas the kite-shape of Strongfist's, although heavier, offered him superb cover. He dug in his spurs, thus gaining an extra burst of speed from the dun and rode onto the impact. His longer, heavier lance spitted the Saracen and carried him straight over the back of his saddle. The impact jarred the dun, and sent the bay to its knees. Strongfist thrust down on the shaft as if spearing a fish, dragged the point back up and out and pivoted the recovering dun with his knees. Close by, Fergus was still howling as he cut with the axe like a woodsman chopping spills for his hearth. To either side, his sons wielded sword and mace with grim concentration.

The battlefield became a patchwork mêlée of struggling men and horses. Dust floured the air and the warriors choked on their grunts of effort, their screams of pain. A metallic tang of blood wove through the haze like a scarlet ribbon, its underside tainted with the stench of excrement and spilled horse entrails. Strongfist's destrier trod on something soft that screamed and then was silent. Hacking, slashing, beset on all sides to the limit of his ability but never beyond it, Strongfist thought that this must be how it felt to stand in purgatory, but at the mouth of hell rather than the doors to heaven. Sweat rolled down his cheeks like rain down a stable door in a thunderstorm but he had no time to replenish the moisture loss. He felt as if someone had kindled a fire at the back of his throat. The only consolation was that no matter how much he was suffering in his heavy armour, the lighter-armed Saracens were suffering too. Not so much from the heat and dust to which they were long acclimatised, but from the weighty force of the Frankish assault. Hand to hand, the Franks had the advantage and with grim determination were cutting into the Saracen superiority of numbers.

Strongfist, Fergus and the two younger men developed a rhythm and pushed forward, guarding each other, battering aside their opponents, driving a path. They took minor blows, but even if a Saracen scimitar did win past the kite shields, the bulk of mail and gambeson absorbed the cut and the bruise of the hit. The Saracens with their flimsy armour and small round shields were far more susceptible. Even so, the Franks were not entirely without casualties. Now and again a destrier would be brought down by the flash of a scimitar and its rider either crushed underfoot or cut to pieces before he could recover. Sometimes a footsoldier would be sloppy with his shieldwork and pay for it. Exhorted by their commanders, certain that their superior numbers would carry the day, the Saracen wave continued to batter the Frankish rock. 'Hold firm!' Joscelin of Edessa's voice bellowed out and the horns continued to sound the note of advance. The standard of the True Cross rode high above the Frankish lines and beside it flew Baldwin's banner and slowly, but steadily, they forged forwards.

Strongfist's breath was tearing in his throat and, despite the bandage at his brow, his vision was a salty blur. Fergus's Gaelic expletives had long since diminished into grunts of effort and the swings of his axe had grown haphazard and less controlled. Strongfist knew that they were teetering on the edge of their endurance – that they would either have to retreat because they were too exhausted to go on, or die because they could no longer protect themselves from the slashes of the Saracen blades.

Just as he was contemplating pulling his exhausted dun from the line, there came a shout to his left and the horns blared out the advance again and again. It was a cry of harrying triumph, a command to gather all reserves that remained and push. 'They're breaking!' Fergus wheezed, his complexion emperor-purple. 'Praise God, the bastards are breaking!' He raised his voice in a cracked bellow of triumph.

Strongfist didn't have the saliva for speech, but he dug in his spurs, adjusted his grip on his sword and, knowing that he would either die or win through, surged forward, shoulder to shoulder with his old battle companion.

The Saracen camp was a scene of abandoned chaos. Il Bursuqi's troops had fled the battlefield without time to collect their belongings. Those who had tried had been cut down in the attempt. Tents were still pitched, cooking fires still burned under small brass cauldrons and food that owners would never return to eat simmered in earthenware pots. Loose horses plunged among the shelters, creating minor havoc, and a large tent caught fire as it was knocked sideways into an untended brazier.

Strongfist dismounted outside one of the bigger pavilions and ducked inside. There was a glass flagon of sherbet on a coffer, set out as though waiting for the owner to return from a day's hunting rather than the enormity of a battle. Strongfist lifted the flagon and, after a sniff, drank straight from the lip. The cold liquid ran like new rainfall down his parched throat and was the most wonderful sensation he had ever felt.

Finally he lowered the flagon, wiped his dripping moustache on the cuff of his gambeson, and glanced further round the tent, taking time now to notice the silky gazelle hides beneath his feet, the camp bed with good woollen blankets and a coverlet of fringed silk, the inlaid table on which the flagon had stood. A brass lamp hung from the tent roof on delicate chains and the scent of frankincense lingered in the air. Here was no common soldier's tent, or even that of a moderately prosperous landowner. This must belong to a higher lord, the Saracen equivalent of a baron at least.

Wedged against the side of the tent and topped by a cushion of tasselled red damask was a wooden chest carved with ornate geometrical designs. Strongfist caught his breath. Setting the flagon aside, he sat on the bed and used his sword hilt to break the lock. When he threw back the lid, gold bezants shimmered at him, layer upon layer like the scales of a carp. Strongfist's stomach clenched. His eyes burned, but he did not have the moisture to spare for tears. This would go a long way towards the hostages' ransom. He closed the lid and bound the coffer with cord stripped from the side of the bolster. Going outside, he commanded two of his serjeants to stand guard over the pavilion and its contents, and gave them his banner to plant at the entrance as a symbol of his possession.

There was no hard pursuit of the Saracen army. The destriers could not have kept pace with the swift, light ponies and the Franks had learned to their cost the danger of chasing an enemy who could outrun them and then skirmish from a distance. The carnage of the battlefield and the chaotic baggage camp told their own story of an overwhelming victory.

That night, Strongfist was too exhausted to celebrate. Collapsing onto the pallet of the Saracen lord whose tent he had appropriated, he slept almost as deeply as the dead on the battlefield. In the morning, however, he set about assessing the sum he had gained. To add to the coffer of gold bezants, he had found a smaller one of personal effects: turban jewels, rings, brooches and buckles. Most were of Saracen work, but among them was a jewelled cross on a chain and a set of prayer beads in pearl, amber and gold that had obviously been seized at some point from Christian hands.

Fergus, nursing a wrenched arm from the vigorous axe-wielding of the previous day, eyed the trove with a gleam. He was wearing a green silk tunic that had come from a Saracen lord's abandoned clothing chest and the collar was stiff with embroidery and gems. 'The King will have enough to ransom the hostages twice over,' he said. 'I suppose you've heard that every knight is to pay a contribution.'

'Yes, I'd heard. He can have it all, if it buys back my family.' Strongfist cast an almost disparaging look at the opulence surrounding him. 'It makes no difference to me whether I drink out of a golden goblet or common earthenware.' He rubbed his back and felt the sharper twinge of bruises above the ache of strained muscles. Not only had he slept like a corpse, he was as stiff as one this morning.

Fergus grunted. 'It matters tae me. I like my comfort when I can get it, but you're welcome tae everything I have for your womenfolk and the wee scrap . . . aye, and the lad too. You can even have this tunic. The collar's fair irritating me tae death.' He hooked his finger into the neckband and tugged it away from his chafed flesh.

'That is beyond duty. You don't have to . . .'

'I know I don't, but they're my family too.' He grinned at his cousin. 'Besides, I don't have a choice. Baldwin will hang every knight by the heels and shake him until the bezants fall out of his braies.'

Strongfist chuckled at the image. Whatever the situation, he could always count on Fergus to lighten it.

'As soon as the money's gathered and counted, a deputation's to be sent to il Bursuqi.' Fergus watched Strongfist move gingerly across the tent to the entrance. 'Do you think you'll be fit to offer yourself up?'

Strongfist gazed out on the battlefield. The Saracens had come under flag of truce to remove their dead and to open negotiations about the hostages. The corpses that went unclaimed were to be buried in a grave currently being dug for the purpose. He could hear the scrape of shovels as the footsoldiers toiled. Other than their daily pay, their reward was whatever they could strip from the bodies to use or sell. The Frankish dead had been borne with ceremony to Azaz for their interment. All had to be done swiftly. Already the smell of corruption flickered on the air like a buzzing fly waiting to settle. 'I'll be fit.' His tone was grim but resolute. 'Not even the mouth of hell would stop me.' He clenched his fist on the tent post. 'Indeed, after yesterday, I doubt that the mouth of hell would be much of a challenge by comparison.'

Chapter 38

Sabin raised his shield and fielded the blows that young Joscelin of Edessa launched at him. The wooden sword struck the blazoned leather with a dull thud and rebounded.

'You see,' Sabin said. 'While I hold it tight to my body, and high, you cannot pierce my defences, but if I am careless thus . . .' He slackened his grip and showed the boy the vulnerable space into which a blade could slide. 'You must ever be on the lookout for your enemy's weakness while never lowering your own guard.'

Joscelin nodded. His freckled complexion was pink with exertion and his eyes were aglow.

'Now, come at me again. Surprise me.'

The boy attacked with suddenness and vigour, feinting high for Sabin's head and at the last moment cutting low. Sabin's shieldwork was swift and automatic as was the practised ease with which he turned Joscelin's wooden sword with his own and flipped it out of his hand. When the youth looked disheartened, Sabin grinned at him.

'No, that was good, and you were using your head. More practice, more strength, more speed and you will be formidable.'

Scowling, Joscelin went to pick up his sword from the dust. 'But for now I am too slow and weak.'

'I did not say that. You could outmatch most youths of

your age, and I would not go up against you lightly once you have your manhood.' He lowered the shield to blot his brow. Joscelin gave a yell and launched himself at Sabin, and this time the sword connected with his teacher's body.

Sabin's breath whooshed out and he doubled over. Joscelin lifted the wooden blade and laid it to Sabin's throat. 'That's two killing blows,' he said perkily.

'Both dishonourable!' Sabin choked.

'You said I had to surprise you.' Joscelin hesitated, torn between triumph and dismay. 'If you were my enemy, I would be mad not to take advantage.'

His arm across his midriff, Sabin gingerly straightened. 'Indeed you would,' he said with a wry smile. 'But when it's your tutor, it is decidedly underhand!' He tousled the boy's hair to show that he was jesting.

Joscelin's good humour returned. 'Then I did well?'

'Well enough,' Sabin said, carefully judging his level of enthusiasm. He was pleased with the boy, but did not want him to grow over-confident at this stage. Assurance and ability always worked best together when they were matched.

They had an interested audience of Saracen guards. One in particular was eyeing Sabin and fingering the hilt of his scimitar. He was called Faisal and his brother and cousin had ridden to join il Bursuqi's alliance against the Franks. Faisal had remained at Shaizar and was taking every opportunity to bait the male hostages.

'If that is the best that you Frankish warriors fight, small wonder you dare not face us,' he yelled.

Sabin ignored him. 'I think that will do for today,' he said quietly to Joscelin. 'Even if you are not worn out, I am.' He started to leave the courtyard. Above his head three doves clapped their wings as they took flight from a roof, circled and flew out over Shaizar's walls. If only, he thought.

'You are all cowards.'

'Keep walking,' Sabin said as Joscelin's eyes grew dark at the insult. 'He would like nothing better than an excuse to fight.'

'Go on, run like women!' A handful of flung stones pattered against their backs. Joscelin made a small sound as one struck his neck and the sharp edge drew blood.

'Inside,' Sabin said, pushing the boy protectively in front of him. But before they could reach the safety of the door, Faisal had run to block their escape. The other guards looked on uneasily. There was some shuffling of feet, but no one moved to intervene, although an older man did sidle away in the direction of the Emir's apartments.

'Get past me, Frank, and you can go hide behind a woman's skirts,' Faisal said as he drew his scimitar from its sheath. The thin edge gleamed, mocking the crude wooden blade in Sabin's hand.

'Let the boy go within,' Sabin said.

The Saracen's dark eyes narrowed. 'No,' he said, his lip curling. 'He wants to learn? We will show him.' The scimitar came down in a slice of light. Sabin parried with the shield and heard the thud of the blade against the hide-covered linden wood. His sword was a toy, and he wasn't wearing any form of body protection. All he had was the shield and his speed . . . and the latter would not last.

The Saracen circled and came in from the side, feinting as the boy had done but with considerably more skill. There was nothing in his eyes to give away what he intended. Sabin guessed right and again thwarted the blade on the shield's hide binding. Faisal snarled and cut high. The edge of the scimitar clipped the top of the shield, narrowly missing Sabin's skull, indeed shaving a lock of hair. As the strands scattered in the breeze, Sabin leaped forward and butted the shield into Faisal's stomach. The iron boss struck him square in the gut and Faisal doubled up with a grunt. Sabin discarded the shield, grasped the muscular brown wrist and twisted. At the same time he brought up his knee into the Saracen's face and felt bone give beneath the pressure. The scimitar dropped from Faisal's fingers and before it struck the ground, it was in Sabin's hand.

'Inside!' Sabin snarled again at Joscelin. 'Now. Do it. Don't argue.' Seizing his shield, he backed to cover the boy's retreat.

Faisal huddled in the dust, crying out like a wounded hare, blood running from his tooth-punctured lip and broken nose. Beyond Faisal, a half-circle of guards fingered their hilts and assessed their chances. Assessing his own, Sabin began a silent recital of the Lord's Prayer and prepared to die. There was no sign of anyone coming to intervene from the Emir's apartments, and one dead Frankish knight would make little difference to the overall hostage agreement. He took several paces back until he was standing in the doorway. As yet the space behind him was clear of guards. He could have turned and run, but decided he would rather face his death than feel it slam hilt-deep into his back.

'Come,' he said. 'What are you waiting for? I am only a single Frank.'

Still they paused. On the ground between him and them, Faisal staggered to his feet, his lower face streaming with blood. Spitting red saliva, he reached for the dagger on the right side of his belt, but before he could draw the weapon, there came a cry from the gateway and a hunting party galloped into the courtyard. The horses were sweating from a hard day's riding, and the dogs ran with lolling tongues and lowered tails. Astride a dappled mare with black points, Usamah took in the scene at a glance and spurred across the courtyard. The guards parted in haste to avoid being shouldered by the horse.

'What is this?' he demanded. His gaze darted to the scimitar brandished in Sabin's hand.

The soldier let forth a torrent of indignant Arabic, his words slurring through his lacerated lip. Blood dripped steadily from his nose.

'He baited me,' Sabin said with quiet vehemence. 'First with words, then stones, then steel.'

Usamah looked between the two men. A gesture and some rapid words cleared the ground of the onlookers. He spoke to the bleeding guard in a voice that was edged with ice. The man bowed his head and, making an abject gesture, shuffled aside like a whipped cur. The glance he cast towards Sabin was murderous, but he did not dispute whatever rebuke had been meted, and swiftly made himself scarce.

Usamah dismounted from the mare and gave her into the custody of one of his grooms. Then he held out his hand for the scimitar. 'I hope you are not going to be foolish,' he said. 'If you make a wrong move now, not even I can save your life.'

Sabin reversed the hilt and handed the weapon across. 'Or your own,' he said.

Usamah thrust the scimitar through his hunting belt and smiled without humour. 'Fortunate that we know each other.' The smile faded. 'I will speak with Faisal and he will be given duties elsewhere. Perhaps you will refrain from training with the boy for a couple of days until the dust has settled.'

Sabin had no alternative but to agree. Besides, he was grateful to be alive. Joscelin was waiting for him at the foot of the winding stairs that led up to the Frankish apartments. Eagerness and anxiety warred in the boy's expression, and there was more than a glimmer of admiration.

'Will you teach me how to do that?' he demanded.

'To do what?

'Fight like . . .' Joscelin sought for a comparison ' . . . like a common footsoldier.'

'You need years of tavern brawling to get that good,' Sabin retorted curtly. 'I doubt your father would approve. My relatives certainly didn't.' Feeling queasy in the aftermath of the tension, he thrust the shield into Joscelin's hands and began to mount the stairs.

Joscelin ran his fingers over the vicious slashes gouged into the leather hide and grimaced. 'He came very close,' he said. 'Weren't you afraid?'

'I didn't have time,' Sabin said. 'All I knew was that I had to put him down and make sure he stayed.' He glanced over his shoulder and managed the semblance of a smile. 'The fear comes now, in the aftermath. Any man who tells you he is never afraid at some point in a battle is a liar.'

Joscelin said nothing until they were almost at the door of the hostages' chamber. A pair of guards lounged on duty, but barely looked up from their game of chess.

'I . . . I am often afraid,' Joscelin confessed, 'but I would never dare say so. If my father heard me, he would have me whipped.'

Sabin stopped and turned. 'You have nothing of which to be ashamed,' he said. 'Your father will be proud of you, I promise.' Joscelin looked wry.

'You think your father fears nothing?' Sabin laid his hand on the boy's shoulder and gave it a small shake for emphasis. 'He fears for you, his flesh and blood, and because he is a great lord and all eyes are upon him, he fears to show it. There will be no talk of whipping when you return.'

Sabin entered the chamber and was immediately assaulted by Guillaume, who dashed up to him, struck his thighs and bounced off. Sabin swung him up into the air and tossed him until the toddler squealed with delight. Finally, tucking him under his arm like a bundled-up saddle blanket, Sabin carried him over to the corner where Annais sat cradling the baby.

Joscelin went to prop the shield in a corner, facing inwards, but not before Annais caught sight of the blazon.

'Dear Jesu, what have you been doing?'

Sabin shrugged and flicked Joscelin a warning glance. 'Nothing,' he said. 'The hide is flawed and fragile. I will ask Usamah for some new skins and varnish to recover it.'

'Even so, a wooden sword would not do that kind of damage.' Her gaze nailed him. 'I did not spend my entire life in a nunnery. I know the difference between a scrape in practice and what I see there. No,' she said to Joscelin. 'Don't try to hide it.'

'It is nothing,' Sabin repeated quietly. 'One of the guards wanted to show off his prowess and, as I said, the hide is of poor quality.'

Annais studied him through narrowed lids. Sabin returned her look with one of bland innocence.

She drew breath, not prepared to let it pass so easily, but the baby came to Sabin's aid by screwing up his face and letting out a high-pitched wail of pain. Immediately her attention diverted. 'It's the colic,' she said and, putting him over her shoulder, gently patted his back. The wails continued. 'And, I suspect, a conspiracy of males,' she added darkly.

'The counterpart to a suspicion of women,' Sabin answered with a smile. 'Here, give him to me.' He took little Edmund from her arms and carried him around the room. Ostensibly, it was to soothe the infant, but it literally got Sabin out of a tight corner.

Dusk was approaching and a servant arrived to kindle the oil lamps. He glanced swiftly at Sabin, and looked astonished to see him bouncing a squalling baby against his chest. He had been one of the bystanders in the courtyard and Sabin could tell that he was trying to reconcile the notion that a brutal Frankish warrior could perform a woman's task with equanimity.

Clucking his tongue, the man turned to the door, but stopped in consternation at the sounds echoing down the corridor. Had they been closer they would have drowned out the baby's wails. As it was, they formed an eerie back song, rising and falling, rising and falling in a swollen ululation. The hostages exchanged glances. They had been here long enough now to know the manner in which Saracen women gave vent to agitation and grief, and to realise that something terrible must have happened.

Chapter 39

Under a flag of truce, the Frankish delegation brought the ransom payment to Aleppo, there to receive the hostages that il Bursuqi had taken into his custody.

'It's a grand jest, is it not?' Fergus said as he and Strongfist waited with the horses.

'What is?' The barrels of money had been removed from the covered cart that was now being prepared to house the hostages. Chattering, silk-swathed women were piling the interior with cushions, bolsters and brightly coloured rugs.

'That the ransom money comes from il Bursuqi's defeat. We might have been years raising it otherwise. Now he has to use the hostages to "buy" back his losses.'

'Mayhap it is a jest, and fortunate for us, but I do not feel much like laughing,' Strongfist growled.

'Ach, you will do soon.' Fergus unfastened a small flask from his pouch, took a quick swallow and passed it over. 'Burn some o' that down your gullet. It'll do you good.'

Strongfist eyed the flask dubiously. Fergus's usquebaugh was notorious and he was not sure that his need was yet that dire. He shook his head. 'I want a clear head,' he said, 'and I'd rather not greet my wife with a kiss tasting of drink . . . . My daughter either.'

'Suit yourself.' Fergus shrugged. 'They'll not care what you smell of, just that you're here for them.'

More provisions were piled into the cart: boxes of

sweetmeats; rush baskets filled with dates and pomegranates; flasks of sherbet, lemon-scented water for refreshing the hands and face in the heat of the day. Strongfist marvelled at the way that the Saracens made such implacable enemies but could be the most generous of hosts.

'If they've been treated to all this luxury then they won't want to come home,' Fergus said. 'Maybe they've developed a taste for harem life.'

Strongfist gave him a withering look and deigned not to answer. It was the same as in church. When confined to inactivity, Fergus had to fidget. His sons, who had formed part of the escort, had thankfully inherited some of their mother's tranquillity and were leaning in the shade of a wall, talking in a desultory fashion and slapping at the numerous flies with horse-hair switches.

It seemed an eternity since Baldwin's deputation had entered the Atabeg's residence, although Strongfist knew that his anxiety was making the time drag. Negotiations had to be conducted in a courtly and delicate style – more than half the reason that he and Fergus were waiting outside. Their role was to act as tough, Frankish knights, not diplomats. A group of olive-skinned small boys had gathered to study them and their weaponry with avid curiosity and not a little bravado. One of them had picked up a stone and was rotating in his hand. Strongfist could almost see his mind rotating too. Yes, no, yes no. Setting his hand to the hilt of his sword, he cast the boy the kind of glower intended to help him make the right decision in short order.

Two women emerged with more bundles for the cart. One threw a glance over the situation and rounded on the boys with a torrent of Arabic and some expressive arm-waving. They fled in noisy, chaotic unison, like a flock of sparrows. The woman turned her attention to Strongfist. He removed his hand from his sword hilt and returned to leaning against his horse. She presented him with a jug of sherbet, the expression in her eyes carefully neutral, for no Muslim woman was permitted to smile at a Christian man. He thanked her and avoided looking at her. Unfastening his drinking horn from his belt, he filled it and passed the jug to Fergus.

More people emerged from the tower. Strongfist raised the horn to his lips and lowered it again, the sherbet untasted. There were men and women, Saracens and Franks. His gaze sped over them with greedy anticipation and more than a little fear. Wordlessly he murmured his wife's name. At first he was unsure, and then he saw Princess Joveta clinging tightly to a sturdy woman clad in a dark-coloured gown complemented by a headdress of shimmering blue silk, fringed with tiny gold beads. For an instant, his gaze skimmed the woman, thinking 'Saracen' because of the headdress, but almost immediately, he cut back to her. The name he had spoken without sound now emerged on a husky whisper, then again as a breaking croak. Dear God, almost a whole year. Months and months of wasted time.

He thrust his cup into Fergus's startled free left hand and strode towards the party. Some Saracens reached for their scimitars but he did not see them for his focus was all on Letice. Her eyes were brimming. As he reached her, she threw her left arm around his neck and let out a single sob. Uncaring of the shocked and censorious stares of the witnesses, he set his arm around her waist and pulled her against him, feverishly kissing her temple, her cheek, her mouth. 'Thank Christ you are safe . . .'

'And you,' she gasped. Her hand gripped his hair and she clung to him as hard as he was clinging to her. Then she stepped back and composed herself. 'There is time later,' she said shakily. 'For now, the Princess has to be my first concern. It has been very hard on her.'

Strongfist looked down into the anxious, pinched little face of Princess Joveta. The child had been thin before, but now she was skin and bone. She clung to Letice even more fiercely than Strongfist had done in the moment of greeting, hers a fear of being parted rather than the joy of reunion.

A feeling of unease stirred within him. His eyes had lit on his wife and he had gone to her, now he sought other reassurance and found it missing. 'They are not here,' Letice said quickly and touched his arm. 'But they are safe – still at Shaizar.'

'They separated the Princess from Annais?' He looked at her incredulously. 'I do not understand.'

'They had no choice. We should take Joveta to the cart. You are holding up the procession.'

Strongfist moved to her left and paced beside her in the customary position for a knight protecting a lady.

'I am,' he said distractedly. 'And glad of it. What do you mean they had no choice? What has happened?'

'Annais was great with child; she will have borne it by now. You will have another grandson, or mayhap a granddaughter.'

Strongfist almost stopped in his tracks, but Letice nudged him and he managed to put one foot in front of the other.

'I said I would go with the Princess, since she was used to me.'

He shook his head. 'A child? What was Sabin thinking . . . ?'

'Men seldom think with their heads when tempted,' Letice said drily. 'But, to be fair, neither she nor Sabin knew she was with child when they entered Shaizar.' She gave his arm a gentle shake. 'Once the last part of the ransom is paid they can go free.'

'I cannot help but be concerned. I was expecting you all to be together, or you, Annais and Guillaume at least.'

'That time will be soon,' she said, striving to reassure him at the same time as she reassured herself. Stooping, she lifted Joveta into the travelling wain. 'For now, let us count the blessings we have.'

'I am counting,' he said, with a smile that was both genuine and preoccupied and turned from the conversation as Baldwin's steward claimed his attention with a question about arrangements for the road.

A contingent of il Bursuqi's guards were to accompany

them on the first part of their journey, which was still in Muslim-held land.

'We saw no trouble on the way,' Strongfist said, eyeing the Saracens who had clattered into the courtyard on their tough Arab mares and geldings. There were as many of them as there were Frankish guards. Unconsciously he fingered the hilt of his sword and wondered if there was treachery afoot.

'Perhaps not, but there is word that the Emir of Homs is smarting from the defeat at Azaz, and he has neither hostages nor money to compensate his losses. He may consider a rash move. Atabeg il Bursuqi deems it honourable to offer an escort – at least until we leave his territory.'

Strongfist grunted, acceding but less than overjoyed. After the recent hard and bitter fighting, he did not relish the prospect of riding with Saracens at his back. Somewhat reluctantly, he mounted his horse and shouldered his shield with exaggerated movements. He also made a great show of adjusting his sword. The Saracens responded in a similar wise.

'Ach, you're worrying too much, man,' Fergus said cheerfully as he mounted his own grey. 'It's a matter of honour that they protect us. If they don't, they'll be skinned alive.'

'If they don't, so will we,' Strongfist said grimly.

They rode out in the direction of Antioch and the safety of Christian-held territory. Once, from a distance, Strongfist saw warriors watching them from a sunburned hillside, but they swiftly vanished into the shadows of some ancient columns built by a civilisation long gone and forgotten. The Saracen guards posted outriders and one of them sent several arrows winging into the ruins, but he killed nothing save a goat, which he brought back across his saddle.

After that, there was no more trouble. The goat was roasted over the evening fire with herbs and spices. Although Strongfist received a strong impression that they were being watched and marked, the danger came no closer than an unpleasant prickling at the back of his neck. Their escort remained with them until they reached the Frankish-held fortress of Harenc and then turned back.

Strongfist delivered his charges to the Patriarch in Antioch, spent one luxurious night in the arms of his wife, and set out again for Shaizar to redeem the rest of the hostages, including one of whose tender existence he had not known until now.

Chapter 40

'I have news for you,' Usamah said. He did not sit down at the chessboard, but leaned against the table on which it stood, his arms folded.

Sabin had been expecting it. When the cries of grief had sounded through Shaizar, he had known that something momentous had happened. Several days had passed and the hostages had been told nothing, but he had known that Usamah would eventually speak. 'I am glad of it,' he said. 'We have speculated until we have run out of notions . . . and many of them have not been pleasant.'

Usamah regarded him with a brooding stare, the hazel in his eyes quenched to dull brown. 'And you would be right. There has been a great battle before the walls of Azaz, between your King and Atabeg il Bursuqi.'

Sabin remembered the ululations of grief and knew who had lost. 'What implications does that have for the hostages? Are we to be set free, or made to pay?' He kept his expression neutral, his voice even.

Usamah ceased to lean. 'Have a care,' he warned.

'I intend no insult,' Sabin said steadily, 'but I cannot easily forget what happened to Waleran of Birejek and Ernoul of Rethel.'

'That was different, a matter of honour, and it was your King who caused the death of those men by his perfidy.' Usamah's eyes narrowed. 'How do you know the outcome of the battle?'

'We heard your womenfolk grieving, which they would not do for a Saracen victory.'

Usamah's nostrils flared. 'Il Bursuqi tried to overpower your armies by weight of numbers, but he failed and paid for it. He lost many fine warriors and his baggage camp was seized.'

Sabin drew several careful, shallow breaths. He could not say he was sorry, but neither was it politic to grin with exultation. 'At least the men of Shaizar were not involved,' he said.

'Some were. A contingent rode with il Bursuqi, including the brothers of Faisal ibn Hamidh . . . and they will not be returning.' He cast Sabin a dark look. 'Faisal has sworn death to all Franks.'

Sabin shrugged. 'He had already so sworn before news of the battle arrived.'

'Well then, his hatred has only grown. I am sending him away from Shaizar for a short while. By the time he returns, you and the others will be gone.'

Sabin gave him a swift, surprised look.

Usamah nonchalantly studied his nails. 'A messenger came from il Bursuqi to say that a Frankish deputation is on its way, bearing the remainder of the ransom money. When it arrives, you are to be set free.'

Sabin heard the words, but they lay like oil on water. He had been so long a prisoner that now he was shown a key to the door, he mistrusted it.

Usamah gave a dry smile. 'You do not believe me.'

He shook his head. 'I do not believe myself . . . How soon?'

'That depends on the Franks. It might be the morrow, it might be next month. Soon I hope. A pleasure though it has been to play chess with you, it is past time that you were gone.' He spread his hand and, turning, indicated the board at his back. 'Although perhaps we should play one final time for friendship's sake.'

Sabin was glad to sit, for his mind was turning upon the

news, working the information into the crevices where comprehension lurked. Usamah clapped his hands and sent an attendant to fetch sherbet and sweetmeats. By the time the man returned, Sabin had managed to respond to Usamah's opening gambit with some semblance of intelligence, but it was hard to ground his thoughts.

'We will part as friends, but the next time we meet, it may be as enemies,' Usamah said as he contemplated the board. 'I will not stay my scimitar, and you will not stay your sword.'

Since there was no denying the fact, Sabin said nothing.

Usamah eyed him. 'You should take your wife and your sons and go back to your homeland,' he said. 'There is naught here for the Franks but the death of their race. Mayhap not in your lifetime or mine, but in the years to come. What of your sons if they grow to be men? Or your grandsons should your people endure that long? Will you see them dead in the heat of a battlefield, pinned to the earth by a Saracen lance, their blood watering the soil?'

Sabin looked at the chessboard, the mingling of dark and white pieces in a battle of wits. 'What you say may be true, but unless you claim the power of prophecy, you do not know for certain that the Franks will not endure in Outremer. Besides,' he added, 'this is my homeland now. It has seeped into my skin with the sun and the dust. This is the land where my children were born, and God willing others will follow.'

'So you will not heed me?'

Sabin smiled. 'Would you if our places were reversed?'

'I would like to think so.'

'But beyond like.'

'I do not suppose that I would,' Usamah said with a shake of his head. He pushed the chessboard aside. 'Perhaps a final game was not such a good idea after all. There can be no winner.'

Annais had brought Guillaume to watch Sabin and Lucifer in the sanded yard that the warriors of Shaizar used to exercise their mounts. Sabin was teaching Joscelin the art of sword-fighting from the back of a horse, as opposed to the same on foot. It was a month since the incident with Faisal, and the latter had been sent from Shaizar, together with any hotheads who might have caused trouble. Now it was certain that the hostages would soon be ransomed, the Emir wanted to keep them whole in order to receive his share of the gold.

'Can I ride with Papa soon?' Guillaume's voice was high-pitched with impatience.

'Yes, soon,' Annais replied, wondering how much grace she had before the fidgeting and whining set in. For a child of his years he was stoical and well behaved, but she knew his limit. In addition, the harem women had spoiled him. They were always feeding him sweetmeats and telling him what a good boy he was – neither of which was entirely beneficial.

Edmund, thank all the Saints, was for once sound asleep in the rushwork basket at her feet, his skin protected from the sun by a muslin shade stretched across the top end of the basket. She knew that the blessing would not last, for he was not an infant who required much sleep . . . like his father, she thought with a wry glance at Sabin. Never needed more than a couple of hours at a time and had a surplus of energy when awake. A part of it in Sabin's case was the constriction of being a hostage, she knew. Once they were back at Montabard, once he had numerous matters, administrative and military, with which to deal, he would be less edgy. And of course there was the tension of waiting. Each moment listening for the cry at the gate that would herald their freedom.

She watched Sabin guide Lucifer with his thighs and heels. The stallion's coat shone like opal in the sun. He twisted and manoeuvred with a sinuous grace the equal of his master's and, watching the partnership, Annais felt a pride so strong that it almost stung her eyes.

Joscelin jabbed his own smaller pony forward and raised his sword. Sabin talked him through the moves, drawing his blows, compensating for the lad's smaller size and lack of experience.

Guillaume wafted his own miniature wooden sword around his head and shouted. Annais winced. The toy had caused as much trouble to the adults as it had pleasure to her son. Yesterday she had caught him about to poke Usamah's pet cheetah in the ear with it. This morning he had aimed a killing blow at Joscelin's head and hurled a tantrum when the plaything had been temporarily confiscated.

The baby snuffled. Annais turned to look at him. He rubbed a little fist over his nose, yawned, revealing a pink expanse of gum, and continued to sleep, although the sucking motions he made with his lips warned her that her time was short. In the brief instant that her attention was diverted, Guillaume launched himself out of her lap and dashed into the courtyard, wafting his sword above his head. Annais sprang up and ran after him, frightened that he would be kicked by one of the horses.

As she caught up with and grabbed him, a troop of riders clattered through the gates, the iron-shod hooves of their mounts striking sparks from the ground, the banners of Edessa and Jerusalem rippling on spear hafts. Guillaume, who had been about to scream, forgot his rage and stared wide-eyed. So did Annais. The leading knight rode a golden-dun stallion and wore a surcoat of blue and gold silk over his hauberk. Although a mail coif and helm concealed most of his face, there was no mistaking the line of his jaw, outlined by a close-cropped blond and silver beard. He drew rein, dismounted and looked around. His gaze met Annais's, dropped to the little boy in her arms, and then he was striding across the courtyard, his arms open and a wide smile filling the space between the end of the nasal bar and throat protector.

'It is your grandfather!' Annais told Guillaume who had backed against her skirts, considerably less bold than a moment before. 'He has come to bring us home!'

'Sweetheart!' Strongfist reached them and engulfed Annais

in a huge bearhug. Then he swept Guillaume into his arms and held him aloft.

'And how's my fine soldier, eh?'

Guillaume deliberated between bawling his head off and accepting the stranger about whom there was a vague sense of familiarity.

'Here, see, do you not remember?' Seating the child in the crook of his left arm, Strongfist tugged off his helm and pushed down his coif.

Guillaume eyed him for a further moment and decided that, since his mother appeared joyful, there was no threat. 'I've got a sword,' he said, thrusting it beneath Strongfist's nose. 'My papa made it.'

'And very fine it is too,' Strongfist said, his voice awkward and choked.

'Of course it is. And named Durendal for the sword of Roland, greatest of our heroes against the Saracens.' Drawing rein, Sabin flung down from Lucifer and strode to clasp first Strongfist, and then Fergus, who had followed more slowly on his cousin's heels.

In the midst of the emotional hugging, backslapping and tears of reunion, a baby's fractious wail added to the wonder and chaos of the moment.

'His name is Edmund,' said Sabin as Annais brought the infant's basket to the men.

'Did ye title him afore or after he opened his mouth?' Fergus enquired as the wails rose in pitch and volume. 'I can aye see the resemblance.' He peered dubiously into the basket. 'He's no' the bonniest bairn I've ever laid eyes on, but no' the worst either,' he said judiciously. 'My own were the worst, although my wife would box my ears for saying so . . . and now look at them.' He thumbed towards the two red-haired young men standing by the horses. 'She calls them handsome, but I'll not have it that they're better looking than me. The girls think they're bonny, mind, but then what do women know, eh?'

'More than men,' Annais retorted and retired to privacy in order to feed her son.

Fergus looked mildly wounded. 'What did I say?'

Strongfist chuckled in her wake. 'I always thought I wanted a meek and biddable daughter,' he said, 'but I am glad that she has found her tongue.'

'Aye, well, you're an unnatural father. Women's tongues are the sharpest weapons ever devised.' Fergus rolled his eyes. 'The wounds I've taken in my time . . .' He turned to Joscelin of Edessa who had dismounted from his pony and was standing a little to one side. 'I hope you are listening to all this, lad, and storing it up for the future.'

The boy smiled but looked bewildered . . . as well he might, Sabin thought.

'He's grown.' Fergus came to stand beside Joscelin. 'Another handspan and he'll be as tall as me.'

'Not difficult,' Strongfist said. 'And half your height is your hair.'

The men's banter, much of it used to cover up strong emotion, was curtailed by a summons from the Emir to attend him in his apartments.

'I need to speak to you,' Strongfist murmured to Sabin as they followed the Saracen guards towards the main complex.

Sabin gave him a swift look. 'Is there trouble?'

Strongfist's shrug was eloquent. 'I hope not, but it is best to be prepared. I know your tendency to tell Annais the bald truth about everything, but what I have to say is no more than rumour, and I count on your good sense to keep it to yourself. I do not want my daughter worrying herself over Guillaume and the babe when there may be no cause.'

'Tell me and I will decide.'

They had paused in the outermost chamber that led to the Emir's apartments. Cushions for seating were piled down each side of the room and a brightly patterned rug covered the floor. Strongfist still had difficulty accustoming himself to the fact that the Saracens walked on their fabrics as well as hanging them on the walls. 'We were warned that the Emir of Homs might try to snatch us on our release. He lost men and valuables beyond count at the battle for Azaz and we would be useful to use as a lever – especially the lad.' He cast a sidelong look in young Joscelin's direction. 'We have seen nothing on our journey here and, God willing, we will come back without incident . . . but it might be wise to sharpen your blade when they return it to you. From what I saw when I arrived, you have kept your skills fresh.'

'After a fashion,' Sabin said, 'but I have not been training every day.'

Strongfist grunted. 'You looked fit enough to me.' He narrowed his eyes. 'You are not going to tell my daughter of this.'

'I might not tell your daughter, but deciding whether to tell my wife is a greater difficulty,' Sabin said. 'She is entitled to know.'

Strongfist's frown deepened, setting three harsh furrows across his brow. 'She is a woman . . .'

'A moment since you were saying that you were glad that she was not meek and biddable,' Sabin argued.

'I am . . . but neither should she be worried without reason . . . especially when she has a babe to feed. She will curdle her milk.'

Sabin's brows rose in proportion to Strongfist's lowering glare. 'If I were not such a respectful son-in-law I would say that you were talking from a hole in your body lower down than your mouth,' he said. 'If her milk were going to curdle, it would have done so long ago after the trials we have endured. Yes, she is a woman, and as gentle and as tender as a snow-flower bloom in early spring. When I watch her nurse my son, or play with Guillaume, or breathe at my side in the night, I want to hold the moment for ever because I am so afraid that I will lose her.' He pinned Strongfist with his gaze. 'If that were all, I would tell her nothing. I would keep it to myself in order not to see a frown trouble her brow or watch her mouth droop. But she is also a woman who carries a honed English scramaseax in her sewing basket, who has been the chatelaine of a fortress and the companion of a queen. She has put herself into the maw of danger for the sake of a child not her own. Do I reward that sort of courage by silence? If so, perhaps I am then a coward.'

Strongfist's jaw tightened, showing grooves of muscle between cheek and mouth. 'Do as you choose,' he growled, 'but choose wisely.'

At that juncture, the Emir's attendants came forth to usher them into his presence and there was no further opportunity for conversation.

Annais watched Sabin from the corner of her eye. He was checking his weapons, which had been restored to him from Shaizar's armoury. He had been delighted that his sword had been oiled and the leather scabbard nourished to prevent it from drying out and cracking. Now he was carefully examining the rivets in his mail shirt for damage and rust. He had been silent throughout the scrutiny, but not from concentration, she thought. Several times he had seemed on the verge of speaking but on each occasion had drawn back, the last time with an irritated glance at Strongfist. The latter was sitting on the floor with Guillaume, playing a game of flipping dinars into a small brass pot, but Annais could tell that her father's attention was divided.

Finished with his hauberk, Sabin set it to one side, but only to fetch his shield. He examined the handgrip and the long leather carrying strap. Annais saw her father compress his lips.

Again, Sabin threw him a wordless glance.

'Is there something you are not telling me?' Annais asked.

'Why should you think that?' Sabin busied himself with the buckle on the strap, shortening it by a notch.

'The way you are checking your equipment as if riding to war. The way you and my father have been passing silent messages ever since you returned from the Emir's apartments.'

Sabin shrugged. 'It is a precaution,' he said. 'The better armed, the less tasty a morsel we will appear to passing brigands . . . Is that not so, wife-father?'

Strongfist flushed. 'That is so,' he said. 'But you do not need to make a parade of preparing your weapons. You will make everyone think that the risk is greater than it is.'

'Better in the bosom of my family than lurking in a corner,' he said. Satisfied with the shield, he set it aside.

Annais looked at Sabin and murmured, 'And how great is the risk?'

He shrugged. 'Probably negligible, but your father did not want me to tell you . . . he thinks you should not be worried lest it curdle your milk.'

Annais raised her brows. 'So you tell me through gestures instead.'

He gave a wry smile. 'I was beginning to wonder how obvious I should become. It was getting to the point where I was running out of equipment to sort through.'

She bit her lip to control a smile. 'There is still my knife,' she said. 'Do you want to inspect that in case I have to use it?'

Her father cleared his throat loudly and frowned. Sabin began to laugh. The sound attracted Guillaume who abandoned his game to pounce upon his stepfather.

'Your mother', Sabin chuckled as he rolled the child in his arms, 'is an Amazon.'

'Ama . . . Amazon?' Guillaume tested the new word with stumbling curiosity.

'Don't be so foolish.' Annais pretended to put her nose in the air. 'They only have one breast . . . and I most certainly have two and in good working order.'

Chapter 41

'May Allah protect you on your journey,' Usamah said as Sabin gained the saddle and drew the reins through his fingers.

The dawn was a red flush in the east and, below the steep walls of the fortress, the River Orontes gleamed like the inside of an oyster shell. Morning smells of bread, hot oil and fresh dung from the stables mingled on the air. Sabin savoured each one because they were seasoned with the scent of freedom. He wore his mail lightly with his shield at his back and his newly honed sword positioned at his left hip – the first time that weight had hung there for a year. Although he welcomed it, the familiarity would have to be relearned.

'And may God watch over you,' he responded. 'If we meet again, may it not be as enemies on the field of battle.'

'*Inshallah,*' Usamah said, placing his hands together and bowing his head.

Sabin settled his helm on his head, easing it down over his arming cap. Reining about, he leaned to take Guillaume from Annais's arms and placed him before his own saddle. There was no baggage wain; everyone was riding astride. Annais carried the baby in a sling; her mount was a smooth-paced black mare, which had been a parting gift from the Emir. Other gifts, such as bolts of silk, goblets of rock crystal and finely woven rugs, were loaded on sturdy pack mules. The Emir could afford to be generous, given the amount of gold that had just trickled into his coffers. He had replaced the grey pony that young Joscelin had outgrown with an Arabian roan, complete with gilded harness.

Banners fluttering in the dawn wind, the later heat of the day less than a whisper, as the Frankish party rode out of Shaizar, crossed the bridge into the citadel and wound its way through the narrow streets of the town. Usamah had sent one man with them as a guide and companion to escort them on the first miles of their journey: Abu, one of Usamah's huntsmen, a slight, swift warrior who was an expert with the bow. He was of an amiable and curious disposition and rode in the middle of the troop, exchanging the occasional word with the knights.

As they left the shadow of the citadel, boys and youths crowded behind them like a swarm of hungry midges. Abu stood in his stirrups and commanded them to be off, but in a good-humoured way. Fergus had a handful of quartered silver coins and a bag of sugared almonds. He flung these offerings vigorously far and wide, and the smaller boys dived in a feeding frenzy, scrabbling in the dust. Sabin grinned at the sight and, expanding his lungs, drew his first breath of free air in a year. Feeling the deep movement in his stepfather's breast, Guillaume looked round and up in curiosity.

'Going home,' he said. He wasn't quite sure what that meant, but he had been told that they were 'going home' today, and everyone had seemed excited at the prospect. He could sense their happiness, but also the underlying tension. It made him feel happy too, but with a squirmy feeling in his mid-section like when he woke in the dark and could not find his favourite scrap of blanket.

'Yes, going home to Montabard.' Sabin ruffled his curls and Guillaume responded to the smile on his papa's face. 'I don't suppose you remember Montabard . . . where you were born.'

'Yes I do,' said Guillaume, not because he did, but because he wanted his papa's approval.

Sabin smiled and tightened his arm slightly, giving the child a gentle squeeze. 'I hardly know if I remember it myself,' he said. 'Except for the falcons wheeling around its great walls, and the river sparkling in the distance – a little like Shaizar.'

'Edmund's not seen it,' Guillaume said and leaned in the saddle to look round at his mother who was cradling his little brother in a sling. Guillaume liked the idea of having a brother, but at the same time he was jealous. A bit like the mixture of happiness and the squirmy feeling. At least he was a big boy though, and Edmund was only a baby.

'No, it will be his first time.'

'I'm the first,' Guillaume said stoutly, raising his chin. When his papa said nothing, he swivelled to stare up at him. 'I'm the first,' he repeated.

'You are the firstborn,' his papa said. 'Now stop wriggling, or else I will begin to think you are a fish, not a boy.' He negated the comment by cuddling him and making Guillaume squeal and wriggle even more. However, after that, reassured, the child settled for the journey.

They wound their way along the river valley with steep hills to their right and the sun climbing in the sky. Behind them, if they chose to look round, the walls of Shaizar stood high sentinel, dominating the landscape. Of the party, only Abu chose to do so, and that because he was judging how far he should accompany them before riding back to report them safely on their way.

He trotted up to ride beside Sabin and engaged him in a brief, fragmented conversation, but barely had he opened his mouth when yelling riders erupted from a thicket at the river's edge and blocked the road. Scimitars flashed in the air and the hard light of the risen sun bounced off shield bosses and mail. Abu's mouth dropped open.

'Go!' Sabin snarled. 'Bring help!'

Abu wrenched his bay mare around, kicked her flanks and swiped her rump with his switch. She took to her heels like a gazelle pursued by a cheetah. Arrows whistled overhead and clattered to the ground in the dust churned up by her flying hooves. The Franks drew their swords and raised their shields. Sabin reined Lucifer to Annais's side and handed a screaming Guillaume across to her. 'In the name of the Emir of Shaizar, let us pass!' Strongfist rose in his stirrups to bellow.

The reply was hostile and filled with mockery. 'In the name of the Emir of Homs, most certainly you may pass and enter the realm of his hospitality.'

'Over my dead body,' Strongfist snarled, drawing his sword.

'Christ on the Cross,' Sabin muttered and, threading his shield onto his arm, kicked Lucifer towards the front of the line.

'That can be arranged,' the Saracen said. A flick of his fingers brought an archer forward, arrow nocked. 'Why should I grieve over one less Frankish knight?'

The archer had sighted on Strongfist but, as Sabin spurred forward, his aim swivelled. Sabin had an instant to recognise Faisal, whose nose he had bloodied in Shaizar's courtyard, a moment of locked eyes and statement of intent. Then, faster than a blink and more slowly than waking from deep slumber, Faisal loosed the shot. His aim was true and Sabin's horrified reactions slow. The arrowhead sank not into wood but mail. A second and third followed in rapid succession. Lucifer reared and Sabin was pitched from the saddle to hit the ground with a sickening thud. A rivulet of blood crawled from beneath him in the dust and he lay as still as a slaughtered sheep. Lucifer bolted back down the road, reins trailing.

The Saracen leader shouted furiously at Faisal and knocked his arm, so that a fourth arrow flew wide, bounced on the hillside and clattered into a gully.

'You filthy sons of whores!' Strongfist roared, his voice cracking with shock and rage. He would have charged into their midst and given his life to take some of theirs, but now the bows were not aimed at him, but at Annais and Guillaume, at the baby and the ashen-faced Joscelin of Edessa.

'You will yield,' their leader said, 'or I will kill the woman and the children.' Another swift signal sent his men among the troops. Weapons were seized and confiscated. Annais was so numb with shock that she could neither think nor move. It was only when a Saracen tried to take Guillaume from her arms that she rallied enough to fight. But it made no difference. She could not hold a baby and a small boy. The Saracen mimed that he would cut Guillaume's throat if she continued to struggle and so she gave him up while his screams pierced her ears and rang in the hollow of her skull. She swayed in the saddle and instinctively tightened her grip on the reins. She must not faint. If she fell with the baby . . . if she fell . . . Her eyes went to the still form in the dust, the red crawl of blood, the outspread, slack hand. She choked and had to retch over her mount's side. What use was her seax now? All the jesting, all the bold words counted for nothing. She wanted to fling off her horse, run to him, take his head in her lap, hold the outspread hand. But she couldn't. Her son was screaming. The baby had woken and was adding his roars in counterpoint. It should have been enough to stir the dead, but it wasn't.

Archers and lancers hemmed the group around, and the horses were prodded into a rapid trot. Faisal lingered near Sabin's still form. He gave it a vicious kick and spat on it. His commander shouted at him again and drew his scimitar. Reluctantly Faisal mounted his horse and joined the troop. Several times he looked over his shoulder as they jogged along the road, before finally settling down behind Annais's black mare.

'Your man is dead,' he gloated in accented French. 'Soon you will wish that you were dead too . . . and your children.'

Annais swallowed bile and fixed her gaze on the Saracen in front who was carrying Guillaume. The little boy's screams had faded to whimpers that now and again carried back to her. Edmund continued to wail fractiously and she jogged him against her body.

'Do you know what they do to Frankish male children? Did the women at Shaizar not tell you?' Faisal's voice was a sibilant whisper. 'Some say that we thrust spears through their buttocks, out through their mouths and roast them whole over a slow fire, but such tales are told by ignorant fools.'

She felt him watching her, judging her response, and sweat crawled down her back like a cold worm. She swallowed and willed herself not to be sick, to show nothing. Against her side, beneath her cloak, she could feel the leather sheath of the seax and wondered if she would have the courage and swiftness to use it. Inside she was silently screaming Sabin's name. If not her soul, then she had lost her soul's mate.

'No,' Faisal whispered hoarsely, 'we take them and, as we do with our colts not used for breeding stock, we geld them and make of them our slaves. The boy, he will make a pretty catamite, with those eyes and the fine curls . . . if he survives the gelding, of course. Not all of them do.'

Annais clenched her fists around the bridle and held herself as straight as a spear.

'It will go hard for you. If you had been fair-haired or blue of eye, you might have entered a harem as a favoured slave. Our emirs and atabegs enjoy pale, Frankish women, but you are too like one of our own. Doubtless you will be put to work in the kitchens, or sold to a man of lesser means . . .'

He was baiting her, she told herself. None of it was true. Even if the Emir of Homs took them, they would be ransomed. Let it flow past like murky water down a river in spate.

'Perhaps I will offer to buy you,' he speculated as he rode alongside her. 'It would not compensate me for the loss of my brothers, but it would go a certain way.'

'I would rather bed with a leper,' she said stiffly.

He narrowed his eyes. 'That could be arranged. Perhaps an entire colony of lepers, eh?' He nudged his horse closer to hers and Annais's hand inched across the bridle leather towards the knife sheath concealed under her cloak. She met his stare with loathing.

One of the other Saracens reined back and spoke sharply to Faisal, tossing him a lance. Faisal grunted a response and, looking less than pleased, cantered off to what was obviously his turn on reconnaissance duty. The man whom he had relieved rode in silence beside Annais, and even in the midst of her abject misery, she found a spark of gratitude for small mercies. Bowing her head over the baby, she prayed, reciting the words that she had learned at Coldingham Priory during a different, tranquil life. In the burning heat from the sun, the tears that filled her eyes were salty and scalding but as nothing compared to the pain welling and welling like a swift new spring from her core.

Hot, hay-scented breath gusted into Sabin's face. He heard the jingling crunch of a horse champing a bit, and the stamp of hooves. Raising his lids, he stared at stones, at settling dust, and at a whiskery grey muzzle with a triangular snip of pink between the nostrils. It breathed on him again and gave a loud snort.

Sabin tried to sit up and the pain rushed at him like a wild boar. It crashed through his skull and gouged his side. Gasping, he forced his will through the pain and struggled to a sitting position. Lucifer was considering him with dark, liquid eyes. His reins trailed in the dust, the loop broken where the stallion had stamped on them. Sabin looked down at himself. Three arrows were embedded in his mail. Two had been caught in the mesh and only the tips had pierced the thick cotton quilting of the gambeson beneath. The main damage came from the third arrow that had punched through close to one of the others. The initial arrowhead had weakened the links, allowing its companion to drive through and pierce the skin over Sabin's ribs, skewering him like meat on a spit bar.

Sweating with effort, he gained his feet and set about

manipulating the arrows out of his hauberk and gambeson. Had his mail been made of inferior quality rivets and less well maintained, he would have been dead. As it was, the vicious throbbing of his wounds told him that he was alive and not too badly injured. Clenching his teeth, he laid his hand to the inch of protruding shaft at his ribs, and pulled it from his flesh as if taking a large stitch in a tapestry. Blood ran over his hands, hot, slippery and red, and for a moment his vision darkened. He knew he mustn't faint and he clung to consciousness with grim determination, pressing his quilted tunic against the tear until the bleeding eased. Catching Lucifer's rein, he rested his head against the stallion's solid silver hide and let the horse take his weight. There was a waterskin hanging from the saddle and, after a moment, he was able to unhook it and take a long, deep drink. Then he cupped a palmful and swilled his face.

His sword was still in its sheath, his shield lying in the middle of the road. Casting his glance around, he saw the discarded weapons in the scrub. There were no bodies, which meant that the others must have been taken for ransom. He did not know how long he had been lying in the road but he did not think that much time had passed, for it was close to Shaizar and must be well used.

A small object caught the corner of his eye. Leaving the horse, he went to it, stooped with an effort and retrieved the small wooden sword with its handgrip of overlapping strips of leather. The hilt was slightly sticky, evidence of the honey cake that its owner had been eating earlier. Sabin's throat swelled with grief, rage and a feeling of utter helplessness. He did not dare to imagine what Guillaume was experiencing. Pushing the toy sword through his belt, he returned to the horse. The effort it took to mount made his vision blur and his side burn as if seared by a brand. His struggle had deafened him to the sound of hoofbeats on the road, but now he heard them, coming from the direction of Shaizar at a fast drum. Gathering the broken reins in his hands, he swung Lucifer to face the sound. The stallion pricked his ears and pawed the ground. The sun beat down on Sabin's mail like a molten hammer and his side throbbed as if a part of that sun was embedded in his flesh. He drew his sword as a score of riders pounded into view and the sun caught flashes and starbursts on lances and Saracen mail. The leading horse was a grey with charcoal rings of dapple on forequarters and rump, and its rider wore a helmet with a spiked point. The rest of Usamah's garments consisted of his dusty hunting gear, with his light mail coat hastily donned on top. Abu rode at his side, his expression grim. 'In the name of Allah the merciful, what has happened?' Usamah demanded.

Clutching his side, Sabin gave him terse details and Usamah's expression darkened.

'This is a stain upon the honour of Shaizar,' he said. 'We must make haste.' He gestured at Sabin. 'Are you fit to ride?'

'For this . . . yes,' Sabin said grimly. 'Even were I at death's door, I would have you strap me to my saddle.'

Usamah gave a curt nod. 'We will pursue these bandits and we will yield them no mercy for they have insulted our honour.' His gaze flickered to the black-fletched arrows lying in the road, evidence of the assault. Cursing fluently, he lashed the reins down on his horse's neck and it sprang straight from its hocks into a gallop. Sabin spurred after him. Lucifer had the strength and stamina to endure. All he had to do was hold on hard and match those qualities.

The men of Homs rode through the burn of the midday sun, for their leader was eager to be as far away from Shaizar as possible by nightfall. Everyone suffered in the heat, which, as the day wore on, became merciless. Having the river nearby was a mixed blessing. While they had access to water, it also meant that swarms of biting flies plagued them and their horses.

The Saracen leader had relented his initial harshness and

Guillaume had been handed to Strongfist to carry. The little boy had ceased to whimper and scream. His thumb had entered his mouth and stayed there and his eyelids had drooped. Annais recognised the signs for she had seen them frequently enough in Joveta. Unable to cope with the terrors around him, her son had retreated into himself, burrowing down into his own private world like a small, frightened animal. She would have done the same herself had she not had the terrible responsibility of parenthood. As it was, she shied from the knowledge of what had happened a few hours since. For the moment she could not cope with it, and so drove it from her mind. She could feel it pushing against the door she had created, however, if she did not look to see a widening crack, then for a while longer she could maintain the illusion of sanity.

In the hour after noon, they had to stop to rest and water the horses at a wayside pool. The hostages were dismounted and herded into a corner and a guard set over them. Annais took the opportunity to feed Edmund, sheltering her modesty beneath the covering of her light cloak. Strongfist sat at her side, Guillaume in his arms.

'I cannot believe this has happened,' he said. It was not an invitation to converse for he did not speak again and his stare was as glazed as his small grandson's.

Fergus was muttering under his breath, but in the Scots Gaelic into which he lapsed during battle frenzy. The sounds meant nothing to Annais. She felt the tug and pull of the baby's mouth at her breast and gazed down into his eyes. They were amber-green like Sabin's, and his brows were feathery black. He didn't know he was fatherless yet. He still had the security of her arms, the softness and sustenance of her breast, and it was all he needed. While she . . . Oh Jesu . . . Annais swallowed and bit her lip. The crack widened to a gap through which tendrils of madness reached for her. She must have made a small sound, for her father laid his hand over hers in a steadying grip. Still he did not speak, but she felt the strength flow from him into her and was able to patch her defences. They would hold a little longer yet . . .

She had given Edmund one breast and was about to transfer him to the other when a shout went up from one of the Saracens posted on lookout. Another scrambled up the rock to join him; there was a brief conversation, followed by a rapid flurry.

'About time too,' muttered Fergus, emerging from his Gaelic monologue to glance darkly at their captors. 'There's going to be blood spilled, and it willna be ours.'

The hostages were gestured to their feet and ordered to mount their horses. More gestures and jabs with reversed spear hafts commanded them to make haste. They set off at a rapid pace. When before they had been moving at a gentle trot, now they jogged briskly, the Saracens keeping up the hostages' momentum by whipping their horses and poking anyone whom they suspected of slowing down with the haft of a lance.

Faisal rode close to Annais again and she saw the hatred glittering in his eyes. 'Do not think that you will be rescued,' he hissed. 'Even if they catch up with us, there is no escape for you.' He drew an inch of scimitar from his scabbard.

Annais stared at him, meeting him eye to eye, as no Saracen woman would ever do. 'Do you think it matters to me?' she said. 'Threaten what you will, I care nothing.'

'Not even for your children?'

'Kill them and you render me dead. What is the difference?' She did not know if he understood, nor did she care.

He drew his scimitar completely from its sheath and flourished it on high to threaten her. One of the other guards shouted at him in reprimand and turned his horse to intervene. Annais could not understand what was being said, but she could well guess. The Emir of Homs would not be best pleased if half the hostages died on the journey.

As the men argued, she heard the sound of hunting horns close behind. The quarrelling ceased and the two warriors drew apart to look back. Their leader joined them, a worried frown set between his eyes. He drew his own sword.

Uttering a sudden yell, Fergus turned his stallion and dug in his spurs. The destrier slammed into the leader's lighter mount and sent it staggering. Fergus grabbed the man's wrist, wrenched the scimitar from his hand, and used it. Howling, he turned the dripping blade and cut at another warrior. Following a hiatus of shock on both sides, Saracens and Franks engaged, the latter heavier, mailed, but mostly weaponless, the former recovering swiftly from their surprise to fight back and retrieve the situation.

'In God's name get the women and bairns out o' here!' Fergus bawled at Strongfist. 'I'll hold these devils! Go on, man, go!' He spurred the destrier side-on into another Saracen mount and clashed blades. One of his sons joined him, a lance in his fist that he had won from a downed warrior.

Strongfist whirled his stallion and spurred towards Annais. 'Ride!' he cried. 'Ride, daughter!'

She could see Guillaume's wide grey eyes peering from the shelter of his grandfather's breast. The numbness encasing her splintered and exploded. She cried out with the pain of it, caught up the black mare's reins and dug in her heels.

Faisal cursed and spurred after them, his scimitar poised on high. He avoided the mailed man and the child and rode onto the outside of the black mare, intent on making Annais his prey. Annais was aware of Faisal's horse thudding up close. She could hear its breath, sense its straining forequarters. Bound in his sling, Edmund was screaming. And she was screaming too. The mare was at full stretch and still she could sense Faisal gaining. Any second she would feel the bitter cut of the blade.

Her father squeezed a last burst of speed out of his destrier and knocked into Faisal's horse. Uttering an oath, Faisal struck at Strongfist, missed, and cut a gouge in the destrier's neck. Although not a mortal slash, it was deep and cruel and the stallion veered away with a scream of pain.

The diversion had allowed Annais to gain a few more yards and now Faisal had to work his mount hard to catch up. The hunting horn sounded again, almost upon her. Glancing beyond her straining mount, she saw the warriors advancing on them. With their turbans, lances and scimitars they looked no different to those from whom she was fleeing, and yet, even if she had wanted to, she could not draw rein. All that lay between herself and certain death was the black mare's fleetness of foot.

Closer, closer. Her eyes stung with sweat, her body screamed with the exhaustion of holding the mare to her course and clinging on for her life and the life of her child. One slip, one wrong foot and it would be over. Faisal uttered a battle howl and brought the scimitar slicing down. At the same time, a white-fletched arrow slammed into his raised arm, piercing the upper muscle. Faisal's blow lost momentum and went awry, ripping Annais's dress and breaking the strap of the sling. But Faisal did not drop the scimitar; he merely transferred it to his left hand.

Clutching a screaming Edmund who had almost fallen from her arms as the sling broke, struggling to stay on the mare, Annais was defenceless. She watched in horror as the curved edge came at her again, and then she saw it caught on a straight steel blade and turned from its purpose. Sparks flew from the connection. Faisal's eyes widened in astonishment and fear. The silver horse thrust its rider side-on to his bay. The sword clashed upon the scimitar again and sent it spinning from Faisal's hand. Annais's vision blurred at the edges and her skull rang with the sound of battle. She was terrified that she would faint and tumble from the mare. With grim determination she held on and watched Faisal fall and his horse bolt. It all seemed as slow to her as a scene acted out in water. The man on the silver horse turned to her and beneath the iron browband of his helm she met his green-gold eyes. And then she was falling too with that same slow-fast rhythm. The exhausted black mare had trembled to a halt and Annais did not strike the ground hard – enough to bruise, enough to wind, but not to cause serious injury and she had instinctively cupped the baby's skull.

Sounds roared in her ears . . . hooves thundering and fading, the shouts of men, the screaming of her baby son. Her vision cleared and darkened by turns.

'Christ, Annais . . . Annais.' A hand touched her face, her throat, feeling for the life force. She was lifted to a sitting position and cradled against hard, sun-hot rivets. A rim was pressed to her lips and she tasted the appalling burn of Galwegian usquebaugh. Choking, she pushed the drink aside with shaking hands and looked up into Sabin's face. He had removed his helm and his sweat-soaked hair dripped at his brow. There was a long smear of dust on his cheek and dried blood caked his hands and beneath his fingernails. He was kneeling and she was lying against the left side of his chest. Edmund yelled with lusty indignation from the ground between Sabin's knees. 'Annais?'

She blinked at him. 'You are alive,' she croaked. 'I saw you shot . . . I saw you fall . . .'

'My hauberk took the blows . . . I am not injured beyond a scrape.' It wasn't entirely true, but it would serve for now. 'It's all right . . . everything is all right.'

Beyond him Faisal's corpse was sprawled in the dust in a grotesque parody of the way she had seen Sabin lying. The blood, the curled hand, the arrow quilling the corpse. She buried her face against Sabin's breast to hide the sight, but he cupped her jaw and made her look up.

'We can go home now,' he said. 'It is all that matters . . . home to Montabard.' He lowered his mouth to hers. The kiss tasted of salt and blood and dust. But it tasted of survival too, and hope and passion. What had been so nearly an end made the prospect of a new beginning all the sweeter.

It was too far for the hostages to ride back to Shaizar to recover from their mauling at the hands of the Emir's men.

Three had been captured for ransom; three, including Faisal, killed; and the rest had fled. A camping place was made beside the river within the shade and protection of a stand of licorice trees. Usamah posted guards on the high ground and sent a messenger back to Shaizar with news of the successful pursuit and details of where the party was spending the night.

A fire was kindled under the trees and water heated in small cooking pots for the bathing of wounds and the cooking of food.

'I do not think we will be troubled further,' Usamah said, crouching beside Sabin who had gingerly removed his hauberk, gambeson and shirt so that Annais could tend to the arrow gouge in his side. 'The Emir of Homs may take an opportunity like any man, but he is not foolhardy. He knows that to dare again on our territory would make him the enemy of Shaizar.'

Sabin tried not to wince. 'I hope that you are right.'

'I always am.' Usamah's teeth flashed with a hint of self-mockery. He looked at the wound and gave a small frown. 'You were fortunate. A fraction deeper, a different angle, and it would have pierced your ribs.'

Sabin grimaced. 'A timely reminder of God's mercy.' He looked at Usamah. 'You saved my life and that of my wife and children.'

'A matter of honour.' Usamah shrugged. 'I would not want you to think I make a habit of kindness to Franks. The debt is cancelled now. Next time we meet on neutral ground.'

'I would hope in friendship,' Sabin said.

'There is always hope.' Usamah's tone was dry. 'If you have need of opium I have it in my pack.'

Sabin shook his head. 'No. The injury is painful but not beyond bearing.' He managed a smile. 'It reminds me that I am alive.'

Usamah left them then and joined his men at the main cooking fire. The smell of broth and spices wafted on the evening breeze. Although the Saracens and Franks sat together, there was a sense of constraint, of an imminent parting of the ways and alliances. This last act of rescue had drawn them together and driven a wedge between them.

Annais bound Sabin's wound with clean strips of swaddling band, first smearing the injury with honey from the cooking supplies. The children were asleep, Guillaume twitching now and again with exhaustion, his fist pressing an edge of his favourite blanket to his nose, Edmund tightly wrapped in his swaddling.

'I wish I could sleep too,' Annais said wistfully as she wiped her hands clean on a spare scrap of bandage.

Sabin studied her. 'The juice of the white poppy that Usamah carries would grant you oblivion,' he suggested.

She shook her head. 'I would fear to sleep like that,' she murmured. 'I have been close enough to death today without drinking its semblance from a cup. Do you think we will ever reach Montabard?' Her eyes were shadowed and she gave a small shiver that owed more to her doubts than the breeze, chill now that the sun had almost set.

He touched his bandaged side. 'If we were going to die untimely, it would have been today, but the sword has passed over our heads.' He reached his hand to her and pulled her against his good side. 'If not for ever, we have tomorrow, and such days beyond that as heaven sees fit to grant us . . . and I pray for the grace to grow a little older yet . . . with you.' He pressed his lips to her temple.

The Saracens had moved en masse from their fire and in the red of the sunset had approached the stream to bathe themselves and prepare for their evening prayers. Fergus and Strongfist were displaying the skills they had learned many years ago as youngsters on the Crusader route and were cooking flat bread on a round Saracen shield. The healing sound of camaraderie and laughter wafted from their endeavours.

Annais sighed and savoured Sabin's closeness, so nearly

lost. The warmth of his body was like a benediction. 'I have never lain beneath the open sky with you,' she said.

She felt him smile against her temple and his hand tightened at her waist. 'Is that a proposition?'

She pressed against him, but carefully, mindful of his injury. 'I am a modest and dutiful wife,' she replied through lowered lids, 'what do you think?'

'I think that never was there a better reason for making a bed to watch the stars,' he said.

In the dawn when the Franks rose, the Saracens had gone, leaving weapons, food and several spare mounts as parting gifts. Poking the embers to light, Sabin saw two shahins winging westwards towards the receding bank of night-cloud, and it seemed to him a good omen. He pointed them out to Annais, who was sleepily feeding Edmund, her dark hair still unbound from slumber.

'Home,' said Guillaume, following Sabin's stretched arm.

'Yes,' Sabin said with a tired, contented smile. 'Home.'

Author's Note

My first unpublished historical novel, written when I was fifteen years old, was inspired by a children's television programme titled *Desert Crusader*, and it set me on the path to my chosen career – although it was another fifteen years before I achieved my ambition. Although *The Falcons of Montabard* is set during the period of the Crusades, it tells a somewhat different story to my starter effort and involves a very different set of characters. However, in a way I still feel as if I've come full circle.

As usual, I have intermingled fact and fiction, although a reader might be hard-pressed to judge which is which, so improbable is the truth at times. The author's note is my chance to explain where I've used imagination and where the facts have spoken for themselves.

Sabin makes a brief appearance as a newborn baby in the novel before *Falcons*: *The Winter Mantle*. His name is Simon in that particular book, but as a grown man he is known by the masculine version of his mother's name (mainly to avoid confusion with his half-brother and father, both also called Simon). While researching, I discovered a single tantalising reference to Simon de Senlis's illegitimate son, but unable to find out anything else apart from his existence, I have used him as the starting point for *Falcons* and given him my own story. I hope he doesn't mind.

Although Annais, Strongfist and Fergus are fictitious, they

xist against a background of firm historical fact. King Baldwin of Jerusalem was indeed captured while out hunting and imprisoned in the fortress of Kharpurt together with Joscelin of Edessa and a few surviving knights from the massacre on the banks of the Euphrates. He and Joscelin were later rescued by a daring raid that could have come straight out of a Hollywood blockbuster. It is documented fact that allies of Joscelin and Baldwin came to Kharpurt in small parties so as not to cause suspicion and, when within the castle walls, threw off their disguises and overpowered the garrison. They were helped by some women from the harem who were Christian slaves. Joscelin went for help and had to negotiate the Euphrates with 'waterwings' made from goatskins. Baldwin held out, hoping for his army to arrive, but Emir Balak rode up first. There was hard fighting, but Balak undermined a tower and gained access to the castle. All save the King and a very few knights were thrown over the walls, including the women who had helped the Franks.

Baldwin continued to be held a prisoner while his wife, the indomitable Queen Morphia, strove to raise a ransom. His release was finally agreed in return for a promise of money and aid, and the provision of several juvenile hostages, including his own small daughter and Joscelin of Edessa's young son. The hostages were held at the fortress of Shaizar in the care of the Munqidh family, of whom Usamah ibn Munqidh was a prominent member. In his old age, Usamah wrote his memoirs and they have come down to us today as a fascinating glimpse of life in the Middle East in the twelfth century. I have loosely borrowed several strands from Usamah's memoirs, including the pet cheetah, which did indeed live among the family. The boar hunt is taken more or less from fact, and I have used Usamah's descriptions of bathhouses to flesh out the scenes in Jerusalem. Usamah also spoke of a Frank who was like a brother to him, so I had a perfect opening to develop the relationship between him and Sabin. Waleran of Birejek and Baldwin's nephew, who is thought to have been called Ernoul, were indeed killed when Baldwin reneged on part of the ransom agreement.

Shaizar itself, although often under threat from the crusading forces, never succumbed to the enemy. The most destruction was done by an earthquake in 1157 which effectively finished the rule of Usamah's family.

While I can take a bow for sketching the drama of the grand finale, the idea again isn't mine, but actually happened. The Emir of Homs did attempt to snatch the hostages as they were on their way home and Usamah came racing to their aid in a day-long pursuit. The only liberty I have taken is in placing young Joscelin of Edessa at the scene, when it is likely that he was ransomed earlier with Princess Joveta.

For those readers wondering about the rapidity of Annais's marriage following Gerbert's death, it is a known fact that widows were remarried at speed in the Holy Land. While I might have exaggerated that speed slightly for dramatic input, the operative word is 'slightly' and the truth is not far out.

I feel I should say a final word about Sabin's horse. You will find Lucifer's descendants today in the Akhal Teke breed. Akhal Teke horses have been around in one form or another for at least three thousand years. Today they are valued for their enormous stamina, their speed and their superb ability as dressage mounts. Their coats, as stated in Falcons, are renowned for having an overlying metallic sheen.

For anyone wanting to read further on the Holy Land during the twelfth century, I would highly recommend the following books. They have been very useful to me – and Usamah's biography in particular was a delight.

I welcome feedback on my work and can be contacted either from my website (which is updated regularly) at www.elizabethchadwick.com or by direct email at elizabethchadwick@live.co.uk.

Bibliography

Boas, Adrian J., *Crusader Archaeology: The Material Culture of the Latin East* (Routledge, 1999), London and New York.

Boas, Adrian J., *Jerusalem in the Time of the Crusades* (Routledge, 2001), London and New York.

Hillenbrand, Carole, *The Crusades: Islamic Perspectives* (Edinburgh University Press, 1999), Edinburgh.

Hitti, Philip K., trans., *An Arab-Syrian Gentleman & Warrior in the Period of the Crusades: Memoirs of Usamah ibn Munqidh* (Columbia University Press, 2000), New York.

Molin, Kristian, *Unknown Crusader Castles* (Hambledon, 2001), London and New York.

Prawer, Joshua, *The Crusaders' Kingdom: European Colonialism in the Middle Ages* (Phoenix Press, 2001), London.

Riley-Smith, Jonathan, ed., *The Atlas of the Crusades* (Guild Publishing, 1991), London, New York, Sydney, Toronto.

Rodinson, Maxime, Arberry, A. J., & Perry, Charles, *Medieval Arab Cookery: Essays and Translations* (Prospect, 2001), Trowbridge, Wiltshire.

Runciman, Steven, *A History of the Crusades, volume 2, The Kingdom of Jerusalem and the Frankish East 1100–1187* (Penguin, 1990), London.

The Eleanor of Aquitaine Trilogy

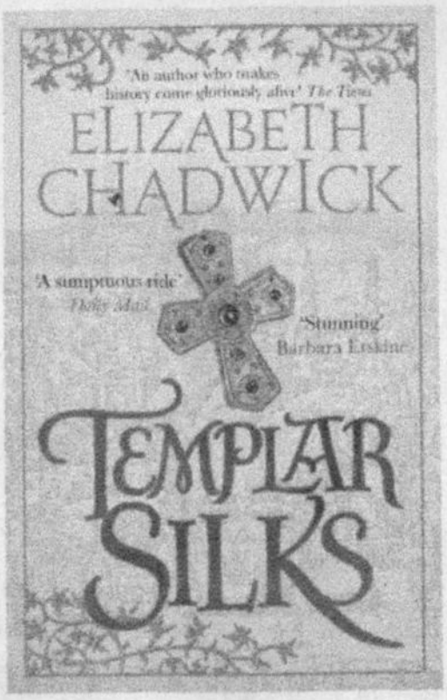

To save his soul William Marshal takes the perilous road to Jerusalem, but the greatest danger he faces there is losing his heart.

England, 1219

Lying on his deathbed, William Marshal, England's greatest knight, sends a trusted servant to bring to him the silk Templar burial shrouds that returned with him from the Holy Land thirty years ago. It is time to fulfil his vow to the Templars and become a monk of their order for eternity.

As he waits for the shrouds' return, he looks back upon his long-ago pilgrimage with his brother Ancel, and the sacred mission entrusted to them – to bear the cloak of their dead young lord to Jerusalem and lay it on Christ's tomb in the church of the Holy Sepulchre.

Jerusalem, 1183

In the holiest of all cities, the brothers become embroiled in the deadly politics, devious scheming and lusts of the powerful men and women who rule the kingdom. Entangled with the dangerous, mercurial Paschia de Riveri, concubine of the highest churchman in the land, William sets on a path so perilous that there seems no way back for him, or for his brother. Both will pay a terrible price and their only chance to see home again will be dependent on the Templar shrouds.

*

'Chadwick's research is impeccable, her characters fully formed and her storytelling enthralling'
Historical Novel Review